"A rich and wintry world  gods and monsters, with epic
battles, dangerous mag... is a
heroine both powerful... ...ney."
Sue Lyn...
Daug...

"Brimming with magic and intrigue, *Barrow of Winter* is a
spellbinding read. Thray's northern quest had me turning pages
late into the night, as did Long's beautiful winter-sharp prose. A
vivid story that lingers long after the last word."
Rebecca Ross, internationally bestselling author of *A River Enchanted*

"A world so vividly rendered you'll feel the ice on the pages."
Richard Swan, *Sunday Times* bestselling author of *The Justice of Kings*

"Evocative, lyrical, and brimming with fierce magic. Another
brilliant addition to this clever, Norse-inspired series."
Sunyi Dean, *Sunday Times* bestselling author of *The Book Eaters*

"Sharp as the winter wind, *Barrow of Winter* grabbed my attention
and wouldn't let go. Long's latest is a compelling portrait of a woman
coming to know herself—woven through with betrayal, darkness,
thunderingly epic stakes, and a cast of prickly immortals I couldn't
get enough of. It's fantasy at its very best."
Allison Epstein, author of *A Tip for the Hangman*

"*Barrow of Winter* reminds me why I love the genre. It pulls you
in and doesn't let go. It's a masterclass in world-building, with
descriptions so visceral you can almost feel the icy winds. Thray is
a complex, powerful character I would follow into the cold again
and again. A superb new addition to the Hall of Smoke universe."
M.K. Lobb, author of *Seven Faceless Saints*

"Epic fantasy teeming with adventure and wonder."
Christopher Irvin, author of *Ragged*

"An epic journey into a strange and wintery world filled with intrigue, adventure, secrets, loss, battles and monsters. At its centre is Thray, a young woman who is half mortal, half god and determined to discover the truth of her own immortality... Her bravery and fragility captured me from the very first page."
Kell Woods, author of *After the Forest*

"H.M. Long has done it again! ... *Barrow of Winter* offers all the action and adventure of high fantasy while also taking the time to offer deep, thoughtful exploration of the meanings of life and death, family and enmity... the perfect read for any reader looking for fascinating magic, adventurous heroines, and a fantasy world that feels real enough to book a plane ticket to visit."
M.J. Kuhn, author of *Among Thieves*

"H.M. Long goes from strength to strength. Transportive and charged with intrigue, *Barrow of Winter* has a heroine in Thray whose appeal is in her turmoil and her flaws. She's unsure yet indomitable as she journeys through a story steeped in ancient, terrifying magic and potential betrayal at every turn. With layers of lore and a sense of a vast, intricate history, Long expands on a world so vibrantly wrought I could taste the winter winds."
Hannah Mathewson, author of *Witherward*

"Steeped in natural beauty cold to the touch and yet crackling with warmth, *Barrow of Winter* is about a young woman on an age-old quest of self-discovery that nevertheless feels as fresh and crisp as new snow. For fans of fantasy and adventure, this is a must read."
Olesya Salnikova Gilmore, author of *The Witch and the Tsar*

"H.M. Long is a master of her craft... *Barrow of Winter* delivered exactly what I look for in epic fantasy: an immersive world of gods and warriors, with badass characters who will stick with me long after I reach the end."
Gabriela Romero Lacruz, author of *The Sun and the Void*

BARROW
OF
WINTER

Also by H.M. Long and available from Titan Books

Hall of Smoke
Temple of No God

BARROW OF WINTER

H. M. LONG

TITAN BOOKS

Barrow of Winter
Print edition ISBN: 9781803360027
E-book edition ISBN: 9781803360034

Published by Titan Books
A division of Titan Publishing Group Ltd
144 Southwark Street, London, SE1 0UP
www.titanbooks.com

First edition: January 2023
10 9 8 7 6 5 4 3 2 1

This is a work of fiction. All of the characters, organizations, and events portrayed in this novel are either products of the author's imagination or are used fictitiously. Any resemblance to actual persons, living or dead (except for satirical purposes), is entirely coincidental.

A CIP catalogue record for this title is available from the British Library.

Printed and bound by CPI Group (UK) Ltd, Croydon, CR0 4YY.

To Dad, with love.

ALGATT, EANGEN, AND THE NORTHERN TERRITORIES OF THE ARPA EMPIRE

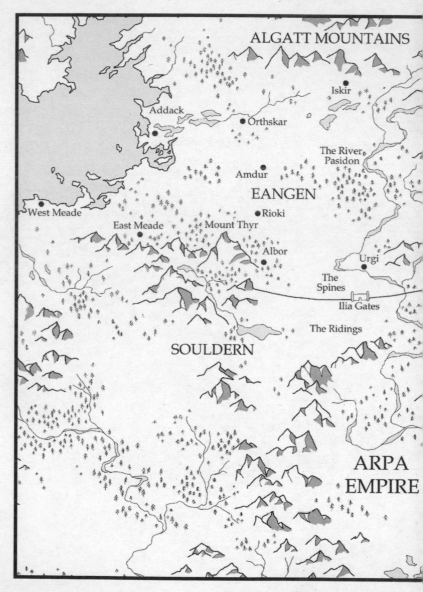

The White Lake

The
Headwaters

Nivari Gates

NIVARIUM

Mircea

Alathea

APHARNUM

Apharnum
City

ONE

I smell iron, dank fur, and carrion breath. Dirt, too, damp with blood. I try to lift my arm, but it won't move. I start to stand, but I falter. I end up crouched, my good hand braced in the frost and cooling blood—the same blood that coats my face, my arm, and clothes.

Across the creek, against a stark backdrop of trunks and dying undergrowth, a second beast prowls. She's massive, a creature between a bear and a dog that emerged after the Upheaval, when so many strange beasts escaped the High Halls. A savn. Her mate lies at my feet, two arrows in his barrel chest and my bow snapped beneath him. Not that I could draw the weapon anymore, even if it had been whole.

Courage, I urge myself, but my head feels light and my senses dim. Late autumn branches clack overhead and the afternoon sky beyond is a thick, snowy gray. *It can't kill you. This is why you're here. Fight.*

I rise, every muscle complaining as I unfold to my full height. I'm tall for a woman, even taller for an Eangen, and I've complained a thousand times that I look all but the largest men in the eye. But now I appreciate it. Now I value the breadth of my shoulders and the strength of my arms, here in the wild, in the dirt and the blood.

The beast shuffles. She's wary of me, but she still sees food—and vengeance.

She drops her head and stalks closer. Seven black claws punch through the thin ice and water rushes around her paw, washing my blood from matted gray fur.

I pull my bone-handled knife from its sheath at my hip. Mud and grit grinds between my fingers as I turn it, angling the weapon out to one side. At a push of my will, it lengthens into a short spear, birch white with a handspan of deadly tip.

The beast growls, low and deep. I feel it in my chest, even though we're half a dozen paces apart. Doubt claws up my spine and I start to tremble, deep in my core.

Perhaps she can kill me. Perhaps my father's blood spared me and, in moments, I'll follow my mother into death.

I want that, I tell myself. The answer, the closure, the end to my uncertainty. But my body wants to run. It wants to push the sun back across the sky and talk myself out of my own recklessness. My village would have tried to dissuade me, if they'd known my plans when I left. But I'd been too quick and too foolish, and all of them too trusting.

I want more than to turn back time. I want to scrape the memory of my mother's pyre from my mind, and claw out the fear that I will never follow her into death. That I'll live on, while age and sickness, beasts and axes claim everyone around me.

I'm terrified and trapped. If I turn and run, the savn's jaws will find the back of my neck. I'm not sure I want to live, but I am sure I don't want to be eaten alive. Would I be aware of each moment? When the beast tired of me, would my fleshless limbs grow back? Would my consciousness live on in a pile of bones?

My mind spins, jittery and edged with hysteria. But another part of me whispers, calm and calloused, *This is what you came for.*

The beast stalks closer, splashing through the cold water and into the mud on my side of the creek.

I've no choice. I brace, settling my weight into my shaking legs, and raise the spear in a firm grip.

The beast roars. Her mate's body lies between us, but I feel the heat of her breath and the force of her rage.

I lower my chin and hurl the spear in one fluid movement. It slams into her chest, right beneath the taught muscles of her throat and the fang-rimmed abyss of her jaws.

Her cry cracks into an agonized whine, but she still flies toward me. I grab the end of the spear as I roll aside and it slips from the wound, re-forming into a curved sword.

I snap the blade back out just as my feet hit the ground again. My boots slide, my muscles shriek, but the blade bites deep. Blood bursts over my face.

The next thing I'm aware of is lying on my side. The sword has re-formed into a small knife and lies in the muddy leaves beyond my fingertips. I squint at it, noticing fresh snowflakes on its blood-splattered grip. There are blood and grit on my lips, too, iron and earth.

I look up, past the bulk of two felled beasts, to the gray sky. More snow drifts down, placid and patient. The breeze is colder, rustling the dead beasts' fur, but I'm burning hot. My ears roar like the sea and my thoughts clatter in my skull, increasingly distant and muffled.

Is this it? The moment when my question will be answered? Will my soul slip from my flesh and settle in the earth, or will I live on, in agony, until immortal blood binds me back together?

A form materializes in the snow—*of* the snow—on the other side of the savn. A man, with flesh and hair and muscle and warm, richly embroidered clothing of gray and white. His hair is pale like mine and his eyes blackish blue, like the underbelly of an iceberg in a spring sea.

I try to push to my feet, but my head spins.

The sound of the wind, my ragged breath and the man's footsteps fade to a distant roar as he crouches beside me. His features are the jagged edges of ice and the contours of wind-smoothed snowbanks. He smells like winter, true winter—sharper and crisper than the late autumn around us. The flakes continue to fall and as they do, the scent of him—his presence—intensifies.

Despite my pain, relief seeps through me. I manage a weak smile and don't bother trying to rise. I don't reach for my knife. This man has led me through enough storms to prove he's safe. Not human, not gentle, but safe.

"Granddaughter," he says. His voice and expression are impassive except for the narrowing of his eyes. "What are you doing?"

"Trying to die," I whisper. The admission makes my heart flutter and I twist to look at my arm. My tunic is black with blood, but its welling has slowed. If I had more energy, I might have started to panic again, realizing what that meant.

But I'm past that point. Fear fades, and I have the presence of mind for one whisper before blackness washes over me.

"Please take me home."

I awaken to the crackle of a fire and the insipid cold of dusk. I lie close to the flames on a bed of cedar boughs and moss, and the snow falls everywhere except my bed.

I'm not home, however much I wish I were. Most of the trees around me are birch with barren branches, rasping, curling bark and dead undergrowth, shriveled ferns, and blanched grasses burdened with white. There's no birch grove near Albor.

I sit up slowly. As I do, I catch the thread of voices off in the forest, but the shadows beyond my orb of firelight are thick enough I can't see the speakers. I recognize one voice, though: my grandfather's, low and deep.

I wear no bandages and my torn tunic is gone. Instead, I wear a new shift of soft linen and a pale blue kaftan I've never seen before. It smells of lavender and pine, as does my skin, and it's beautifully embroidered with geometric patterns, lined with gray fox fur at the collar and cuffs. Strangest of all, my wounds no longer hurt. When I lift my arm, there's no pain.

The Great Healer has been here—her lavender and pine scent, as much as her work, betrays her. Goosebumps prickle down my neck. She might still be close by, if one of those voices belongs to her. One is certainly female.

I'm awed and sickened by the realization. My test is nullified. Am I alive because of her, or my own inability to die?

The last voice is another male, and I spy his broad figure through the snow. His beard is braided with horsehair and he wears a heavy cloak, but his head is bare. Gadr. Not a human, but a Miri, a higher being. Like the Healer.

Two former gods and Winter himself have visited me in the forest, tonight.

My nerves prickle, but I force myself to ignore it. Instead, I sit straighter and check for my belt. It's intact, along with the bone-handled knife. I draw it, expecting the weapon to still be covered in blood, but my grandfather has cleaned it.

I stare at the blade, at its keen edge near the calloused skin of my hands. The moment stretches too long, and forcibly, I sheathe the weapon again. *That* route to answers is not an option. I promised my mother it would never be. Now she's dead, and I'm trapped in my word.

The voices in the forest go quiet and my grandfather returns alone. He strides into the firelight and surveys me with his usual impassive expression. He's carrying a new bow, I notice, and a set of arrows. They're all as bone-white and unnatural as my knife.

"For you," Winter says, setting the bow and quiver within reach. The arrows clatter softly in a quiver of dark leather and intricate stitching, its darkness a contrast to pale shafts and fletching. "The quiver will never run out of arrows, and the bow will never break."

No ordinary weapons, then. Miri creations, like the knife at my belt.

"I don't deserve them," I murmur wretchedly, looking from him to the weapons without truly lifting my eyes. He barely looks like a grandfather; other than the white hair knotted at the back of his head, he has no wrinkles or other visible signs of age on his snow-pale skin. But he's older than mountains and seas, and no one who looks into his eyes could forget that.

He shows no emotion at my self-pity. "Your bow is broken, and these collect dust in Eang's Hall."

"I can get a new bow anywhere."

Grandfather looks at me long and levelly, so I stay my tongue.

"I've sent an owl to Albor." He changes the topic, practical as ever. "But you roamed far from home. There is another village a day's walk south. The High Priestess will meet you there."

I choose my first words carefully. I haven't seen my grandfather in four years, though I've sensed him and heard his voice every winter since I was a child. He's not doting, ever on the periphery of my life. So why bring me gifts?

"How did you know I was in danger?" I ask. "And why was Gadr here?"

He sets my new bow and quiver on a rock and crouches to stoke the fire. He doesn't require the heat, but it doesn't bother him, either. "You are my only blood south of the mountains. I am always aware of you. As to Gadr, he was curious. He's oddly fond of you, given his history with your family."

That makes me feel… warm, watched over, even if my grandfather's expression is flat. It's a feeling I don't often have, not in a world that distrusts my blood and whispers of my brother's strangeness, my father's crimes, and my mother's weakness for bedding him.

I feel something else too. Longing. It makes tears prick at my eyes and my throat thicken.

"Do you visit your other grandchildren, in the north?" I ask, eager both to know and to shift the conversation away from myself.

He finishes feeding the fire and sits back, forearms resting on his knees, fingers entwined between them. "No."

"Why?"

"They're too much like him."

Him. My father. Ogam, Son of Winter, Son of Eang; the immortal, matricidal traitor who nearly burned our world to the ground during the Upheaval—the year I was conceived.

"Are they…" I look down at my bandages, hesitate, then press forward. "Immortal, like him?"

"Many are."

I think of the blood pouring down my arm and the roar of the blackness before I passed out.

"Am I?" The question comes out hoarse. Guilt and grief and dread wash across my skin, and the fire does nothing to soothe me.

My grandfather looks up, expressionless as always. "We will not know that until the day you should have died."

"That wasn't today?" I press, though my lips feel numb.

He shrugs, a small, stiff gesture. "Your father's children might be able to tell you more, but I cannot. I am myself. You, all of his get, are something other."

"Other," I repeat bitterly. "That's what the Eangen say. I'm not like you, not like them. Everyone like me is on the other side of the mountains."

"Yes," he agrees impassively. "And it's best they remain there, and you here."

"So I should stay here forever?" The words burn. Tears stream down my cheeks and I know I must look terrible, red-eyed and wet-nosed, a child rather than a near-woman, but Grandfather still shows no concern.

A log shifts in the fire and sparks dance up into the bare branches overhead. The sight and smell of it takes me back to my mother's funeral pyre, and for an instant I feel the emotions of that night over again. The emptiness. The disbelief. Her death had been so sudden— drowned when a riverbank gave way and the current trapped her underwater. I feel the High Priestess's arms around me, see the empathetic looks of distant relations, but they're all droplets in the empty well of my heart.

And my mother's other child, her son by her first husband? He didn't reach for me that night. His black curls hid his handsome face on the far side of the pyre, but I still saw his tearless eyes.

He is duty personified. Stoic and steady.

I am conflict.

"Perhaps you will live a mortal life and die soon. Perhaps you will remain here forever. But when forever comes, I will be here too," my grandfather tells me, and I can't tell if he's trying to comfort me or stating a fact. I want to believe the former. "We will stand together, you and I, at the turn of the age."

"My father's children will still live too," I point out, my voice weak. My siblings, the ones who might be able to tell me if I'm immortal. Because short of finding another beast to bloody me, or an enemy I can't best, I will not be finding out on my own. My courage is frail, my promise to a dead mother binding. The bone-handled knife remains at my belt, quiet and sated.

"Yes." Winter's eyes grow flinty, the first sign of emotion he's shown. He murmurs again, in a voice so cold I shiver, "They will be there too."

TWO

I hear a voice on the breeze. It steals away the last of the summer warmth, rustling the dune grasses as I trudge from one sandy crest to the next. The sea lurks to my left, muffled in violet dawn and heavy fog. Waves swell, charge, and crash. I stay well beyond their reach as they wash away the tiny, three-pronged footprints of darting shorebirds, and drum in hollows of rocky outcroppings.

Granddaughter.

The word comes to me laden with moisture and salt. I plant the end of my spear in the sand and take in what little I can see of the coastline, searching for a shadow or a shape in the fog. But I'm alone, save for scuttling shorebirds and the muted cries of gulls.

"I'm listening," I say to the breeze.

There is no response. I hesitate for a few breaths, then resume my course. My soft leather boots slip in the sand and my muscles complain at so much activity early in the day, but there's a reason my grandfather's voice is drawing me up the coast. Autumn is here again and winter, the heart of his power, isn't far behind. He's waxing, reaching for me, and it's my duty to answer—even if I'd rather be back in the hall, in the warmth of my bed. There are few perks of being a village priestess on the edge of the world, but lying in my bed past dawn is usually one.

The dunes give way to smooth, gray rock, and the rush of waves grows to a steady boom. I carefully skirt tidal pools, catching glimpses of my own distorted reflection—tanned skin, windblown white braid, practical tunic and leggings. I jump shallow, freshwater falls, their journey from the glaciers of inland mountains finally ending at the sea. Lichen crunches beneath my boots in the drier reaches and valiant, stubby purple flowers quiver in rocky anchorages.

Granddaughter.

I stop beside a creek to catch my breath. Water trickles past my boots, over a ledge into the crashing waves. I eye the froth, fighting the urge to distance myself from it, and focus on the sounds around me.

I pick out something other than water and wind and the gust of my own breath. This sound is sharper, steadier.

Ships' drums, and the grind of oars.

Fear scorches away my fatigue as the fog peels back. Seven ships materialize, thick-masted, with simple, reefed gray sails and many oars. Their prows are high, each decorated with the head and shoulders of a beast—whales, eagles, bears and serpents.

The drums beat, the shapes of men and women row in time, and the ships forge south. South, toward the waters where the Eangen fishing boats will be out for morning. Toward the settlement I've learned to call home.

But these are not Eangen ships. They're too large, and despite the distance between us, something about the people on deck—their clothing and profiles—strikes me as distinctly other.

Perhaps I'm wrong. Perhaps they're Arpa explorers, I think desperately. There have been more of those heading out in the world in recent years, or so I've heard. But even though I'm a child of peace, a lifetime of stories and warnings have taught me better. The Empire to the south does not build ships like this. Theirs are flat and heavy, made for rivers and shallow seas, while these are narrow and predatory, with high prows and sterns.

No, these are strangers, and strangers mean raiders. Raiders coming not from the northern mountains or over the great wall to the south, but from the sea.

"I see them," I murmur to the wind. The breeze dies and the fog swirls back in, hiding me from sight as I heft my spear and draw a deep, settling breath.

I rise, turn my feet south, and run.

My lungs ache as I pound over the wooden walkways of Iesa. The fog is lighter here and the settlement quiet—the rush of early morning has long ended. The faint colors of dawn have faded into a solid, obscure gray, and there are no fishing boats on the beach.

More than half the population will already be out at the nets, including Havar. The image of his face as we parted last night slips through my mind, and I pick up my pace.

Villagers stir as I pass. A clutch of women carding in a pool of sunlight turn to stare, surrounded by baskets of raw, clean wool and a scattering of chubby, playing children. An older boy with an apron full of eggs peers around a corner and two old men, eyeing a huge deer hide stretched on a frame, mutter as I pass.

"Are you well, priestess?" one of the men calls.

I cast him a distracted, flat smile and keep moving. I might be the village's priestess, but it's not my place to throw its occupants into a panic. I must speak to the headman before anyone else.

"Thray!" This shout comes from a young man on the path ahead. He sets down a half-empty pack and hunting bow and snags my arm in one hand. "What's wrong?"

I tug away. "I'm in a hurry, Branan."

The concern in his eyes is tempered by offense. He gives a soft snort. "I can see that, but—"

I'm tired, sore, breathless, and in no mood for his needling. I brush past and make for the hall, ignoring the stares of other villagers.

The village of Iesa is perched on a network of smooth rock shoulders, overlooking the sea and punctuated by windblown pines. It once had walls, but now the settlement's defenses are reduced to its vantage, the twenty-foot drop from ridge to sandy beach, and the spears of a hundred fisherfolk, weavers, crafters, and traders. Only the headman's personal guard of ten, a few old raiders, and myself have undergone more than cursory martial training.

The great hall sits on the highest point of the ridge, looking over the beach and the waves. It's smaller than the one I grew up in, but has similar heavy beams, a steep roof, and a door carved with intricate runes, declaring the history of the local people and the strength of the headman's line.

The doors stand open to the fresh air as I stumble inside, the smoke-and-sage scent of home filling my ragged lungs.

Three huge hounds bark as they tangle about my legs. I brush them off, not without affection, and search the shadows. Curtains are pulled back for the day, the central hearth has burned down from breakfast, and all but two of the hall's denizens are absent. I'm grateful for that—it gives the headman and I more time before the inevitable panic—but it also worries me. How long will it take to get everyone to safety?

"Thray." Ossen, the headman, has already seen me. He leaves the bench where he's been sitting with one of his daughters and approaches me. Behind him, the daughter pauses over the garment she's embroidering. Her eyes, a usual Eangen brown in a tawny, freckled face, watch me curiously.

"Seven ships coming down from the north. Large ships—I've never seen them before," I tell him rapidly, speaking low enough that the girl won't hear. My lungs hurt and my muscles shudder, but I'm too tense to rest.

The dogs, still nuzzling at me, give up and go back to their spots near the hearth.

"At least fifty people on each ship," I add. "They'll have to round the peninsulas, but we've hours at most."

Ossen is quiet for a long, strained moment. His gray hair is free about his aging face, casual in the walls of his own home. But there's nothing casual about his tone as he asks, "They're not Arpa?"

I shake my head. "I don't think so."

"Nor the mountain folk?"

"Definitely not."

Another tense breath. There are no other seafaring peoples, not that we have a name for. I see that knowledge in his eyes, and I know it's reflected in mine.

"Did they see you?" the headman presses.

I think back to the cliff, the fog, and the distance. "I doubt it."

He moves then, striding past the hearth, his staring daughter, and the curtain to his sleeping quarters. A moment later he returns with his hair swept up into a knot and a long, curling horn in his hands.

His daughter stands, mute in shock, as he makes for the main door and the cliff beyond. Villagers have already started to gather, I see through the broad frame. They shuffle, murmuring to one another and holding back unruly children.

"Pray, priestess," Ossen tells me as he passes.

I nod, my expression all determination and courage, but my stomach curls. If only I *could* pray.

The headman puts the horn to his lips and for the first time in over twenty years, a war horn sounds in Iesa. It begins as a low moan, swelling and oscillating as Ossen's lungs strain. Then it crests, so loud I wince, and ends in a sonorous crack.

The village goes silent. The cries of gulls die out. The breeze itself seems to hush and there, in the quiet, I hear the drums.

Doom. Doom. Doom.

THREE

I watch fishing boats drive onto the beach, my breath lodged in my throat as their prows lodge in the furrowed sand. Each boat brings some measure of relief, one more familiar face returning to the marginal safety of shore, but drums still resound through the fog.

No sooner do the boats halt than fisherfolk sprint toward the village, sweeping up waiting family members and trading places with Iesa's best warriors.

"Priestess, you should go into the forest with the others," one of the warriors chides me. She's older than me by twenty years, old enough to remember raids and have the scars to prove it. She's also been one of the most critical of my appointment here, and after two years of service I've yet to earn her trust—even with something as simple as my own life.

"I'll stay," I reply, expression cool.

She glances at the bone-handled knife at my belt. "The chief priest still isn't back?"

I shake my head. My elder counterpart left for a yearly journey to Albor three weeks ago. Last year he might have made the trip in those three weeks, but the villagers don't seem to realize how lazy their priest has become since my arrival. I've little doubt he's meandering his way back along the eastern road as slowly as possible, filling his belly at hospitable hearths and singing tales to the wide-eyed children of every woodcutter and charcoal burner from Albor to the coast.

The thought would have made me smile, any other day.

"I doubt he'll be back until first snow," I warn her. "I'll stay."

The warrior realizes I will not back down and gives way with a nod. She jogs after her companions, who are hauling the boats into a defensive line along the shore.

I maintain my calm facade, but it isn't until I see Havar's boat that I breathe freely. My betrothed leaps into the surf at the same time as Udr, one of his brothers, holding fast to the gunnel and running the boat into the sand. His sister-in-law, Jara, comes last, leaping out gracefully and grabbing their satchels.

He brushes off his hands and scans the beach as I start toward them, my pace urgent but measured.

Havar's eyes find me. He's a handsome man, with typically burnished Eangen skin, his head shaved at the sides, beard well-kept, and his body honed by a lifetime on the waves. His eyes are usually warm and soft, the color of autumn earth. Today, however, they're hard and urgent.

He doesn't bother asking why I'm still here instead of hiding in the forest, and I'm grateful for that. I embrace him, anchoring myself in his scent of salt and fish and waxed wool.

He crushes me in return. I feel his pulse at my temple and his breath in my hair for a few moments, then we step apart, resuming the careful distance I've cultivated since our betrothal last year.

"They're raiders?" Havar asks, as if he still can't believe it. No one can.

"We don't know," I reply. The drums, the fog, and the beach surge back in as his arms retreat, and I steel myself. The ships are closer now. Somehow, despite the fog, they're finding their way toward us. They know we're here.

How? Uncertainty trickles through me. Perhaps they're following the fishing boats into the harbor, or they caught the echo of Ossen's horn? But the fog is too close, too distorting, for that. Not to mention the shoals and jagged coastline, which threaten all but the most seasoned local sailors.

Belatedly, I let my priestess's senses roam. Despite being gifted with the Sight as a child, it still doesn't come naturally to me—ever an afterthought, a tool at the bottom of a dusty chest. Life in Iesa, where the greatest threat is the weather and the occasional disgruntled bear, hasn't helped.

But now I stretch my senses, searching for a presence on the wind or a glisten of foreign magic. My own magic suddenly hazes around me, amber-gold and tasting like honey on my tongue. Havar can't see it—only other Sighted can—but to me, it's as real as the fog.

As I search, I feel Jara's eyes on me, and the eyes of many others on the beach. I'm their priestess—my response to this situation dictates theirs, almost as much as the headman's. So I stand straight and keep my chin level, showing caution but no fear.

A single gull cries in the distance. There's nothing out of the ordinary here, save the ships.

"Are we running, or arming?" Havar includes his siblings in the question.

"Arming," a voice answers from behind us, where Havar's eldest brother and mother approach. His brother grins broadly and hefts the double-headed axe that usually resides above the family lintel, newly sharpened and unhooded. "Though if you want to hide, I'm sure Mother will hold your hand."

Their mother frowns at him, her wrinkled eyes narrow. "I didn't raise cowards." She drops two shields and unshoulders a bow and quiver, which she passes to Jara, before she gives all her children another hard look. Havar, her youngest. Darag, the eldest. Udr, the middle child, and Jara, his wife.

She doesn't look at me.

"Don't leave me with Sare and all your babes," she warns, naming Darag's wife, but I see the worry hidden in the lines about her mouth. "We'll be in the forest."

The woman's disregard for me sits heavy in my chest. I'll be one of her children by the end of the summer if I hold to my promise, but she does not see me as a daughter. Not with the white hair of a dead immortal drifting across my eyes in the breeze, and the questions that go with it.

Though if I'm honest, I do not blame her.

Jara kisses her mother-in-law's temple, then the older woman joins the flow of villagers back through the settlement. I'm left with

Havar, his brothers, and Jara, who fits her quiver onto her belt with shaking hands.

The five of us stand together, gazes glancing off one another as we turn toward the sea. Darag hefts his axe. His grin is still there, but it's deeper now, darker and tucked in around his black-lashed eyes. He, of all the brothers, remembers war the clearest. He was old enough to run when the Old World fell, but not old enough to fight and die. And, like so many of that generation, he eventually turned to raiding the Empire to wet his axe with blood and prove himself. He's one of the few true warriors in the village.

He catches me watching him and gives a dry, subtle wink. "Stand behind me, little sister."

A smile creeps into the corner of my mouth. "Probably wiser to stand behind me."

He smirks and, without warning, the drums in the fog cease. Darag's expression closes like shutters to the wind and everyone on the beach stills, straining their senses and raising their shields.

The thudding of the drums resumes—this time a stately double beat. The heartbeat of a sleeping giant.

"Warriors!" Ossen bellows.

Havar gives me one last glance, his eyes full of unsaid things, then he and the others sprint into line. I follow, falling in beside Ossen as a wall of painted round shields lock into place before us. More warriors hunker behind the beached boats just ahead. Jara and a handful of other archers—hunters, the lot of them—form a back row. And then we wait.

Threat hangs as thick as the fog. The figureheads I saw earlier emerge in eddies, carved like wolves and whales and more unfamiliar beasts. They're followed by the sweep of high prows and masts, and I strain to make out the figures on their decks. Most sit at their oars but others cluster in the center of the vessels, standing straight and impassive. I see the glint of spears, and my hand tightens on my own weapon before I consciously relax it.

I hear a shout in a foreign tongue. The lead ship turns, dividing the shallow water in a shushing, frothing ripple. The oars give two more great hauls, then angle skyward in a dripping, clattering forest.

Our warriors brace as the ships drive through the shallows toward the beach. I look at Ossen, wondering why we're letting the strangers make landfall without loosing a single arrow. But the headman's gaze is narrow and shrewd, and he does not move.

The first vessel grinds onto the shore, followed by two more in a frothing run. The last four, the largest ships, remain out of bowshot in the fog.

Foreigners leap from the beached vessels with the ease of riders from horseback. Most of them remain near the ships, heedless of the cool waves lapping at their boots. Three come forward, all unarmed, the central figure with hands extended.

"Eangen!" the leader, a woman, calls. "Lower your spears, cousins."

The words are not spoken in our language, but I understand them. I stiffen. She's speaking in the Divine Tongue, the language of the Old Gods, universally lucid, yet impossible for any human tongue to shape. The Miri speak it—those like my grandfather, the Great Healer, and Gadr.

So, this newcomer cannot be human. At least, not wholly. My senses converge upon her and I touch my priestess's senses again. From one blink to the next, silver hazes the heavy, moist air around the stranger.

My heart twists, not in fear, but disbelief. I glance at Ossen—I doubt he has heard the language before, but I can see in his face he knows this is no human greeting.

"Let me go first," I say quietly, barely able to hide my urgency.

He looks about to protest, but gives in. "I'll be right behind you."

I step forward. The shield wall parts, the nearest warriors looking up at me in something between incredulity and curiosity as I leave the safety of their lines. I feel Havar's eyes among them, but he doesn't move.

I lead Ossen down the beach. I pass our fishing boats and the staring warriors behind them, then step onto the open shore, in full view of both Iesa and the ships.

The newcomers' leader is perhaps ten years older than I, at least to the eye. Her hair is white, like mine. Her frame is tall, like mine, and her eyes deep blue, threaded with black in a way that reminds me of my grandfather. She is paler than me, and her eyes have a dulcet, youthful shape uncommon among the Eangen.

I recognize what she is with a fierce and sudden clarity. I manage to hide my shock, but I cannot look away.

She, in turn, examines me. Her eyes travel my face, my hair, and stature. She turns up the corner of her mouth in satisfaction and offers an open hand, long, graceful fingers gently crooked.

"My name is Siru, of the Duamel in the north," she says. "Greetings, Daughter of Winter, sister of mine."

FOUR

My thoughts come too fast and too many. All I hear is a disjointed hum. Siru has Father's eyes, my hair, my very scent; a cool, crisp memory of winter that never fades from my skin. It twines between us despite the breeze and the stink of wet sand, fish, and decomposing seaweed.

"We are explorers." Siru speaks to Ossen with a shallow bow and an unfamiliar gesture, tapping the middle three fingers of her right hand to the center of her forehead. She wears a long tunic, nearly a gown, slit from knee down, with a short sealskin cloak belted at the waist. Her clothing is clearly well-made but plain, with muted blues and grays faded from salt and sun.

"It has been centuries since our peoples met," she says. "But the world has changed, or so we've heard. They say Eang is dead, and a new god rules the south."

The south? My humming mind untangles her words. She said she's of the Duamel in the north—far enough north that Eangen is south? The thought is a strange one.

The rest of what she says is simple, and true. Many of the Miri we once worshiped as gods are dead, including my grandmother Eang, from whom the Eangen derive their name. But if our peoples haven't met in centuries, how would she know that?

"Yes," Ossen answers, hesitantly. He speaks Eangen, though Siru still speaks the tongue of the Old Gods. "You... understand me?"

Siru gestures to her two companions. "I do, and I will translate for my people."

Her companions, standing a pace behind her, haven't spoken yet. A man and a woman, they're a little shorter than her and their coloring is fair, mild brown hair with honey-hazel eyes and skin that must rarely see the sun. Their jawlines are narrow and the man wears a short, clean beard without braids or adornment.

"I am Ossen, of the Addack clan of the Eangen," Ossen says, hesitancy fading. He's still guarded, though—I see the tension in his neck and the way he holds his hand obviously away from his sword. He asks one of the questions on my mind. "Where did you hear Eang is dead?"

"From our spirits." Siru's icy blue eyes drift back to me. "They travel far, as our father once did."

Our father. Our shared features. Her scent.

Daughter of Winter, sister of mine.

This is real. This woman is my half-sister.

Havar, his brothers, and Jara are my family, as much as my other Eangen kin from my mother's line. But I've always known that my father's descendants were somewhere in the far north, brothers and sisters from my father's line, who my grandfather warned me of on a snowy, bloody day.

My grandfather's caution seeps through me now, tempering my shock.

"You came to explore with seven ships?" I prompt in Eangen. Siru and I might look alike, but I do not speak the tongue of the gods. Or at least, I don't know if I do, and that thought alone sends a trickle of yearning through me. I keep my expression neutral, cool, and direct. "Seven ships could easily be mistaken for a war party."

She gives me an odd look, perhaps at my choice of language, but it's fleeting. "Our ships have regrouped after a summer of exploration in the west. We thought it best to land here in strength, given the Eangen's bloody reputation. We do, however, come peacefully. We want to explore, learn, and trade. Nothing more."

I feel the shift in Ossen. "Trade?" he asks, interest wheedling through his guardedness. "What do you offer?"

Siru gestures to the boats behind her. "Knowledge. Goods. Tools and maps, the warmest wool and furs, oils that will burn for many days. Black pearls of uncanny beauty. Skills of medicine and shipbuilding."

The headman considers Siru for a moment, then nods toward me. "Give us a moment?"

Siru opens her arms in a gesture of acquiescence and retreats toward her companions.

Ossen murmurs to me, still watching my half-sister. "What do you say? What does the God say?"

"The God has yet to reply," I answer, but do not elaborate as to why. "I do not trust that woman."

"Is she your kin?" Ossen asks, even more quietly. "Another of Ogam's daughters?"

I clear my throat as my father's name is finally spoken. It seems so much weightier than its two, simple syllables. "Yes. That is why I don't trust them. My father was a traitor."

"We trust you," Ossen points out.

I smile, small and wry. "Not all of you do."

The headman grunts at that. "Fools mistrust what they do not understand. I see opportunity. I saw it in you, and I see it here."

"So you're wise?" I quip, because I doubt his faith in me is deserved.

"I am." Ossen glances back at the newcomers and sucks his teeth before he asks, "Will you oppose me if I invite Siru to the village?"

I hesitate. I was honest when I told the headman that I don't trust the newcomers, but I'd be lying if I said I don't want to learn more about them. I need to. Siru draws my eye like a flame draws a moth.

Besides, our people have gone into the forest and runners were sent to neighboring villages—within hours, they'll reinforce us. There's a chance we'll be dead by then, but perhaps if we're careful… the risk is worth the reward.

"If they leave their weapons on the beach," I reply.

"We'll offer a hostage too." Siru's voice carries to us.

Ossen and I look back to her, both realizing she's overheard our conversation. She beckons a boy from the boats, barely older than twelve with pale skin and brown hair. The boy lifts his tunic, showing he's unarmed.

Ossen glances at me once more, then grins deeply. He beckons the boy forward, smiling like a benevolent uncle.

"Welcome to Iesa," he declares.

Havar pulls me aside as soon as we enter the high-vaulted hall, tugging me through a curtained doorway and into a shadowed room.

The curtain rustles closed behind us and hanging herbs brush my forehead. Light pours in through an open shutter, illuminating a table full of jars and bowls and neat lines of bundled plants. My hip jostles the table as we slip into the confined space and two clay jars clatter together, loud in the quiet.

I note all this in the half-breath before Havar backs me into the wall.

He takes my face in his hands and kisses me. Startled, I almost push him away. This is exactly the kind of moment I've avoided since our betrothal, but he's all worry and tension, and I haven't the heart to chastise him.

Besides, despite my better judgement, I'm kissing him back. I anchor myself in the moment, in the warmth of him, as I let my heart catch up to my head.

The ships didn't attack. None of us died on the beach. We're safe, at least for the moment. And from the way Havar's kissing me, he's as grateful for that as I am.

His lips withdraw. I crack one eye open, then both.

"I'm sorry," he says, looking anything but. His lips quirk in a coy smile and he smooths his beard with one hand. His other hand slips from my cheek to my arm, then to my hand. Our fingers entangle.

I smile wryly. "Were you worried about me?"

"I was. I am. She's one of them?"

I nod. "I suppose it was inevitable, meeting one."

He lifts my hand to his chest and presses my fingers into the embroidered collar of his tunic. I feel his heart thundering, and it's that, more than his words and the reminder of Siru, that steals the last of my smile.

Hearts like his are so easily stilled. What if the Duamel had attacked? What if he had died today?

What if I had not?

All at once, I wish the room wasn't so small, we weren't so close, and we hadn't kissed like that. I thought I'd reconciled myself to the possibility of watching him die, whether by accident, violence, age, or infirmity. Reconciled enough to agree to marry him. But until now, his mortality never felt so real.

"Your father might have children where Siru is from, but your *family* is here," he says, and I catch the strain in his voice. This, I sense, was part of the force behind his kiss. "You never even met Ogam, and your mother only lay with him to stay alive. And she was Eangen. I am Eangen."

My thoughts flick back to the way his own mother disregarded me on the beach, but the pain is shallow.

"I'm not going anywhere, Havar."

The anxiety in his face doesn't change. "Even if they can tell you what you are?"

My blood still races from the kiss, but now the feeling shifts—from heady anticipation to a spark of hope, and a thread of unease. I don't show him any of those emotions. I let myself shrink and look down, because I know if he feels he must comfort me, he'll smother his own concerns and let this conversation drop.

It's manipulative. But I've grown up in a world that held me at arm's length, that mistrusted my bloodline and potential. I've learned how to protect myself, to guard my emotions and my secrets.

Sure enough, his fingers tighten around mine, still against his collar. "I'm sorry. I'm still afraid one day I'll wake up and you'll be gone. You've the blood of the Old Gods. How can your life be as small as mine?"

I catch his gaze. I dislike it when he belittles himself like this, but his fear is justified.

I hope he can't see that in my face.

Voices rise beyond the curtained doorway. A second later the heavy fabric sweeps aside and an older woman peers in at us. Girda, Ossen's wife. Her coils of gray hair are braided and set with the ornate bone pins the coastal people favor. Her overgown is a pale red, heavily embroidered, strung with glass beads at the breast and fastened by brooches.

She gives me a narrow-eyed frown. "This is *not* the time. Come, now. Both of you, you foolish children."

She vanishes back through the curtain. Havar steps away from me, as far as the small space will allow.

"We can talk later," he relents.

"I'll hold you to that." I'm already moving toward the curtain, quietly grateful for Girda's interruption.

I push beyond the curtain and Havar follows. Ossen, several prominent villagers and our Duamel guests have taken seats in a circle of chairs at the other end of the hall. I lead Havar past the low-burning fire pit, sunk into the earthen floor and lined with stone.

I take my chair beside Ossen, while Havar fades into the background with dozens of other villagers to watch and listen. Our hostage sits with them, quiet and unmoving. One of the warriors offers the boy a flask, which he sniffs in distrust.

Girda sits on Ossen's other side, easily exchanging greetings and niceties with the newcomers, with Siru as a translator. I'm grateful that's Girda's task, not mine. I'm free to watch, listen, and study my white-haired sister.

She's charming and smooth, steady and clear-eyed. She smiles at the right times and speaks respectfully, but boldly. She's confident and seems to feel no need to hide her... otherness. I don't trust her yet, but I can't deny that I like her.

Soon, Siru and Ossen begin to discuss why the visitors have come; exploration, friendship, and trade. Again, these are not my tasks, but

I listen and watch as the travelers produce pouches of beautiful beads and black pearls, samples of herbs, precious metals, and rare furs. In turn, the Eangen produce dyes and glass, Soulderni iron and pouches of gray salts. Iesa isn't the richest or best-connected settlement, but they make a fine show of it.

The visitors say little about where they're from, other than they are called Duamel and they live in the far north, above the Algatt Mountains, beyond the Hinterlands. They worship wind spirits and I gather that Siru is tied to them. Though she translates, the Duamel obviously revere her. Their eyes drift to me too, respectful and curious.

By the time the discussion wanes, the sun is past its zenith.

"We will feast tonight," Ossen says, standing and planting his hands on the edge of the table. "Our meeting is a momentous thing and it should be properly celebrated. Besides, warriors from several neighboring villages are on their way, ready to save us from raiders, so we must at least appease them with good food and drink."

It's a tactful warning and Siru's small smile shows she's understood. This meeting has gone well, but there's still room for betrayal, especially under cover of darkness.

The foreigners outnumber the occupants of Iesa, but not for long. We have friends with axes, and they're on their way.

FIVE

F irelight fills the rafters of the hall and pours out the open doors. Villagers on the ridge cast long shadows on the beach below, where most of the Duamel camp beyond reach of the tide. Their tents are simple hide and their own campfires glow in the night, surrounded by indistinct figures and distant conversation.

In the hall, the feasting has nearly ended. Several dozen Duamel guests sit across from Eangen from Iesa and the neighboring villages, some passing pitchers of mead and laughing over fumbled attempts to communicate, while others watch warily.

I sit quietly in my carved chair beside Ossen and Girda as the food is cleared away and more mead rolled in from caves beneath the village. The barrels are tapped, and the Eangen begin to sing.

They harmonize traditional songs, throwing in growls and churrs to punctuate the final lines. I haven't seen Havar all night, but as the song fades I finally spot him stationed near the hostage, the boy's captivity little more than a formality now, with our peoples so intermingled. The child sits surrounded by curious Eangen children, who show him toys and natter at him, even though they have no common tongue. The Duamel boy remains aloof.

Havar watches over them, leaning against the wall with spear in hand. He's endeavoring to look casual, but I know him well enough to recognize the angle of his chin and tightness around his eyes. He's wary, and the Duamel's good behavior and the music have done nothing to lighten his mood.

My chest aches a little, watching him. I like him. I've agreed to marry him, and don't regret that—most days. I want to spend my days with someone, and Havar is a good man. He'd make a good husband, a fine father.

But that ache feels more like uncertainty than love.

I'm not going anywhere, Havar.

Even if they can tell you what you are?

I'm about to go to him when a Duamel man stands on his chair. The last notes of an Eangen song fade as he claps his hands over his head and waves for the room's attention. Quiet falls. Meeting the eyes of his kinsfolk, he begins to sing and nod encouragingly. They seem reluctant, but the leader's mood is infectious. Soon they're singing, and someone produces a drum. They begin to pound a steady rhythm, interspersed with taps on the heavy frame.

A sensation fills the air, amid foreign words and displaced notes. It feels like a memory, half stirred and snatched away, but its essence remains—heat on a frigid winter's evening. It's at odds with the warm autumn night, but that hardly detracts from the magic of it. It intensifies it, frames and contrasts it.

When I touch my Sight, silvered magic billows like dust with every beat of the drum. Magic. Magic drums. My aunt, the High Priestess of Thvynder, once told me that my father mentioned such instruments when he spoke of his centuries in the far north.

Now I know those centuries were spent with the Duamel. And one of the children he fathered during his sojourn is here, standing on the other side of the fire with craftsmen and merchants from nearby villages. She translates as the men and women converse, ignoring the music for the sake of oils and white bear fur.

Siru catches me watching her. Deciding to take the initiative, I nod to an empty bench on one side of the room. I rise and head toward it.

A moment later, she joins me. Nearby guests cast the pair of us sidelong looks and draw away.

"Little sister," Siru greets me in the language of the gods. "Your people are very welcoming."

I glance at the knot of merchants and craftsmen. "You've intrigued them."

"I'm surprised," she admits. "You have trade with a great empire in the south? When I heard that, I feared we would not have much to offer you."

"My people are easily bored… Your arrival has opened the world again." I let my gaze drift across the hall. "We warred for centuries with the Algatt—the mountain folk, just north—and the Empire to the south, but now we're at peace. The young are restless because they've never known war, and the old are restless because they've never known anything else. Trade and exploration are a good outlet."

"And you?" she asks. "Are you bored of peace?"

Something in her tone prickles the back of my neck. "No," I say firmly. "I know enough of war from my aunt, and mother before she died. They both lost their first husbands to it, and I've no desire to lose those I love."

"You're not afraid to die, yourself?" Siru pries.

I look at her directly, her glacial eyes locking with my earthen green. I don't want to be hostile, but I sense she knows exactly what she's asking, and I dislike the backhanded way of it.

"I don't know if I can," I reply.

She glances at my white hair and raises a cup of mead to her lips. She says into the brim, "Have you had opportunity to… find out?"

I think of blood-muddied snow and a roaring, charging beast. I had, but my grandfather stole it. "I don't know," I say, rather than confess that.

She looks at me more closely, her gaze traveling the lines of my face. "How old are you?"

"Twenty-five."

She nods slowly. I expected more of a reaction—among the Eangen, it's odd to be unmarried and without children by my age. But perhaps the pattern of life is different among her people.

"Immortality usually becomes apparent within the next ten years," she tells me. "You'll stop aging. We can speak more of this later, but Thray... I have questions."

I wait for her to go on.

"How did our father die?" she asks.

"Your spirits don't know?"

She shakes her head. "They heard he drowned. But he was immortal, so there must be more to the story. Did your new god find a way to slay him?"

I choose my words very carefully. I consider outright lying, but the story of Ogam's death is widespread. She will find out the truth eventually, if her people continue to interact with the Eangen. "There's a sacred lake, in the mountains. Our God slept there for a long time, and the water was... saturated with their power. Eang drowned Ogam in that water."

Siru is quiet for so long my palms begin to sweat. Should I have lied? Will she see the lake as a threat to her siblings' immortality, or will she blame the Eangen for the actions of our former god?

"Then our High Priestess slew Eang," I add pointedly. "My aunt."

My sister looks at me in surprise. "Your aunt is Hessa? We've heard of her."

I nod. "She's not my aunt by blood. She and my mother were close friends, and she was like a mother to me too. Especially after my own died. She drowned too, like Father. Though it was an accident."

I force myself to add the last two sentences, recounting the events dispassionately, as if the pain has healed, my chest doesn't ache, and I'm not awash in unwanted memories.

"Mothers do that... they die," Siru murmurs into her cup. I watch her face, looking for more hints to the emotion of her statement, but they're hidden away. "Strange that they should have both drowned."

I nod without comment. It was a cruel twist of fate, to be sure—and the reason I look at the sea with such distrust. I might yearn to learn the truth of whether or not I'm immortal, but not like that. Not with water in my lungs. Not enduring the same terror my parents must have, in the last moments of their lives.

"You should come north and meet your brothers and sisters."

Siru gives the invitation so casually that it takes me a moment to react. "Come with you? Now? When?"

"Before the weather turns." Siru taps the brim of her cup against her chin in thought, then sets it aside. "I see the way these Eangen watch you, Thray. They mistrust you. But see the Duamel? See the way they look at *us*?"

I cast my eyes through the crowd again. At first I can't identify anyone watching us, then I catch the glances, the covert stares of pride and want. They all come from the Duamel, and they are not just directed at Siru.

"They praise spirits in the wind," Siru continues, dropping her voice. "But it's our voices they hear."

I close my lips for a long, tense moment. "Are you saying they worship you?"

"No, no," Siru protests, her smile gentle. There's the barest hint of condescension in her eyes, but it isn't directed at me. "They worshiped our father and now that he's gone, they worship what he left behind—whether or not they understand what that is. Spirits. Children. We're all voices on the winter wind, if we choose. Some of us, like me, act as intermediaries, revered and adored and wanting for nothing. You could be one too."

Her last sentence makes my heart skip an unruly beat. I'm tempted in a vague, unsettled way. What she's describing is certainly better than mistrust, but it *is* worship, whether or not she gives it that name.

"I am a priestess of Thvynder, one of the Four Pillars of the World," I remind her and myself. "I do not want worship. I'm just a woman."

"Perhaps." She sits back against the wall behind us. "Some of Ogam's Get are 'just' men and women. They live and die like their mothers. But you've yet to learn what you are."

I feel as if Siru is peeling my soul bare, prodding the questions and fears that have plagued me since I was old enough to understand who my father was.

"I don't want to be more," I say, and the coldness in my words is almost a physical thing. My skin prickles.

Siru reaches for one of my hands. I draw away, and she settles her hand back in her lap.

"Your want doesn't change anything. It will trap you here, watching everyone in this village die and be replaced by their children, who will also die some day." Once again, her words gouge into me, too knowing, too insightful. "We do not die. We live on, together. I've stood two hundred years by my siblings' sides, and I'll stand a thousand more. Together, we're as strong as our father ever was. We are Ogam. We are Winter himself."

Two hundred years. I stare into her face, which looks barely older than my own, and marvel at how young I must seem to her. How naive and unseasoned. That irks me.

"My place is here," I say, though the words feel dull on my tongue. "I'm the next priestess of this village. My God is in this land, and I'll be married in a few months."

Siru sits up straighter. "Married? To whom?"

"An Eangen man."

I can't read her expression. It might be distaste, but maybe it's pity. Whatever it is, it's usurped by her gentle sincerity.

"Then think on it," she says, picking her cup back up and taking a long drink. "We won't leave for a few days, and there is always next spring. I'm sure we'll be back when the ice breaks up."

I almost tell her not to bother. She smiles a knowing smile and taps her cup against my arm, then sets it on the bench and leaves.

It's not until she's merged into the crowd that I glance down into her cup and see its contents have turned to ice—a perfect impossibility in the warmth of the feasting hall.

Are you sure you're not more?

I need air. I navigate the edge of the hall, slipping past knots of murmuring guests and stepping over others, seated on the floor with extended legs and half-drained mugs of mead or ale. A child tugs on my skirt, and I don't have the presence of mind to acknowledge them.

The night air is cool, salty, and light. I head inland, through the village toward the forest that sheltered most of the population earlier today. The sounds of the settlement are replaced by the susurration of wind in the pines and the melancholy calls of night birds.

There's a small shrine, just inside the trees. A boulder forms a natural altar, flat-topped, knee-high, and stained from centuries of sacrifices. Once, priests of Eang bled seals and seabirds and goats here, even themselves, but those days are long passed. Now only a black stain remains, and an offering bowl carved into the stone.

There's a small box at the foot of the altar. I retrieve a nest of frayed birch bark, kindling, and herbs, clear out the offering bowl with a puff of breath, and lay the new material inside. I pull iron and flint from my belt pouch, and, still kneeling, close my eyes.

"Thvynder," I say to the shadows. "I need council."

I strike flint to iron in a rain of sparks, then another. Light and warmth from my little fire play across my cheeks, and the scent of the curling herbs fills my nostrils.

A presence brushes across the back of my mind, but otherwise my God does not reply. Parts of Thvynder remain here, in Eangen, but the uniting force that is the God is absent. They have been for over a year—a secret carefully kept by the priesthood.

Still, the prayer and that presence settles me. My God is not gone or neglectful, just distant. I could send an owl to the Watchman or the Vestige and get the council I need, but they're both bound by place and time. It would take days to receive a reply, and the Duamel might not stay that long.

"Grandfather," I venture, reaching again for the voice that led me up the coast. But he's silent too.

I sit back on my heels and fill my lungs with a deep breath. Siru.

Ogam. Siblings. Havar. I take each thought and separate them, giving each its own space to root. I need to see each of them clearly, to weigh them logically.

But I don't want to be logical tonight. Tonight, I burn with the reality that another of my father's daughters is here in Iesa, and with her answers and possibilities I'd thought were out of reach.

My eyes drift open and my hand falls to the bone-handled knife at my belt. I set it on the edge of the stone altar, a line between myself and the fire. The weapon is another connection to my father's bloodline, the half of me I've never had the chance to explore.

Once the Duamel leave, will the possibility of answers go with them? If trade is established, I could go north next year, but by then I'll be married. I might even be with child, and it will be time for me to take over as chief priest in Iesa. I won't be tramping off into foreign territory to investigate spirits on the wind. I'll be nestled into the rhythms of ordinary, mortal life, and bound to its obligations.

No, once Siru and her boats sail away, my chances of exploring my heritage go with them. And I need answers now, before I give myself to Havar—and my blood to a child.

I eye the knife. At a push of my will, it lengthens to a curved, sickle sword with a soft scrape of rock and bone. Firelight plays across the blade, white and smooth as folded steel.

I become aware of footsteps approaching from the village. I hold still, hoping whoever it is will change their mind and leave me be. I'm on the edge of a decision, one I desperately want to make.

"Thray?" Havar's voice asks. There's a hard edge to it, an unspoken question that immediately makes me feel guilty.

I look over my shoulder as he stops a respectful two paces back from the altar. I meet his eyes, and my indecision gives way to painful knowledge.

My duty is here. Outside of a directive from Thvynder themself, I cannot leave Eangen.

"They're saying Siru asked you to come back north with her,"

Havar says. His voice is carefully low and level but his stance is coiled, leashed. Possessive. His eyes flick to the altar and the fire burning there. "Are you..."

"Considering it. I... came to pray," I reply honestly. I pat the earth beside me. "You can sit with me."

He closes the space between us and drops into a squat, but doesn't touch the altar in any way. He doesn't even look at the fire. That is a self-imposed restriction. To the Iesan, the altar and its flames are the realm of priests and priestesses, not fisherfolk.

"What did the God say?" my would-be husband asks. He and the common Eangen do not make offerings like I've done, and they certainly do not pray.

The God says nothing. But I cannot tell him that. For all Havar knows, Thvynder spoke to me from the night sky and commanded me to go north with the whole of Eangen in escort.

That thought, the opportunity and the simplicity of it, makes my breath hitch.

Havar notices. "What? Thray, what's wrong?"

For a moment I see him as he'll be in fifty years—aged and bent, eyes already fixed on the High Halls of the Dead. Will I have aged too, or will I kneel here just as I do now, with strength in my limbs and not a crease around my eyes? Will we grow old together, hand in hand, or will I remain young, caring for him until the inevitable dawn when I awake and he does not?

The decision rushes close again. Just a few words, a simple lie, and I could be free. Free to go with Siru. Free to find the answers I so desperately need.

But to falsely claim a divine mandate is the gravest of transgressions for a member of the priesthood. If I was discovered, I'd face exile—or worse.

It is rare that a Vynder priest be executed or exiled nowadays, but I've seen it happen; a priestess exiled for using false visions to control her village headwoman, a priest executed for taking bribes in a judicial ruling and covering the transgression with false affirmation from our God.

Right now, my lie would affect only me. Surely my punishment would not be so severe.

I push punishments from my mind. I can't think about them now, vague possibilities that they are. Havar and his worry, however, are present and tangible.

Can I lie to him? He'll be devastated if I leave. Even now he's handsome in the firelight, his attention centered on me, his shoulders broad and his concern sincere. He wants me. He trusts me. I trust him, and all at once, the thought of leaving him fills me with a yawning ache.

Sensing my conflict, he shifts onto his knees and takes my hands in his, giving me plenty of opportunity to pull away. Our eyes are level but his hands are larger and warmer, enfolding mine.

"I'm to go with Siru," I say before I can talk myself out of it. The words feel like they come from someone else's mouth, some part of my mind disconnecting from the magnitude of what I've just done.

I plunge ahead, my brazen tongue harried ineffectually by my own, horrified, good sense. "I'm supposed to go north and return next summer," I state.

Havar's hands tighten to the point where they hurt, but I don't point it out.

"You're sure?"

"Yes. We'll have to marry after I come back."

I flex my fingers meaningfully and he releases them. For a long moment he's silent, then he clears his throat. "I'll go with you, then."

"No," I immediately protest, but as soon as I say it, I doubt myself. I've already acknowledged I don't want to leave him, but I also want to go with Siru. Can I… have both?

The deepening lie twists in my stomach. I'm backing myself deeper into a corner, and I need to be sure I'm making the right decision. What if the High Priestess discovers my deception? A lie that only risks myself is one thing, but one that puts Havar at risk?

I waver. What if I forget about Siru's offer entirely? What if I marry Havar and mother children, and watch them grow old and die, one by one? Pyre after pyre. Even if I do not marry him and choose a different life in another village, everyone I form a bond with will end in the stench of smoke and crisping skin.

No. I cannot do that. I need to know the truth. And I want Havar to come.

It's my turn to clutch his hands. "Come with me."

A grin creeps into the corner of his mouth. His gaze drops to my lips, and a little shiver creeps down my arms. He kisses me lightly and I close my eyes, letting the brush of his skin soothe my bewildered conscience.

His breath is warm on my lips as he challenges, "Just you try to leave me behind."

SIX: INTERLUDE

"This is where the Old World ended," my aunt tells me. "Where the gods fell."

We stand beside a pale lake, nestled in the mountains and girded with barren, rocky slopes. My mother's other child, Vistic, is nearby, watching tiny ripples on the water as if the lake is speaking to him.

For all I know, it is. There was a day when he'd tell me such things, when we would curl up together against a cold night and he'd describe his dreams and conversations with the God. But that was before I became a woman, he a man, and his duties as Vestige consumed him.

My aunt dips a toe of her boot in the water with a soft splash and looks over at me. I'm eighteen, nearly grown, and she's shorter than I am. But her dense musculature and the hooded axe at her belt more than make up for her height. She's the image of a warrior goddess with warm sunlight on her ruddy, freckled face—her long black braid, her scars. But she's human, flesh and blood, even if that blood is a little more gold than usual.

Hessa, High Priestess of Thvynder, points down the shoreline and several paces out into the water. "That's where Eang drowned your father."

She says the words simply, without softening them. I never met my father, and his death is something I've long grown accustomed to speaking of. But here, in the place where his immortal life ended, it is weightier than usual.

48

I draw mountain air in my lungs, settle myself, and examine the lake. It's so thick with minerals that it looks like milk. It's harmless to Hessa, and the boot she dampened in it. But the power of Thvynder lingers here, in the water that sheltered them for thousands of years. In the lingering power that can kill the immortal, that drowned my father in its murky waters.

That power doesn't bother my half-brother, standing on the shore with the breeze rustling his Eangen-black curls. Despite his connection to the God, he's as mortal as Hessa.

I shift my weight back in my heels, separating myself slightly from the placid lake.

"Where did you kill Eang?" I ask.

"There." Hessa points to a spot near where my father died. "Ogam had turned the surface to ice. Eang and I fought on it."

"And his body?"

"There was none. It turned to snow by the next morning and blew away." She watches the spot on the lake, brown eyes thoughtful. "That's all he often was. Wind, snow. Formless."

There's a moment of silence between us. I stare at the water without seeing it. "This is the only place I can die too. If I'm… like him."

Hessa's hand closes on my forearm and Vistic looks up at us for the first time. His eyes have their usual distracted blankness, but there's a flicker in them, a passing concern.

"Yes," Hessa says. The simple admission shocks me, as does what she says next. "But if you are like your father, Thray, there's much, much good you can do in this world. Fate weaves and you're an integral thread. Perhaps you are a long one too. Swear to me you will not touch this water until your purpose is fulfilled."

I imagine my father, drowned here by Eang's hands. I imagine my mother, drifting to the riverbank below the rapids that killed her. It would be fitting to end my days, but the thought of it horrifies me.

Wind traces ripples across the surface of the lake, lashing stray, white hair into my eyes.

"Thray?" my aunt prompts.

"I swear," I reply, though I've no idea whether I'm lying. This matter is too personal, too bound up in my fears, to give a binding answer.

"As to the whether or not you're immortal," Hessa continues. "You swore to your mother you would not force an answer to that question. Not by your own hand."

Tension skitters across my shoulders like ripples across the lake. But maybe that's because Vistic watches us. Knowing and distracted. Human and divine.

"Yes," I affirm, though again, the line between truth and lie eludes me. "I promise. I'll keep my word."

Hessa smiles at me, then nods back to a forest on the southern side of the valley. Trails of smoke mark a settlement among the trees, almost entirely of priests and their families. It is the heart of the Vynder priesthood. Our priesthood.

"Then come, my feral children need to be found and fed. Will you help me?"

I smile, but the expression feels empty. "Of course."

As we leave the lakeside, I catch Vistic's eye. He still watches me, another flicker of concern cracking through his distraction. Does he sense my lies? Does he know how the question of my mortality burns in my chest? Can he foresee the lengths it will drive me to?

If he does, he does not speak.

SEVEN

Two days later, Duamel oars cut through the waves again. I sit beneath an awning in the stern of the ship with Havar and three other Eangen companions, while ships divide the waves to either side. Rowers line both gunnels, their spears tucked into racks midship and their sealskin cloaks belted tight against the wind.

Anxiety roils in my belly with the rhythm of the waves. I battle not to look at them, not to contemplate the water surrounding us or how easily it could swallow me, as it did my mother and father. My fear of the water is instinctual and visceral, embedded in my bones in a way that rational thought cannot root out.

Yet now I've taken to sea, bound myself to a ship for what will most likely be weeks. I have to bear it. So I will.

I swallow a rise of bile and gaze at Iesa's ridge and hall, tiny formations and drifts of hearthsmoke on the horizon. But all too soon they slip away, engulfed by the sea. All that remain are the white-crowned waves and the hazy, indistinct rocks of the coastline, interrupted now and again by the creaking swing of the boom as the ship tacks.

I close my eyes and turn inward, reframing the tremor in my belly as excitement. I'm on my way. Answers to the questions that have haunted me since childhood are just over the gray clouds of the northern horizon. They lie with my sister at the prow of the ship, sequestered in her own thoughts. And they're in the hands of the hundreds of siblings I'll soon meet, men and women just like me—half mortal, half divine.

This is more than I ever hoped for, and I won't let anything spoil it—not my dread of the waves, nor my nagging fear of discovery.

I know, objectively, that I was wrong to lie to Havar about Thvynder sending me north. The matter has already gotten out of hand, with three more Eangen deciding to join us on our journey, including Havar's eldest brother Darag. But my conscience is silent.

I need this. And I need Havar with me.

My betrothed watches the spot where Iesa was for a long time before he looks back at me. I expect him to look grim—Darag does, staring back as if he can still see his wife and children on the cliffs.

But to my surprise, Havar smiles. It's a lithe, crooked expression.

"This feels right," he says, lacing an arm around my shoulder to pull me into him. I let him, shifting into his side, and the seaspray in his beard dampens my cheek. "You and me, heading into the unknown?"

"I'm here too," Darag reminds him sourly. He squints glistening eyes, and I suspect that the wind isn't the only reason for their watering. "Fool that I am."

Despite Havar's excitement and my earlier resolve, Darag's words prod at my determination. I'd barely thought about how leaving might affect my future brother-in-law. I worried briefly for his wife and children, but in my experience fathers are always absent things. I didn't expect him to struggle with leaving. But Darag clearly does—his eyes are tight and he never lifts his gaze from the south-east.

Still, he insisted on coming, as did the other Eangen in our small party—Seele, a merchant, and Branan, the hunter who interrupted my journey to the hall on the morning the Duamel arrived.

The people of Iesa would not allow their priestess to go off without a guard, even if that priestess is possibly immortal and has martial skills to rival the best of them. It also didn't help that warriors from the nearby villages were present over the last few days, judging and *tsk*ing over the risk of it all. The pride of the people of Iesa was irked, and they had to make a good show.

I sit straighter beside Havar and tug my cloak tighter around my shoulders. "Thank you for coming."

Seele, a woman near thirty with thick freckles, grunts. She's better kept than the rest of us, her hair tightly braided and her deep purple apron dress pinned with fine bronze brooches beneath her black sea cloak. She's small and pretty, in a shrewd kind of way, and it's her that will be overseeing the mercantile aspect of our journey.

"All of you," I clarify, then add coyly, "except for you, Branan."

The others chuckle. The hunter frowns at me and tips his nose up to the wind. He inhales, and his shoulder-length black hair lashes across his face. "Of course, priestess."

Throughout the day, I watch the coastline, ignoring the water in between as stolidly as I can. The seaspray-shrouded rocks transition to cascading waterfalls and smooth, pebbled beaches. Forests come and go, and the Algatt Mountains to the north grow larger, peaking through a layer of heavy cloud. Glaciers glisten between them, twisting rivers of ice. Sea eagles ride the wind and, on outcroppings of rock, seals bark and bask.

When the sun is high, I join Siru in the stern. She offers me a bowl of cold fish and flatbread smeared with butter, which I take, and settle at her side.

The smell of the fish turns my already unsettled stomach. But I spoon some into my mouth and force myself to chew.

"What's in the west?" I ask between careful bites. "You said your people explored there this summer?"

"You don't know?" Siru looks at me quizzically.

"My people spent most of their existence fighting the Algatt and shedding their blood for Eang," I tell her, sniffing at the bread. "We had no time for exploration. Eang was Goddess of War, not conquest."

"Or victory," Siru observes, "if the war lasted so long."

I shrug and try the flatbread. It's fresh from Iesa, seasoned with salt and herbs, and goes down much more readily than the fish. I wonder when I'll taste the likes of it again.

"All blood shed in worship strengthened her," I say. "She'd no reason to seek victory. So what's in the west?"

"Islands." Siru settles back against the bulwark in a way that makes my knees weak with apprehension, wind tugging at loose strands of her white hair. "A barren coastline, in the south. We found ruins, here and there, signs of a lost people. The land around them was flooded, though. Destroyed. No forests, no arable land. We did find rivers heading south, but hadn't the time to explore them."

My imagination sparks at her words. "My people came from across the Western Sea, long ago."

"Before they worshiped Eang?"

"Yes. Eang came to them in the first winter, here on the coast. Some chose to worship her. Others moved farther north. They became the Algatt."

"Mm, the Algatt." Siru glances toward the coast and the distant mountains, now almost entirely shrouded in cloud. "Their god is still alive?"

"Gadr. But he's not a god."

My half-sister turns her gaze to me, critically. "Ah. Yes, I understand there is only one being you call a 'god,' now?"

I chew a bite of bread, choosing my words carefully before I reply. "No. There are four. The Four Pillars, who made the world, including the Miri and humanity. Our God is Thvynder. Eiohe is absent, but his echo remains in the Arpa Empire. Fate weaves time itself."

Siru furrows her brows at my mention of Fate, then she asks, "Who's the fourth?"

"Imilidese," I reply.

"Where are they?"

I tear at my bread again, buying myself time. This question is precisely why Thvynder has left Eangen. "She abandoned creation, long ago. Before the first Miri, the Gods of the Old World, rebelled and drove the Pillars away—except Thvynder, who they bound in the White Lake I told you about."

Siru lowers her bowl and considers me. I'm not sure if she believes what I'm saying, but she doesn't contradict me. Instead she says, "Father told us of the Old Gods. Their tombs are in Duamel."

A shiver creeps across my shoulders. "You've been there?"

"Yes, and I can take you."

I watch her, flatbread, fish, and unsettled stomach forgotten.

"Unless you don't want to see them," Siru says, mistaking my silence. "Perhaps a Vynder priestess would have... qualms about visiting such a place."

"No, I want to see them," I say, and I mean it. I'm fascinated, awed, perturbed—and it's an intoxicating combination. "I want to see everything."

Siru's smile is wry. "Then you will. Though I'm afraid Duamel is a rather barren place—our people are not so numerous as the Eangen and the Algatt. Our cities are large, but widespread, and most people still live in very small villages in the forests. But it has its beauty."

She trails off, and I follow her gaze up the side of the ship to the rowers. Havar is there, stripped down to a light undertunic, muscles straining at an oar, wind drying the sweat on his face. He catches my eye and grins.

"He's yours?" Siru asks, contemplation in her blue eyes. "You're fortunate he followed you."

"I am," I murmur, breaking Havar's gaze. I don't want to talk about him—there's so much more I need to know about Duamel and my siblings. "With the seas like this, how long until we reach your homeland?"

"Two weeks, perhaps." Siru glances up at the sails, then the northern horizon. "A week to the north coast, a week on the river. Longer if we encounter obstacles, or early winter storms."

I nod my understanding, trying not to show how uneasy the thought of two weeks at sea makes me. Still, it's better than I hoped.

"What kind of obstacles?" I prod.

Siru raises her face to the wind like a hound. Fine braids, already stiffening with salt, flutter in the wind. "Unfavorable winds. Early ice and winter storms, as I said. The serpents. They breed in the northern seas at this time of year, before they freeze into the ice. At the first whisper of snow on the wind, they'll converge, and the sea will boil."

My sister lifts a hand and pulls up her sleeve, disentangling three bracelets. They are circles of unbroken bone, carved with geometric patterns and foreign runes. Each marking is outlined with what I think might once have been a rust-red paint, though now it is little more than a stain.

"Cuttings from a serpent's fangs," she says as she shakes the bracelets down to her wrist and lets me examine them.

I touch one, warmed and smoothed by Siru's skin, and turn it. Imagining a serpent big enough to produce something like it is staggering. "Did you kill it yourself?"

"Not alone, but yes." Siru watches me examine the item, then pulls her sleeve back down. Her focus is distant, and her smile reticent. "But first, I rode it."

I can't help it. I gape, sure my half-sister must be lying.

She smiles, nearly a smirk. "We have our amusements, we children of Ogam. Immortality is emboldening, if nothing else."

That night, we shelter in an inlet, and I'm so thankful to be back on land that I stand rooted in the sand for a long moment, buffeted by the breeze as the Duamel disembark.

We've traveled far enough that the low forest and broad sandy beach are unfamiliar, but precisely how far we've come isn't clear. Clouds overtook the mountains to the north-east hours ago, and even Havar, who has sailed the coast of Eangen since he was a child, is unsure where we are.

"There are hundreds of inlets between Iesa and the mountains." He shrugs, where he stands at my side, watching the Duamel anchor their largest ships in the shallow waters. The smaller vessels have already been run ashore around us, depositing most of the company for a night on dry land. "I don't know all of them."

"That's all right, as long as we haven't crossed into Algatt territory." I rub at my cheeks, exhausted by the sun and wind and the nagging threat of the waves. I'm harboring a small hope that I'm growing accustomed to being at sea, but I'm not sure it's true. "Gods forbid they think the same thing we did when the Duamel put ashore. We'll be dead before morning."

"We can't have moved that quickly." Havar hefts our packs and looks up the shore to where the other Eangen gather around Darag. "I'll get us settled?"

I nod absently and he leaves me alone on the sand.

I watch the Duamel make camp. They raise tents of hide and oilcloth with oar frames, arranging them in circular clusters that likely highlight divisions between tribes or familial lines I've yet to learn. Wood clatters, iron strikes, and fires ignite along the shore, surrounded by busy figures and drifting voices. No one shouts commands but there's an obvious order to the proceedings, each person aware of their role and completing it with efficiency.

Only Siru does not work, wandering through the assembling camp as she absently braids her hair. The hems of her clothes ripple in the breeze and her gaze is vigilant, but calm. The Duamel have likely done this a hundred times over the course of their summer exploring the Western Sea, and she's at ease.

But worry stirs at the back of my mind. I glance north-east again, searching the waning day for the Algatt Mountains. The Eangen and the Algatt have been at peace since before I was born, but my generation still knows the stories—farms raided, loved ones carried off into slavery, and villages burned. Our conflict sated the Goddess of War and ensured that no one, even I, am oblivious to the threat of landing unannounced on Algatt shores. Let alone landing with several hundred armed foreigners.

Duamel scouts leave the camp, heading for a sandy ridge and low pine forest. I follow their progress, eyes lingering on their spears, and come to a quick decision.

I unshoulder my bow and start after them. I clamber up the short incline, wedging my feet between exposed roots and pushing drooping boughs out of my path. The scouts are almost out of sight, but I don't rush, content to make my own observations.

I tuck frayed, salt-stiff hair behind my ears and trail the scouts, bow in hand and half my attention on the forest around us. If there is an Algatt settlement in the area, there should be signs. The Algatt aren't a subtle people and since the peace, they've grown particularly pointed in marking their trails and sacred places.

I catch a sound—not the scouts, heading north along the edge of the inlet—but farther inland. I pause. The beach is out of sight and the roar of wind in the boughs merges with the crash of the waves, but I can still hear the slight scuff of footfalls.

A shout goes up from the scouts. The cry is followed by an Algatt war horn, so close and so loud I curse.

More shouts erupt from the trees—war cries I know in my bones. The Duamel scouts reappear, sprinting toward me with shock and dismay in their faces.

A dozen Algatt thunder behind. Pale-haired and armed with axes, spears and round shields, they roar. They're barely armored, wearing little more than padded tunics with the Algatt's signature triangular hemlines. Some have intricate vests of boiled leather plates and only one has a coat of mail—but the Duamel scouts wear much less.

I sprint toward the fleeing Duamel, meeting them halfway, but instead of continuing toward the beach they fall in behind me, as if they expect me to protect them. I stare, then my thoughts are full of charging Algatt warriors, axes raised, blond hair smudged with blue and yellow paint, and faces twisted in challenge.

"Stop!" I shout in Eangen—close enough to the Algatt dialect that there's no chance of misunderstanding. "I'm a priestess of Thvynder, stop!"

The Algatt come up short. One, a man with a thick beard, an axe, and round shield, calls in reply, "Then who are *they*?"

"Duamel, from the north, returning home after explorations in the west," I explain, trying to soothe him with the steadiness of my voice. "Have we trespassed?"

"You have." This voice comes from the forest beyond the Algatt. A huge man steps out from behind a cluster of pines and squints, taking in me and the Duamel. He has a shaved scalp and a thick blond beard, braided and augmented with horsehair in various hues. His feet are bare, and he wears slim trousers and a worn green tunic with its laces undone, revealing a hairy chest of blond and gray.

"Back down, I know this woman," Gadr, Miri and former god of the Algatt, says to his people.

They're slow to comply, but gradually, shields and axes lower—only to snap back up again as more Duamel swarm into the forest from the beach. Siru is at their head, but when she spies Gadr and I, she throws up a hand.

The Duamel halt. Siru continues forward alone without slowing her pace, soft boots sinking into the sand, needles, and moss of the forest floor.

Gadr notes her, narrows his eyes, and looks back to me. "Do your uncles know you're so far from home?" He pauses a moment, then adds with more feeling, "Does your aunt?"

I almost smile, hiding the expression in the corner of my mouth. My hand had strayed to the knife at my belt but I release it, easing my weight into my heels. "As if you'd tell them."

"I would not," he acknowledges, ducking his chin and wandering closer. His gaze shifts to Siru, and he scowls. "Is *that* what I think it is?"

Siru steps up beside me. "Are you what I think you are?" she asks, returning the insult.

"Unhappy to meet you and wondering why you're on my land? Yes." Gadr waves at his Algatt and they fall back half a dozen paces off into the forest. Their eyes are still wary, but their trust in Gadr is stronger.

"You know this creature?" Siru asks me.

"He's the Miri Gadr," I tell her. "Former god of the Algatt."

"Before Thvynder showed me the error of my ways and I took a life of humble kingship," Gadr elaborates with a stiff smile. "Why are you on my land?"

"We're going north," I tell him, before Siru can speak. There's no use denying it, but I don't have to tell the whole truth. "This is Siru, and her people are the Duamel. They live in the far north."

"Duamel who?" Gadr squints. Behind him the Algatt still hover with their axes and round shields, and behind Siru, the Duamel wait with their spears and tall shields.

The breath of silence before Siru answers stretches long, and I become overly aware of the hush in the forest. Even the distant sounds of camp have gone quiet, and I imagine the hundreds more Duamel on the beach, watching the forest and waiting to attack.

"The Duamel are the people of Ogam, my father," Siru replies. "I assume you were there? The day he was murdered."

"Yes, I was," Gadr replies, watching my half-sister with a flinty eye. "I wonder why you were not. Or did he not bring his spawn on his expedition of treachery and ruin?"

Siru meets his stare, cold fury behind her eyes. "You know nothing about my father."

Gadr laughs a dangerous, warning laugh, and I glance to the long knife at his thigh. I know he would do nothing to harm me—his relationship with my Eangen family has always been tense, but he and I have an understanding. Siru, however, is a different story.

Gadr abruptly grunts and scratches his beard, jutting his chin forward. A few stray hairs fall on the front of his tunic, he brushes them away, and the tension shatters.

"You must be what I remember as the Erene," the Miri concludes. "I haven't heard of them in many long years. Didn't realize there were any left."

At the name, Siru stiffens further. "We are called the Duamel," she corrects.

Gadr shrugs, unaffected. "You're too young to remember, anyway."

"I've two centuries."

"Two centuries!" Gadr raises his eyebrows in mock admiration. "What are centuries to me? I remember when Esach first sought my bed in midwinter, Addack himself walked the sands of this very coast, and the Great Bear took his mortal wound. I also remember the day your grandmother cut your father from her swollen belly and left him on a mountaintop to die."

I see Siru's nostrils flare, and I think she might lose her temper. For a moment I see the three of us from a distance—ancient Miri, centuried Winterborn, and... myself. I am so young in comparison, so new to this world, ignorant of its histories and unsure of my place.

Not for long, I remind myself.

"If you've finished being difficult," I say to Gadr, "perhaps you and I can escort your warriors away from the beach. We'll be gone by dawn, I assure you."

Gadr shoves both thumbs through his belt and sniffs at Siru. "Have a safe journey north, Daughter of Ogam. And be warned—the Algatt do not take kindly to unexpected ships on their shores."

Siru's smile is hollow and her eyes remain sharp. "We'll be gone by morning, as Thray says."

"Good." Gadr turns to me and nods back toward his people. "I've more to say to you, pup."

I turn to Siru: "I'll be back soon."

My sister waves to her people. They vanish toward the beach and her white braid is the last I see of her in the fading afternoon light.

Gadr's already walking in the opposite direction, so I jog to catch up.

"Hessa doesn't know you've run off with a Winterborn?" he asks. The Algatt cast cautious glances over their shoulders, but do not wait.

"I haven't run off," I inform him. "I'm going north to learn what I am. Mortal. Immortal."

The admission comes easier this time. Gadr was there the day I faced the savn. He saw the blood, and he surely knew what I'd tried to do.

I imagine saying the same thing to Havar, and my throat feels clotted.

Gadr cocks his head to one side, but whatever he thinks of my latest attempt to learn what I am, he doesn't say.

"Well, I can hold my tongue. For a price," he informs me. "There's an old door to the High Halls in the area, you see, and if I was to wander through, I could have the entire High Priesthood here within... oh, an hour?"

I darken as I feel a flash of fear and surprise. It's a reminder that, even if this man and I have a peaceable relationship, he's not safe. "What do you want?"

Gadr stops walking and rounds to face me, until we're only a pace apart. "There's a lot more in the north than these Duamel. The tombs of the Old Gods are there too, and other... things. Bring me home a gift, Thray, Daughter of Winter. Hessa and Imnir will find out about your little escapade soon, I'm sure, but bring me something pretty, and they will not hear it from me."

A chill creeps over my skin at mention of the tombs. But his request is a simple one, and though I suspect a trap, I do not ask for more detail. Gadr's motives are a problem for my future self.

"All right," I agree. "I'll do it."

Gadr nods with gravity. "Good. Keep the Erene on the beach, and no harm will come to them."

"Keep your Algatt in the forest and no harm will come to them, either."

I wait until he's out of sight before I release a long breath. I feel simultaneously relieved and doomed, but I've ensured word of my departure doesn't reach home until I'm long gone.

Home. I realize belatedly that if we've trespassed into Algatt territory, I've officially left Eangen behind. Sometime that day, in the wind and waves, we passed an invisible divide.

I am on my way north, and nothing will turn me back.

EIGHT

The sea ends in a lattice of peninsulas and narrow islands, shoals and high cliffs. The cold wind carries a sodden, salty chill that frosts Havar's beard and the fur collar of my kaftan, where it peeks out from my heavy cloak.

Around us, the Duamel exhibit a skill in sailing that has Darag muttering and Havar camped by the tiller, studying every heading, trim, and tack as we weave through the treacherous waters. But though my fear of the waves is as leashed as I can manage, sailing and ships still hold no interest for me. I think only of the future, and how I wish for the warmth of a fire and shelter from the wind. I take to pacing down the center of the ship, between the rows of benches, but end up in the way of the sailors.

So I shed my outer clothing and take up an oar, relishing the burn of exertion that flushes my skin—though I can't tell whether it's the cold that raises gooseflesh on my skin, or the slosh and rush of the water, just on the other side of the hull.

We sail through a narrow strait between several islands. Dense, moody clouds converge in the western sky, wrapping us in premature gloom. Thin rays of golden warmth are snuffed out and the wind shifts, turning from crisp to tooth-shattering. Above my oar bench, the sails luff with a rippling, sighing snap.

I shiver in my sweat-soaked undertunic and pause to ship my oar. I jerk my wool overtunic back over my head and tug it down around my hips. The bite of the wind immediately lessens, but my sweat is still icy against my skin.

"Hold!" Siru shouts. I tug my braids from my collar as she hastens to the prow, where she confers with several wary-looking Duamel. Other northerners scatter to drop the sail and the pattern of the oars changes, maintaining our heading but ceasing to draw us forward.

Curiosity piqued, I glance around. A Duamel woman, anticipating my need before I voice it, steps forward and gestures to take my oar. There's an urgency about her and a discomfort, and I'm not sure it's entirely to do with the change in the wind. She seems relieved to see the oar leave my hand.

Disconcerted, I nod my thanks and, snatching up my cloak, join Siru. I pass Havar at another oar. He opens his mouth to speak to me but I ignore him, not out of maliciousness, but practicality. Something is happening, and it has Siru worried.

I see his expression close, wounded. But I'm too cold and distracted to turn back.

"What is it?" I ask Siru, pulling my cloak tight and trying not to shiver. In the back of my mind, I hear my mother's voice chiding me for putting on my outer clothes before my sweat dried.

"I don't know," my sister tells me, eyeing the strait. The rocking of the ship increases—we've nearly stopped now. I spread my stance wider, ever wary of the gunnel and the waves beyond. "I'd wonder if it's Grandfather but... I do not sense him. Do you?"

I stretch my senses. I do feel him, but only in the distant way that always accompanies the coming of the winter season.

I shake my head. "No. Just an early winter gale?"

Siru looks between me and the Duamel sailors she'd been speaking with, all of them bundled against the cold, long-lashed eyes narrowed and cheeks windburned.

"We make for the lee of that island and anchor for the night," she says, nodding east. One of the islands that brackets the strait looms there, its rocky ranges sprawled through the waves like the arms of a dead squid, tossed onto shore. Waves crash against its peninsulas and a scattering of huge, lonely boulders to the south-east, I think I spy what Siru has—a sheltered inlet.

The Duamel eye the island, the wind, and the choppy waves in between for a long heartbeat. I see the uncertainty in their faces, though they try to hide it, and I think they might disagree with Siru. Then they murmur in their language and move to the task.

I remain with Siru as the ship begins to come about, guided by a new pattern of the drum. My nerves sing as the deck rocks and I grab for a line, anchoring myself in place. Waves slap against the hull, each one more jarring and unpredictable than the last. The wind tears froth from their peaks, spraying salt into my eyes, and I swallow a surge of trepidation.

The other Duamel ships, spread out across the sea behind us, slowly follow us. There's the creak of booms, the strain and grind of oars, and the rush of the prow through the waves alters. Then the sails loose, fill, and the ship straightens out.

I let out a shaky breath as we begin to cut through the waves again, now heading east with the wind behind us, away from the stormfront. The gale whisks past Siru and I, sending our braids and the edges of our cloaks fluttering. I can't help but watch my sister sidelong, beautiful and regal with massing storm clouds at her back. She looks like a hero from a tale. She looks like a goddess.

My earlier trepidation retreats into a knot of emotion and yearning. The pull of her, of the Winterborn, redoubles.

Do the Duamel look at me the way I look at Siru? A thread of guilt and self-conscious embarrassment—cinches around my chest, but it quickly relaxes in the face of my sister's presence and power.

"I need to know if I'm immortal," I admit suddenly. I'm sharply conscious of the wind, toying with our words, and the ears it might carry them to. But I mirror Siru's composure, her presence and dignity. Part of me is aware of the childishness of that act; part of me does not care.

"You will," Siru assures me, as if my request is some banal, daily thing. She touches the back of my arm and gives it an encouraging squeeze. "There's a ritual we will perform, one to test your immortality without requiring your death. But we can speak more of that when we're with the rest of the Winterborn."

I nod, somewhat soothed.

Anything more we might have said is lost as the light dims further and the wind picks up. Siru and I look past the rowing Duamel as the ship rocks and the straining masts creak.

I taste the snow before I see it, flakes swirling past us in streaks of white. It snags on my clothes and hair and I lift a hand to catch some, watching it melt on my palm.

Siru makes a sound, somewhere between relief and resignation. "Ah. There is our answer, then."

"The storm?" I ask, but something else has caught my attention. Nearby, a tousle-haired boy perches on the ship's rail, clutching a line. I flinch, seeing him so close to the water, but contain myself. This isn't the first time I've watched the Duamel, or even the Eangen, tempt the hungry sea.

I recognize the boy—he's the hostage we'd hosted in Iesa. He's as aloof now as he was then, taunting his caretaker in Duamel as the man calls for him—presumably—to get down. The boy laughs, feet dangling, careless and unworried.

"The serpents," Siru says, and gestures to the boiling waves. "They—"

I've just turned to gape at her when a wave strikes us broadside. The whole vessel lurches. I stagger, water gulps over the deck around the laughing boy, and he topples backwards over the rail.

I do not think, not on Siru's words, not on my actions. I lunge for the child and grab his tunic just as the dark ocean swallows him whole. I feel his hands clamp on my arms, see his mouth open in a gargling scream through a sheen of rushing water. I've just enough time to feel horror at the sight—then we're both in the sea.

My world becomes one of numbing, liquid cold. The air punches from my lungs and I spasm, but I instinctively pull too.

Thin arms clamp around my upper body. Salt stings and blurs my eyes. I can barely see, but I feel a small frame: ribs through layered clothing, a knobby elbow, and warm flesh.

When I was a child, my aunt, Hessa, taught me to swim under the winter ice. After my mother's death I refused to continue the tradition. Yet now, as shocking as the plunge into the sea has been, it's a familiar shock, and the disorientation is fleeting.

My shattered awareness pieces back together with the speed of an indrawn breath, but that consciousness is a curse in itself. I feel everything. The weight of my muscles and wet clothing pull me down. The water presses close. The boy's panicked arms lock around my neck and bubbles escape from his lips in a screaming rush. They slip over my skin and drift up, too lazy and calm for the terror of the moment.

A crashing heartbeat later the child is tangled up in me, and I can't swim. We sink farther, my cloak and braids drifting around us on a strange, rising current.

Urgency blazes through me, bright and light and all-consuming. Terror comes with it, memories of my drowned mother and drowned father flaring like sparks. Siru's words are there too, echoing and repeating.

The serpents.

I tear the child off me and thrust him upward, after his own drifting bubbles and into muted, rippling daylight. He strikes out wildly, a blur of shadowy limbs. I see him break the surface next to a greater shadow of ship and surge after him with great, strong kicks.

One moment I'm swimming, legs churning, arms reaching, then something strikes the side of my head.

I blink, long and languid. In the fractured moment of disorientation, I realize I'm limp in the water, just below the surface. Rows of oars bar my path upward, some half retracted, others stretched out as if to reach me.

The serpents.

I look down. There below me, I swear I see the coiling of a great, lithe beast in the murk. Its scales are pale and opalescent, its broad, serpentine face crowned with arched, twisting horns.

I make out the shape of another massive shifting body, and another. A hundred. Beneath my drifting legs is a tapestry of sea serpents entwined in one another, twisting and surging.

Not one looks up at me, locked in their circuitous dance, but I feel them—the movement of them creating a clash of currents and turning the sea to a boil.

Adrift in my own flesh, I lift my eyes upward. The strange current made by the serpents has kept me from sinking too far and I see the oars have retracted, shafts of shadow retreating into the belly of the ship. Muted light dances in my eyes and I register Siru, her face accompanied by a fringe of white braids. She does not reach out to help me, but I imagine our eyes meet.

I see my pale hand between us, reaching with limp fingers.

Something lands in the water beside me in a blur of bubbles. The next thing I know is frigid air assaulting my face, hands grabbing me under the arms, and the hard rail of the ship digging into my side.

I topple onto the deck, hit an oar bench in a burst of pain, and vomit. Fingers rake my hair back from my face and arms stretch over me, warding away a crowd of dismayed, jostling Duamel.

I blink salt from stinging eyes and waver into a sitting position. My forehead feels as though someone is pressing a hot coal into it, and I sense something warm trickle down the side of my nose. When it reaches my lips, I taste iron. My shoulder screams too from where it struck the oar bench, but that pain is secondary.

Havar kneels before me, equally sodden. He brushes the blood from my lip and wipes it carelessly on his trousers.

"Serpents," I try to croak, but the word is cut off in a fit of coughing.

"You're all right," Havar soothes.

I blink again, noting a cloud of red as blood seeps into my eye. It vaguely occurs to me to wonder what hit my head—an oar? The kicking boy? One of them, I'm sure.

"Serpents," I wheeze, clearer this time. "Someone tell Siru. There are serpents below us."

I see someone move—Seele, shouldering away into the crowd. I see the boy I saved off to one side, crying into the chest of a pale-faced man. The man nods to me, gratitude and guilt in his harrowed expression.

Blood runs into my eyes again, clotted by snow—which blows even more thickly now—but I manage to nod back.

It's only as I'm ushered under the awning that I finally spy Siru. She directs the Duamel with brusque efficiency, her eyes on the waves.

Despite the chaos, my mind slows. And in that lull, I recall seeing my sister through the water.

How I'd reached for her, and she had not reached back.

"She didn't help me."

I don't realize I've spoken aloud until Seele makes a noncommittal sound. The smaller woman works at the clasp of my sodden cloak and peels it—already stiff with ice—from my body. I immediately feel lighter, but not in a pleasant way. My head spins.

We're in a tent on shore, sheltered from the biting wind by the bulwark of a huge, pine-crested ridge. The snow has given way to rain but the wind from the west barely reaches our camp, here in the lee. The moan of the gale whistles through craigs in the rock and the bellies of the beached ships—safe from the waves and the coiling serpents in the depths.

A fire burns just outside, filling the canvas with light, if not warmth. The rest of the Eangen move around it, organizing our packs and building the fire higher. There's an undercurrent of solemnity and unrest to their efficiency. It reminds me what might have been today, and it threatens to overwhelm me.

Today one of my deepest fears had been realized, and at the same time, the answer to my questions of immortality were within my grasp. I'm left unsettled, uneasy, and suspicious.

"Your sister?" Seele clarifies, as she examines my headwound.

Outside in the hastily constructed camp, Duamel call and struggle to erect more oar-framed tents. "She's the one that found you in the water. She told Havar where to dive."

I tug at the memory. It's vague and fractured, clouded by disorientation and memories of the serpents, coiling below.

"How long was I in the sea?" I ask. She steps back and I pull my overtunic off, careful to avoid my aching forehead.

"Moments." She takes the garment. "You and the boy went over. He came right back up. Siru saw you, Havar jumped in and then you were flopping on the deck like a fish."

"Spewing all over me," Havar adds from beside the fire, where he strips. He grins at me through the door of the tent, but he's shaking with cold and his hair is a clotted tangle of black curls. He looks harried, like someone woken from a nightmare.

Which, I reflect, isn't far off the mark. I feel haunted too, still brimming with the cold bite of the sea and the burn of salt in my eyes. The imaginary teeth of a serpent, piercing the flesh of my belly.

I smile at Havar in return, but the expression feels forced. "I'll try to vomit into the sea next time."

He holds my gaze momentarily, the naked muscles of his upper body taut with cold, skin reddened and goosefleshed. There's sympathy in his eyes and he smiles despite his shivering, but there's no power to it. Just the dark reality of what might have been.

Abruptly, Darag throws a bundle of dry clothing at Havar. My betrothed staggers backward, flinching at a face-full of rough wool, and Darag grins. Branan laughs, Seele snorts, and the tension breaks.

"That's no way to treat a hero," Havar says to his brother. His chest vanishes under a fresh linen undertunic and thick wool overtunic. Then he hops his way out of sodden trousers and into a clean pair, cursing the dirt and pine needles stuck to his feet.

"Hero," Darag scoffs. "For what, going for a little swim?"

"Thray is the one who went after the boy," Seele points out, and is ignored.

"All I want to know is how many serpents there were," Branan says at the same time, looking to me.

I suppress a shiver and scratch at dried blood on my face. "I couldn't count them."

"Siru says such things are normal in breeding season," Seele says, turning to dig around in my bag. "They're unlikely to attack as long as we stay in deeper waters and do not disturb them."

"She told me she rode one, once," I say, turning over the image in my mind. Now that I've seen the beasts, the notion seems doubly ludicrous.

Darag laughs. "Don't believe everything your big brothers and sisters tell you," he warns me in an overly paternal tone, his eyes dancing. "They lie."

"Don't I know it," Havar quips and hurls his sodden tunic at his brother. Darag catches it with a wet slap of fabric.

The men descend into banter and soon all remnants of tension fade from their voices. They jest as they work, building the fire high until its heat even reaches me, in the tent.

I change, donning one of my two spare sets of clothing. By the time we gather next to the flames and I ask Seele to see to my wound, my memories of the water have eased, some aspects fading, others clarifying.

I see the moment Siru's and my eyes met through the water for what it was, now—half a breath of time, too quick to be acted upon, bracketed by chaos and unexpected peril. Perhaps I've come to think too much of my half-sister, as if her long years separate her from the fears and flaws of humanity.

I know enough of the full-blood Miri to know they're not without fault. And the blood of a human mother also runs through Siru's veins, twined with Ogam's.

Just like mine.

NINE

I sit beside the fire with Havar in the windy, sullen darkness of night. The camp is quiet and the storm has broken, though the air remains sharp with the scent of snow. Darag snores inside the men's tent, the sound rippling over the constant crash of waves, and I see the flicker of an oil lamp beyond the canvas of the shelter Seele and I are sharing. Every so often a Duamel wanders past, faceless in the dark, and Havar and I look up. But for the most part, we are alone with the flames, wrapped in blankets and lost in our thoughts.

My mind wanders, relaxing in the warmth and solitude. I imagine lying down on the earth, resting my head in Havar's lap. I imagine leaning into his shoulder, kissing his cheek, and drawing on the warmth and steadiness of him. We already sit close, our knees brushing.

"Are you angry at me?" he asks suddenly.

I look up, taken aback. "What?"

He looks at me sidelong, and I'm surprised to see resentment in his eyes. He lets out a heavy breath and tilts his head to one side, as if bracing himself. "The way you look at Siru… it's worrying me, Thray."

"Look at her how?" I reply, pulling away. The light touch of our knees vanishes, cold air slipping between. "Why would I be angry at you?"

Havar stares into the night without seeing it, eyes narrowing, thoughts inscrutable. "I thought we were on a journey, you and I. Together. Yet on a ship smaller than Ossen's hall, you seem to forget I'm there. Siru has all your attention. She whistles, and you run like a hound."

"A hound?"

He shrugs in affirmation. "I risked my life for you today, and you haven't said a word to me for the past hour."

"I've much on my mind," I protest, trying to shrug off the weight of his accusations, but they settle heavy in my stomach. Perhaps I have been too distracted. But right now I'm tired, my head and shoulder ache, and my lungs can't shake the searing need for air. "I nearly drowned in a sea full of serpents."

"And I pulled you out," he points out again.

I frown at him. "So you can hold it over me?"

"No, no. I would have done the same for anyone. But… I love you." Havar gives a long-suffering sigh. There's a shudder to it, though, betraying his hurt. He must realize it too, for he straightens and reaches to take more firewood from a nearby pile, then sets it on its end and leans it into the flames. I watch his long fingers move, taking care not to be burned.

"I love you too," I say, guiltily.

He watches the flames lick around the edges of the new firewood before he speaks again. "You've a purpose coming north, I know. Thvynder has given it to you, and we've all sacrificed to obey."

I pull my cloak tighter and wet my lips, ready to confirm his words. But the lie won't come this time. I stay silent instead.

"And if getting close to Siru is part of your task, I will not begrudge you," Havar says. "But don't forget about me."

His words and the images attached to them, the hopes and the plans, punch the air from my lungs as surely as the icy sea. I shift onto my knees, and put a hand on his cheek to make him look at me.

He does. I see a spark of hope in his dark eyes, a simmering want. A wash of wounded pride.

He covers my fingers with his own.

"I'm sorry," I say.

"Just promise you'll come home with me. To me. After this is done."

I hope I can. I think of the moment we crouched beside the altar in Iesa, where my deception began. But the day has been too long, too eventful, and there is no more room in my mind for reflection.

"I promise," I say, and rest my head on his shoulder.

The sea takes on an even more ominous quality. The Duamel keep constant watch for serpents, or the slightest change in the clouds. At night I dream of water in my mouth and fangs in my flesh. I see myself sinking into the boiling mass of the serpents, crushed by their coils. I see Siru's face through the water again and again, and a new imagining joins her—another face, a male one, looming at her side and obscured by saltwater and waves. Ogam, himself.

Finally, seven days after our departure from Iesa, an unbroken coastline materializes across the north. The sight fills me with impatience and restless energy.

"We'll be at the river mouth by the end of the day and carry on into the night," Siru tells the other Eangen and I, but as she continues, she looks at me. Above us, the thick canvas of the awning snaps slightly in the breeze. "There is somewhere I want to take you. We'll rest there."

"What is it?" I ask, pulling my cloak tighter around my shoulders.

"A sacred place," she replies with a half-smile, then leaves us.

"I don't see a river," Branan mutters without looking at my sister. "All I see is rock and sea."

"Perhaps Ogam's Get has better eyes than you," Darag suggests.

Seele gives a disapproving hiss and looks at me, as if she expects me to be offended.

"She does." I can see a slight variance in the coastline where Siru pointed—a dip where the sky bleeds in between two cliffs. "The river is there."

"Good," Branan says, hunching a little farther into the bulwark and forcing Seele to move out of his way, her expression disgruntled. Over the voyage I've wondered many times why he accompanied us, other than his own pride. He's had brighter moments, usually when laughing at someone else, but his mood has steadily darkened since we left home. "Because if we spend any more time out here, I'm going to get myself put ashore and walk back to Eangen. I'm a hunter, not a sailor."

"That's a long way to walk," I point out, a little amused at his vehemence. "A month, at least."

Branan shrugs. "Better now than once we're in their 'north.' Then we'll be trapped."

The back of my neck prickles with unease—he's right—but I don't let it show. "You volunteered to come," I remind him.

"Yes, you did." Darag glares at the younger man. "Complain like that again and I'll make sure you walk home. Alone. Through a long, hungry winter."

Branan doesn't speak again, but the image of that long, solitary trek lingers in the back of my mind.

I turn back to watching the coastline.

We reach the river by the end of the day. As we pass through the choppy waves where the two waters meet my fear crests and breaks, and I nearly laugh in relief. After the sea and the serpents, a river holds all the threat of a placid forest creek.

Few trees line the waterway's rocky, vaulted banks, and those I do see are stunted by wind. They're girded by hardy shrubs with foliage of deep burgundy and burnt orange, interspersed with swaths of late yellow flowers that bloom despite the hints of snow clinging in the shadows of the rocks. Above, gulls call and eagles cry, and on the open rock beneath the cliffs seals sun themselves in the last of the daylight.

We row through dusk and on into a moonlit night. I doze under the awning, wrapped in my cloak, until the first rays of sun break in the east. The cliffs have retreated from the riverbanks, slipping back into low mountains of windblown forests, skirted by seasonal floodplains. Muddy puddles reflect the dawn, and odd circular boulders sprout between enterprising rushes and dead marshflowers, laden with seedheads. Migrating shorebirds arrive in thundering, ribboned clouds, and far in the distance, I watch a fox leap upon some unseen prey.

The Duamel camp beside one of these floodplains on an elevated peninsula, anchoring the larger ships offshore and driving the smaller vessels onto the beach.

I drop onto the beach with the rest of the Eangen, bleary and exhausted from the restless night aboard ship.

"What is this?" Havar scoops up some of the stones beneath our boots. He holds out his hand, showing that they're perfectly round like the boulders on the floodplains, though these are no bigger than the nail on my smallest finger.

"I've no idea." I take one and turn it between my fingers. It's smoother than the most perfect pearl. But these are stone, and the same color as the larger, more irregularly shaped boulders I can see poking out from the conifers around us.

The forest is thick with the scent of sap and the water, just as the coast of Eangen would be, but here there are noticeable differences. The round stones, for one, along with thinner, narrower ferns, tufts of reddish grasses, and pale, yellowish moss.

I continue to toy with the pebble as the Duamel move around us, setting up camp. Darag gives us a long-suffering glower as he hauls our packs off to one side. "I wonder where the locals are?"

"There are none," Siru replies. She gives Havar a glance—not warm, not cool, but passably polite. "Let's go, sister."

Havar looks as though he wants to protest but I stop him with a hand on the arm. "How long will this take?" I ask my sister, slipping the round stone into my pocket.

Siru glances to the sun, which is fully over the horizon now, painting the sky with orange. "We'll be back by noon."

My half-sister and I leave the camp behind, striding deeper inland. The ground rises steadily, building into one of the low mountains I noted from the ship. Loose stones—broader here, less round—crunch beneath our boots as we ascend and after over a week of limited activity, I'm quickly out of breath. The breeze here is sweet though, crisp and clear, and the cold is pleasant on my sweating brow.

At the top of a rise, I stop to catch my breath and glance back at the camp. The Duamel and Eangen are indistinguishable from this distance, all pitching their tents among the trees. They race the weather; a sky of dense, warning cloud looms above them, but the air smells of rain instead of snow.

"That storm is coming in fast," I observe to Siru. "Are we going much farther?"

My sister waits a few paces ahead, following my gaze. "Are you afraid of getting wet?"

I crack a smile, because I feel like I should. But though I'm tired and aching, my curiosity is alight. "Not at all. Lead on."

By the time we reach the summit, the camp is ready for the storm; the forest is dotted with tents and the smaller vessels line the shoreline like scales in the thickening stormlight. But here on the mountaintop, daylight still pools, edging around the clouds. Loose rock gives way to a great shoulder of gray stone, swirled with quartz and salmon pink. The swirl tightens the closer it gets to the center, where a burial mound has been carefully constructed.

The structure is as tall as I am, some four paces wide across the middle, and its walls formed of carefully stacked stone. Despite patches of lichen clinging to the facade, it's lovely and solemn, and there's the feeling of a temple about it—weighty and aloof, vast and intangible.

"It's beautiful," I murmur.

Siru stands a few paces back from the mound, so I go no closer. "It's a barrow," she says. "One of Father's wives is buried here."

"Wives?" The term surprises me. "He took wives?"

"A few," Siru tempers. "This one was his only lover for four decades. They had six children, but only one of them was immortal. That child was his last... before Father left the north. That was forty years ago."

The weight of the place multiplies, now a physical pressure on my chest. To think my father stood on this mountain and mourned, not hundreds of years in the past, but mere decades? Did he stand right here, where my boots are now?

I turn the questions over, and the emotions they dredge up are too complex to unravel. But one thought seeps through.

"Was that why he left?" I ask. My voice comes out harder than I expected. "Losing her?"

Siru's expression is pensive, but I see pain around her eyes. Ogam was a real person to her, a father she saw and touched and spoke to. And despite who he was and what he did, I envy that.

"Maybe," the other woman says. "He'd lost others before. Many of them. I think he saw this one's death as an end, a clean cut. The closing of an age."

"So he went into the Hinterlands," I state. "Released the Old Gods and tried to destroy the world."

She cuts me a sharp look. "You sound like Gadr. Do you really believe that's what Father was trying to do?"

I hesitate. My father's villainy is so widely known among the Eangen, it has never occurred to me that Siru might believe something different. That, maybe, the truth *is* different.

I cut that last thought off before it can take root. I know the truth of Ogam and his actions—whatever Siru says won't change that, but it might explain it.

"He deserved recognition." Siru turns on me, every inch the elder sibling now. "The other gods feared his immortality, so they shunned him. He should have sat in Eang's Hall. He should have been worshiped by more than the Duamel. He was greater than all of them, save the Old Gods."

Her words prickle across my skin like droplets of icy water.

"He released the Old Gods, though," I point out. "They would have ended all of us."

Siru surveys the barrow for a long, hard moment. There's tension in every line of her, and she reaches up to rub a knuckle along her clenched jaw.

I'm sure she's about to ridicule me, and I feel myself waver between conviction and regret. I want to be her ally, her sister, but I must remain cautious.

"It doesn't matter what he did or why," I decide, trying to pacify the situation. "He's gone. The world is as it is, and we're the ones left in it."

She drops her hand and looks at me again. Her tension is still there, but her smile is wry. "Yes, I suppose we are. There's one more thing you should know, Thray."

I'm quiet, waiting for her to go on.

"The Duamel's ruler, the Inheritor, is a grandchild of this woman." My sister gestures to the barrow. "He's our kin, though his blood is thin and his power weak. I must take you to him in Atmeltan, the Duamel capital city, to introduce you before we can go on to the rest of the Winterborn."

"How long will it take? Can we reach Atmeltan before winter?"

Siru's smile is lean, and a little sad. "You're going to Duamel, Thray. Winter is already there."

By the time we return to camp, the skies have opened and soaked us to the bone. Siru bids me farewell and I make for the Eangen tents, where Darag and Branan fight to set up a steep tarp over the sputtering fire. Seele fusses over wet packs while Havar watches from the shelter of his small tent, chewing a strip of smoked meat and wiggling pale, wrinkled toes. His boots are upended over sticks beside him and he's shirtless, despite the chill of the rain.

I stop beside the tent flap.

"You're not coming in here with those wet clothes," he informs me. His tone is flat but there's a crinkling around his eyes, beneath a fall of damp hair. "I'm finally starting to dry. But if you take them off, you're more than welcome."

I blink at him, taken off guard. "You're bold today," I observe.

He leans back on his palms. His gaze is intent and prompting, but I see the shadow of another conversation behind it, beside the fire on a rocky island. "I'm getting impatient. And seeing the way these Duamel look at you? Perhaps you should share my tent."

"Not tonight." I point to the other Eangen, blinking and cursing in the rain. It's not that I wouldn't appreciate it—the thought of it has kept me up many long, cold nights. But lying with him is a line I will not cross, not until I'm willing to commit to a life with him and the possibility of children. "We should help Darag."

"I got us our firewood *and* supper." He waves a hand to a nearby bucket with half a dozen fish inside. They're already cleaned and gutted. "That's enough work for the both of us. Besides, I'm warmer than that fire is going to be, I promise."

My lips twitch into a smile. Temptation creeps closer, but the image of the barrow is fresh in my mind, and with it, the ever-present threat of loss. I waver.

"Just sit with me." He's still grinning, but I notice an edge of pleading in his eyes. "Please."

I glance at the others once more, then relent. I pull off my sopping tunic and sink down next to him in the narrow tent mouth in my slightly dryer undertunic. Our arms brush as I settle in at his side.

"Where did Siru take you?" he asks, voice low enough for just the two of us. His breath is warm on my ear, and my damp skin prickles.

"The grave of one of Ogam's wives," I reply, equally quiet.

"Wives?" He looks at me more directly. "He married?"

"I reacted the same way," I admit.

"How many did he have?"

I shrug. My father's marriages remind me of possibilities I would rather forget; the very reason I keep the boundaries between us high, even as Havar tries to tear them down.

I say, "A few. He lived a long time… but they were mortal, of course."

Havar's quiet for a moment, perhaps reflecting on the same fears as me. "Why would Siru show you that?"

I shrug, trying not to think too deeply on the question. I suspect Siru was making a subtle point about my relationship with Havar, and it worked. But: "It would be odd not to, with us already passing by."

He either accepts this or senses I don't want to talk about it. Closing the topic off with a bracing smile, he pulls the bucket of fish closer and raises his voice to call to the others: "Who's making the bread?"

TEN

We rest on the riverside until the next morning, enduring constant rain and rolling thunder, then set out once the weather clears. Despite our efforts to stay dry I've been damp for days, and when the sun breaks through the clouds to strike Siru and I near the prow, I turn my face to the warmth with a sigh. The light dancing off the surface of the water makes it easier to ignore the strength of the current sweeping us inland, and the implicit threat the water still brings.

Siru watches me before looking back at the river. The rest of the ships have spread into a long line before and behind us, and the oarsmen keep easy time to the lead vessel's drum.

"Enjoy this while you can," Siru tells me, lacing her arms across her tunic. "A few more days, and light and warmth will be a memory."

I glance at her, reminded of what she said yesterday about the Duamel winter. "I thought you were exaggerating. It's barely past harvest."

"We call it the Winter Night—it isn't what you southerners believe," my sister says, stroking the end of her long, wrist-thick braid where it hangs at her waist. "Or what it used to be. There was a time when it came only in the heart of winter. But that was when Father ruled. After his death, the night began to grow longer. Two years ago, it stopped leaving at all. Now the darkness and the winter rule Duamel."

I shift to look her fully in the face. "You live in endless winter?"

"No, and yes." She searches for words, and gestures at the land along the riverbanks. "There's variance, especially on the borders. Here, at this stretch of the river, the world will freeze and thaw as anywhere else—enough for a short growing season, in any case. That's what's kept us alive, fed our livestock, and kept our cellars from emptying. But the deeper we go into Duamel, the more... permanent the night becomes. It's one of the reasons we've begun exploring farther afield. Some still hold out hope that the night will lift—perhaps it's an effect of Father's death? We don't know. But the people cannot live in darkness forever.

"We"—when she says the last word, she holds my gaze, including me in the word—"are what keeps the Duamel from abandoning their land entirely. We sustain them. Give them hope."

Trepidation works its way up my spine. "Why didn't you mention this before?"

Siru shakes her head. "Why would I? It doesn't change what we can offer to the Eangen. But it's something I want you to know, now, and you should prepare your people for. You're a Winterborn, and the Duamel will recognize that. Like I said, we sustain them in the Winter Night, and sometimes their need can be... aggressive. But we'll protect you until you come into your power, after the ceremony."

I've more to ask, but her words stir me. We've spoken of the ceremony to judge my immortality several times, though never in depth. "When will that be?"

She glances at me, her smile true, but distracted. "Soon."

That evening, as the waning sun fights its way through regrouping stormclouds, we sight our first Duamel settlement. Imel boasts several thousand inhabitants and spreads across the riverbank and up into the hills beyond, fortified with a stone wall and multiple gates. The houses are of hefty wooden beams and artfully layered, slate-gray stones. Smoke rises from hundreds of chimneys, gathering in the gloom and scenting the air with the promise of hearths and an evening meal.

Townsfolk stare as we disembark. Siru gestures for me to follow her and leaps off the prow of our ship, landing lightly on the rocky beach. The wind whips her loosened hair like a white banner as she strides toward the crowd, calling out a greeting, and I could almost swear I see a glimmer of silver on the wind.

I leap down after her, ignoring the feel of hundreds of eyes that follow me across the beach. Despite them, with the river and the water behind me, I breathe a little easier.

I join Siru as she speaks to a short young man. He quickly bows to me and puts three fingers to his forehead in the Duamel salute, murmuring in his own language all the while.

"You're thoroughly greeted," Siru translates dryly. "This is Elin, the son of the local headwoman, and we're to spend the night at their keep. Come, your people can follow."

I glance back looking for Havar and the others, but can't see them in the crowd of disembarking Duamel explorers.

"Thray," Siru urges.

Reluctant as I am to abandon my Eangen in a new city, I give in.

We enter the streets of the town and begin to trudge inland, following a way lined with staring locals. With their characteristic large eyes and pale skin, cheeks red with the cold, they're more subdued than I expected. Their admiration for Siru—and me, by my white hair and proximity—is not a boisterous thing, not joyful or celebratory. There's fear to it. A need, a desperation. It makes my skin crawl.

Siru keeps her head high. She doesn't falter or meet anyone's gaze until the crowd parts around a large, cloaked figure. He pushes his hood back.

I see... my father. Or my father as I always imagined he was. This man is a handful of years older than I with a broad-shouldered, leanly muscled form and a white, braided beard studded with black beads. His hair is white too, jaw-length and windblown in the way of some Duamel men. His skin is light but his eyes are a deep, warm brown, and he wears a knee-length kaftan with a broad belt beneath his fluttering cloak.

We stop in the street and the headwoman's son, Elin, stands respectfully to the side, hands clasped behind his back.

"Siru," one of Ogam's sons says, touching three fingers to his forehead. He's taller than both Siru and I by a head, and a veritable giant next to even the tallest Duamel onlookers. "We worried you would not return this year. Who is this?"

His warm eyes, such a contrast to his icy pallor, travel over me. I feel a pang in my chest, a sharp and sudden longing that strips me down to my bones. This man, this vision of my father, is my own flesh and blood. A half-brother.

Emotion clouds me, and I can't decide whether it's happiness at meeting another sibling, or sadness for the memory of another brother, lost to duty and divine fervor.

"Thray," I tell him, collecting myself and leveling my chin. "I am Thray, of the Eangen, Priestess of Iesa. Daughter of Ogam and the woman Sixnit."

The Winterborn man glances at Siru, some unspoken question and answer passing between them. He seems oblivious to the silent clusters of Duamel in his shadow.

"I'm Kygga," he says. "It is odd, to hear Eangen from one of our lips. Much of you is odd, now that I look."

He peers at me, no doubt noting the tawny Eangen undertone of my skin. I feel the pattern of the air around us change. Sounds muffle, and I realize he's dampening our conversation. The Duamel stand close, but from the startled looks in their eyes, they can no longer hear.

Kygga can control the wind, as our father could.

"Freckles?" he murmurs, still examining me. "I wonder what other... gifts, your mother gave you. A green-eyed, half-Eangen sibling?"

"The mother's blood always affects the gifts of the child," Siru tells me before turning back to her—our—half-brother. "She hasn't yet come to her power."

"Ah." Kygga is directly in my face now, examining me. I don't concede ground, straight-spined, the heels of my boots firmly planted in the hard-packed dirt of the street. I study him as openly as he studies me.

"I'm said to be the only child of Ogam by an Eangen," I say. "Perhaps I will surprise you."

Kygga's smile is so subtle, I question whether it was there at all. He steps back, granting me space to breathe again, and looks at Siru. "I'm only here for the night. Take dinner with me?"

He must have lifted our muffling veil, for at this, Elin, still standing patiently off to one side, bows low and shuffles closer. He says something in Duamel that I interpret as an apology, from his tone and posture, and then makes an offer.

At that moment, Siru's entourage from the boats catches up with us. My Eangen companions are among them, and Havar's eyes widen when he sees Kygga standing over Siru and I in the twilit street. He stops, our packs heavy on his shoulder, and gives me an inquiring look.

I smile to console him, but I'm distracted. My eyes keep dragging to my newfound brother, sorting through his features and wondering which of them best reflect Ogam. I feel more than a little awe, and as soon as I recognize that, I swallow it down.

If all goes as planned, I'll be meeting hundreds of siblings like Kygga and Siru in the next few months. I cannot give them any reason to see me as young and naive and easily impressed—as Siru already does.

"Very well." Siru nods to the Duamel man and Kygga. She notes our newly arrived companions with a passing glance and adds, "We can speak more in the privacy of the hall."

The home of the local headwoman is built into one of the hills, multiple stories clinging to the slope. It has a central hall with a smaller outer chamber, which has an ornate outer door. The door is accessed by a broad staircase from the busy town below and its beams are square and simple, its facades stone. It's not all that different to Eangen design, a practical result of the similar climate and resources at hand. But one characteristic of Duamel is immediately clear: the colors. Each beam, outlining walls of stone and moss, is stained bruise blue or rust orange. Patterns are painted across these colored beams in black, a series of slashes and shapes that fill the beams from top to bottom.

"Are those Duamel runes?" I murmur to Siru as we climb the stairs. Kygga shadows us two steps behind.

"Yes. They're blessings and curses. Blessings on the house and land, curses on enemies and those with ill-will. Prayers to keep the Winter Night at bay."

"Do they have any power?"

My sister shrugs. "Perhaps."

I eye her and glance back at Kygga, looking for more information in his handsome face, but he doesn't appear to have heard us. He's looking out over the land to the west, watching the last of the sunlight fade with a guarded wistfulness about him.

Elin gestures us through the outer door. We enter a chamber, packed with rows of hanging cloaks and hoods and warmed by a central brazier. We add our outer clothing to the pegs, then pass into the central hall.

This space is broad but low, its wooden floors layered with woven reed rugs and its walls decorated with patterned hangings. I spy staircases leading to upper chambers to each side, and hefty, aged ceiling beams stretch low overhead.

Items are tucked here and there among the beams. Some are obviously practical: jars, bundles of herbs. Others are more interesting. I spy an idol of a woman in windblown furs at the center of one, carved of smooth gray stone. Another shaft is inlayed with hammered metal disks, while others boast arrays of carved bones and tusks, animal skulls, and other unidentifiable relics and trinkets.

At the far end of the hall the ceiling lifts into a high facade built into the hill itself. A hearth pit stretches there, preceded by two heavy tables and girded with fur-laden thrones.

The headwoman rises from one of the thrones as we enter and sweeps the length of the chamber toward us. She's a sturdy, short woman in an ornamented, floor-length wrap dress of pale yellow wool, and as she bows, firelight flashes off the lattice of gold threads that cradles her hair at the back of her skull.

Elin joins his mother, and Siru translates as they welcome us. Kygga nods once, then sits in a throne and pulls off his boots without waiting for the pleasantries to end. His socks come next, damp with travel, and he lays them out on a rack beside the hearth to steam dry. The headwoman eyes him, but he ignores her and begins to examine his bare, spread toes.

I bite the inside of my lip to stifle a laugh and remain politely poised beside Siru.

"Our sister, Thray," Siru introduces me, reclaiming my attention.

I conjure a smile for our hosts, but since I can't understand their greetings, I focus on their body language and mannerisms. They're stiff and reverent, earnest in an almost pained way. This doesn't ease until a third party enters the room, a man in a knee-length blue kaftan lined with brown fox fur.

"A priest of the Diviners," Siru introduces him to me.

The priest bows deeply and holds out the palms of his hands to us, fingers splayed, head bowed. For a moment I mark the gesture as some Duamel oddity, then I notice the scars on his fingers and palms. There are dozens, perhaps hundreds of them, so thick he cannot straighten his fingers.

I recognize them immediately, and shock nearly empties my face before I catch myself. He wears the same scars as my High Priestess—sacrificial scars. But where hers are old, memories of an abandoned tradition, this man's are pink and fresh, his left thumb cleft with a fresh scab. As he strains to hold his hands flat, I see the scab crack, and a trail of blood trickles down his pale skin. It congeals on the end of his thumb and falls in one scarlet droplet to the stone floor.

My eyes drag to Siru and Kygga. She nods at the scarred priest in affirmation and he retreats, ducking another, lower bow before straightening next to the headwoman and her son. Kygga simply watches him, unflinching and unamused, then calls for hot water to soak his feet.

He proceeds to do so in front of all of us, and stops only once his feet are red and wrinkled. Then he pads his way over to the table where Siru and I already sit with our hosts. His barefoot saunter destroys any formality and I vacillate between awkwardness and amusement. Frequent glimpses of the priest's scars further complicate my feelings, and the priestess in me burns to ask what they mean.

Fortunately, the meal does not last long. Our hosts depart as soon as our plates of mutton, roast vegetables, and bowls of steaming mushroom are clean, leaving Kygga and I to settle by the hearth. Siru briefly confers with the Diviner priest at the foot of the stairs, then he, too, is gone.

I'm alone with my siblings and the crackling of the fire.

"You've not been blooded, yet?" Kygga asks, holding up one of his socks to the light and checking for dampness. Satisfied, he begins to pull it back on his long-toed foot.

"Blooded?" I repeat with a raised eyebrow, turning over possible meanings. "As a warrior or a woman?"

A small, illusory smile flicks over his lips again. "I see scars and breasts. I've no questions about those. I mean as a Winterborn."

"He means the day you should have died," Siru explains. She fetches a pitcher of wine and tops up her wooden cup, one hip perched on the side of the hearth. Her loosened hair falls heavy down her back as she twists, setting the pitcher on a nearby bench. "The day your mortal life ends and your immortal begins. It doesn't necessarily include blood, but it often does."

I glance between the two of them, the silence of the hall suddenly pointed and overpowering. Beside me, the fire pops. "Honestly... I don't know."

"How can you not know?" Kygga asks. He eyes Siru's cup until she scowls. She picks up the pitcher again and passes it to him, and he proceeds to drink straight from its mouth. He turns his gaze back to me, awaiting my answer as amber mead drips into his mustache.

"There have been opportunities, but they were all... thwarted," I admit. My voice is light, but I shudder at the memory of salt water in my mouth and the piercing, numbing cold. "I nearly drowned on the voyage here."

"Hm," he grunts. "What of the other 'opportunities'?"

I run my fingers over the knuckles of my opposite hand, feeling the scars there. I earned most of them from accidents—and one very intentional fist to the teeth of a young man—but I'm thinking of the thicker scar that laces my arm, under my clothing. "I killed a pair of savn, and I should have died doing it. But Grandfather intervened, and Aita came. She healed me before I could die—or live."

"Winter intervened in your blooding?" Kygga's brows rise high. He sets the pitcher down and wipes the mead from his beard, making his black beads and golden droplets flash. "Truly?"

I nod.

"Was that the first time he did something like that?" Siru asks, leaning on one palm.

"No. I was lost in a snowstorm once, as a child. He led me home." I let my memory drift back to that day, etched in my mind with fear and cold. "I would have died, otherwise. From cold or beasts. I was only six."

"Why were you out in a snowstorm so young?" Siru pries.

"I was playing with older children, from the village," I reply, letting no emotion show. "They left me behind."

Kygga makes an unsurprised sound, and Siru's mouth twists in sympathy.

"It wasn't easy, being Ogam's only Eangen daughter," I add, conjuring a wry smile. Though we sit next to the fire, the memory chills me. One would think carrying the blood of Winter exempted me from such feelings. And from the way Kygga and Siru sit close to the fire too, it's the same for them. Our human halves long for light and warmth.

And our inhuman halves, I wonder, *what do they long for? Recognition, like our father?*

"Winter prevented her blooding," Kygga repeats to Siru, pulling us back to topic. "Why would he do that?"

Siru holds Kygga's gaze momentarily, then offers her cup of mead to me. I take it, but don't drink, pointedly waiting for an answer.

"He favors her. He's protecting her," my sister decides. "It's strange—he despises the rest of us—but it seems you're Father's last, Thray. Perhaps he thinks to make an ally of you."

"Or prevent her from coming into her power." Kygga takes another thoughtful drink from the jug.

That idea unsettles me. I think of our emotionless grandfather, trying to align my memories of him to Kygga's suggestion, but it does not match. He may not dote upon me with smiles and embraces, but he gifted me the white bow and preserved my life. The fact that his actions have stayed off a possible inheritance from Ogam is simply an aside.

The lull in conversation is thick, almost palpable, and I sense an undercurrent between my siblings. My pondering wanes into vague suspicion, and all this talk of my grandfather reminds me of his distrust for my siblings.

There's something they're choosing not to say. I want to press them, but between Kygga's disregard and Siru's general crypticness, I doubt I'll get a straight answer. I decide to bide my time.

I change the subject. "Why does that priest have sacrificial scars?"

Siru is carefully neutral. "Because he is a priest, and that is what's expected."

"In Eangen priests used to bleed themselves in worship of gods, but the Duamel have no real gods," I point out. "Just spirits on the wind. Which… are you."

"We are whatever they need us to be," Siru answers, mollifying.

"If they call us gods and sacrifice to us, it's because they want to." Kygga sets the jug on the floor with an empty *clunk*. "We protect them from the beasts that hunt their children. We preserve them during the endless winter and distribute the goods that keep them and their livestock alive. *We* answer their prayers, not your southern god or any pure-blood Miri. Because we do have Miri blood, little sister. Perhaps you've forgotten that Eang was Ogam's mother? Rule is our inheritance."

My conscience turns, but it's always been a stunted thing. "I haven't forgotten. But blood sacrifice gave the Miri power. Does it do the same for you?"

"No." Kygga laughs. It sounds odd and, as when we were out on the street, I realize the air around us has shifted again, cocooning us in a bubble of silence. "Gods below, no."

"But the Duamel believe it does," Siru tempers. "They believe it gives them some small control, something they can do to secure their lives when the night is long and the beasts are at their doors. Would you take that from them?"

The way she looks at me, all gentleness and controlled exasperation, reminds me just how naive she thinks I am. I hold my tongue, weighing my response.

"Can the Night not be broken?" I ask at length. "How did it begin?"

"We don't know," Kygga answers. "It started the year Father left. Some say it's a curse from Winter. Punishment for what Ogam did."

I frown slightly. That doesn't sound like something Grandfather would do, at least not without a clear purpose. He's cold, but not vengeful.

"Or," Siru tempers, "Ogam held the Night back while he lived, and when he died his power broke. He ruled Duamel for as long as these people can remember."

"Surely he would have warned you of that," I point out. "In case he didn't return."

"He had no reason to think he wouldn't return," Kygga mutters, and though he hides it well, I think I catch bitterness around his eyes, and the echo of an indignant kind of sorrow. "It's Winter, cursing us."

"Have you asked him?"

Siru takes her cup back from my hands, where it had been forgotten, and sips. "The old man does not speak to us. Or save us from dangers."

Both my siblings' eyes drift to me.

"He... does speak to me," I admit. "Sometimes. Maybe I can ask him."

"Don't bother," Kygga says carelessly. "I'm going to sleep."

He stands and stretches broadly. The firelight throws his shadow across the hall, a giant of muscle and shadow and wild hair.

"When will you leave?" Siru asks, looking up at him.

Kygga scratches his scalp with crooked fingers. "Early. But I'll meet you in the capital in a few weeks."

Siru nods and, to my surprise, he pulls her up into a strong embrace. She leans up to kiss his cheek, smiles, and then lets him go.

"Thray." Kygga turns to me and ruffles my hair like he might a child's. I'd have been offended if my chest hadn't suddenly grown so warm. The touch, the familiarity of it, strikes a lonely chord. "Keep well. Or rather, don't—the sooner your blooding is, the better."

"Kygga," Siru chides, but there's a hard undertone.

Our brother gives me one last pat, more of a light slap on the back, then strides away across the hall. Siru looks down at me, and I rise to face her. My cheeks are warm and my thoughts a muddle of new information, suspicions, and possibilities, but I swipe them all aside and smile at my sister.

"I'll see you in the morning," I say. "Goodnight, Siru."

ELEVEN

The next day is gray and muted and the wind once again smells of snow—winter, creeping ever closer.

I eye the gloomy horizon from the window of the chambers the Eangen and I have been given, worried that Siru's unnatural winter night has already come. But there's a reassuring glow beyond the eastern clouds, and every so often a beam of light dances on the river or trails across the mountains. The sun is still here. For now.

"Will you come see the city with me?"

Seele draws up to the window to join me. The smaller woman is already bundled against the cold, legwraps thickly wound and a separate hood fitted over the shoulders and chest of her layered tunics. The hood itself is pushed back, revealing a tightly woven crown of braids and two of the bone hairpins the coastal Eangen favor. The hairpins are slim and delicate, longer than my hands, and protrude from her braids just over her ears, like horns. And like horns, they can be deadly when necessary.

Seele mistakes my silence for a prompt. "I didn't come north solely to be your companion, priestess, though I mean no disrespect by that. If this is the most southern Duamel settlement on the river, it could become an important center of trade. I need to—"

"I understand," I break in, stepping away from the window and glancing at the door to the main chamber. The men's room is beyond that, and I make out soft snores in the quiet. "The men aren't awake yet?"

Seele's snort is answer enough. "I'm not waiting for them. The day will be gone."

I grin knowingly. For men that arise before dawn nearly every day of their lives, Havar and Darag can sleep like the dead if given the opportunity—and the Duamel's eerie, dark dawn is deceptive to southern eyes.

"We'll go together, then, you and I," I decide. A little voice warns me that this is a risk, but I doubt we'll encounter trouble so early in the day. And I'm capable of handling anything short of a riot. "Do we need Siru to translate?"

Seele shakes her head. "I already asked her. She's gone with your brother and the priest. I'll just look today, if that's all I can do."

My curiosity sharpens. Kygga said he'd be gone by dawn. What could be important enough to make him stay, and draw Siru away without an explanation? "Gone where?"

The other woman tugs up her hood, settling its fur ruff behind the points of her hairpins. "Into the city. The priest came to get them."

Crossing to the foot of the bed, I pull on an overtunic, then my kaftan. I belt it and settle my knife, then grab my cloak on the way to the door. "Let's go."

The Duamel city is unfamiliar, but finding the market is no task. The smells of fresh bread and cooked fish draw us down a broad street and into an open area not far from the headwoman's home. Here, carts and tents cluster, displaying every kind of ware from lamps to fabrics to grains. Horses stamp and braziers burn. Breath from humans and animals mists in the air, and mounds of manure steam on the frost-christened ground.

Despite the language barrier, Seele goes right to work. I shadow her as she passes from stall to stall, smiling at merchants and communicating over wares with a series of gestures and well-placed Duamel words. She even helps me exchange a slim bronze armband for one of the Duamel's warm hoods, a fine slate-gray wool lined with equally fine linen, rimmed with black fur and edged with intricate tablet-woven trim.

"I didn't realize you'd been learning the language," I say to her as I settle the hood on my shoulders and bundle my sea cloak in my arms. The admission leaves me feeling oddly ashamed. It hadn't occurred to me to try and learn Duamel, not when the potential for the Divine Tongue is in my veins.

Seele shrugs as, together, we start off through the market again. "I listen."

"I listen too, but I don't understand anything these people say," I reply. "Well, I've a few words, 'priest' and such, but little else."

"I have to learn," the other woman says, eyeing an array of knives and scissors as we pass an ironsmith's stall. "Like I said, I didn't just come here for you. There *will* be trade with the Duamel. And I will make myself invaluable to that trade."

I am impressed by the conviction in her voice, but the smell of bread tugs my eyes past her to a local woman passing around loaves out of a shuttered window in exchange for the Duamel form of currency—rings kept on a thread about the neck.

I nudge Seele. "Go buy us some bread, then, translator."

Seele gives me a three-fingered Duamel salute—the tips of her fingers pressed into her forehead, between the eyes—and veers off toward the baker.

The clouds thin as I wait, texturing the rooftops and marketplace with varied degrees of light and shadow. A swath of light passes right over me, pulling my gaze farther up the street to a circular structure. It's built entirely of stone, roofed with wooden shingles, dusted with frost. The ends of its beams stick out like the spokes of a wheel, each hung with feathers and strips of braided cloth. They both flutter in the wind, thickest around a small, heavy door.

A woman approaches, wrapped in a heavy cloak, and goes inside. The wind gusts just then, carrying a thread of warmth and scent to me. The former is tempting; the latter arresting.

Widow root. I'd know the smell of the plant anywhere. It's a key ingredient in yifr, the drink the High Priesthood of Thvynder use to leave their bodies and visit the High Halls of the Dead.

This building is a temple. A temple to whom? To my father? My siblings?

Seele is deep in conversation with the woman at the window now, or as deep as her limited Duamel allows. The woman smiles and gestures, and Seele laughs.

I catch her eye and point to the temple. She waves her understanding and turns back to her halting conversation.

The interior of the temple is quiet and dark. Solid pillars of pine mark out the eight sides of an octagon, each punched out into a shallow alcove with a bed and a drape—some open, some closed. It's blissfully warm in here, so much so that sweat immediately prickles down my spine. I nudge back the edge of my hood, but don't uncover my hair.

In the center of the room a fire burns in a stone oven with a narrow chimney, but there are other fires too. In front of each alcove is a small brazier, and set atop some of these are small metal pans. Oil and herbs release a delicate steam, and devotees sit or lie on the beds, inhaling with soft, measured breaths. One or two glance my way, but otherwise ignore me. Any other devotees present are fast asleep, thin curtains pulled for privacy. Only their motionless feet are visible.

Over them all hangs the scent of widow root, and other herbs I cannot quite identify. They bring a new dimension to the forms lying listless in their beds. Their bodies might be here, but I suspect their consciousnesses are somewhere else entirely.

As I look around, a priest rises from a stool beside the main fire. Dressed in an undyed kaftan of rough brown wool, he's younger than me, gangly but pretty with his round Duamel eyes. He says something, but of course, I cannot understand.

He approaches with a welcoming, questioning smile on his lips. In the last moment before I must pay attention to him, I search the shadows for signs of magic or inhuman presence. There's something in the air, beyond the smell of widow root. It's a sense of… vastness, but I can't identify who it belongs to.

The priest asks me something.

"I don't speak Duamel," I say, unhelpfully.

The priest looks at me more closely. I see his gaze touch on my freckles, then my pale eyebrows and lashes. A little caution creeps in around his eyes, but even if he thinks I might be one of the Winterborn, he's not sure.

He touches his chest and says what I recognize as the Duamel word for priest, "*Aul.*"

I touch my chest too.

"*Aul* of Thvynder," I say, watching his face for any recognition. Siru knew of Thvynder and the Eangen people before coming south, but I've no idea if those things are common knowledge. "Eangen."

He smiles a sudden, elated smile and holds out both his hands, obviously intending for me to take them. He nods toward one of the empty alcoves.

I shake my head, keeping my hands at my side. "Thvynder," I say. He's a priest—he should understand that I'm not about to participate in another religion's rituals without understanding them. I don't even know who he worships.

"*Aul* of Thvynder," I repeat, pointing to myself, then him. "*Aul* of…?"

"*Aul* of Eirine," he immediately replies, picking up the Eangen preposition. His face is alight as he points to the alcove again.

I've never heard of Eirine, but Gadr's mention of the Erene drifts into my memory. The name is close. Yet it's clear the Diviners, like the priest I met last night, are the primary religious order in Duamel. Are these worshipers of Eirine tied to an older religion?

"Thray!"

I look over my shoulder as the door to the outer chamber opens. Seele darts inside, accompanied by a rush of cold air. The fires flicker, smoke swirls, and the curtains flutter. She clutches two rounds of bread, forgotten in her hands.

"Something's happening," she says, breathless.

We step outside as the market is overtaken by startled shouts, running footsteps, and barking dogs. The priest of Eirine follows us, peering out as a horde of newcomers floods into sight. They run and shout, and in less time than it takes me to grab Seele's arm and pull her behind me, they're upon us.

They act like an invading force, rushing and aggressive, but I realize the people streaking past us are simply women and men, children and elders, clutching bundles and bags and one another's hands. Every one of them is pale and sickly, with the hollow eyes of beaten dogs. Livestock mills among them: goats tugging on leads and frightened, bleating sheep.

"What is this?" Seele asks, dumbfounded.

"Travelers," I say. It's the only answer I can think of. "Refugees?"

"Refugees of what?"

My gaze drags unconsciously north to the looming, pressing darkness. But before I can share my suspicions, the tide of humanity begins to thin. Slowly, gesturing for Seele and the priest to stay back, I step out into the street and look in the direction the refugees fled from.

A savn roars. There's no mistaking the sound—nor the way it turns my guts to water as the cry echoes through the streets. The merchants and tradesfolk, up until now standing protectively by their goods, draw back. Horses panic with clattering hooves and a toppled brazier spills orange, blazing coals onto the hard-packed earth.

I toss my bundled cloak into the temple, tug my knife free, and flick it into a spear.

A savn prowls into the market with its huge head lowered and nose questing. Warriors flood around it, dozens of men and women armed with spears and tall wooden shields. They thunder after the fleeing refugees, the tallest men dwarfed by the huge beast in their midst.

No, not just one beast. Two more savn lope into the market, monstrous and predatory.

And… mastered.

Seele gasps, but I've lost my breath altogether. Warriors ride the savn like horses, the nightmarish beasts of the Eangen wilds transformed into saddled war dogs. It's an image out of myth, an impossibility I can't wrap my mind around even as they lope past me. They leave a fetid, bloody stink in their wake, and my stomach roils.

A hand grabs my arm and I look down into the priest's pleading face. He points after the last savn as it vanishes up the road, leaping one of the refugee's forgotten bundles and diverting down a side street.

The priest asks me a question in Duamel.

"He's asking for help," Seele says. Her cheeks are pale but her back is straight. "He knows what you are."

"What does he want me to do?"

Seele shrugs, looking helpless. "Protect those people? There're children, Thray. They're using savn to chase *children*."

I've made my decision before Seele finishes speaking. Duamel matters shouldn't be my concern. I should hold myself aloof, but I can't. My muscles itch to run. Even if the savn are mastered by Duamel riders, they're my enemy.

Besides, I've a feeling all this is connected to Kygga's lingering in the city. The Winterborn are involved, and I should learn why.

"Stay here?" I ask Seele.

"I will." She glances at the priest, who seems to understand. He nods firmly.

I take off at a run after the savn riders, spear at my side. A gust of wind blows my new hood back, ruffling its black fur and exposing my hair to the merchants of the marketplace, but I don't bother to pull it back up.

The streets have cleared except for warriors, disappearing into houses and emerging from side streets—searching for the refugees. I spy a woman on the ground, blood running from a gash on her temple, and a man being wrestled from a home by two warriors. He shouts and pleads with his captors, but when he spies me turning into the street, his cries take on a fevered pitch.

The warriors turn to stare. More filter out of alleyways and one, his knee-length kaftan marked out by a white sash, calls to me in Duamel and drops to one knee.

I slow, cursing my lack of understanding.

Kygga materializes in a gust of wind. He snaps something to the warrior and faces me, his cheeks lightly flushed and a sword in his hand.

I wonder briefly how the sword—not to mention his clothes—can travel with him on the wind, but now is hardly the time for such trivialities.

"What's happening here?" I demand. "Who are these people?"

"Refugees who broke down the north gate, despite being ordered back to their villages," Kygga replies, then snaps at the warriors' commander: "Control your people! You've a task—must I find someone else to do it?"

The Duamel warriors scatter, but the refugee who called to me remains in our street under guard. They've gagged him but he stares from me to Kygga, pleading in his eyes.

It makes my heart ache, but I try to hold the feeling at arm's length. "Why did they leave their homes to begin with?"

"The Winter Night." Kygga casts the dark northern horizon a brief, caged glance. "They're hungry. Game is fleeing south, and so do they. There's food here in Imel, and they know it. *But* they've been told help will come if they stay in their villages."

There's bitterness in his tone, but I can't decide if it's directed toward the disobedient refugees or whoever gave that order.

"I see." I look from the captured man to the bleeding woman on the ground. Part of me whispers again that this is none of my concern—I came to find my siblings, not insert myself into a foreign land's unrest. But I ignore her. "What can I do?"

Kygga, who has been watching the street and the soldiers, looks back at me. "Nothing, not without the language. Go back to the keep and make sure your people don't get caught up in this mess."

With that, my brother disappears. One moment he's there and the next he's gone, leaving a cold wind to brush my cheeks and stir the hairs escaping my braid.

I watch, silent, as the Duamel warriors move down the street. They carry off the injured woman and the bound man. The latter doesn't look at me anymore, but tears stream down his face.

Conflict coils inside me, but I know Kygga's right. I can't do much without a common tongue, and inserting myself between refugees and guards isn't my place. Watching over the Eangen is—but that means more than just returning to the keep. What's happening raises questions about the state of Duamel and its inhabitants, ones I can't ignore if our peoples are to enter a peaceful alliance.

I pull my hood back up over my hair and start walking. By the time I find Siru, I've passed into an entirely different section of the city. Refugees are herded into a courtyard before a closed gate. More than a few are injured, and bright flashes of red blood stand out against pale skin and hollow eyes. Babies wail, children cry. Most of the livestock has vanished, along with packs and bundles.

I finger my spear as savn riders guide their beasts around the crowd. Unsurprisingly, no one dares run.

Siru appears atop the gate. Her mane of white hair is bound in a thick, simple braid today but the wind plays with the end of it, lashing it across her stomach as she surveys the assembly.

"I am the voice of the Winterborn, the face of the spirits in the wind," she tells them, her gaze grave and kind and disapproving all at once. "And you have disobeyed."

There's a strained ripple among the refugees, desperation and panic barely contained.

Siru continues, "You were to remain in your villages and rely on the faithfulness of the Winterborn to provide for you. You did not. You arrived at the gates of Imel and were told to turn back, but you did not. You invaded a city of your brethren like feral dogs, bringing suffering and fear to yourself *and* your kin."

The rustling of the crowd has turned to a painful silence now, only the whimpering of a few infants breaking the hush.

"You will return to your villages." Siru's verdict cuts through the air with sudden, icy cold. Kygga appears next to her and wind ruffles her clothing. "My brother will accompany you, watching you on the wind to ensure your obedience, as will the savn riders you see around you now. You will be safe, unharmed, and provided for—so long as you obey. If you do not? All protection and provision will be withdrawn from you and your settlements. You choose the death of your children, and the end of your lines."

A man suddenly shouts, and though I can't understand what he says, some of the other refugees—and some of the citizens around me—stir in response.

"The sun will not sustain you as the spirits do," Siru replies coolly. "But go over the mountains if you wish. Go to the Algatt and the Eangen of the south, and see how long you survive their wrath."

Wrath? I understand her intention, but she's painting my people as a threat—hardly conducive to forging healthy bonds between our peoples.

"Go home," Siru finishes. She gestures to someone on the ground and there's a heavy *thunk*, then a grind as the doors of the gates open.

First a trickle, then a rush of refugees begins to move through. The savn herd them like sheep, and Kygga vanishes back to the wind. When I touch my priestess's Sight, all I see of him is a fine haze of silver.

I watch until the last refugee stands in the open space, surrounded by churned snow. He's the same man who shouted at Siru, and now that the crowd is gone, I can see the little boy he holds by the hand.

He looks at my sister long and hard, then says something clear, concise and full of belief. I catch one word.

Eirine.

Siru's face darkens, but she only watches the man lead his child through the gates of Imel and into the snow beyond.

TWELVE

I find Siru on the riverbank below Imel, staring at the river through fine snow. It melts on the muddy bank between our beached ships, clings to the branches of a few conifers, and turns the distant sun into a haze of dusk in the west.

Siru squints at me as I approach. For a moment she looks tired, haggard, then she pulls strength into her spine and lets her hands fall to her sides.

She meets me in the shadow of a tree. Snowflakes susurrate in the boughs above, only a few flakes making their way down to the soft bed of needles beneath our boots.

I give her a half-smile in greeting. "Did Kygga tell you I was in the city today?"

Siru shakes her head. "No, but I'm not surprised. It was disruptive."

"What will happen to the refugees?"

"If they're wise, they'll go home and they'll be cared for," Siru replies with finality.

I've more questions about what went on today, but it's clear Siru doesn't want to talk about it.

"I saw a temple," I say instead. "I couldn't communicate with the priest but I heard the name of their god. Eirine. Is she one of us?"

Siru pauses in the middle of brushing snow from her sleeves. She lifts her blue eyes to mine and cocks her head. "No. She's not. We call her worshipers the Sleepers—perhaps you saw the beds, in the temple? They send their people into dreams with a poisonous smoke. Father...

tolerated them, and instructed us to do the same, and so they remain in the land. They're a cult, Thray. An old one."

"I smelled widow root in the smoke. It's not poisonous. The Vynder use it in our initiation to visit the High Halls, and I've used it other times besides."

"The High Halls? You know how to access the High Halls?"

I catch myself, too late, and close my lips. These are secrets of the Vynder priesthood, and I've no right to share them with Siru—even if I do trust her.

"How?" Siru steps closer. "Thray, we have no access to the Halls. If you can teach us… You'd change everything."

I'm tempted to point out that the Sleepers likely already have access to the High Halls, though whether they realize they do isn't clear. There are two ways into the upper realms—physically, through a door like Gadr mentioned, or spiritually, through death or yifr. If the Sleepers are inhaling widow root on a regular basis, they've likely visited the Halls in a spiritual way. As to the physical, anyone with Miri blood or Thvynder's leave can open an established doorway, and the former would include all of Ogam's children.

But Siru doesn't know any of this. Perhaps there are no doors in Duamel, or the High Halls functions differently here than in Eangen.

I've information, then, that my siblings want. I'm not sure what to do with that yet, but I tuck it away like the round pebble in my pocket.

"There's little I can tell you," I inform Siru. "The Halls are dangerous, and their secrets closely guarded by the High Priesthood."

"So you don't know how to reach them?" Siru prods.

"I didn't say that."

My half-sister watches me for a long moment, snowflakes drifting between us, then tucks a wry smile into the corner of her mouth. "I see. Perhaps we can discuss that in the future. But for now, I'd encourage you to stay away from the Sleepers. Perhaps I'm too protective of my little sister—I forget you're a priestess. But they are not our allies."

I'm simultaneously warmed and insulted, which, I reflect, are becoming my default feelings around Siru.

"Who is Eirine?" I ask, returning to my earlier question. "What is she?"

Siru starts walking back toward the docks and the city, shrouded now in a fine white veil. "A fevered dream," is her only reply.

I squint blearily into the sunrise from the deck of the ship as we depart Imel the next morning. The sky is clear of cloud for the first time since our arrival, the water is placid and demure, and warm sunlight spills over the eastern horizon. The snow of the afternoon before has already melted, and I can almost fool myself into believing autumn is not yet gone. The sails fill with a crack of canvas, and the rowers sit at their ease as the warm wind bears us north.

But just beside the fiery orb of the sun, I see a haze of black. The Winter Night is a physical thing now, a lording presence over the northern horizon. From our vantage it looks solid and unbroken, but as the days pass and the darkness stretches its fingers overhead, I begin to pick out stars in its depths.

This duality in the heavens is a bizarre sight to Havar, Darag, Seele, and Branan. Once it must have been strange to the Duamel too, though now they cast it little more than grim glances.

To my eyes, however, it's nearly familiar. It reminds me of the High Halls, which Siru and I spoke of on the riverbank. There, the divisions between realms can always be seen, chiseled across the sky. But this division is less defined, more insipid, and I cannot decide if the similarities between the two are coincidental.

Suddenly my own concerns—immortality, siblings, Havar—seem less significant. Foreboding settles on my skin like dew, and there's little sunlight to burn it away. Why would my grandfather do this to the Duamel, if it's actually his doing? And if not him, who—or what—is causing it?

I wish the High Priestess were here. Hessa has spent more time in the High Halls than any other human, save her husband, who serves as Shepherd of the Dead. She might know more.

I consider praying, but even if Thvynder was close enough to hear, reaching out to them would be unwise.

I remember my deceit and its possible repercussions: death, exile, atonement. They're one more burden in the back of my mind, seething and restless, pushed down with the memory of saltwater in my mouth and the hurt in Havar's eyes beside the fire.

Promise me you'll come home.

I push the thought away. Remembrance and pondering will not serve me now. I need to stay focused.

There is someone safer I might reach out to, though.

"Grandfather," I murmur toward the darkness. "Where are you?"

Havar appears at my side and I cut myself off. We've had little time to speak since our arrival in Imel and I should be happy to see him, but irritation flashes through me.

He reads my face and recoils, eyebrows raised. "Am I interrupting?"

I bridle myself and shake my head. "No, no… It's just that." I indicate the dark sky before us. "It's unnerving."

"Ah." He follows my gaze. "It is. But you were sent here for a reason, so what have we to fear? It won't harm us, or else Thvynder would have warned you."

"It's harming the Duamel," I remind him, though my thoughts linger on the rest of his words. *Thvynder hasn't warned me because they haven't sent me.* "The refugees looked so desperate. Sick. Hungry."

"Seele says the merchants in Imel asked mostly about food." Havar leans beside me, broad shoulders spreading as he relaxes back into the rail. Wind lashes stray strands of his black hair into his narrowed eyes and I distantly think that I should braid it for him. "But back in Iesa, her people only spoke of salt and iron and glass."

I consider resting my hands on the rail next to him, but the water is too close. "They didn't want us to know what state Duamel is in. Not on the first meeting."

Havar gives a grunting nod. "So, they chose to begin our relationship with lies?"

"Not lies," I correct, feeling oddly transparent. "Omissions."

"There's a difference?"

"Yes. In any case, the Duamel's concerns aren't mine, or yours. Seele's, perhaps, but this isn't our land. We're here for one reason, and it's not to interfere with the Duamel."

Havar straightens, and I read the question in his eyes as readily as runes.

"I know it's not my place," he says. "But since the island… I've been thinking. I want to know the real reason Thvynder sent you. We all do."

I feel a sudden rush of blood to my limbs, nearly a fight response. Does he suspect I've lied, or just that there's more to my mission than I'm letting on?

"The Winterborn have information I've been tasked to learn," I say. I watch his face closely.

He takes this quietly, then asks, "Siru knows that's why you've come?"

I nod.

The ship rocks slightly, and Havar shifts his stance with practiced ease. "Here I was wondering if you were an assassin…"

I start to laugh, then cut myself off. "What? Why would you think that?"

"The last time an Eangen priestess was sent beyond our borders, it was to steal the Arpa throne." Havar shrugs, a grin tucked into the corner of his own mouth. There's relief in his eyes, so keen and fresh I realize just how burdened he's been. "Then we learned of the Winter Night, and there was violence in Imel. You draw that knife at every shadow, and you're so secretive. It… seemed possible."

"I'm sorry I can't tell you more," I say, and it's nearly true. I shift closer to him, softening. "But I'm grateful you're here."

He shrugs one shoulder, his eyes on the darkness up ahead. "I know."

I place a light hand on his back. Together, for a time, we watch the Winter Night close in. And despite the physical contact, despite the steadiness of my determination and the man next to me, foreboding turns in my chest.

I'm stirred from a doze under the ship's awning by a large hand on my shoulder. I look up to see Darag's face, backed by reefed sails, an untimely night sky, and drifting snow. My breath fogs before me—the cold has deepened, and snowflakes take too long to melt on my cheeks. I'm freezing.

"You need to see this," my future brother-in-law tells me in his low rumble.

I quickly climb to my feet, pulling my blanket tight like a cloak and rubbing at my icy cheeks with the back of one hand.

The rowers still row and the riverbank passes steadily by, but we've slowed. I follow Darag's pointing finger to the prow, where Siru stands alone. Her white hair is uncovered to the starlight, tugged by a northern wind, and her posture is one of preparation.

The rowers watch her. The Eangen, stirring around me, watch her too.

I leave Darag and join my sister at the prow.

Her eyes are closed and her chin lifted to the river ahead of us.

The water is locked in ice. It sheathes the surface of the river in a jagged line, clotted with frozen debris and creeps, I imagine, steadily southward. The riverbanks are high, treeless, and layered with white, and the dark river between us and the ice swallows the flakes that drift onto its ravenous surface.

Our ships will strike the ice in moments. I grab a nearby line in a flush of dizzy premonition and instinctively turn to warn Siru, to break her from her stupor.

Before I can speak, I hear a great crack. I clutch the line harder and twist, sure that one of the ships has wrecked, that I'll be back in the water within moments, lungs burning and mouth open in a muffled scream. But the Duamel continue to row with measured intensity, unconcerned.

Siru opens her eyes. She smiles a distant half-smile. "The ice, little sister."

More cracks ripple through the unnatural night as the barrier of ice begins to break apart. Great chunks fold into a crevasse, bobbing and thudding and splintering in the rushing silence. A rim still clings to the banks but, in the center of the river, a channel has opened.

We slip through. More cracks punctuate the night, but not once do our oars brush ice.

"This is my gift," Siru tells me, her voice low and her gaze on the river ahead. Snow catches in her hair and eyelashes. "Or rather... part of it."

"What is the rest?" I need to know.

She reaches to squeeze my hand, then braces her palms on the gunnel and looks back to her task. "The better question, sister, is what is yours?"

THIRTEEN: INTERLUDE

The pyre burns low, at the edge of the forest outside Albor. The leaves of the trees rustle, hidden in the shadows beyond the waning firelight, and the wind is gentle. But my cheeks are scalded from standing too close to the flames, and the warmth of the summer night stings.

The torch-lined path back to the settlement is empty. Not even my aunt is visible in the gate, watching for my return. She's left me—us—to our grief.

Together, my half-brother and I linger. Though, judging by the vacant look in his eyes, he's not truly here.

"Do you feel nothing?" I ask him. The words come out in a rasp; my throat is raw and my eyes dry after days of crying.

"I feel a great deal," he says without offense. He looks from the coals to me, orange light seeping into his golden eyes and lending them a soft glow. "But she's in the High Halls waiting for us, Thray. Just here. Just beyond."

I force my eyes to follow his pointing finger as he gestures to the space between us. I stare at the spot, and though I know what he says must be true, all I see is hard-packed earth where the villagers and priests stood earlier that night, watching my mother's body burn.

"I can feel her," Vistic says.

"I can't," I bite back.

He looks at me directly, as if seeing me for the first time that night. "Why are you so sad? I'll take you to visit her. We can climb the mountain and—"

"It won't change anything—" I choke on my own words, and curse. I cover my eyes with my forearm as a new wave of tears threatens me, but they never arrive. I convulse instead, sobs wracking my chest and tearing at already torn muscles.

"Thray." His voice is closer. "This is not the end."

I jerk back, lowering my arm and squinting at him through aching eyes. "For you. You can…" My next word sticks to my tongue, clotted with a tremulous, anticipatory grief. "You'll die too. You can be with her. And I'll stand beside your pyre, here, alone. Eventually there will be no one left but me. At least *part* of your soul will be with Mother, but mine…"

His fingers wrap around my upper arms. The touch is light, but it shocks me.

I stiffen. He hasn't touched me since we were children—the hugs and tussles and familiarity fading as his awareness of his place in the world grew, and the shard of the God that resides within him took control.

"You do not know that," he says, each word weighty and firm. "And even if you are immortal like your father, I'll still take you to see Mother, when I can."

I hiss in hurt and frustration. "So I can—what? Feel this pain over and over, every time I leave?"

Vistic's feather-light touch drops away. "I'm trying to comfort you."

"Nothing can comfort me. Especially not you!" I hear my voice rising, but I'm powerless to stop it. It feels good to speak, to shout, to unleash. "You're barely human anymore! You're not my brother. You stopped being him a long time ago. Now you're a shell with my brother's face—"

My voice cracks again. Vistic has backed away, watching me with a stunned kind of caution that sends me into a blinding fury.

"Don't look at me like that!" I scream, and I'm sure they can hear me in the village. "I'm not a monster! I'm not his daughter! I'm her daughter, and she's… she's…"

My head feels light. I claw at my burning eyes and turn away, letting the shadows hide my shame. I want to shrink, to hide. And in the same breath I want to scream and shatter the world with my grief—to make Vistic remember what it is to be my brother.

It takes time for my rattling breath to settle and my emotions to clear. I feel dizzy and light-headed, and I'm beyond spent. I've no more words. No more strength.

Vistic is seated on the ground a few paces away, waiting for me. He doesn't reach for me again or offer comforting words. But as I stumble toward the village, half-blind and wholly broken, he follows without a word. He watches over me as I return to our mother's empty house, curl up in her bed, and slip into unconsciousness.

But when I wake in the morning, he is gone.

FOURTEEN

The Duamel capital of Atmeltan fills the horizon, crowned with moonlit snow and drifting smoke. The houses are built of gray and pink stone in concentric circles up one of the region's low, smooth mountains, each layer elevated in tiers above their fellows. Their windows are small—only occasional slits of light peer out as the ships draw into a stone-lined harbor on the river's east bank. Pines bow above the rooftops here and there in the outskirts, and the center of the city is dominated by a huge circular structure. It caps the city as the barrow capped the hill by the sea—a fortress against wind and chill, illuminated by moonlight alone.

Around Atmeltan more mountains rise, as clear in the moonlight as they might be at midday. These are truer, harsher mountains than those we've seen so far in Duamel. Swaths of forest lie between them but their slopes are sheer, gilded with snow and draped with glinting glaciers. The rock is as dark and forbidding as the perpetual night. It's melancholy, cold, and beautiful.

The Duamel throw ropes up to waiting hands on a dock. People swarm, glutting the mouths of streets and passageways. Children peer from the shutters of upper windows while their parents cluster in the streets before heavy doors. Here and there braziers burn and many in the crowd carry lanterns, warm light glowing through intricately patterned gratings. These cast strange shadows across the faces of their kin—everything from lattices to stylized animals and scenes from myths. Racing wolves, each leaping and open-mouthed, sway across the stone quay beneath my feet.

Havar and the others gather around, forming a knot of familiarity in this strange, uncanny world. As beautiful as I find Atmeltan, I'm grateful for the brush of their clothing and the curl of their breaths.

Havar adjusts our packs on his shoulder. He murmurs, eyeing the Duamel, "They're so pale. Not Arpa pale but... they look ill."

"They still look better than the refugees," I whisper in reply, though only the other Eangen and Siru can understand us, and she's already farther down the dock.

I look to the lightest part of the horizon, in the south where the sun hides, and a shiver passes up my spine. We've endured the darkness for days already but there's something about seeing so many people, living in these shadows, that freshens my dread.

"I'm surprised there's even needles left on the trees," I add, gesturing toward one of the windblown pines that speckle the city. "There's nothing natural about this night."

"How can they live like this?" Branan mutters as the rest of the Eangen cluster in. "I'd go mad. I'd leave."

"This is their home," Seele reminds him. "You wouldn't easily give up on the land that bore you."

"If that land couldn't feed my children I would," Darag says. He glares up at the sky.

"They can't leave. The Winterborn have promised to save them." I take a step in Siru's direction. She's speaking with a knot of cloaked figures, and from the way the crowd holds back, they're obviously important. "I should be with Siru."

I slip off and Havar, wordless, falls in behind me.

"Sister," Siru greets me in the Divine Tongue as I approach. Her face is illuminated by the cross-hatched pattern of a lantern, suspended over their heads on a pole. One of her eyes is fiercely blue and bright, while the other rests in a bar of shadow.

The pole is held by a lanky youth with cold-pinched cheeks and a fur-lined hood. He stands just behind the rest of the group, who all wear heavy cloaks and separate fur-lined hoods like mine, with generous swaths across the chest that fall to points. Small metal disks hang from the points, flashing in the light. I only have time for a brief glimpse, but I notice three different symbols among them, all heavily stylized runes. Different orders, perhaps?

The Duamel shiver toward me as one, bowing their heads like flowers in a drought.

Behind me, Havar eyes the supplicants.

"These are the Diviners," Siru informs me, scrutinizing the bowed assembly with something between distaste and indifference. She conceals it with a gracious smile. "Those who seek the Winterborn on the wind, and have earned our favor."

I'm surprised—these priests are much better dressed than the Diviner in Imel. Members of the High Priesthood, perhaps?

One of the foremost Diviners, a middle-aged woman with a small mouth and short, horizontal lines tattooed at the height her cheekbones, lifts her face to mine. The others follow her lead and I see they wear the same tattoos, though some are partially hidden by the ruff of their hoods. The woman doesn't speak, but her deference is clear.

"This is Per, chief priestess. She's offered to take us to the temple," Siru informs me. "Apparently the Inheritor is absent from the keep, and they wish to keep us to themselves. I've just asked her where the Inheritor has gone."

The priestess blinks, brief offense and distress darting through her eyes, then she conceals it. She explains something in Duamel, each word given with painstaking care.

Siru cuts her off. "Tell me where he is."

I'm also curious as to where the Inheritor has gone, but I marvel at the way Siru's every word, every shift of stance or expression draws reaction from those around her. It's discomforting to watch but at the same time, I enjoy it—like a child throwing stones into a pond, just to see the fish scatter.

Per says something with obvious regret, and veiled disapproval.

"The Great Bear was seen heading east," Siru translates, a line appearing between her brows. Her skin is particularly pale in the moonlight, a reflection of the snow all around. "I don't know your people's name for him, but he bore a grave wound, and was healed by a fire-haired daughter of the gods."

"Aegr," I supply, my curiosity deepening. The bear is an integral figure in Eangen legend, and my aunt spoke of him occasionally. He had a soft spot for young women, she said, and had saved her from an unbound demon when she was young. "He escaped the High Halls before I was born and hasn't been seen in Eangen for... ten years, perhaps. Why would the Inheritor hunt him?"

Siru lifts her eyes to the distant fortress on the hill, then looks back at Per and repeats my question in the Divine Tongue.

The priestess nods, murmuring obvious apologies and regrets.

Siru lets out a harsh breath. "She says he wishes to tame him—taming beasts is a hobby of his, the fool. He has enough of Father's blood to be a menace, and too little to be competent. He was likely just bored of his other projects." She glances at the priestess, including her as she finishes, "I'll send for him. Aegr will not be harmed."

I doubt the bear could be injured by humans, but I'm relieved all the same. I've no desire to see a raging, legendary bear tear through the Duamel capital in pursuit of vengeance.

The Inheritor's absence also raises a possibility I don't like.

"We'll have to wait for the Inheritor to return before we go to the Winterborn?" I ask Siru.

She still appears unhappy. "Yes. Come. We'll go directly to the keep—I've no intention of sleeping in the temple."

Per's expression crumples at this, but she doesn't try to convince Siru. She does try to fall in behind us as we set off but Havar slips in between her and I, merging with my shadow. Darag and the others come close behind, bearing our packs and openly staring at the Duamel. Only Seele offers an occasional smile at the locals, and those fade as we go on.

Crowds and lanterns line the street all the way to the fortress, but the Duamel here are even more subdued than those in Imel, like a people half-woken from sleep. Yet their eyes track Siru and I with unsettling intensity.

"I'm glad you're here," I murmur to Havar as we ascend worn, stone-paved paths up to the fortress.

"There's nowhere else I'd be," he rumbles back.

Water sloshes and Havar's bare back disappears into a waft of steam. I strip off my sweat-stiff traveling clothes and hand them to a bath attendant with outstretched hands. Like the Duamel on the journey north, the servant shows no qualms about nakedness, or the fact that we Eangen bathe together. They simply take our clothing and leave our weapons stacked beside the sprawl of natural, steaming pools.

The others' voices drift to me through the haze, laughing lowly, tension easing out of them. I hesitate at the edge, looking at the water and steeling myself. I haven't been submerged since my near drowning, and there's the barest trembling in my hands, now.

Before anyone can see my hesitation, I sit on the edge and slowly lower myself in. My feet meet the bottom of the pool before the water touches my navel, and relief ebbs through me with the prickling warmth of the water. My muscles ease, and my trembling stills.

"I hope they're bringing us something else to wear," Seele mutters as the servants vanish through a carved archway and up a set of stairs to the keep proper. She's already waist-deep, her soft stomach cutting a swath through the water as she wades deeper. Her hair is still bound in its thick braids, but she begins to unravel it. "Or do they expect us to dine naked?"

At the side of the pool, Branan watches her with only his head above the water. Darag, noticing the direction of the younger man's gaze, wades over and places his own large, bare backside between the pair. Leaning to scoop up some soap from a clay pot, he begins to pointedly wash his underarms with a squelch.

I stifle a grin as Havar fetches the clay pot and brings it to me, offering me the yellowish soap paste within.

"Can I wash your hair?" he asks. He stands close, all warm bare skin and searching eyes. While I'm grateful for his presence in this unfamiliar world, with its perpetual darkness and unknown dangers, I can't let the barriers between us fall.

"No, I'll do it myself," I say, gently but firmly. Avoiding his eyes, I dip my fingers in and begin to lather my skin, lifting days of dirt and sweat with each stroke. When he doesn't leave, I look back up and murmur, "Thank you."

His smile is wan. "I'm patient."

"I'm not," Branan interjects, looking around Darag toward me. "How long will we be here? Thvynder sent you to the Winterborn, not the Inheritor, whoever he is."

I steel my courage and submerge myself, letting the warm water lift the soap from my skin. When I resurface—whole, unharmed, and not drowned—I smile in satisfaction.

"He's the ruler here," I remind Branan. "And we're trying to establish peaceful relations. We have to stay until the Inheritor returns, then Siru will take me to find my siblings."

Havar places the jar of soap on the edge of the pool and lets himself drift in the water.

"May I stay here?" Seele asks. She sits at the side of the pool now, black hair floating around her. "It's an honor to travel with you, priestess, but my task is better served in the cities."

"You can't stay alone," Branan says, still submerged up to his chin.

"I've no intention of staying alone," she replies coolly. "Stay with me."

He gives her a long, inscrutable look.

"There's no need to decide these things yet," I jump in before the conversation can grow tense—or awkward. "When the Inheritor returns, we'll figure out what to do next, and who will go where."

That sates Seele, Branan, and Darag, but as they return to their ablutions—or simply floating, listless in the warmth—Havar asks in a low voice, "You don't intend to go with Siru without us, do you?"

For a moment, I can't reply. I had intended the Eangen to accompany me all the way to the Winterborn's hearth, but now the thought of Havar beside me as I meet my siblings feels like an intrusion. I remember the way he looked at Kygga on the street in Imel—the guardedness and caution in his eyes. Jealousy, I feel, will not be far behind.

"Thray, it's not safe to go alone." Havar seems to read my thoughts, echoing Branan's challenge to Seele moments before. "We're too far from home, and you know nothing about the Winterborn."

He must see something in my eyes, because he falls silent.

"Yes, I don't know them, and I don't trust them, but I'm here for a reason," I reply, keeping my voice low. "We'll discuss this another time."

"Then why does it seem like you've already made up your mind?"

Guilt pierces my carefully built walls. I asked Havar to leave his homeland and lied to him to make him believe it was necessary. Blocking him out now is more than unfair; it's cruel.

I reach out and cup his face, tracing a gentle thumb across his bearded cheek. His eyes widen, startled by the unexpected intimacy.

"No matter how the next few weeks play out, I'll be safe," I say, giving him the words like a promise, and kiss him gently.

Silently, I hope that promise will persuade me as well.

Siru and I sit on either side of an empty throne as the Diviners spread a feast out before us. Members of the Inheritor's household, the Eangen and various priests fill the keep's central, circular chamber with movement and chatter, but we sisters are isolated. On a tier below us, they gather around low tables filled with rich foods: thick bread studded with nuts and berries, stews of root vegetables and squash, slabs of roasted meat swimming in juices. The scene is one of festival, though it's more subdued than any Eangen festival would be. There are no laughing children or running dogs under foot. There are no bear hugs between old friends, good-natured insults shouted across the chamber, and no couples entwined arm in arm on the benches.

My Eangen companions look as unsettled as I am, seated at their own table off to one side, with three servants in broadly belted robes hovering. Darag drags out his chair and sits before the servants can do it for him. Still standing, Branan cuts a piece of meat from a steaming flank with his belt knife and eats it, staring down at a third tier, which holds the blazing central fire pit. Only Seele takes the seat a now frantic-looking servant offers, arranging her skirts and scanning the room through keen eyes.

Havar raises his eyebrows, communicating his skepticism about the proceedings. He looks strange, clad in a long Duamel tunic with fine-woven wool, sealskin boots, and beaded trim—we all do—but he's clean and handsome. Despite our conversation in the baths, or perhaps because of it, the affection in my smile is genuine.

"I should sit in it," Siru mutters beside me. She eyes the Inheritor's throne, which sits empty between us. It's made of sturdy wood, each arm carved like the arm of a bear, with furled claws at the ends. At its top a carved bear's head roars at the ceiling in stylized relief.

Siru settles deeper into her own chair, adding with a glare toward the priests down below, "It would panic Per, and I can remind these sycophants what Ogam's blood truly looks like. Both victories, in my opinion."

"You and the Inheritor don't get along?"

"He's too arrogant for his thin blood," Siru replies, picking up a cup of what looks like hot milk, scattered with herbs. "Try this, it's quite good."

"So you are more fit to rule?" I don't look at her as I ask the question. Instead I reach for my own cup and sniff it. I recoil. "Is this wine?"

"It's a fermented milk," my sister replies distractedly. "Sweetened with honey, and the herbs give it flavor. Each cup will be a little different, but don't have too many. It will go to your head quickly."

I tentatively put the cup to my lips. At first all I taste is sourness, and the creamy texture turns my stomach. But soon the sweetness of the honey hits my tongue, and the dusky flavor of the herbs. The combination is wholly foreign to me. I sip a little more, then put it discreetly aside.

"I do not think I'd be fit to rule," Siru answers me after a long moment. Below us Per begins to speak to the assembly with gravitas and the rest of the room falls silent, so Siru lowers her voice. "I'm better placed as a mediator. Besides, the Inheritor's bloodline—weak as it is—is entrenched in this city, and our father ordained their rule. I'd have to marry him to take the throne peacefully."

"He's family. You wouldn't marry him."

Siru watches Per, calculation in her eyes. "Great-great cousin, if we're being technical. But that means less among the Duamel. Even less so to the Inheritor himself."

The fermented milk sours in my stomach. I open my mouth to protest further, but anything I might say is drowned in a wave of murmuring and raised cups in our direction. Per has turned, raising her own cup to us. Siru smiles benevolently and nods, so I follow her lead.

It's not until the clamor dies down that I notice Siru has rested one hand on the arm of the throne, her pale fingers overlaying the carved bear paw.

Drums beat in the unnatural night, waking me from a restless slumber and luring me from the warmth of my bed. Soon after, I lift my hood, tucking away my sleep-frayed braid, and hope no one will recognize me as I wend through the keep. Several servants give hasty bows as I pass—obviously my disguise isn't as good as I hoped—but they don't stop me.

By the time I stride through the main door of the keep and out into the untimely night, I'm filled with a grim satisfaction. I haven't been alone like this since we left Eangen and, between that and the cold, I'm exhilarated. I'm in a foreign land, unable to communicate, but I feel free.

Some part of me reflects that I should at least have told the Eangen I was leaving, but the sounds of steady breathing from their chamber had been too peaceful. Besides, I don't intend to be long. Take some fresh air, investigate the drums, and return to the fire in my little chamber.

I approach the source of the sound—a building just below the keep with a high doorway, triangular and formed of two thick slabs of rock. It looks older than the rest of the buildings and is bracketed by burning torches. The rock is painted too, colored lines intersecting black ones to form Duamel runes.

The scents of smoke, char, and damp hit me as I enter a long, narrow corridor. It's pitch black except for a light at the far, far end, where silhouettes and shadows pour from a large chamber. They all hover, kneeling or sitting around a central point. A temple?

I move closer, not creeping, but not announcing my presence, either.

My sister kneels in the center of a hard-packed earthen floor, surrounded by devotees. Across from her kneels Per, and between them is the bloodied pelt of an animal. As I watch, tucked into the shadows of the doorway, Per lifts a small, glistening knife. I assume she will cut herself, offering a blood sacrifice, but Siru takes the knife instead.

With unflinching, practiced movements, Siru slits her palm. Blood spills over her pale skin and begins to drip onto the animal pelt, which Per lifts to catch the crimson flow. But slowly, the bleeding stops. Before my eyes and those of the onlookers, Siru's wound heals.

Siru speaks in the Divine Tongue, her words flowing with the rhythm of frequent repetition. "Burn this to sate the shadows."

The Duamel murmur back in their own language, and though their voices are low, I hear more emotion in them than I've yet seen from the reserved people. They're moved. Awed. Grateful.

Siru stands. Chanting begins, backing a rising, sweet melody, all of which she endures with the same passive expression. The animal skin is burned somewhere out of my sight, adding the stink of singed hair and charred leather to the air. Then my sister inclines her head to Per and starts toward the passage where I linger.

The Duamel's eyes follow Siru's progress. I back off, avoiding their gaze until Siru is in the hallway.

She stops and cocks her head at me. "How long have you been here?"

"Long enough. I saw the bleeding," I say. There's an edge to her demeanor that suggests I've walked in on something I shouldn't have, but she isn't quite sure what to do about it. "And how you healed. You told me your gift was ice."

"One of my gifts is." Siru gestures toward the door. "Some of us have two gifts, rarely three. Healing is one of the least common."

I open the door and we step out into the cold street. "Even the Miri do not heal that fast."

"Aita does," Siru replies, naming the Great Healer. "You remember what I told you about the blood of the mother affecting a child's powers?"

"Your mother was a devotee of Aita?"

Siru nods. "From a wandering Duamel tribe. Long ago they roamed to the very back of the Algatt Mountains, before they settled in the cities."

"That seems a little… unfair," I decide. "You've immortal blood *and* Aita's healing?"

My sister grins crookedly. "Why do you think I'm the sibling that chooses to travel the world, to take the greatest risks? I cannot be slowed or stopped. It's also why I'm the one whose blood we give to the Duamel."

That thought catches me. "There was no power in that ceremony, though," I state, and I know it's true. I saw no magic in the temple, no tell-tale glisten of gold or silver.

"No," Siru agrees as, by unspoken agreement, we start back toward the keep. It lords over us, the torches lining its long stair the only relief against the night. "But the Duamel believe there is. Per confided in me that there is… unrest, in the city. With both myself and the Inheritor absent, voices have been amplified that should have remained quiet. So I took steps to renew the people's trust."

"Whose voices?" I glance around the quiet houses, shrouded by snow and latticed by hard-packed footpaths and cartways. There are few Duamel in sight, and those we do see are as reserved as always. "These people are all so… meek. They adore you."

Siru's laugh is thin. We start up the stairs and she glances back down at me, blue eyes black in the night. "Not all of them. Do you remember that cult I warned you of? The Sleepers?"

We reach the main doors of the keep and I open them, allowing Siru to pass through ahead of me. "I do."

"They've always been a thorn in our feet. Father made a kind of peace with them—they were passive, insular, unconcerned with the world around them—but since his death they've grown bolder." Siru lowers her voice. "Their ranks are small but there's a movement beginning… we've seen the signs and heard the whispers. They gather in secret and paint their lintels with symbols of the sun. Think we do not see or understand, but we do."

We pass through the entrance chamber of the keep, shedding snow from our boots onto the stone without pause. I've still only a basic understanding of the keep's layout, and my sister sets off down a side passage I've yet to explore.

I think of the earnest young Sleeper priest I met in Imel. He hadn't seemed divisive, just sincere. But without knowing the Duamel language, my understanding is shallow. Perhaps there was a maliciousness beneath the sweet smoke and welcoming smile.

"What are they doing?" I press. "Or preparing for?"

"I don't know." We've reached the door of Siru's chamber and she turns to me, one hand on the latch. From her posture, she's not inviting me in. "But I intend to find out."

FIFTEEN

Three days pass. I see little of Siru during that time, and the Eangen and I are left to our own devices. I'm restless, itching to continue north to the rest of my siblings, and there's little to distract me. I can only sleep so much, spend so much time with Havar or listening to Seele ramble about trade enterprises and prices and plans for the future.

So, I wander the keep. I open doors and follow staircases, stare down hallways lined with the Inheritor's hunting trophies—skulls, antlers, horns, skeletons, and serpent fangs—and run my thumb over the brightly painted Duamel writings on each doorframe. I spy idols and trinkets, tucked atop beams. I watch the servants, who work and chat and flirt until they see my eyes on them, then become quiet and reserved as mice. I study the guards, noting the places they protect and gather, the way they move and watch me without ever looking my way.

At first, I wander to take the edge off my restlessness. But as time goes on, I realize that I'm preparing. For what, I don't know. But I do know that Siru has secrets, and my grandfather's distrust in my siblings has yet to be proven wrong—or right.

I discover that the keep extends into a broad compound. There are two tiers, both built into the side of the mountain. The first is high-walled and contains numerous outbuildings that spill smoke, light, sound, and scent across the hard-packed snow.

Beyond this is a huge open space, lined with a short wall that runs along the edge of the mountain with a single gate. There are no other buildings there, except what almost looks like abandoned living quarters to the north. White-mantled rooves are nothing but mounds in the endless night. No smoke rises and the guards don't bother to patrol it.

The guards do, however, utilize the open space as a training ground, merging with the ranks of general warriors. Pells and targets are set up and the area is well maintained by the servants, who clear the snow and light torches for company after company of the Inheritor's trained men and women.

Branan finds me the second day as I watch them. He takes up position at my shoulder and follows my gaze, arms crossed over his chest.

Down in the yard, archers nock arrows in sequence, draw and fire. Projectiles slam into targets with a chorus of soft thuds and the shout of a commander. Another volley flies, followed so quickly by a third that I barely see the archers move.

"They're very good," Branan observes, a little grudgingly. He shifts on his feet, fidgeting from cold or restlessness, I'm not sure. "Have you noticed the savn tracks?"

"Where?"

He nods down to the training yards. "I found some yesterday morning in the yard. I haven't seen the beasts yet, though."

I find that unsettling, but unsurprising. While I turn the savn riders over in my mind, I admire the Duamel's display of cohesion and skill below. I rarely see an arrow stray, even when the wind gusts and the snow swirls. They change distances, practice sequences under varied commands, and even begin to shoot and run. I catch laughter on the wind, what I surmise are jests and good-hearted ridicule and encouragement. It makes the torch-lit figures more human, but I still feel the shadow of a threat at my back.

"Why are we waiting for this Inheritor, Thray?" Branan asks after a time. "We're here because Thvynder sent you to your siblings, not him."

"We're strangers here," I say, though I feel much the same. "We can't simply wander off into his domain without introducing ourselves, particularly not if we want peaceful and profitable trade."

"You sound like Seele." Branan makes a face. "Is this really the Inheritor's domain? I thought it belonged to your siblings."

I haven't discussed my siblings' relationship to the Duamel with Branan or any of the others, and in usual Iesan fashion, they haven't pressed. But they see the way the Duamel look at Siru and I, and if there's one thing the Eangen people are particularly sensitive to, it's false gods.

"My siblings rule in a spiritual sense," I hedge. "But the Inheritor has direct power over the people and the warriors. There are other voices too. Like the Sleepers' cult."

Branan watches the archers disperse, some flowing toward us and the keep, while others set aside their bows and take up spears. "I saw one of their temples. Not as big as the one in Imel but not small, either."

I pause. "Where?"

He shrugs. "Between here and the market, in the lowest tier of the city."

"Could you find it again?"

He watches me curiously. "It wasn't hidden. Why?"

"Siru suspects the Sleepers' cult is causing unrest among the Duamel," I explain. The wind gusts, frigid and tasting of snow, and I tug at my fur collar.

"What does that have to do with us?" Branan asks.

I give a wry, half-laugh and turn back toward the keep. A troop of archers passes nearby, some nodding at me, others touching the tips of three fingers to the center of their foreheads in the Duamel salute.

"Nothing, I suppose," I say. "I'm only curious. I'll see you tonight?"

I see a flicker of genuine regret passing over his face. "Where are you going?"

"The baths," I lie smoothly, and smile. "My toes are frozen in these boots."

I leave him standing in the cold, watching the Duamel at their spear drills—thrusting and advancing, blocking and retreating in a coordinated mass of movement.

I've no intention of going to the baths, or even returning to my quarters. I pull up my hood and make for the market—and the Sleepers' temple.

Drums beat and rumble through uncharacteristically empty streets, even for the Duamel's eternal gloom. But this time they do not come from the Diviners' temple, near the keep. They come from deeper in the city. Down near the market, where my booted feet are already carrying me.

Between my solitude, the darkness, and the drums, my skin begins to crawl. The heavily shuttered houses are dark and the moon is partially veiled. It's eerie, and the cold is deep enough to freeze my breath in my eyelashes. I bury my chin into the collar of my hood and carry on.

I consider how Havar and the others would react to my venturing out alone during what I suspect is a Duamel religious ceremony, but I'm already here. Besides, bringing them with me would have increased the chances of Siru finding out. I've no desire to lie to my sister about this outing, but I want to form my own conclusions about the Sleepers, without her present.

I join people flowing in the same direction as me, hooded and cloaked against the cold. There are adults and children, leaving the elevated doors of their homes and descending into the street. Between the darkness and my Duamel clothing they barely look at me, intent on the drums and their distant destination.

It's hard not to be carried along. Soon I'm surrounded by the locals, but without Siru to interpret, their murmurs and chatter mean nothing to me.

I head for the origin of the music—the central meeting grounds at the foot of the city hill, broad and open and lined with torches on high poles. The Duamel flow toward it like a river, and in the newfound light people glance at me curiously. I keep my hood up and my face shadowed.

Just as I enter the meeting ground, it begins to snow. Wind sweeps across the open space with renewed chill but the drums do not falter, and the Duamel seem undeterred. They surge through the drifting white and pool around a low, central mound.

I'm taller than most of the crowd and have little trouble seeing the Diviner priests, marked by their layered robes, dangling talismans, and facial tattoos. They're clustered on the mound, backed by three drummers. Two of the drums are an average size, like I've seen in the Inheritor's court, but one is three times larger than the others. While the small drummers' tippers fly in rapid sequences, the big drum carries a steady, deeper beat.

I touch at my priestess's senses, and silver flares in the night. It drifts with the snow around both drummers and priests, visible only to me. It's finer than dust, but there's power to it. It leaves me feeling enraptured, breathless, awed—all feelings I can't find the source of, other than the magic of the drums and the contagious energy of a worshiping crowd.

"Thray!" I startle as Seele appears, bumping into me for lack of space. Her cheeks are flushed from the cold and she's breathless, but not from apprehension. She looks as curious and enraptured as me. "Priestess! What is this?"

I ignore her question. "What are you doing here?"

"I came to hear the drums," she says, straining on the tips of her toes to see over the crowd. I'm reminded of how small she is next to me, and I feel suddenly protective. The Duamel are packing in tight around us, jostling and worshiping. If anything were to go wrong…

"I was already out, looking for Dova in the market," Seele says. "I saw you go past."

"Dova?"

"One of the Duamel merchants, we traveled north with him. You saved his son." The other woman's tone is vaguely reprimanding. It irks, but I understand—in my eagerness to forget the incident, I'd never bothered to ask the name of the boy or his guardian. And they'd never dared to approach me except to offer brief thanks aboard ship.

"Are those priests?" Seele asks.

"Yes." I glance again at the hill, with its robed figures and drummers, and my tension surges.

Carefully, I look around. On my other side, a Duamel woman stands on her toes as Seele did, a hungry glint in her eyes—not unlike a child listening to a fireside story. Her clothes are worn and less colorful than many in the crowd, and her hair is covered by an embroidered wrap, brimmed with fur. She clutches a large pack to her chest, as worn as her clothes. A refugee?

She's not alone. Beyond her, a group of men with equally worn clothes and packs watch the drumming with varying measures of intrigue or awe. It's an odd expression on their weather-hardened faces; too honest, too sincere for these reserved people, and if I look harder… I see flecks of silvered magic from the drums around them.

My priestess's instincts coil. Refugees have arrived in Atmeltan.

"We should go." I slip an arm through Seele's and begin to tug her toward the edge of the crowd.

She resists—again, another oddity. She glances from my arm to my face in shock, as if she didn't intend to struggle. Then she gathers herself and nods firmly.

I push through the crowd, releasing her arm so she can follow close behind me. Duamel faces blur. I feel trapped, claustrophobic, and despite the frigid wind sweat prickles down my spine.

I search for my original goal and potential shelter: the Sleepers' temple. I'm not happy that Seele's with me now, but she has enough reverence for the priesthood that I can likely convince her to stay quiet about my visit.

The crowd thickens around us. Disoriented by torches and too many staring faces, I walk right into a man. He's big, the same height as me and broad as a bear. He spits at me and pushes me aside. I stumble into a woman holding a small child and she recoils, her own rebuke on her tongue. I tug away, looking back to make sure Seele is keeping up. She's there, right behind me, eyes wide.

In my haste, my hood slips. Snowflakes land on my cheeks and I jerk the garment back into place, but not before my white braid tumbles free over my breasts.

The woman I stumbled into draws a sharp breath and starts to babble something, bowing.

The rhythm of the drums changes. There are no words to this song, but the impact doesn't need translation.

The priests are pleading. They plead against something, something dark and overbearing, something that surrounds us. Images come with the pounding drums, glimpses of bitter cold and a predator's glinting eyes, falling snowflakes and a waning sun. The Winter Night. There's mourning in the air, and hopelessness. That feeling feeds into the crowd, into me, and I find myself yearning for a rising, golden sun.

Seele's hands dig into my arm. "Priestess, what—"

A flurry swirls right toward us. It buffets Seele and the nearest Duamel, but it wraps around me, snatching my hood back again and leaving my white hair exposed to the watching throng. They stare and point, and I curse under my breath. I jerk my hood back up, but the damage is done.

I swear I hear a voice on the wind. It taunts, urges, and as it does I see the Duamel stir. They're all turning, and with each set of eyes that finds me, the crowd presses closer. Seele's fingers on my arm turn to claws.

Up on the mound, the drums come to an uncoordinated stop. One of the priests shouts over the assembly, but no one is listening.

The closest Duamel, a refugee, reaches for me. I instinctively slap her hand aside and wade for the edge of the crowd. A man grabs my sleeve, begging. A woman shouts—then another and another.

The crowd erupts. The priests shout for order, but the Duamel press in. I make it three paces before my hood is pulled back one last time. I don't bother catching it, and the sight of my father's brand drives the crowd to hysteria.

"Stay behind me!" I shout to Seele, who holds on to me as if she's drowning.

I draw my knife and, with a push of will, transform it into a short, bleached staff. I swear I can understand the Duamel's shouts as I do, though I know that's impossible.

Lift the darkness, Daughter. The beasts take our children, Daughter! Please, please, please.

A Duamel woman bars my path, her face a mask of grim desperation. I'm propelled toward her, herded by the crowd, and she reaches for my arm.

I see the knife just as it stabs toward me. I step back, cracking my staff off her wrist. I nearly trample Seele in the process and stumble, catching myself on a faceless Duamel and shoving them aside just as quickly.

"Thray!"

Over the heads of the crowd, I see a large form shove his way toward us. Light from a waving torch flashes over his face and I recognize Darag, with Havar and Branan behind him. Guilt and relief crash through me and I start to wade in their direction, but there are so many hands, so many bodies pressing, begging, clutching.

Another knife slashes. I bring up my staff, but the blade gouges into my hand, jagged and raw. I cry out and yank my hand back as two more Duamel seize my arm. Someone drags a piece of fabric over my skin, collecting the blood, then bolts back into the crowd.

Another knife, this one heading for my shoulder. I jerk free and duck the blow, driving my fist into the aggressor's jaw and spinning my staff back in front of me.

For a moment the Duamel scatter, and the reality of what they're doing crashes over me.

The blood. The cloth. Siru, spilling her blood in the Diviners' temple. If the Duamel believe the blood of my siblings has power to keep the Winter Night at bay—mine would too. Nevermind whether it's willingly given.

Seele's grip on my arm slips and I spin to see a Duamel hauling the Eangen woman out of his way. Seele screams, reaches for me, and is swallowed by the crowd.

I do not intend to hurt anyone. But between the magic in the air, the memory of the knife, and the sight of my terrified companion, my temper snaps.

My staff becomes a curved, sickle sword, short and liquid smooth. Blood blossoms down the blade and I whirl, careless of the path it carves. Duamel scream and scatter, clutching wounds and staring from me to the blade in horror.

Havar bursts into the space behind me. Darag shoves in with him, but I don't see Branan, and Seele is still gone. The Duamel, seeming to realize my impending escape, crowd in with renewed fervor. I see more weapons now, and someone is shouting orders. I know what they're calling for. More blood.

"We need to go!" Havar shouts.

"Seele was here!" I reply, turning on the Duamel in a wave of desperation and fury. "We can't leave her!"

There. I see the Eangen woman behind a wall of Duamel, eyes frantic, hands reaching.

I smash the hilt of my weapon into the face of the closest worshiper and lunge past them. Havar is right behind me, pushing two more Duamel aside so I can grab Seele by the wrist and haul her forward.

Her scream is half panic, half pain, but in a moment she's between Havar and I.

"We have to get to the keep!" The voice is Darag's, so close I can't see his face.

Branan shoves in front of us, firelight sliding down the blade of his own sword. "Move!" he bellows at the crowd.

They part just enough for him to shoulder in. I don't hesitate. I dive after him, bundling Seele with me. Havar and Darag come close behind.

I glimpse the edge of the meeting ground ahead, its high torches blazing before a backdrop of empty space and snow-laden Duamel homes, with their carved posts and painted beams.

"Go!" I push Seele. She takes her chance and bolts.

I'm a step behind when someone slams into me. The air leaves my lungs. I stumble into more bodies and instinctively shove, trying to open space around me. I win a few inches and my weapon lengthens in response, driving the Duamel back. Half a step. A pace. I wield a spear now, with a long, deadly head.

"Thray!" I hear Havar shout.

"Move!" I roar at the Duamel. I'm half-blind with rage now, blood roars through my skull and my mind is full of violence. I'm on the edge of my control. "Move or I will butcher you!"

Whether they understand or not, whatever the crowd hears in my voice crashes over them like cold water. They scatter. Some fall to their knees. But still they do not leave. I'm trapped in a circle of churned earth, the wall of flesh around me tightening like a noose.

Then I see her. The crowd's retreat has revealed something on the ground. A body—the body of a small woman, her hair black in the shadows.

Seele.

I lunge forward, terrified of what I'll find, but the body—the corpse—isn't her. It's a Duamel girl, and she's not moving. Blood pools around and one of her hands is stretched out on the ground. It's crushed and red, burst at the knuckles—every bone broken by stomping feet.

Cold wind caresses my cheeks like a mother's touch, soft and gentle. Then it bursts back, scattering the crowd even further and leaving me with a clear path into the city. I see Havar and the other Eangen calling for me, with bloody weapons in hand. My muscles scream to run, to leave the crowd and that limp hand, but my eyes are trapped by the dead girl.

"Thray!" Havar bellows again, pleading in his voice.

I flee.

SIXTEEN

My ears roar as Havar ushers me through a door. Heat hits me like a wave; I'm in a fog, my blood humming with killing rage and my head full of the dead girl's crushed hand.

A voice drifts through a large chamber. I force my head up, fingers cinching on my bone spear, but instead of a pressing, hungry throng I see a lone priestess. A Sleeper priestess, with a simple brown kaftan and intricate woven belt, who rushes forward.

A bar slams down over the door behind us. The sound cuts through the roar in my head and I feel as though my ears pop, the details of the moment surging toward me with renewed clarity. The clamor of the crowd is outside now, beyond a heavy door with a sun painted over the lintel and stone walls punctuated by alcoves. I find empty beds and hefty wooden pillars, every way I turn.

We're in a temple. The Sleeper temple.

Darag lingers by the now-barred main door. Seele sits against a wall, cradling her face in her hands, and Branan crouches before her. I want to go to her, to make sure she's not hurt, but my body won't respond.

Havar turns me to face him. "Are you all right?" he asks earnestly.

"Yes," I lie without hesitation, but my eyes gloss over him. I've seen death before, sought it and inflicted it. I've been in situations where I thought my life might end, or I might lose someone I cared for. But the broken hand, the drums, the screaming crowd. That was different.

The priestess's voice wheedles through my shock, and I've distant impressions of questions about tea and assurances of safety. The woman swings a full pot of water over the central hearth and stands back, wringing her hands. She looks as terrified as Seele, her gaze flicking between me, my spear and the Eangen men. All the same, the sight of her big Duamel eyes and the sound of her voice threatens to panic me all over again.

But eventually, my racing blood begins to slow. Maybe it's the warmth, or the familiar threads of yifr in the smoke. Maybe it's Havar's closeness, and his hand on my back. Maybe it's my spear in my hand, its grip gritty with dirt and blood.

I draw a deep breath.

"We're trapped until the crowd disperses," Branan states, not leaving Seele. He refuses to look at me directly, but I feel anger radiating off him. Does he blame me? For going into the city alone and placing them all in danger?

I stare at my bloody spear.

"There's no other way out?" Darag directs the question at me and the frightened Duamel priestess.

I look at the priestess, who's on her way to one of the alcoves. This alcove looks lived in, with bags and clothing hung on the walls. She glances at Darag without understanding but pulls a chest out from under the bed and opens it, revealing neat rows of bandages, pouches, and sealed jars.

"Is there another way out?" I ask the woman, even though I know she can't understand me. I point to the door, then the other walls. "Another door?"

"No, I'm afraid not," she murmurs and takes up several pouches of herbs. She beckons me, setting them out on a table by the hearth, and holds one out for me to sniff. "I want to make a tea, for your companion, for her nerves..."

I go still. How does this woman know Eangen?

I look at Havar. In his face I see the same incomprehension as Darag and Branan—they've no interest in what she's saying or the fact that she's said it in our tongue. They didn't understand.

But I did.

"You understand me?" I ask the priestess. Havar looks at me oddly.

"Yes, Winterborn," the woman says, giving me a guarded look. She points to Seele, then holds the herbs out again and indicates the boiling water. "I can make a tea, to calm her."

Winterborn. Her use of the title strikes me harder than usual. She understands me and I understand her, though the Eangen do not.

I'm speaking the Divine Tongue. Was that why the Duamel at the riot suddenly retreated? They actually understood my threat to butcher them? Horror spikes through me.

I'm not a monster.

The priestess is still holding out the herbs. And as mundane as it is, in a strange temple in a rioting city, I obligingly sniff.

The pungent scent of Sweet Tear rushes into my senses and I immediately feel myself steady. I start to nod my acquiescence, then think better of it and hold out my hands. "Thank you, I'll make the tea myself." The words, now that I focus on them, feel sharp and warm on my tongue. I can sense they're not Eangen.

The Duamel's smile is hesitant. She passes me a cup along with the herbs and watches as I fix the tea for Seele, then hand it Branan. He hovers over the distraught woman, blowing gently on the hot water before he touches her shoulder, speaking softly.

Seele takes the tea in careful hands.

I turn back to see Havar circling the temple, pulling back each curtain and looking for another door. Thankfully there's no one else here, no sleeping devotees to panic or stare. Just the priestess, who watches my betrothed nervously as she lays out more herbs and bandages on the table.

She offers me another brave smile and gestures to the items. "Take what you need, please, Winterborn."

Havar, assuming I haven't understood her, calls over her, "There's no other way out. What do you want to do? Try to reach the keep?"

Fists pound on the outer door. Seele curses in a voice thick with tears and Darag hefts his axe, facing the barrier with an even stance.

"The doors will hold," the priestess tells me, tangling her fingers over the curve of her lower belly. Her smile is hesitant and a little wry. "This is not the first assault we've weathered. You're welcome to stay here as long as you need."

"Thank you," I say, though I'm still not at ease. Hiding from a riot in the temple of a cult my sister perceives as a threat is not a situation I want to be in, and the presence of my Eangen companions does not help.

By now, Havar's caught on that the priestess and I are communicating. He cocks his head, staring at me, and for an instant I think he's upset. But he says with pride in his voice, "I knew it would come."

I can't quite manage to smile. How and why the Divine Tongue came to me today I've no idea. And that blast of wind that pulled my hood back, or opened the crowd as we fled—where had that come from? Not me, surely. Another Winterborn, one like Kygga? Perhaps Kygga himself?

More fists pound on the door. Havar takes up station beside a shrewd-eyed Darag, touching my arm as he passes. Seele and Branan now sit on the floor together, and she sips her tea with one eye on the door.

I take up my spear and return it to its usual bone-handled knife form, turning it over in my palm. My hands are covered with blood and dirt and it takes me a moment to see the terrible gash where the Duamel's knife cut. In the shock and the cold, I can't feel the pain, but the sight of it makes my stomach flip.

"Winterborn." I look up to see the Sleeper priestess offering me a damp cloth. "Here."

I take it. The cloth is hot and soothing, and it cuts through the blood and grit with ease. Even though my nerves feel raw, I offer the woman a small, grateful look. "This needs to be covered."

"Of course. I'm Rana. May I help you?"

"Yes," I reply. "I'm Thray."

Rana immediately takes up a pot of salve and gestures for me to sit on a stool. I comply and lay my hand on the table, watching with no little anxiety as she begins to clean the torn flesh on the back of my hand and apply a pungent salve. Across the room, I feel my companions watching too.

I feel no pain as Rana skillfully stitches and binds, and my mind drifts. I recall the questions I hoped to answer today, ready and waiting on my tongue. They feel less pressing, given what just happened, but when will I have this chance again?

"There are some things I would like to know," I say to Rana. "About your god."

Rana is obviously pleased, but flicks her gaze to Seele. She tucks the end of my bandage in. "I am happy to answer them. But may I tend to your friend, first?"

I flush at my own lack of consideration. "Of course, of course."

Time crawls past. I wait on my stool as Rana guides Seele to a bed and settles her there. Outside, the city rages. Seele still won't quite look at anyone, but Branan settles in beside her with his own cup of tea. He doesn't say anything and they do not touch, but the kindness of the gesture doesn't escape my notice.

Eventually I rise and pace, but the temple isn't large enough to work out my tension. I approach Rana, who has retreated to her own bed and is rearranging the items in her healing chest.

"May we speak now?" I ask.

She points to the other end of the bed. I sit and glance over the chest's contents.

"Widow root." I pick up a pouch of dried, gnarled plant, careful not to inhale too much. The scent is bitter and putrid. I find another familiar herb next to it, both of their pouches marked with the same yarrow-dyed thread. "Henbane. This is what you use to summon visions?"

"Yes, to visit Eirine."

"Who is Eirine? Is she like Siru?"

Rana packs more herbs back into her chest as she answers me, her voice firm but gentle, as if she expects me to be offended. "Eirine is a true goddess, one from the beginning, before those who bore your father. Before Siru or Midvyk or any of the others came to be."

"Who is Midvyk?"

"One of your oldest sisters."

I take a moment to sift through her words. She could be saying that Eirine is one of the Gods of the Old World, who Eang defeated, but there's more. Her choice of words, combined with the presence of widow root, prickles at my mind. A true goddess. Herbs that can take the Sleeper to the High Halls of the Dead—or, at least, the Duamel region of the Upper Realms.

"What is she a goddess of?" I ask, searching for more clues.

"Dreams. Visions. What is and should be. What can be, what has been." Rana pauses as she tucks the last of the herbs into her chest. She glances at the next brazier. "I can send you to meet her, if you desire."

The prickling at the back of my mind begins to solidify. "Do you mean Fate?" I ask, nearly breathless.

"Fate? What is and should be? Yes." Rana seems perplexed by my question. "This is Eirine."

I take a sharp breath. I try to temper myself, to remember that I could be misunderstanding. But... If I take Rana's words at face value, I can't help but conclude that Eirine is Fate herself, sister-god to Thvynder. One of the Four Pillars of the World.

If this is true, it makes sense why my father allowed the cult to continue in Duamel; he would not risk offending Fate herself.

"Rana," I begin, lowering my voice, "does the name Thvynder mean anything to you?"

Rana's eyes widen as fists pound on the door, shattering the silence. Darag, Branan, and Havar stand to attention in the entryway and Seele looks up, fingers digging into the side of the bed.

"Thray!" Siru's voice slips through the wood. "Thray, let me in!"

The men look at me and, to my surprise, I hesitate. I need to ask Rana more, but I doubt Siru will allow it. And I fear for the priestess if I show her any regard in front of my sister.

"Tell no one we spoke," I say, rising quickly.

Rana nods, standing after me in obvious distress.

The Eangen men wait for me at the door, though Seele hasn't moved.

"Do not tell Siru that I speak the Divine Tongue," I say to my companions, making a conscious effort to speak Eangen. The warm spark that marked the Divine Tongue earlier leaves my lips. "Understood?"

The three of them nod and back on the bed, Seele inclines her chin.

"Thray!" Siru shouts again.

Havar lifts the bar free. The door opens and torchlight spills in, accompanied by swirls of wintery air and Siru's tall form.

"Come," she says, not bothering to ask for an explanation. "We need to get you back to the keep."

"You have to be more careful." Siru turns on me as soon as the door of her chamber closes behind us. "At least you weren't alone but, Thray, I warned you. The city is restless. And the Sleepers! Why would you run to them?"

"It wasn't intentional," I admit. I don't even have to lie about that— I'd had no idea the door we burst through was to Rana's temple. That had been Branan's doing.

My fear and fury have dulled into a cool exhaustion, and even Siru's ranting fails to ruffle me. "But the Sleepers did us no harm. The Diviners, though? That riot was no accident."

Siru is pacing across her chamber, but at that she turns on me. "What?"

"The drums put the people in a fervor. There was magic in the drums and in the air, silver like yours. Yes, I can see it. And the wind pulled back my hood. It made sure the people saw what I was. Then it cleared my path out of the riot."

In any other context, between any other people, such a statement might be laughable. But we are both daughters of Ogam, and though I might not be well acquainted with my other siblings, I know enough.

Siru sinks onto a low, cushioned bench and stares past me. All at once, she looks as tired as I feel. "One of the Windwalkers, perhaps..."

I trail over and sit beside her, waiting for her to go on.

"Have you noticed the three talismans the Diviner priests wear?" Siru asks.

I nod, recalling the symbols I first saw on the docks the day we arrived.

"The powers Winterborn inherit usually fall into three categories, symbolized by those talismans—there are other smaller groups, but those powers are from a mother's blood. There are the Icecarvers, like me. The Stormbringers, who influence the weather. And the Windwalkers, who travel on the wind itself and control it, like Kygga."

"Would Kygga expose me like that?"

Siru's lips twist in something that isn't a smile. "I doubt it. But there are those among our number who see Ogam's unblooded children as… simply, lesser. It's entirely possible they wanted the crowd to attack you, perhaps even kill you. Then, if you are immortal, you'd be blooded. And if you aren't—"

"I'd be dead," I finished for her.

Siru nods slowly.

"Could they have amplified the magic of the drums?" I ask. "The feeling of them, the sound… It changed."

"Yes, and no. Three of our sisters make the drums and give them their magic, but they can't windwalk and none of them are in the city, so there could be no amplification. It's likely that whatever Windwalker was there just whispered to the priests to play a… more dangerous rhythm. They would obey without question."

I am quiet for a moment, processing all this, before I hold up my bandaged hand and admit, "The Duamel took my blood."

Siru says something under her breath. It takes me a moment to realize she's speaking Duamel and doesn't intend me to understand. But my new gift translates.

"Damn you, Arune."

Arune. Are they the sibling Siru suspects of instigating the riot?

I tuck this away and blink past it, as if I haven't understood. "So one of the Winterborn tried to kill me today, and nearly killed my kin in the process."

Siru stands again and paces across the floor, stretching her neck and letting out a long sigh. "Yes. But... Thray, don't think of it that way. They just want to know if you're like us."

Just. A flicker of my earlier rage flares in my chest at the casual word. "Oh? What if I'd died? What if Havar had, or Seele, or any of the others?"

"A foolish risk, which I will rebuke them for," Siru assures me, focusing on my latter question and glossing past the former. "I think I've miscalculated, Thray."

Her admission shocks me enough that I abandon my earlier questions.

"No one has found one of Father's children in decades, and that's aside from the fact that you're the only half-Eangen sibling we've ever met. You're an anomaly. You're too interesting, and some of our relations cannot see the difference between mischief and harm." Siru rubs at her cheek, and I'm struck by just how weary she looks. "I need to go to the other Elders—we're the council of the Winterborn's oldest siblings. I need to warn them before I take you out of the city. I need to make sure they do not let something like this happen again."

I blink at the implication that Siru herself is one of these Elders—I hadn't realized she held so much power. But that, and any repercussions, are thoughts for another time.

"Surely I will be safer outside the city," I protest. Distrust coils through me, but I can't find the root of it. "I'm not going to sit in a keep being stared at and plotted against while you go off without me."

"It's not that simple," Siru counters. "You will be safe here. There's little that any troublemakers would do inside the Inheritor's keep. Not openly. There are too many priests, and we must keep face. Kygga will be here soon too. He can take my place watching over you and serving as your translator. Until then, you must stay in the keep."

I deflect the thought without even considering it. "No. If you go to the Winterborn council, I'm going with you."

"No, you're not." There's no waver in Siru's voice. It's the voice of a leader, of a queen whose word is absolute law. "You will stay. You will meet the Inheritor and protect your people. And when the time is right, I'll come back for you."

Protests build in my throat, but at mention of protecting my people, they die. I think of the trampled girl, and recall my terror when I first saw her—that she was Seele. What about Havar? What of Darag and Branan? Could I bear to see any of them fall, human casualties in a game of immortal siblings?

Whatever expressions slip onto my face, Siru seems to know she's won. "I'll leave in the morning," she tells me gently. "I'll be back in three or four weeks, as quickly as I can."

Four weeks. I cringe at the number but force myself to nod, to ply a small smile. Even when I close the door to Siru's quarters and wander back through the hallways of the keep to the Eangen rooms, I do not let any emotion cloud my face.

But inside, I burn.

SEVENTEEN

I dream of drums. The sound merges with the wisps of a dream: a barrow on a lonely mountain. The beating of tipper on hide resonates beneath my bare feet, disturbing fine shale and cracking the crust on patches of snow.

I look from my feet to the barrow. It's much larger than the one Siru showed me on the coast and, I sense, much more important. I also understand that the thudding I hear is not drums, but the heartbeat of a fallen god.

All at once the heartbeat is gone. Silence overtakes me, the empty, whisking silence of a lonely mountaintop, then a new sound begins—a shushing, tap, and creak. A loom. The smell of widow root fills my nostrils and I inhale deeply, my senses easing through the boundaries between worlds and into…

I open my eyes. I'm back in my chambers at the Inheritor's palace, alone in the darkness. The scent of widow root fades, replaced by the pleasant musk of the blankets clutched beneath my nose.

Just a dream, I tell myself. But my mind is wide awake and my senses sharp, as if I've been awake for hours.

And that clacking sound. I know from my aunt's stories that it is tied to the presence of Fate. That doesn't mean my dream was a vision—it could simply be a symptom of the turmoil of the day and my conversation with Rana. But it's not impossible.

I want to speak to Rana again. I want to know if the Sleepers worship Fate, and what they're preparing for. But Siru's warning to stay in the keep lingers with me.

Unable to fall back asleep, I climb out of bed and dress, fitting my knife at my belt and pulling my Duamel hood over my head. I head for the practice yards without seeing a single servant. It's the dead of the Duamel night, and I'm grateful for the solitude.

The practice yards are equally empty, sheathed with blowing snow under the weak starlight. I haven't been this exposed since the riot, and the cold creeps in warning across my cheeks. But after two days in the keep, I need this scrap of freedom, dangerous as it is.

I know I'm tempting fate, but that only makes me more defiant.

I pull the knife from my belt and level it out before me. It lengthens at my will, taking on the shape of the sickle sword I wielded against the crowd. I half expect to see blood on the blade in the starlight, but it's clean, as white and opalescent as ever.

I turn my thoughts to the weight of the weapon, the bite of the cold, the rush of blood and movement of muscles.

I loosen my grip and let the sword swing in a clean, tight sweep. I shift my stance as I do, slipping into the movements that my uncle Nisien taught me. The tall, dark-skinned Soulderni fought in the Arpa cavalry in his youth and lent me his expertise, when he saw I favored the curved sword more than straight Eangen blades— though I've spent equal time on those, under the tutelage of Eangen's finest warriors.

One movement flows into the next. I step and cut, over and over until my muscles are warm and sweat breaks across my forehead. My wounded hand aches, but I ignore it. I shed my hood, then my kaftan. Wind-borne snow rushes past my legs and intermittent clouds pass over the stars, but my sword is bright.

"Thvynder," I pray when I pause for a handful of labored breaths. "Find your sister soon and return to us. I need your council."

The wind sweeps my words away and I push harder, weaving sequences together until my limbs shake and I'm desperate for water. Finally, I stop, shifting my sword into a staff and stabbing it into a snowbank. I scrub snow across my face and melt some on my tongue, drawing the cool into my body.

Then I pick up my staff, transition it into a spear, and start again with new sequences, new patterns. Step. Thrust. Cover. Sweep. Pivot.

By the time Kygga steps out of the night, my sweat-sodden tunic steams in the cold. He appears with a gust of wind, barely cooling my fevered brow. One moment, the night is empty, the snow smooth. The next, my brother's boots puncture the surface and he watches me with a calm, critical gaze.

"Little sister," he says in greeting, looking from my spear to my tunic, stuck to my stomach with sweat. "Where is Siru? Her chambers are empty."

"She left," I answer, careful to speak in Eangen. I try not to lean too obviously on my spear, but I'm sure he can see my exhausted quaking. "To go to the other Elders, after a Winterborn tried to kill me in a riot."

I watch his face, looking for any sign that he already knows this. But though I don't see any surprise in him, I do see amusement, then passing concern.

"Are you blooded, then?" he asks. He steps into the area where I've been practicing, leaving large footprints beside the chaos of my smaller ones.

I shake my head. "Sorry to disappoint you."

Kygga's eyes flick to my weapon and though his expression is closed again, I take a half-step back into a preparatory stance.

My brother shakes his head at that. "Thray, I've no intention of harming you, though cutting your throat would be a simple thing. You want answers? That's one way to get them."

"I still want to live, even if it's a mortal life. I'll wait for Siru's test."

"Fair," Kygga concedes. His lips contract as if he intends to smile, but the expression never forms. "Well, I suggest you return to the keep. And visit the baths. The Inheritor has returned, and he will not wait long to summon you. It's nearly dawn, in places where there's still a sun."

The Inheritor. My breath, still thin in my lungs, snags. "Finally," I breathe.

Kygga continues, "It seems he's had an eventful journey. But he will tell you all about that, I'm sure."

I'm curious to know more, but Kygga is right. I need to get cleaned up and prepare. My mind skips ahead, however, and I step closer to my brother. I know him less than I know Siru, but after what passed between us before she left, my trust for him is at an equal level.

"After I've met him, will you take me north?"

Kygga tilts his chin to one side, but the expression is more of curiosity than denial. "Siru will do that. I've other tasks."

"Siru said she would be gone at least three weeks." I step closer. "Eangen are not a patient people."

When I don't break his gaze for a long, chilly minute, he gives a slight nod. "I'll consider it, but only under the condition that you leave the Eangen behind. The journey is not easy, and I refuse to become caretaker of four breakable humans. You are more than enough trouble already."

The smile that was forming on my lips falters. My people and I haven't discussed this topic since the baths, and my own feelings remain unsorted. But at Kygga's assertion, my stomach turns in regret.

I consider protesting. I almost open my mouth to do so. But then I think of traveling north with Kygga alone, so soon, and I close my lips again.

This journey is mine and mine alone. Perhaps it's best if I leave the Eangen behind—safest for them, and easiest for me. I won't need to care for or consider anyone else.

I think of a trampled hand, Seele's terrified face and Havar's worry. I could spare them so much, leaving them in the warmth and safety of the keep.

"All right," I agree. I lift my spear as I do so and transition it back to a knife.

Kygga watches the change, and from the way his brows arch in surprise, I gather he wasn't here to see its earlier changes from sword to staff to spear.

"Where did you get that?" He falls into step beside me as I start up a carefully tended path toward the keep.

I glance at the knife in my reddened, wind-bitten hand. "A gift from Hessa, High Priestess of Thvynder... After she beheaded Frir and took it from her."

"Gods below." Kygga laughs a short, jarring laugh. "How many Miri has your High Priestess killed?"

"Two," I say. Pride and caution twist inside of me. "Frir and Eang."

"Our great-aunt and our grandmother," Kygga observes with a slow shake of the head. "I struggle to believe a human can be so powerful."

"Magic can't be used against her," I explain, fully aware that I'm bragging. I want to stay in Siru's and Kygga's good graces, but I also want them to know the power my Eangen bloodline holds. That I am not less than them.

"Facing Hessa, everyone is human," I add.

We've reached the keep now, and its shadow swallows Kygga. Passing between darkness and deeper black, he corrects, "Human, but still immortal."

I stride toward the doors of the keep's central chamber with Havar, Darag, Branan, and Seele on my heels. Guilt weighs on me like a sodden cloak every time I look at them. But I smile away Havar's concerned look, and focus on the meeting ahead.

We're all washed and clad in our best Eangen clothing, hair braided and weapons left behind in our chambers. I wear the pale blue, fur-trimmed kaftan Aita left me on the same day Grandfather gave me my bow, its color still bright and its stitches tight, despite the passage of years. My hair hangs long, only its upper half braided by Havar's careful hands.

"Kygga will translate," I say softly. In the rush to prepare ourselves, we've barely had a moment to speak. "Be cautious, follow my lead."

Up ahead, servants open the door. Light and laughter spill out into the hallway, backed by soft music and the barking of dogs.

We enter that wash of light and sound. In the days since our arrival, I've seen only the demure solidarity of the Diviner priests. But though I spy Per and several other priests in the room, speaking with heads bowed, there is nothing reserved about the Inheritor's return.

The tables have been pushed back. Dogs tussle on the floor and several dozen men and women cluster around packs and bundles. Discarded outer clothing covers the chairs and I smell sweat, leather, damp wool, and the fermented sweetness of drink. Servants weave throughout the chaos, laying out food and filling cups.

In the center of it all is the Inheritor. He's stripped to an undertunic and trousers, seated on the throne with his elbows braced on wide knees, laughing down at the antics of two dogs who bark at a huge, shrouded cage in the center of the room, where the fire usually is. A damp cloak with a ruff of muskox fur is cast carelessly over the throne at his back and his pack lies beside him, as if he were a passing traveler rather than a king.

Attan, Inheritor of the Duamel, is in his mid-thirties and has broad features, pretty Duamel eyes, and hair of a dirty, flaxen blond. Only in his short beard do I see streaks of Winterborn white, and his eyes are a brilliant blue.

Those eyes fix on us, just through the doorway, and he stands. He holds a cup aloft and shouts in Duamel, "To the Eangen!"

Half the assembly echoes his cry, raising their own cups. The others are too late and resort to belated cheering and clapping as we round the covered cage and approach the throne.

As we do, the shroud on the cage rustles. I catch a horrible, musky stink that makes my skin crawl, but don't allow my face to show it. There's a beast in the cage, I know that for sure. But it's far too small to be the great bear the Inheritor was hunting. A savn, I suspect.

"Kygga, cousin." The Inheritor descends toward us, cup still in hand, and beckons my brother from a nearby seat. He turns a brilliant, hungry smile on us as he commands Kygga: "Translate for me. I wish to greet our southern guests. Greet them for me."

Kygga unfurls from his own chair, somewhat removed from the festivities. He says in Duamel, "Do not call me cousin."

"Then Great Uncle, Aged and Most-Wise," the Inheritor corrects, smile still flawless. "Please, greet my guests for me. I'm delighted to find them in my city and home, they are most welcome here." At the last, his eyes skim us. They linger on Branan a little longer, then move over to me and my white hair. The hunger in his gaze fades somewhat, but his eyes still drop to my body, examining each curve and line before tracking back to my face.

I feel Havar shift behind me, but I'm grateful he doesn't intervene.

"Attan Winterborn, Inheritor of the Duamel greets you," Kygga says in the Divine Tongue. He's stiff-backed and bland, clearly unimpressed with his role as translator. He adds wearily, "Be awed."

"We are pleased to meet our gracious host," I say in Eangen, pulling at the priestess's formality I've been taught since childhood. I speak directly to the Inheritor, trusting Kygga to translate. "We've eagerly awaited your return. Was your hunt successful?"

Kygga translates.

"Tell them Aegr the Great Bear has been driven from my lands," the Inheritor says, descending another step. He continues examining us over the rim of his cup as he drinks. "A pity. But I've brought other prizes."

As Kygga again translates, the Inheritor strides past us to the covered cage. Without waiting for Kygga to finish he grabs the shroud with his free hand and tugs.

Everyone in the room turns, cluster after cluster, to look upon the occupant of the cage. Conversation lulls and, around me, the Eangen tighten.

There, behind iron bars barely two paces from where I stand, is a savn, just as I suspected. But rather than a raging, fierce beast, the creature I see is bloodied and beaten, its eyes dim with what I can only determine must be drugs.

"She's pregnant," Attan declares. He surveys his captive from within arm's reach, eyes cold and calculating. "The last female we took bore five pups for my kennels. They're difficult to capture, as you can imagine, but in this condition? Just a healthy challenge, for someone as experienced as I am. Tell them that, Kygga."

My scarred arm begins to ache, impossibly, and despite the beast's poor condition, I resist the urge to palm my knife. I feel a spark of pity too, though, seeing the beast cowed and preyed upon in her vulnerable state.

"Those riders in Imel," I begin, turning to Kygga. I'm surprised to find him directly beside me now, displacing Havar, who glares at him. "Did their beasts come from Attan's kennels, here?"

Kygga nods.

Attan scrutinizes us as we speak and I fear he's understood me, but his smile is smooth as ever. "Kygga, tell my new cousin to come sit with me. Her attendants can go."

I nearly react to the Inheritor's casual dismissal of my people, but catch myself. I wait until Kygga translates to pointedly introduce each Eangen, giving Seele special focus. Upon finding out that she represents trade interests on behalf of the Eangen, Attan looks mildly more interested, but still insists on sitting with me alone.

Havar gives me a long look as they retreat to the side of the room. I smile at him, wishing I could help, but Kygga prods me into movement with a discreet finger to the shoulder.

Kygga, Attan, and I retire to the throne, where Attan perches and my brother and I take seats to either side.

"So, tell me, cousin," Attan begins, still addressing me through Kygga. He's less abrupt about it now, speaking directly to me and trusting the Windwalker to translate. "What is it you want from your time here?"

"I wish to introduce my people to yours, and establish a friendly basis for trade," I reply, watching my Eangen. They have cups before them now and murmur among themselves. "I believe our peoples have much to offer one another."

Attan nods slowly. "I am sure. But what do *you* want? I can see your blood, cousin, and Ogam's Get always have their own plans."

Kygga gives a soft snort as he translates.

"I will go north to visit my siblings," I state, delivering the words with no room for sway. The Inheritor's demeanor, along with his repetitive use of "cousin"—trying to shorten the distance between us—has begun to irk me as it does Kygga.

I add, "Kygga and I will depart within the next few days."

"Ah." The Inheritor fingers the bear-paw end of his armrest as Siru did just a few days ago. "Well, I shall not stop you. But I trust your people will remain here? Or will you all abandon me so soon after my return?"

Kygga gives me a sharp look as he translates, reminding me he hasn't made his decision yet. I draw a leveling breath.

"We have not decided," I temper, treading carefully.

"I see, I see." Attan draws from his cup and, finding it empty, tosses the wooden vessel down the stairs. It clatters and topples, the sound nearly lost in the rumble of conversation.

A servant promptly picks it up and whisks it away, wiping a trail of creamy droplets from the stone with a sash around their waist.

"Tell me," Attan says, "are you as Kygga and Siru, immortal, or are you like me?"

I glance at him, unsure why he's pointing out his own mortality. "I'm unblooded."

The Inheritor nods with gravity. "Ah. So, you are a blade unforged. Curious."

"We'll leave tomorrow." These decisive words come from Kygga, startling me. I try to read his face, but it's indecipherable. "The other Eangen will remain, and I'll send another Winterborn to translate for them."

Even though I knew this last was coming, my stomach drops. Now, with a savn in the room, the Inheritor's unsettling words, and the memory of the riot, my doubts about leaving my people renew.

But I need to go to the Winterborn. The journey will be long, cold, and difficult, so in that way, I'm sparing the Eangen. They can remain here, warm and comfortable as guests of Attan, while I do what I need to.

It's for the best.

"Very well." Attan accepts a new, full cup from a bowing servant. "I'll take good care of your followers while you're gone, cousin. I'm vastly curious about your people, your god, and your ways. It will be entertaining! And upon your return, you and I can better acquaint ourselves."

I hold a smile on my lips until it feels genuine. "I'd be grateful."

"Of course, of course," Attan says to me over the rim of his cup, waving one hand. "But you must hurry back to me, cousin."

EIGHTEEN: INTERLUDE

Cloud-laden forest shrouds the temple at the White Lake. The peaks of the mountains are hidden from sight, and even the far shore of the milky lake is obscured. There's no breeze, no wind moaning through the craigs to stir the surface of the water. The high mountain valley is as silent as a tomb.

I stand on the lakeshore with the thin, moist air prickling at my lungs. A door to the High Halls, placed here by Thvynder for the priesthood, glistens half a dozen paces away. It's little more than a crack of golden light, stretching as Vynder priests and priestesses from Eangen's south slip through. Our journey from Albor through the High Halls took mere hours, versus the weeks on foot, and Thvynder's servants are fresh-eyed, alert, and reverent. They keep their voices low and their steps soft, none daring to break the stillness.

The temple's roof is visible above the treetops through occasional eddies in the clouds, and overlooks to the worn path that stretches from the rift to the forest edge.

Two men part from the fog. One appears to be just past forty, though the years hold little sway over him. His tunic is a deep teal, its keyhole neckline heavily embroidered, and half his brown hair is pulled back into a simple knot. Omaskat, the Watchman of Thvynder.

The second man is the younger, a year my senior. His unbraided hair is Eangen black and full of gentle curls, and his beard is short and well-kept. His skin is a shade darker than Omaskat's and he wears one of the tunics our mother made for him, its hems a masterwork of carefully stitched runes. It's a rich green, contrasting the uncanny gold of both his and Omaskat's eyes.

Vistic, the Vestige of Thvynder, turns those eyes to me and ducks his head ever so slightly, but his attention remains with Omaskat.

The elder man approaches the High Priestess. Hessa, her face framed by her legendary axes, takes Omaskat's forearm in a firm grip and exchanges quiet words as more Vynder flow out of the rift. Golden light oscillates and flashes, flowing over her muscled frame and thick black braids. Then she reaches for Vistic, planting a kiss on his cheek as he places one on hers, his hands gentle on her upper arms.

I wonder distantly if my aunt realizes what a powerful statement such interaction with Vistic is. Or if she thinks of him only as her best friend's son, who she loves as her own.

The last priestess steps through the rift: Uspa, another of Hessa's adopted children. With two huge hounds at her heels, a round shield on her back, and a spear in her hand, she's the picture of a warrior priestess—and, if the rumors are true, Hessa's first pick for her successor.

There was a time when I was the one marked for that role, but that was before Uspa carved her name upon the world. I feel no jealousy at that thought—at least, not toward Uspa herself. She's the closest I've ever had to a best friend, though her children and duties have taken priority in recent years.

Uspa glances at the rift and by an unspoken flick of her will, it fades. It shrinks to a slim crack in the fabric of the world and goes dormant, golden light fading like a sunbeam smothered by cloud.

All eyes turn to Omaskat and Vistic.

"Welcome," Omaskat says, his voice carrying effortlessly through the assembly. "Your brethren wait for us in the temple. Follow me."

Vistic stands off to the side as the Vynder begin to flow after Omaskat into the forest, vanishing into pine boughs and fog. He remains there until I reach him, then falls in at my side.

"Thray," he says. His voice isn't cool, but neither is it warm; it's the memory of warmth, from the days before his duties consumed him.

"Vistic." I haven't seen my half-brother in years, and the formality of his tone and posture, rather than bothering me, somehow puts me at ease. He makes no effort to bridge the gulf between us, and for that I'm grateful.

Looking at the path ahead of us, he lowers his voice and says, "I want you to know, my priority remains keeping the Eangen safe."

"What do you mean by that?"

He doesn't reply, and I know him well enough to recognize he will not be forthcoming. I'm better to save my breath and wait.

We travel in silence for a time, following a winding path through the trees. The Vynder give us a wide berth, our combination of Thvynder's Vestige and Ogam's Get warranting more than a little respect.

I don't mind that today. Striding beside Vistic, the separation between us and the Vynder feels right. The power of it. The strength. It could become addicting.

The temple appears through the trees. It's by far the largest structure in the north, built on the ruins of an ancient place, holy to the God Beneath the Lake. Over the years, the Vynder have added to its grand central hall in graceful, calculated tiers, steep secondary rooves sweeping down like layered skirts. Smoke drifts from a dozen chimneys and the great doors of the main entrance stand open to allow the Vynder into its smoky, herb-laced interior.

Vistic leaves me at the door with a brush of his shoulder against mine. I don't let myself look after him, drifting instead to where Uspa sits near the back of the assembly. Her hounds, discontent with being indoors, vanish into the forest to prowl.

Uspa glances at me, smiles distractedly, and pats at the hard-packed earth beside her kneeling legs. She's just a few years older than I, blonde hair woven into a crown and blue paint smudged into her hairline in the Algatt style.

I sink down beside her.

"How is Iesa?" Uspa asks, watching the rest of the assembly settle beneath the lofty beams and stone pillars of the hall.

I follow her gaze, weighing my reply. Vistic, Omaskat, Hessa, and her husband Imnir—blond-haired, narrow-eyed, and slow to smile—gather on the platform at the far end of the hall, around a huge bronze offering bowl.

"I don't mind it," I say.

"Who's priest there now?"

"An old man. It's a quiet post. Births, weddings, and funerals. Lots of fish."

Uspa smiles at that. "I don't mind the sound of that. Though I hear the winter winds are brutal on the coast. What's that the Addack say? 'Swift comes the North Wind.'"

"'Swift steals the North Wind,'" I correct.

"Ah. Well, it shouldn't bother you," Uspa teases absently, citing one of the Eangen's favorite misconceptions about me and my bloodline. As if simply being sired by the Son of Winter makes me immune to human feelings of cold and discomfort.

My smile slips a little. Even Uspa doesn't quite understand what it means to be me.

Omaskat starts speaking, pulling my attention back to the four figures at the front of the hall. I draw a deep breath and settle my hips back onto my heels.

"Of the Four Pillars," Omaskat tells the silent assembly, "only Imilidese remains absent from our world. Eiohe breathes again in the Ascended Emperor of the Arpa Empire, and his eyes have turned back to us. Fate has always remained active in our lives, and now Thvynder's reign is established over the north."

"Imilidese has not been seen since before the creation of the Gods of the Old World," Vistic continues. He stands next to Omaskat with a straight back, golden eyes drifting over the crowd without seeing anyone. Hessa and Imnir linger to either side of them. "Imilidese failed to return when the Gods of the Old World rose up against Thvynder, Eiohe, and Fate. Now, Thvynder intends to find her. The Four Pillars will govern our world together, once more."

"Where can she be, if she's absent from creation?" I whisper to Uspa.

"Perhaps there is another creation," Uspa murmurs without curiosity, her eyes fixed on Omaskat.

"Thvynder will depart today," Omaskat finishes.

Ripples and murmurs of unrest drift through the assembled priestesses and priests. Hessa and Imnir show no signs of surprise, nor does Uspa. If she already knew a secret as great as this, Hessa must truly have chosen her as successor.

"How long will the God be gone?" an elder Algatt priestess asks, yellow and blue paint smudged into the hairline of her many fine braids. There is no concern in her voice but I see it in the faces of many around her; in the widening of their eyes and the shifting of their bodies.

"As long as they must," Omaskat replies. "But the Vestige and I will remain in the land. Thvynder will be too far away to hear your prayers, but with the owls Vistic and I will hear, and we will come. The owls will be offered to you all—only use the runes to summon them. But do not, under any circumstances, tell anyone outside of this priesthood that Thvynder is absent. Those who would be our enemies may perceive an opportunity."

There are murmurs of unease, but also assent.

"Have no fear," Vistic picks up the speech. "Your High Priestess and Priest have proven themselves your faithful protectors time and again. You, yourselves, work tirelessly to maintain peace and order in the north, and provide stability for many generations to come. Thvynder's decision is a sign of our growth and unity—one we can all be proud of."

More questions come and more answers are given, but I only half listen. My focus narrows inward and I look down at my hands, folded in my lap.

"Thvynder," I murmur instinctively. I feel an immediate brush at the back of my mind, warm and present. My God is still here. Tomorrow, once they're gone, what will I feel?

Uspa bumps her shoulder into mine. "Don't be afraid, Thray."

"I'm not afraid," I tell her, and I mean it. I trust our God will return, just as I trust the priesthood to manage any threat in the meantime. "But this deception... I've a hard time believing the priesthood condones lying to the people."

"Omaskat and Vistic remain with us. There's no deception," Uspa says with ease. "Feel no guilt over it. You're obeying your God and serving your people."

But just as I told her I'm unafraid of Thvynder's departure, I feel no guilt over hiding it from the Eangen, either—I'm simply shocked that no one else does. A good priestess should be bothered by this, at least in passing.

I glance down at my white braid and absently strike its length, feeling the contours of intertwined locks.

Shouldn't they?

NINETEEN

"I won't let you go alone." Havar paces the otherwise empty Eangen quarters. The others have already voiced their displeasure, said their goodbyes, and gone out into the hallway to give Havar and me privacy.

He begins another length of the room. "This is stupidity. You barely know Kygga. You don't even know where you're going. You'll be entirely reliant upon him—"

"This is the way it has to be." I linger next to the door, my pack at my feet and my skin crawling with unrest. I hate seeing him like this. "Havar, I need to go. I'll be back as soon as I can. Then we'll take the next steps together."

"Then we'll go home," he corrects and turns on me, measuring me with a shrewdness that reminds me of his mother. That look—I've seen him give it to others, but never me. "Or will you stay here in Duamel?"

"I'm not staying here," I snap. "Stop this, Havar. We're betrothed. I'm yours, but I have to do this, and Kygga will not take all of us."

"Then wait for Siru," he growls.

"I can't," I growl back, advancing on him a step. The lies come easily—he's being unreasonable, too protective, perhaps even a little jealous. "I can't wait, and I can't tell you why. I'm bound by matters bigger than you or I. What do you want from me?"

He laughs, short and bitter, but cuts himself off. "You know what I want. But for now? Promise me we'll leave as soon as you return. There's no need to wait here for spring, not with the Winter Night. We can go back to Imel at least, and head south as soon as the sea ice clears."

"It's hardly safer in Imel," I counter, thinking of Siru's banishment of the refugees.

Havar closes the space between us and takes my upper arms, holding me gently but firmly.

"I feel like a hostage, Thray," he says, low. "I don't want to be here. I don't want you here, and I certainly don't want you running off alone into the wilderness with Kygga."

I shift under his touch, discomforted. "You're not a hostage. You'll be safe and warm, getting fat on good food."

A shadow of distain crosses his brows. "You're being naive."

That hits me hard, cracking my self-control and letting anger seep out. For a moment I'm overwhelmed by it, burning from the inside. I breathe slowly, measuredly, and when I speak, my voice is cold and passionless.

"There's nothing else I can do right now. Kygga will not take you, and I have to go. This is why I came to Duamel, why we all came. I will not give up this opportunity."

Havar's lips cut a hard line in his handsome face and his hands drop away.

I force a smile. "This is difficult for both of us."

He doesn't look convinced. "You seem happy enough with him and Siru."

The jealousy is clear in his voice now, and resentment. But there's something else too, something rawer. He's wounded, and that vulnerability cools my temper.

"I am," I admit, raw honesty in my voice for the first time tonight. I reach out and take his hand. His fingers are limp, unresponsive, but I wrap them in my own. "This journey is a gift from Thvynder as much as it is a burden. The Winterborn are a part of my family I never thought I'd know. No, I can't trust them wholly. But my parents are dead, Havar. I never even met my father. This is the closest to him I'll ever come."

I see the fight leave him. "That I can't blame you for," he says. "It's just… difficult, to watch you go."

His unhappiness is a palpable thing, heavy in the touch of his hand.

I'm overtaken with the urge to wash his struggle away. I embrace him, suddenly and tightly, and his tension eases. I bury my face in his shoulder and kiss him, letting him feel my gratitude and determination all at once, and hiding away my lingering resentment.

Then I slowly step back, take up my pack, and put a hand on the door latch.

"When I return, we'll leave Duamel," I promise, and I pray I'm not lying. "I'll see you soon."

Kygga and I take one of the Inheritor's sledges north, pulled up the ice-locked river by a team of shaggy northern horses and guided by two weather-worn drivers, bundled eye-deep in furs, with their spears strapped to the sides of the sleek wooden craft.

League after league of frozen river and snow-buried landscape pass us by until, at the end of the first day, they drop us on shore and continue their way north. I do not relish our upcoming trek overland, but I am relieved to step off the ice and shed the threat of its hidden, rushing waters.

Kygga and I spend that first night in a small village on the riverbank, at the headwoman's hearth. A fresh layer of snow falls across the world outside, smothering domed houses of layered rock, packed with earth and chinked with moss and clay. Central chimneys let out puffs of smoke, and the scents of cooking bread and fish fill the headwoman's house.

We stretch out on either side of the fire. The headwoman and her family sleep behind a curtain on reed pallets, while we've been given stuffed mattresses and piles of furs. Kygga lies on his like the god our father was, languid and at his ease, shirtless and oblivious to the discomfort our hosts have been left in. I, for my part, try to ignore a spark of guilt as I listen to the headwoman chide one of her children.

"Settle down, pup," she says in Duamel. "The floor is hard, I know, but we've Winterborn at our hearth."

"I'm cold."

"I know, you can sleep right next to the fire tomorrow night. Come here, I'll keep you warm."

Kygga doesn't appear to hear the voices, or if he does, he doesn't care. He lies on his back, staring up at the chimney in the center of the domed roof and drumming his fingers on his muscled stomach.

"Why did you decide to leave Atmeltan so quickly?" I ask him in Eangen, keeping my voice low and giving no sign I've understood our hosts behind the curtain.

"The Inheritor thinks too highly of himself, and he has his eyes on a dynasty," Kygga replies, smoothing his beard and continuing to stare up at the ceiling. "But if that dynasty is to succeed, he needs to marry Ogam's blood."

"Siru mentioned something like that." I mirror him, turning to lie on my back and stare up at the trailing smoke, my braids splayed across the furs. I rest my injured hand on my chest, newly bandaged and distantly aching. "I've no interest in being his consort, if that's what you're hinting at."

"He's not the kind of man who would care about your interest." Kygga gives an ambiguous grunt and adds dismissively, "But he wouldn't do anything until he knows you're immortal."

That, oddly, chafes me. "All the better that I'm already betrothed to Havar."

"The Duamel have little room for betrothals." He dismisses the idea. "Marriages are sealed within a moon of any agreement, or the parties are considered unenthusiastic and the agreement null. Attan would not see Havar as a problem."

A shiver creeps down my arms, despite the warmth of the fire. "I suppose I should be grateful for that," I murmur, trying not to think of what would happen if the Inheritor did consider Havar an obstacle. "But why did that make us leave Atmeltan early?"

"I did not appreciate the way he looked at you," Kygga says flatly. Warmth trickles through me, tempering only slightly as he adds, "You're a daughter of Ogam, not a savn bitch for breeding. You're worth a thousand times what he is."

Only if I'm immortal, I think to myself. My thoughts trail to the caged savn, her belly full of pups that Attan intends to train for war.

"Speaking of savn," I say. "How many does Attan have?"

Kygga crooks a leg beneath his blankets, tenting them and elongating his shadow across the curtains, beyond which the headwoman and her children have quietened into sleep. "I haven't been to the kennels in some time. They're under the keep. Last I heard, he had close to fifty adults, but the pups mature quickly. I can't say how many he has now."

I'm surprised. In all my wanderings of the keep, I'd seen nothing of savn aside from their tracks in the training yards. If they're *under* the keep... there could be a great deal more to the complex than I've uncovered.

"Has he been successful training all of them?" I ask.

"They haven't eaten him yet, so I assume so. But I don't really care, so there's that. Goodnight, Thray." Apparently done with our conversation, Kygga rolls over.

I frown at him, but let him be. His broad back expands and deflates more and more slowly, until I'm sure he's asleep. His soft breathing and the crackling of the low fire become the only sounds left in the house.

At long last, I prod aside thoughts of savn and Havar and Attan, and sleep too.

I dream of a barrow on a mountaintop. It's the same vision I had in Atmeltan, but this time there's no heartbeat or clack of a loom. Instead I hear the rush of wind approaching, coming closer and closer but never reaching me.

Snow begins to fall, smothering me with the huge fat flakes of early winter. The world is obscured, barrow fading, mountaintop slipping away.

Then the wind hits. It brings with it something greater. Someone colder.

I awake with a start. Untangling from my furs I find Kygga already up, standing barefoot between me and the door. The wind howls over the chimney and the remnants of the fire gutter. Behind the curtain, I hear the headwoman shushing her frightened children.

A light knock sounds at the door. Kygga watches it, his back still to me. He draws his sword and braces, staring at the squat, round-topped doorway.

I rise into a crouch as the headwoman slips from behind the curtain. She's brown-haired and green-eyed, in her early forties with weathered skin and simple, Duamel-cut garments on her short frame. Kygga gestures for silence, but indicates she should go to the door. Behind her, four children of varying age peek around the curtain.

She slips past and makes for the door, eyeing Kygga nervously as she lifts the latch.

Cold air sweeps into the room. Kygga raises his chin, sniffing it like a dog. I sense it too—there's someone on the wind.

I draw my knife, slipping it into my good hand.

"Mother." A young woman slips through the door with a baby bundled in her arms and snow melting in her hair. She opens her mouth to speak to the headwoman again, then she sees Kygga looming and me, crouched behind him. She goes very pale and shrinks to the side, shielding her child. "I— I apologize. I—"

The headwoman hastily closes the door, puts an arm around her daughter, and leads her behind the curtain. There they begin to murmur, and I hear the baby fuss.

Kygga eyes the door for another moment, then lets out a breath and glances back at me.

"You sensed him too?" he asks, holding my gaze with an intensity that, I swear, makes the fire burn lower at my back.

"Grandfather." As I say the word, I become more convinced of its truth. That cold presence was Winter, both in my dream and in this village. "But why was he here? Why didn't he say anything?"

Kygga's expression is its usual shade of indecipherable, but I don't miss the tension in the lines of his body and the corners of his eyes. "It doesn't matter. He's a loud dog with no bite."

He loosens his shoulders and gives me an irritated, *oh-well* smile, but suspicion turns through me.

Even if Winter didn't speak, perhaps his presence was a message in itself. A warning.

But it was not for me.

TWENTY

I sleep little the rest of the night, wondering about my grandfather's visitation. I suspect more and more that it was a warning to Kygga, perhaps over taking me to the rest of my siblings. But the fact that Winter gave *me* no instruction leaves me unsure. Why would he come all this way and not acknowledge me? Caution me? Instruct me?

I ponder the incident as we're served a breakfast of boiled grains and cooked fish, and for the space of a few bites, I almost consider returning to Atmeltan or sending for the Eangen to join me, so I have extra eyes to watch my back. But my circumstances haven't actually changed. Kygga refused to take me north with the Eangen in tow and my answers lie with the Winterborn, at the end of our snowy road.

I must move forward.

Kygga speaks up. "We'll head east from here on foot. There's something you'll want to see."

My curiosity deepens. "What is it?"

My brother smiles and for the hundredth time since I met him, I see our father in his face. My drive to know more about Ogam—and myself—reasserts itself. Atmeltan and the Eangen fade away.

"That, little sister," Kygga says with a wagging finger, "is a surprise."

We set out as soon as my bowl is empty, scraped as clean as Eangen etiquette dictates. Conversely, Kygga barely touches his meal and leaves the bowl forgotten beside the hearthfire. My cheeks flush at his rudeness, though I'm hardly surprised.

I watch the headwoman as we cluster by the door, giving farewell. But she shows no offense to Kygga's ingratitude, all smiles and polite bows.

Then, as I slip outside, I notice the headwoman's children pick up Kygga's bowl. They smuggle it back behind their curtain, whispering excitedly and passing the spoon between one another.

Kygga glances at the children so briefly I wonder if he saw them at all.

"Should I not have eaten?" I ask him quietly as we set off through the village. Other villagers, and a large, shaggy gray ewe, watch us from under a mantle of snow. "They gave us their best. I thought it rude to refuse."

"They gave us their best in a famine," Kygga reaffirms, "because we're guests—and we're Winterborn. If we'd asked them to sleep in the snow, they would have. And if I'd finished my food, I doubt the family would have eaten today."

My breakfast sours in my stomach. I think of the children, complaining of the cold last night. Perhaps Kygga had heard. Perhaps I had misjudged him.

"So next time I should not eat?" I ask.

"I doubt there will be a next time." My brother looks beyond the edge of the village, where an endless swath of white stretches away under a half moon. "We're heading into the Hinterlands now."

We set off. A scattering of villagers watch us go in typical Duamel silence, but Kygga does not look back. I do not, either.

If there are roads or paths in this direction, I can't see them. Snow and wind have obscured everything, though animal tracks can be seen here and there—rodents and hares and a lynx. Our snowshoes punch into the crust next to them, their impact and the brush of our clothing the only sound beyond the wind.

We make for a dense line of shadow on the horizon that I assume must be forest, while beyond, the night hides the mountains. I walk in Kygga's footprints, though he makes no effort to shorten his strides for me. In turn I make little effort to keep up, deep in my own thoughts.

I reflect on the Duamel people and their hungry children, the Winter Night and its refugees. I want to ask Kygga about Winter's visitation, but everything about my brother, from his expression to his pace, wards off conversation. I decide to bring it up when we stop to sleep.

But by the time we make camp, I'm so exhausted I can barely think. A sunless day of snowshoeing has stripped me of all my strength, and when Kygga leaves me to hunt, I let him go without a word. I dig down into a cluster of young conifers and light a fire, discovering along the way that the trees, which I'd thought abnormally short, are simply buried in layers of snow as deep as I am tall. Eventually I give up trying to reach the ground and a huge boulder becomes our hearth.

Once the fire is burning I range farther out, spending the last of my energy gathering more firewood. While I'm gone the flames melt the snowbanks back in a yawning circle, textured like a river valley, and I watch each layer sparkle as I wait for Kygga.

The quiet stretches until I finally hear the owl.

Startled, I look up. A large, black and brown bird flutters into the firelight, alighting on a branch. With a pale moon face and a black fringe around its beak, it ruffles its feathers against the cold and churrs.

A vision envelops me like a wave. All at once the Duamel night is gone and I stand next to a hearth in Albor, in the Morning Hall where my aunt rules. The details of the hall are blurred with the distance, firelit beams rising into a haze of smoke, but the smell is there—sage and smoked cedar, bread and humanity. I feel the hall's warmth, though I know it's a trick of the mind. I'm not really there.

Hessa, High Priestess of the Eangen, steps into sight. She eyes me, gaze so intent that I realize this is no simple vision. Hessa is using the owl to create a living link with me, and she sees me just as I am now.

Vistic is here too. My mother's son stands opposite to Hessa, watching me wordlessly. But I sense he's not in Albor, either—the firelight on his face is paler and more distant. The three of us are connected by the threads of the vision alone.

"Are you well, Thray?" Hessa asks. Her black hair has yet to show any sign of graying but the lines between her brows are deep in the firelight.

"I am," I reply, though my eyes drag to Vistic. He hasn't greeted me, so I do not greet him.

"Then what compelled you to lie to your people?" Hessa's gaze is hard and unyielding. "Thvynder did not send you north."

At this, Vistic shifts. The light of his distant fireside changes, and shadows deepen around him.

The hair on the back of my neck prickles. "I had to go."

"To find Ogam's children?"

"Why else?"

Her lips twist in displeasure. "They are not to be trusted."

"I know that. But they're the only ones who can tell me what I am." I glance to Vistic, shrouded and silent. "They're like me, Aunt."

A strained silence twines between the three of us. Distantly, I hear the crying of a baby, the cooing of a mother. Many families live in the Morning Hall, and the sound does not distract Hessa. Vistic doesn't appear to have heard at all.

"I cannot condone your lie," the High Priestess tells me, her voice like iron. "There will be a price to pay. But your journey... that I understand."

I feel relief and uncertainty in equal measures.

Hessa continues, her cool expression granting me no insight into her mind. "Do as you will. But remember the cost and promise me that you will not forget your duty, or the good sense your mother taught you."

Mention of my mother needles at me, as it always does. Vistic has bowed his head, his expression far away.

"Do as you need to and come home," the High Priestess finishes.

"What will my punishment be?" I ask, unable to hold the question back.

Hessa shakes her head in a way that tells me she doesn't know.

Vistic speaks for the first time. His voice is low and calm, each word delivered in its own time—the speech of someone who has never battled to be heard. "Omaskat and I will come to a decision in due time. For now, the owl will remain with you, to watch over you. Send him to me if you are in need."

I stiffen, both at the implication that my brother will decide my fate, and the mention of the owl. I've no desire to be watched by anyone, let alone an unnatural bird doing Vistic's bidding.

"I don't think that's wise," I counter.

"Why not?" Vistic asks, still the most shadowed figure in the hall.

"Ogam's children." I hesitate, choosing my words carefully. "They must know of the owls, and who they serve. They will not appreciate being watched, and it will make me seem even more of an outsider. They won't trust me."

"You want their trust," Hessa observes, judgement clear in her tone. "Be careful, Thray. Do not be drawn in by promises and familial terms."

Vistic nods sagely. "The owl will remain, but discreetly."

My pride is raw, but I keep my composure. My mind continually tracks back to my punishment, the uncertainty of it a sliver beneath my skin.

"Will you intercede for me?" I ask lowly. "With Thvynder?"

"I'll always intercede for you," my aunt says, lowering her voice.

Vistic doesn't move, but I see a thread of sadness in his eyes. He doesn't speak, and my dread coils.

The hall around us blurs and its sensations fade. The owls are powerful, but even they can only hold a connection for so long. I'm left with Vistic in a fog of diffused firelight. Emotion prickles at me, both at what's been said and the fading connection to home. I snatch at our last moment.

"Fate," I say, grasping at the threads of the vision. "There is a cult here who seems to worship Fate. Ogam's children distrust them, but they've sheltered me. Siru—my sister, one of Ogam's other daughters—claims they are preparing for something, and it's causing unrest in the capital city."

Vistic lifts his chin in consideration. "They *seem* to worship Fate?"

"I'm not sure it's her."

"Then learn what you can," he charges me, his face becoming indistinct with each word.

Vistic fades away and I feel the cold of the Duamel night rush around me again. I think to tell my brother of the Winter Night, belatedly, but the threads of the vision are disentangling.

The last I hear of my mother's son is a disembodied voice: "Come home to us, sister."

I startle back into my body. In the tree above me the owl remains, ruffling his feathers and watching with wide, curious eyes.

Sister.

Vistic hasn't called me sister since our mother died. Why use it now? To comfort me, or to manipulate me?

Exhausted and unsettled, I build the fire up and watch the night slink back. I've too many emotions to sort them out now, so I set up stakes, arrange my oilcloth tent facing the fire, and layer its exterior with conifer bows while I wait for Kygga to return.

All the while, the owl watches me. But when my other brother reappears with a string of thin hares, the bird is nowhere in sight.

We travel for a timeless repetition of days. I do not see the owl, though I hear the beat of wings in the shadows once or twice. I think of Vistic and Hessa, and my impending punishment. I ponder the Sleepers and their god. Eventually, I broach the subject of Grandfather's visitation again with Kygga, but his response is disappointing.

"He said nothing. It was a show of his power, nothing else," Kygga says as we stride through a forest, down the center of another frozen river as Northern Lights play across the sky in white and amber.

I feel a distant thrum beneath my snowshoes, and though there's at least a pace of snow between us and the ice, my imagination has me plunging through into the rushing, ravenous current.

"As if we could forget him," Kygga adds, startling me from my imagined death. I'd lost the thread of conversation, despite the weighty topic. "With his night hanging over us."

"If he is causing it."

Kygga glances back at me, white hair touched with pale gold from the dancing sky. "You sound like Siru."

"There could be another explanation," I say, shifting my pack higher. "Winter and the Winterborn aren't the only power in Duamel. There are the Sleepers too, and whoever they worship."

"The Sleepers live in smoke and visions," my brother snorts, "they haven't the power to do this. Their god has never been active, and their priests have no magic."

I don't reply, though I'm inclined to disagree. If the Sleepers do serve Fate, they're certainly not powerless—and if the Winterborn think they are, that may be intentional on the Sleepers' part.

Kygga trudges on and I return my focus to my steps, but my mind continues to turn. I'm struck by how much Duamel and its concerns have come to dominate my thoughts. This isn't my land—the vision of the Morning Hall reminded me of that to a painful degree—but the longer I spend in the north, the more invested in its people and troubles I'm becoming.

Come home to us, sister.

Promise me we'll leave as soon as you return.

More days slip past Kygga and I, unfaltering and unmarked. In the Inheritor's well-lit keep I could occasionally forget about the darkness, but there is no ignoring it out here. Even when the moon is bright I struggle to wake for the day. Only the cold keeps me alert during the long hours of travel, and it takes me increasingly long to fall asleep at night, despite perpetual fatigue.

It does not help that Kygga is a nearly silent companion, or that the landscape refuses to change. Mountains hang in the distance but we are so small, and traveling as slow as we are, their silhouettes never shift.

It's as we pass through another colorless, moonlit forest that I ask Kygga, "How is it that the trees are still alive?"

"I'm flattered you think I know." My brother squints around as he trudges. Here the crust of the snow is so hard, his snowshoes barely break the surface. "Not even the Elders can decide. The moon comes and goes, the weather shifts. The stars follow their normal patterns. Everything changes but the cold, the darkness, and the trees."

We fall quiet again and I focus on our uneven path beneath the dense boughs.

Eventually, the forest ends at a crumbling lookout. The ground before our feet gives way to wind-carved waves of white and exposed, snarled branches, while the land below is a haze of fine powder and glistening, frozen mist. Trees lean precariously over the edge of the short cliff, while others have fallen entirely into the basin.

I stop back from the edge but Kygga carries carelessly on, peering out over the vista. When the land beneath him doesn't crumble, I follow.

"Can we go around this?" I ask.

Kygga shakes his head and points to one of the toppled trees. "You'll have to climb down."

With that, he vanishes into the wind and re-forms below, stretching his arms out to the sides and sauntering off into the mist.

I blink, curse under my breath, and head for the tree.

The climb down is not easy. Branches jab into me and my mittens become sticky with pine sap. Other creatures have used the trunk as a ladder too, the delicate tracks of mice and mink and fox imprinted in the snow. But my graceless descent destroys them, sending powder and needles raining into the basin.

It's only after I jump the final pace to the ground that I notice the temperature shift. Instead of burning the inside of my nose, the air here is nearly… warm. Or at least, not so viciously cold. It eases its way into my lungs on wafts of moist, vaguely sulfurous steam.

There's still white on the ground, but not nearly as much as the world above. It has melted, leaving only rocks, boulders, and fallen trees capped with mounds of white. The earth is black in the dim light, moist, interspersed with puddles and populated by the remains of sparse, hardy plants.

"Hot springs," I decide, speaking half to myself, half to Kygga.

"There are pockets of them all across Duamel." My brother rematerializes at my side in a surge of shimmering silver steam. Moisture condenses on his eyelashes, mustache, and beard, and he rubs at it with one hand. "Come on."

Side by side, we set off across the basin. Here and there pools bubble, banishing the snow in broad circles of sandy minerals that crunch beneath my boots. We stay on the periphery of these barren spaces, Kygga and I both eyeing the bubbling surfaces of the pools with caution.

"Will they erupt?" I ask. I keep my voice low, though I can't fathom why. Maybe it's the eeriness of the place, the sudden warmth in a silent, icy world. Or perhaps it's the weight of the air in my lungs— turning from soothing to cloying the longer we're immersed in the clouds of steam.

Kygga shakes his head. "Rarely. But I've no desire to be doused with boiling water. I've only been here once."

I glance at him quizzically, then recall what he is. "Ah. You fly over it. A useful skill, windwalking. How many—"

My brother comes to a sudden stop, cutting me off. "Something's following us."

I halt and put my back to his as I search the dark mist.

I look for the owl first, thinking Kygga must finally have noticed our companion, but I see no sign of them. Our footprints stretch back the way we've come over the snow-mottled rock, but the mist closes everything else off.

I press into my senses, both natural and gifted. At the same time, I drop a hand to my knife and let one strap of my pack slip, ready to drop it.

Mist. Warmth, laced with hints of the outer world's bitter cold. Fine flakes of condensation shush against my cheeks before it melts again. But there's no variance in the fog, natural or unnatural.

"Do you see anything?"

There's no response. I glance over my shoulder at him, and my body turns to ice.

Kygga is gone. His footprints remain, yawning and empty, but he's nowhere to be found.

A growl ripples through the mist, and I swear the droplets of moisture on the fur of my collar tremble with the sound. Slowly, I turn around.

Eyes glint at me from the mist, more appearing with each shallow breath. One set. Two. Four. Six.

Wolves. I feel a ridiculous wave of relief—it's not savn, just wolves stalking me in the miasma. Then the ridiculousness of that thought slaps me. I draw a sharp breath.

I've no time to untangle and string my bow. I pull my knife and flick it into a spear at the same time as I shrug off my pack. It lands with a heavy *whump* and I step away from it, keeping as many glinting sets of eyes in sight as I can.

"Kygga," I hiss to the wind. "Where are you?"

A wolf charges.

TWENTY-ONE

My world narrows to the point of my spear and the beast in the swirling steam. It's huge and lean, white and gray with black facial markings and bare, snarling teeth.

The night itself seems to contract, trapping the pack and I in a fragment of time—immobile and rife with impending violence.

The charging wolf feints, snapping toward my legs and darting to the side before I can land a blow. Another immediately leaps for my shoulder. I slam it aside with my spear, hard wood impacting with fur and muscle with a thud and yelp. I hear a splash as it skitters out of sight in the fog, followed by a second yelp and a hiss of steam.

"Kygga!" I shout, enraged and terrified at his abandonment. But my body does not freeze—Hessa trained me too well for that. Another wolf comes in and I unfold with a snap, stabbing the spear into the creature's chest.

For one blurred instant I'm sure the blow landed. I feel the resistance of hide and muscle and bone then—air.

The wolf rounds me and snaps at my back. I spin with it, a second too slow, and feel a jaw clamp onto the flesh of my side. Teeth pierce my thick clothing.

I scream. I drive my elbows down at the wolf's face but it's still moving, snarling and jerking as it drags me to the ground. I stagger, a second cry of frustration and panic clawing out of me.

Another wolf lands on my chest. My breath leaves me, but my muscles still react. I catch its jaws on my forearm and knock its head to the side. I roll, desperate to protect my throat, belly, and face.

I press down with my hands and knees and try to lunge back to my feet, only to find myself bowled over again. The world blackens for an instant then I blink—once, twice. My lashes feel thick and my eyes burn. They're clotted with blood and slush, and I'm on my stomach again. In my hand, my spear has retreated to a short knife.

I feel the horrible weight of paws, the pain of wounds and crushed flesh, of jaws dragging me across the clattering rock and bright, cold streaks of snow. I slash blindly.

Blood hits my face in a second, spurting tide. Teeth and claws leave my limbs as the wolves scatter and I try to breathe, but there's blood in my mouth.

I stagger upright, spitting and wiping my face, trying to prepare for the next attack. None comes.

Through eyes rimmed with scarlet and slush, I survey the carnage. The wolf whose throat I cut lies nearby, twitching and bleeding. It's no threat, but more eyes flash in the mist and discontented, anxious canine sounds surround me—yips and howls and growls and whines. The rest of the pack linger, waiting for an opening. Waiting for me to tire.

"Kygga, you bastard!" I wheeze, unable to conceal the panic in my voice. "Where are you?"

Quiet falls, interrupted only by grumbling yips and burble of water. Where is my half-brother? He's gone to the wind, that much I can guess. But not to help me. He'd swept himself out of harm's way and now…

He's letting me be blooded. The realization hits me as the wolves circle in again, watching, loping, regaining courage. Stalking.

I fight through a rush of betrayal. I can heed no more pain, no fatigue, no desperate thoughts. I find my balance, grip my knife, and wait, because there's nothing else I can do.

Stillness falls, in the seconds before the rest of the wolves come to tear me to pieces. Then, one by one, their glistening eyes vanish. They slink away into the night and a fragile relief washes over me.

"Kygga." I hear the word, though I can't feel it on my lips. I can feel my knife, though. Its handle is slick with warm blood, and snow melts on my knuckles. "If you want to blood me, you'll have to do it yourself."

The wind picks up and coalesces into a form. But they are not Kygga. They're smaller, leaner—prettier, in a way that strikes me as neither masculine nor feminine. Their hair is a wild, chin-length mane, barely tamed at the temples by thin braids. There's blood on their lavish clothing, a kaftan with a high collar and black fur at every hem. Their trousers vanish into high, wrapped boots, tied off at the knee with clusters of canine teeth that rattle as they walk. There are teeth in their hair too, at the ends of two, tight braids.

"Well, Kygga," the newcomer says to the darkness. Their voice is masculine, low but sweet. "Will you stop me?"

"Arune!" Kygga appears between me and the newcomer in a flurry of steam. He stumbles, an arm clamped to his ribs and his face streaked with blood. It's his blood, from multiple cuts to the hands. "Stop this!"

Quickly, I piece the scene together. Kygga didn't abandon me. He's been fighting his own battle with this stranger. Another sibling.

My clouded feelings of betrayal abate, but there's no time to enjoy the relief.

Damn you, Arune. Siru suspected someone with this name of driving the Duamel to riot, nearly killing my friends—and leaving that Duamel girl trampled.

"It's so much easier this way," Arune complains. They twirl a knife between their fingers, the blade so fine and the movements so fast all I see is a blur. "She lives and she's of use. She dies and you can stop wasting your time. You can't tell me you're enjoying trekking into the Hinterlands on foot, Kygga. At *least* make her pull you on a sled. She's brawny enough for it."

"We've been over this," Kygga growls. "She goes to the Elders. This is what Siru wants."

Arune *tsk*s in disapproval. Their eyes slide around Kygga's broad form, over the dead wolf and bloodied snow, and land on me. "She's no idea what she's getting into, does she?"

Something else enters Arune's eyes when they say that. There's no malevolence, no mischief to it. But there is knowledge, somehow icy and pitying all at once.

"I came to find Ogam's Get." My leg is quaking, my savaged hip weakening. I steady myself and flick my knife into a sword. "Given who he was, there's little that could surprise me."

A smile creeps onto Arune's lips, their eyes flicking from my face to the sword, which they eye in admiration. They look to Kygga again. "You're set on this?"

"I am, brother," Kygga growls.

"Fine, walk to the Barrow with the outlander." Arune throws their hands up in surrender. "I won't warn you of the wolves again."

My interest tugs at his mention of a barrow, but Kygga is speaking and my pain rises with each labored beat of my heart.

"You hardly warned us." Kygga's expression remains stormy. "You led them right to us and attacked me."

"I warned *you*. And what else did you expect, coming to the one place with open water in a hundred miles? There're always wolves here." Arune waves Kygga's accusation aside. Their eyes flick to me one last time, then they bow to the pair of us. "Enjoy your walk."

With that, Arune vanishes. I touch at my priestess's Sight and see a haze of silver. It swirls and vanishes in seconds, rustling the mist as it goes.

Focusing on the silvered haze, it takes me a moment to realize my leg is giving out. I sink into the ground with a clatter of rock, lowering my weapon in dull dread. Are my injuries worse than I thought? Punctures, those I can feel. Bruising, yes. But this exhaustion…

"I don't know if I'll be walking anywhere," I say to Kygga. My voice sounds perfunctory, over-simplistic. "I need to rest."

He eyes me without coming closer. As usual I can't read his thoughts, but something about his posture makes me wonder if he's reconsidering Arune's words. Should he slit my throat now? It would save him time, particularly now that I'm injured.

Then he shakes the tension from his muscles. He frowns at the dead wolf, picks up my fallen pack, and comes over to me. He offers a hand, pale and smeared with blood.

"We can't stay here. Once we're out of the basin, I'll build a fire."

"Will Arune try to kill me again?"

Kygga glances at the mist, still holding his hand out to me. "No. He knows we're on alert now."

I hesitate a moment longer, still distrustful, but I have no choice. I put my hand in his.

We rest for the night and late into the next day in the shelter of a copse, far beyond the other side of the basin. My wounds aren't bad, as I'd hoped, but I'm simply too tired to go on. The physical exertion of the journey, the wolf attack, Hessa's visitation, and my uncertainty about my siblings have drained me to the marrow.

With shaking hands, I clean a dozen puncture wounds across my hip, back, and stomach, and up my arms. The thickness of my clothes saved me from the worst of the wolves' teeth, but did nothing against the strength of the bites. I bruise quick and harsh, purple-black and tender.

Kygga is hurt too, but not badly. He favors his ribs as he moves about our camp, gutting our meals and clearing snow. He builds a shelter with my oilcloth and conifer boughs, arranges a spit over the fire, and even sets out my breakfast grains to soak overnight, all while speaking as little as possible.

I'm grateful. I tell him that, but he only grunts and returns to his work.

I wake up after the midday meal on the second day feeling immensely better. Kygga is absent, the air cool and crisp outside the warmth of my little shelter. I hobble out into the forest to relieve myself, and immediately see the owl.

It looks at me from high in a branch, its expression judgmental.

"What?" I ask. "Do you need to watch me piss?"

The owl, predictably, does not look away. I ignore him, seeing to my needs and easing my trousers back up over my bandaged middle.

"Do not let Kygga see you," I remind the bird. I add as an afterthought, "And warn me of any dangers, please? Either from people or beasts. Otherwise you'll be making the long flight home sooner than you'd like."

He ruffles his feathers and drops his head in what might have been agreement. I've never been able to decipher how intelligent the birds are, or how much individual will they possess. But the request seems wise.

I return to the fire. I'm badly in need of a bath but there's no hope of that out here. I dig a comb from my pack instead and begin to work it through my hair, rinsing the blood out with melted snow. By the time Kygga returns, I've braided it simply over one shoulder, washed my face, neck, and arms, and feel much better.

"I'm ready to leave whenever you are," I tell my brother.

He glances me over in approval. "Good. I'll pack up. I don't want to stop again until we reach the Tomb of the Old Gods."

TWENTY-TWO

The side of the mountain is a great, black maw. The forests that sheltered Kygga and I for the last days have fallen away and the land around us is stark, all snow and dark rock in the moonlight. Even the mountains before us are barren: treeless, sheer, draped with glaciers and frozen, windblown waterfalls. They're an impassible wall, unbroken except for the maw.

Above the opening are seven runes. Easily a dozen feet across and evenly spaced up the cliff, I recognize only two. The first is the old name for Eang, with its bold cuts and defined lines. The second is a swirling pattern I recognize as Soulderni. It's the name of Oulden, the Miri who once ruled the Soulderni as their god.

The other runes are illegible to me, but I can guess what they say. They're the names of other Miri who bound the Old Gods, now cast from their thrones or dead.

Awe shivers through me, not just because of the gravity of the place, or the fact that I look upon runes carved before my people had a name. Every symbol is shattered, as if a huge beast had ravaged the mountainside—or clawed out of it. Eang's symbol has burst from the inside out, cracking in a dozen directions. Oulden's is slashed clean through. Other symbols have more than one cut, and when I look at the ground beneath them, I see piles of oddly smooth-sided debris beneath drifts of snow. Pieces of the seals, fallen to the earth.

"The top one was forged by Esach and Gadr, and the second down was made by Aita and Dur," Kygga says quietly. He's taken up station at my side, eyes roaming up the cliff face. "See how Esach's seal shattered differently, like Eang's? Lathian broke their bindings from within, but the other seals cracked when the gods who made them died."

I swallow thickly. "And then Lathian was free."

"More or less."

I look past him, down the mountains to the south. There, beyond the horizon, another mountain range hulks—the Algatt high peaks and the White Lake where Thvynder once slept. Being able to see the mountains makes me feel suddenly close to home, though we're many weeks from the border.

"Which seal did our father break?" I ask, drawing my gaze back to Kygga's face. "To start the Old Gods' release?"

My brother points to the yawning cave. "That one. Shall we explore?"

I nod without hesitation. I'm in no way at peace with entering the Tomb of the Old Gods, but just as I told Siru back on the ship, I want to see this. I can't resist. Few feet have ever trodden here, and isn't it fitting that I should walk a path my father once took? This is his legacy, grim though it is. And Gadr did ask me to bring him a gift from this place.

I let Kygga lead me to the mouth of the cave. The runes stretch above us, an arrow toward the sky as we enter the shadow of the mountain.

Our feet crunch over fingers of ice and drifts of snow. I place my steps carefully and pause a few paces in, allowing my eyes to adjust to the gloom.

I hear the strike of flint and steel. Light flares and Kygga raises a smoldering bundle of moss tinder to his lips, blowing it gently into flame, then lays it into a bowl. The flames gutter and strengthen. I catch a whiff of dirty tallow, but I'm glad for the light.

Golden illumination fills the chamber. The rock walls are largely natural, save for every two paces where smooth strips stretch up like pillars into the gloom. On these, the rock is as smooth as a doldrum sea and decorated by countless runes of even size and varied origin.

I'm so focused on the runes that it takes Kygga walking through one of the rougher walls for me to realize they're not whole. Each section of unhewn stone, between the smooth dividers, has a doorway—if cracks in the rock can be called doorways.

"This is where the Lesser Gods of the Old Gods slept." Kygga beckons me through the door. "The ones that began the true work of freeing Lathian. The others were bound deeper in the mountain, with Lathian himself at the mountain's heart."

I drift over to him and peer through the divide. Within I see a perfectly square burial pit in the gray rock floor. Shattered pottery and other unidentifiable refuse surround it.

"Why were they bound instead of killed?" I ask, instinctively lowering my voice.

"Some lesser gods were killed, but together, the Gods of the Old World were simply too powerful." Kygga moves on to the next alcove and I follow him. Inside I see more of the same, though the trough in the floor is a little smaller. "Father used to speak of how he watched his mother lure them all here, into the mountain. She lost them in the catacombs, and slipped back outside before they realized she was gone—or that her allies had amassed outside."

Awe sweeps over me, and not just at the magnitude of events Kygga describes. He mentions Ogam speaking to him so casually—just a father telling his son stories of a long, unfathomable life.

"What was he like?" I ask. I don't mean to speak so gently, but my voice comes out hushed.

"Father?" Kygga glances at me, brown eyes darker in the lamplight, and keeps walking deeper into the mountain. Patterns of shadow skitter across the stone all around him, and I fall into step at his side. "He was..."

Kygga trails off. My brother's face is creased with thought, and whatever he's about to say, it must be painful. But instead he says, "Someone's been here."

Startled, I follow his gaze to one of the alcoves, where I see a clay vessel. It sits unbroken on the stone floor, neither dusty nor worn by time. It's painted with bright colors in patterns that I recognize from the Duamel houses. Their runes.

Kygga passes me our lamp, folds himself through the narrow door and picks up the new vessel. It's an oil lamp, similar to the one I'm holding, but different enough to make my brother pause.

Kygga turns the new vessel, studying its runes as he does. "This is Sleeper," he says, voice hardening. "It shouldn't be here."

I slip into the alcove after him, scuffing debris under my boots. "Why would Sleepers come here?"

Kygga looks from the lamp to the burial pit, then back out into the hallway. "Scavenging, perhaps," he says, but I can tell he doesn't believe that. "It takes a good deal of courage for a human to trespass in a place like this."

"Siru believes the Sleepers are preparing for something," I remind him.

"Siru spends too much time in Atmeltan. She sees conspiracies in every corner," Kygga says dismissively, then looks at the lamp again. "Perhaps it was stolen. We don't know. But we've siblings that visit the tombs regularly. Maybe it was them. At least, they will know more."

We slip back out into the main passage. Kygga slips the Sleeper lamp into my pack without a word, and when I open my mouth to pick up our conversation, he shakes his head.

I feel a draft and glance at my brother again, wondering if he's manipulating the air around us.

Ahead, lamplight slips across a hole in the floor. It's large enough to admit a person, and it's not the result of a natural collapse. Someone has carved their way through the tomb floor and into... a chamber, beyond.

"I'm guessing that isn't supposed to be here?" I ask quietly.

"No." Kygga's voice is the barest rumble. Abruptly he backs away, grabbing my arm and urging me with him. "We should go. Now."

My wounds protest at the sudden movement, but he seems to have forgotten about them.

"You don't want to investigate?" I press. I certainly do. The sight is ominous, yes, but I can't imagine just walking away.

"Here?" Kygga laughs. He glances back at the yawning hole in the stone floor. "Never."

We're not two paces from the mouth of the tombs when snow begins to fall. It starts lightly, tiny pricks of cold melting on my cheeks and building up on my eyelashes. Within ten paces, the wind begins. Within a score, we're trapped in a full winter gale. We might as well be back underground.

"Grandfather." I cringe down into my collar, and the biting wind snaps my words away. "Are you doing this?"

There's no answer.

I squint through the flurry as Kygga turns back to me, standing so close his chest bumps into my shoulder. I free my mouth from my collar long enough to shout, "Can't you make it stop?"

His response is lost in the maelstrom, but it's obviously negative.

"We need shelter!" The cold pries into me, filling my muscles with tension and making my wounds ache fiercely. "Can't we go back to the tombs?"

"Are you mad?" he shouts back.

"Where else are we supposed to go?"

Kygga hesitates, buffeted by the wind, then relents. His hand fastens on mine and he begins to walk. The contact startles me, but I'm more surprised when I realize he's retracing our footsteps. I feel them rather than see them—indentations in the snow that both make walking easier and threaten to trip me with every step.

Kygga doesn't release my hand until the driving snow turns to a swirl and the wind shifts from a torrent to a forlorn howl. Then he releases my hand and stomps into the tombs again, shedding snow like a disgruntled dog.

As I pull off my hat and shake it, flint strikes steel. Again, tinder flares and Kygga's grim face fills with light. He transfers the flame to the lamp we've only just extinguished and an orb of light pushes back the darkness.

"I don't want to be here," he grumbles.

"It's our only choice," I remind him, sounding calmer than I feel. At least he knows he's immortal, and any dangers in the tombs can't kill him. I don't have that luxury.

Still, my eyes are drawn to the back of the cave, to the carefully carved hole in the floor, and my curiosity burns.

I take my pack off his shoulder and set it on the ground. "I'll start a fire if you keep watch?"

He grunts his agreement and we set to work. I find firewood stacked in the first alcove, along with rolls of brittle reed pallets, a shelf of tallow lamps, and several jars covered and tied with leather. They prove to have more tallow inside, and I hope it's enough to keep the darkness at bay until the storm is over.

I start a fire close to the door of the storage alcove, which is graciously protected from the mouth of the cave by a shoulder of rock. I consider making the fire in the storeroom itself, but there's no ventilation for smoke, and no escape if anything… unfortunate occurs.

As for Kygga, he stalks farther inside the mountain, obviously far more concerned with dangers from within than without. He hasn't drawn his short sword but his posture is all caution and coiled power in the lamplight.

"What do you think it is?" I ask when the silence is too much to bear. I kneel beside the fire, scooping gathered snow from my folded cloak into a pot on the fire's edge. "That hole in the floor."

Kygga looks at me across a band of darkness, pooling between where the light of his lamp ends, and the light of my fire begins. At the tomb mouth, the wind continues to howl. "I told you I don't know. I've only been to the tombs a few times… they're not my concern."

"Then guess."

"Something no one remembers," my brother says, and the weight of the words settle heavy in my chest. "Tunnels. Perhaps something the Sleepers unearthed… or awoke. I know there was a great deal of residual power here, after the Old Gods escaped. Great beings like that, and the magic that bound them, tend to leave an impression."

I think of the White Lake where Thvynder slept and my skin crawls. I can't imagine Sleepers like Rana stirring a long-empty tomb, but I only met the woman once. I wish, not for the first time, that I'd been able to ask her more. Or that I'd followed her direction and gone to speak to Eirine. I'm tired of feeling ignorant, ever the student, and never the one with the upper hand.

"Thvynder would know if there was something dangerous left here," I say, half to soothe him, and half to soothe myself. I warm the backs of my fingers on the pot and add, "Especially something that could awaken."

"Thvynder doesn't rule here. Even Grandfather doesn't have much sway, though the winter is born, ultimately, from him," Kygga replies. Leaving his lamp on the floor, he begins to pace back and forth across the breadth of the tunnel. "The Elders will know more. Try to get some sleep, Thray. And don't wander off."

TWENTY-THREE

I have little intention of sleeping. But the raging storm takes on a droning, hypnotic quality, and eventually I drift.

I jerk back awake when a rush of wings settles beside my ear. The fire has burned down to a scattering of languid, licking flames. Kygga's lamp is on the floor half a dozen paces away, its flame flickering in the draft.

I nearly call for Kygga, then see the owl perched on my pack, its eyes a pair of harvest moons in the firelight.

"What is it?" I whisper.

The owl stares off in the direction of Kygga's lamp. I follow its gaze, looking for any sign of my brother. But he's gone.

I push into a sitting position, marveling at how my body can ache in so many different ways at once.

The owl flutters toward Kygga's lamp. Its light wavers in the rush of wings and the bird lands beside it, looking back at me and waiting.

Kygga is not here. Yes, the darkness is deep enough to hide him, but all my senses—human and priestly—tell me that the owl and I are alone.

A mix of fear and anticipation creeps up the back of my neck. "Where did he go?" I whisper to the owl.

Its only response is to take off again, soaring deeper into the cave. The bird, too, it seems, is eager to explore.

Hastily, I shove more wood into the fire and draw my knife, transitioning it into a staff I can lean on as I hobble after the messenger.

I pick up Kygga's lantern on the way, searching for any sign of my brother. But aside from a few curls of snow, caught in the draft from the cave mouth, there's nothing but bare rock.

I'm not surprised when I find the owl waiting for me at the gap in the floor. It perches on the edge with uncharacteristic patience and bobs its head in a gesture I can only interpret as reassuring.

I crouch at the lip, alert for any sign that the rock beneath me is about to give way. But it's sturdy. I hold the lantern down, trying to see deeper into the pit, and I see a series of pale markings in the stone. Chisels. They're recent enough to shed dust when I brush a thumb across them.

"Someone did open this intentionally," I observe to the owl. "The Sleepers? Or one of my siblings?" Kygga had claimed not to know who did this, and perhaps he spoke true. It's clear to me that there isn't complete unity between Ogam's children.

I ease my weight back into my hips to maintain balance. The lamplight pierces the deeper darkness beyond the thick ledge of rock revealing a floor. It's only a couple paces below, barely deeper than I'm tall.

I drop a stone, just to be sure my eyes aren't playing tricks on me. When I see it clack on the cave floor, I sit on the edge, then ease myself down.

I land lightly but painfully, torn muscles, bruises, and punctures punishing me for daring to move at all. In the flickering lamplight, I survey my new surroundings as I wait for the pain to pass.

To all appearances, this is a natural cave. There are none of the smooth sections of the hallway above and both floor and ceiling are uneven. I'm between two shelves of rock, sloping down toward... more darkness.

I see careful piles of rubble. Whoever opened this entrance was meticulous. There was more than one intruder too—I see multiple sets of footprints in a layer of stone dust, leading down toward the deeper shadow. None of them looks large enough to be Kygga's.

The owl remains on the lip of the pit, watching me with his full-moon eyes.

"Warn me if Kygga comes back."

The bird ruffles its feathers and looks away, back toward my campfire and the entrance to the tombs.

Stooping slightly to keep from hitting my head, I set off after the footprints. It occurs to me then, as my aching body struggles to keep balance on the uneven ground, that I'm being unreasonably reckless. Why am I creeping down a tunnel in an abandoned tomb, other than curiosity and the encouragement of an owl that isn't an owl?

I don't stop, though. I sneak on until the shelves of rock end and I drop down into a new chamber. I hear the trickle of water and raise my lamp high.

I'm in another, larger cave. It twists and meanders, smooth-sided from erosion and lined with slick banks. Holes in the rock, like tears in taut leather, let me glimpse further chambers. They're different, but the same—smooth-walled and rambling. The footprints end here and, with no other direction to go, I head for the sound of trickling water.

Tense and breathing shallowly, I continue down a tunnel until a rockfall turns me back, then another, and another—more secret ways into the heart of the mountain, perhaps, closed off with time.

The trickling water comes through one of these rockfalls. It flows around my feet, icy cold, bluish, and thick with minerals. I eye the fallen rock behind it cautiously and try another passage.

Then, I feel… something. I touch my priestess's Sight and see a haze up ahead, a shimmer that clings to the walls and drifts through the air. The remnants of magic. It's many colors and shades twined together, like an opal under the sun.

I follow the magic to its source, in the center of the twisting passageways. It condenses in a cloud in the center of the chamber, above an empty stone pedestal.

I advance, holding my lantern out before me.

The pedestal is empty. It's simple, bearing no markings or ornamentation. But something once sat upon it, I've no doubt of that. Something powerful.

What was it? And who has it now?

A gust of wind heralds my brother's return. I look up from a wooden cup of tea as he materializes in the midst of a lengthy stride, shaking snow from his hair and heading right for the hole in the floor. He scoops up his lamp along the way, which I'd replaced exactly where he left it.

I start to rise, but the wind is still blowing and two more figures appear in mid-stride. I freeze as Arune gives me a distracted half-bow. The third Winterborn, a willowy woman with a band of pale tattoos down the center of her forehead, barely glances my way, calf-length skirts fluttering about her high boots.

I look from her to the knife at Arune's belt and recall how he threatened me at our first meeting.

"Little sister," he calls. He wags a finger at me, walking backward after Kygga and the woman. "You'd best stay there."

I do, hoping and praying my footprints in the dust look no more recent than the Sleepers'—or whoever else was here. But there's no use fretting. I sip my tea and watch my siblings drop, one by one, out of sight.

They're gone for a long time, and it's all I can do not to pace. They're likely all Unsighted and won't be able to see the lingering magic like I did, but the empty pedestal will be obvious enough. Do they know what should be there?

I finish my tea, stoke the fire, and comb out my hair before my siblings return. I'm still wary of Arune, but I continue to braid my hair as he situates himself across the fire with his arms crossed and his gaze on Kygga.

Together, we watch our siblings linger at the mouth of the cave, backed by impenetrable black night and a haze of blowing snow. We do it surreptitiously, by unspoken agreement; as if we can't see one another spying.

The sounds of the storm and a muffling wind shroud Kygga and the woman's conversation. But their body language is clear enough. Kygga speaks urgently, questioningly, and his posture is confrontational—stance broad, chin tilted, gaze sharp. Meanwhile, she's relaxed into her heels, arms lightly crossed under her breasts, and her expression is both patient and placating—as if Kygga is the younger, irrational sibling. Then she bids him an obvious farewell and, in one fluid step, disappears into the storm.

Kygga stands there for a moment with his back to Arune and I, then he comes to join us. He sits, crossing his legs and staring into the pot of meltwater I've set in the fire for more tea. Without a word, he leans to grab a pouch from our stack of packs and dumps the last of the leaves into the pot.

"That'll be strong," I comment cautiously. The tea is a mixture of Sweet Tear and other herbs, good for relaxation and recovery.

"It'll be a long night," he replies, glancing deeper into the darkness of the cave.

"You can always go sleep in your own bed," Arune comments. He slips closer to me, feline in his movements, and holds out his hand for my comb. "I'll stay with Thray. Here, let me have that."

"So you can do what?" I recoil. "Slit my throat?"

"Not with that comb, silly child," Arune chides. "I'll fix your hair."

"That's not…" I start to protest, but catch myself. I don't trust Arune, and perhaps that's precisely why I should take an opportunity to bond with him. Resigned, I hold up the comb, and he takes it.

"I'm not leaving," Kygga mutters in return to Arune's earlier suggestion.

"I'll stay with her," Arune repeats lightly. I feel, more than see him kneel behind me and pick up my half-braided hair. His fingers are gentle, but a chill traces up my spine. Perhaps this was a bad idea.

Kygga snorts. "Not likely."

Arune makes a *so be it* sound and gets to work. But instead of continuing the braids I've already begun, he picks every last one of them out and starts again. I grit my teeth and look to Kygga as Arune's fingers tug, separate and smooth.

"What did you find down there?" I ask innocently. "Under the floor."

Kygga stirs the tea with a stick and sniffs at the steam. "Nothing."

"Anymore," Arune clarifies. He begins to draw tight plaits back from my temples, like he wears. "There was something. A very important something, to be hidden here."

"By whom?"

"Haven't a clue." Kygga shrugs.

Arune doesn't say anything else.

"Do you think the Sleepers took it?" For all Arune's threats to blood me, his fingers are gentle, and pleasure prickles across my scalp. I fight the sensation, but only a little.

"I do," Arune replies. "They've always been troublesome. And with the night growing longer, they're getting bolder. More influential."

"We know nothing for sure," Kygga counters. "Midvyk will take the matter to the Elders."

"Midvyk is the woman with the tattoos?" I ask. I remember Rana mentioning the name, and that she's a Winterborn Elder.

Kygga nods. "In any case, it's not our concern."

Arune makes a considering sound. "Yes, yes, our concern is getting this unblooded pup to the Barrow." He pats the top of my head condescendingly, but lightly, so as not to muss my hair.

"As soon as possible," Kygga affirms. "I'm well past tired of this little adventure."

TWENTY-FOUR

Traveling with both Kygga and Arune is vastly different than traveling with Kygga alone. Arune comes and goes with the wind, vanishing without warning into a night sky ignited by shifting Northern Lights. He reappears walking at my side, high on the banks of freshly fallen snow both he and Kygga clear from my path with gusts of wind. He reports on the landscape ahead and sings to himself, his gentle tenor backing almost every waking moment.

Once, when he reappears at my side, I ask, "How is it that your clothes vanish with you? And that knife?"

"Objects without a soul I can carry at will. Within reason. I can't move a mountain simply by holding on to it," Arune explains. He strides beside me, light-footed and leaving barely any prints. "People or creatures? They're rather attached to their flesh and blood and do not travel so well."

"But aren't you flesh and blood?" I pry.

"I'm flesh, blood"—he lowers his voice dramatically—"and the winter wind."

Two days turns to three. We shelter in caves, many stocked with firewood and caches of meat from previous Winterborn travelers. We sit by the fire as snow drifts outside and the Northern Lights play, taking turns on watch. For all the bitterness of the endless cold and Winter Night, the beauty of this place steals into me. Alone on watch, with my newfound brothers sleeping at my back, I watch the moon rise over the unbroken wasteland of white and rock—nearly full, and as bright as a second sun. We pass a series of frozen waterfalls, glistening like the purest glass in the moonlight. Once, we even pass a small herd of muskoxen plodding their ancestral routes through the land. They peer at us through a heavy snowfall, their great shaggy coats caked with white and tugged by the wind.

"You really should be blooded, Thray. What if you fell in this crevasse?" Arune asks on the third day as we pass a great gouge in the icy earth. We've delved into the mountains now, ascending beside a glacier into a pass, which Kygga tells me will take us to the Winterborn's settlement.

Planting his palms on his knees and looking down into the rift, Arune sniffs. "Oh never mind, this one's not deep enough."

"Arune," Kygga warns.

"Enough," I dismiss at the same time. I'm perturbed, but I do not let it show.

Another time, we hear howling in the distance. Arune vanishes in the wind and reappears a moment later, grinning. "More wolves. They're hungry."

"Obviously," Kygga growls.

"If you don't fight back, it'll be quick," Arune assures me. His smile is wolfish in itself, but I glimpse a strain behind it now.

"No." I'm exhausted, and in no mood for his games. "I've already told you. Even if I fail your test, I want to live. I want my mortal life."

"A mortal life." Arune's smile twists into something closer to a grimace. He glances at Kygga, who trudges on ahead without looking back. I remember this expression on Arune's face a little mischief, a little pity— from our first meeting. Now, in the meek light of a veiled moon, it looks somehow more dangerous. But I sense the threat isn't directed toward me.

"What's that look?" I ask, lowering my voice.

Arune begins to walk beside me. "It will be very painful. The test."

The admission makes my stomach turn, but I'm not surprised. "Did you do it?"

"I did. Not all of us have to… We're blooded by other means."

"Like the wolves."

"Or human violence, or sickness, or accident."

"What is the test? Ceremony?" I lower my voice. "Siru wouldn't tell me, and you know how forthcoming Kygga is."

"There isn't much to tell. It involves herbs, and smoke, and some blood. Obviously blood—and pain." Arune stares at the path ahead of us, lowering his voice to match mine. "A drum. Everything you'd expect from a ritual. And when the Elders are done being all pompous and sagely about it all, you'll have your answer. The blood will tell."

I shift the strap of my pack on my shoulder. "Then it's worth it."

Arune nods, and we let the conversation drop. But something has changed between us, and the next time Arune suggests an untimely end—falling back down the pass we're currently clambering through—it strikes me as more teasing than anything. My only response is a dry smile.

We camp that night in the shelter of a heavy overhang, its narrow roof and back wall blackened by repeated use. It's freezing cold and there are no trees to be found, but the cave is well stocked, as usual, and Kygga has brought a pair of fowl.

Arune insists on combing and braiding my hair again, which I allow without protest. When he's finished, I hold out my hand for the comb. He gives me a curious look but sits patiently as I begin to tend his own hair, plaiting and tying it to mirror mine.

Kygga watches us while he builds the fire and spits our dinner. When the skin of the plucked fowl begins to crisp and brown, filling the night with delicious scent, he says, "We'll arrive early tomorrow, Thray."

My stomach contorts, but I nod and do not falter in my braiding.

Tomorrow. Tomorrow I'll meet the rest of my father's family. Tomorrow I'll stand on ground where he once stood, and I'll learn just how much of his blood runs through my veins.

The next morning, Arune doesn't sing, and the Northern Lights do not dance. The moon is shrouded; we continue in a thick, treacherous darkness. All I can see is the lightness of the snow before us—the sky and the high rock walls of the pass retreat into obscurity. The snow itself is a hard crust, scraped raw by a punishing wind, and without the iron teeth I've replaced my snowshoes with, I'd easily have slipped back down the mountain.

Arune grows impatient with our stumbling and vanishes into the wind. Kygga remains with me, but with an unnatural lightness to his step. His boots leave no imprint, and no bits of ice jangle after his steps like they do mine. It makes me realize that maintaining a physical form hasn't been his only sacrifice during our journey—every footprint he left for me to tread in was a deliberate choice.

"Thank you," I say. After so long in the quiet with only my footfalls and the tinkle of ice, the sound of my voice startles me. The thin air leaves my lungs starved but I manage not to pant as I clarify, "For bringing me here."

"Don't thank me." I can't see my brother's face, but there's no humility in his words, true or false.

"I appreciate you doing this, I know—"

"Truly, don't thank him yet." Arune's voice drifts from the impenetrable black around us. "Thank him when you're back with your lover in Atmeltan."

This is the first time either of them have mentioned Havar, and it catches me off guard. But before I can say more, I sense a change around us. There's a new presence, a pressure that is somehow both foreign and absolutely familiar.

I hear movement up ahead and a torch flares to life in Arune's hand, flooding his face two dozen paces above us at the top of a rise—the top of a mountain peak I didn't even realize we were climbing. We must have left the pass some time ago.

Arune holds the torch high as Kygga and I close in, and then leads us over a crest and down a snow-covered stair.

The wind eases and lights appear in the darkness below—torches and opening doors, though the structures they belong to are indistinct in the dark. Despite our elevation, there's barely any snow to highlight their edges, and no white whatsoever on the warm, stony ground. The terrible cold eases into eddies of frozen mist, then wafts of warm steam, drifting through invisible cracks in the earth.

Relieved, I rake in a breath of warm steam as an eddy passes over us, interrupting the chill, and blink condensation from my eyelashes. There are hot springs here, just like the wolf basin. But here they're harnessed, controlled. There are no deadly, bubbling pools in sight.

I become aware of voices, both from corporeal mouths and on the wind, which picks up around us with curious intensity. Pale-haired figures appear from the shadows and mist and the voices rise, all speaking in the Divine Tongue—conferring, speculating, gathering.

"Thray." Siru shoulders from the murky crowd and into the light of Arune's torch. Her head is uncovered and she wears an indoor kaftan, taking full advantage of the near-warmth here in the village. "Midvyk told us you were coming. Why didn't you wait in Atmeltan?"

"Little sister is impatient," Arune quips, raising the torch and looking back at me. "She wants to know what she is."

Another sister steps up beside Siru—Midvyk, who I saw briefly at the tombs. Up close, her skin is smooth and her age ambiguous; there's a maturity to this woman that I've yet to see among Ogam's children.

Midvyk appraises me momentarily, an eddy of warm steam drifting past her face. "Then we'd best find out."

TWENTY-FIVE

That first night with the Winterborn passes in a haze. I'm overwhelmed, taxed from our journey, and yet I know there's no chance of sleep. There are too many siblings to meet, brothers and sisters who crowd around or watch from a distance, welcoming or weighing, cheerful or wary. I try to hold myself back, fight not to lower my guard. The watchers help, in this respect. They're withholding trust from me as I am from them, and it reminds me to be vigilant.

Midvyk leads me through the settlement, its features clarifying somewhat in the light of torches. The homes are built in rural Duamel style but are noticeably larger, their domed stone structures punctuated by thick chimneys that release smoke into the dark sky. The pathways are stone as well, large slabs carefully laid, and here and there steam vents from beneath the earth. Distantly, I hear goats bleat off in the night.

"There are natural hot springs below the settlement, in catacombs," Arune tells me as we walk. "No matter how heavy the snow, it never lingers long on the ground. And there's always a hot bath to be had."

"Like the place where you lured the wolves to kill me," I comment, without real ire. Now that I'm here, surrounded by my siblings with answers at my fingertips, my elation grows by the moment. I cast Arune a sideways grin.

"Precisely," he agrees, unabashed.

Midvyk opens a low door with a wash of light and warmth, and gestures me into a central building. It's round, with three broad tiers, like the Inheritor's feasting chamber. Light radiates from myriad lanterns, suspended from the ceiling, and the heat is all-encompassing, seeping up from the floor. There is no central hearth. Instead the room pivots around a table or altar, with a wooden surface and a solid, stone circumference.

Someone takes my pack, bow, and outer clothes, and someone else presses a warm, faintly alcoholic drink into my hands. I'm hungry but there's no food in sight, and the liquid goes straight to my head. I don't mind, though—it eases my aches and dulls my worries. I'm among family, after all. And for all my grandfather's warnings, seeing a room full of faces like mine is as intoxicating as the wine.

Three sisters play the drums as we settle in to eat. They sit on low stools, legs bowed, heavy skirts spread as their tippers fly and their silver magic weaves. Images and feelings wash over me like memories—the warmth of fires, the love of mothers, fox kits nuzzling among flowers in the spring.

"Those are the sisters who make the Diviner drums," Siru tells me after I've eaten my fill and my haze of hunger has faded into a murky contentedness. We sit on the tier above the altar. "You're familiar with them?"

Remembering the riot, I take a moment to reply. "Yes. Are the drums the only instruments they make?"

"They've been known to make other things," Arune puts in from where he's draped over a chair nearby, the edge of his cup resting on his full lower lip. "Siru, your ships are blessed with some magics for speed, aren't they? And the sisters made a horn, once. I think there was flute, but someone lost that."

"You lost it," Kygga interjects from where he sits on the edge of our tier, cup in hand and pitcher at his side. "We all know."

"No," Arune replies with overdone patience, "I did *not*. That is pure and spiteful speculation. I told—"

"Binding magic to an object is a powerful gift," Siru says to me, cutting them both off. "They use it sparingly."

"Not least because magic is hard to find," Arune goes on, cup still resting against his chin. "A little of their blood makes a drum, but anything beyond that…"

I furrow my brows. "What's beyond that?"

"Potential and possibilities," Midvyk says, and though she doesn't so much as glance at Arune, I sense she's quelling him.

Suspicion creeps up my spine again, but I'm careful not to show it. I drink like Arune. There are secrets here, and it seems my siblings will not trust me with them easily.

Midvyk continues, taking the reins of the conversation. "Thray, this chamber is where your ceremony will take place. But before that, you should go to Father's Barrow."

"His grave is here?" Dulled by wine and warmth, my caution steps back. Will it be the barrow from my visions?

Midvyk nods and Arune explains, "The Barrow of Winter—not Winter as in Grandfather, of course. Ogam wore his title to the Duamel, and Grandfather left the land—and seasons—here to his rule." He glances at Midvyk. "I'll take her in the morning, unless you'd like to come?"

"Morning," Midvyk repeats. "Strange that these words should still have any meaning, but here we are. I will come. When we wake, we go to the Barrow together. But for now you should rest, Thray, and let us prepare for what is to come."

Arune has already told me what to expect tomorrow but I shift nervously. "That seems wise."

"Follow me." Siru reappears at my side. "I've prepared a place for you."

I bid farewell to Arune and Kygga and the remainder of the Winterborn. Then Siru and I are back out into the misty half-cold, moving down twisting streets until we come to a home with a low, heavy door, thick enough to stop a bear and chinked with wool and resin. Beyond it, two broad, shallow steps lead down to a second barrier of hanging oilskin and furs.

Siru pushes these aside with a wash of heat and reveals an inner chamber. It has a central fire and a raised bed, heavy with blankets and furs. Surrounding them are racks of clothing, trunks, and shelves stocked with jars and trinkets that hint at another owner, at another time. My own pack is already here, my hood hung on a line on one side of the fire. A draped doorway leads to further chambers.

"Through there you'll find the catacombs, where the hot springs are," Siru tells me, gesturing to the draped door, "and the baths. Use them as you will. Anything you need, only make it known. But now I'll leave you until morning."

The stark rise in temperature makes sweat prickle across my brow. I unbind the belt of my kaftan and look at my sister. "Thank you. And thank you for speaking to the other Elders on my behalf."

"We are all eager to know what you are," my sister replies, stepping back toward the outer door. "Sleep well."

I murmur the same. The outer door closes in a sudden cessation of sound and draft, and I'm alone for the first time in weeks. I feel my aching muscles ease, my mind relax, and even the temptation of a hot bath barely convinces me to risk that solitude.

Still, I need to bathe. I strip down to my undertunic and hang the rest of my clothes near the fire to dry, bank the flames, then slip out the door to the catacombs.

Down a steep stair, I find a network of chambers and pools. The one my staircase empties into appears to be natural, with smooth walls, but there's an intentionality to its shape. Did one of my siblings carve this place with water and ice? Did my father?

I'm mostly alone. I hear distant voices through the two arches leading out of the chamber, lively and happy and discussing the antics of a mutual acquaintance, but the speakers are out of sight.

I pull my tunic over my head and step down onto a strategic boulder in the pool. Ankle-deep, I glance over the water's steaming surface and my distorted reflection. My features are obscure—my bruises and scars, the goosebumps rising on my skin. But the shape of me remains, heavily muscled, tall, broad-hipped, and strong-shouldered.

Pride flares in my chest. I might feel weak and aching, nervous and suspicious, but I look strong. I'm the daughter of an immortal. I'm a Winterborn, like all those around me, and I've a right to be here.

I slip into the water and submerge myself. I'm too muscular to float but I let myself drift, toes tapping the bottom of the pool every so often to keep my nose above the surface. I find a dish with drops of sweet-scented soap—honey, sweetgrass, and spruce—and begin to scrub away the sweat of the road.

Sometime later, as I try to talk myself into climbing from the pool and finding my bed, I hear a voice drift through the catacombs. This voice is familiar, though I'm so stupefied with comfort it takes me a span to realize it's Midvyk. I'm even slower to understand. She's not speaking in the Divine Tongue, but another language I can't identify. Thankfully, my own understanding of the Divine Tongue allows me to understand.

"… the Eangen bloodline. They produced the Eangi. Those may be gone but the traits… can be trusted?"

A second voice replies, one I recognize immediately as Kygga. His deeper voice carries more easily on the moist air. "She can be trusted. She's been alone among the Eangen her whole life, Mid. Even if she is rebellious for a time, we owe it to her to be patient."

I bite the inside of my lips, as conflicting emotions lance through me. Kygga is clearly defending me, which warms me. But what is he defending me against?

"… have centuries to reconcile." Midvyk's voice fades slightly, perhaps as they pass behind a wall.

"It won't take centuries."

"Perhaps… she learns…" Midvyk's voice fades even more. "The Eangen will not…"

My spine snaps straight at the mention of my people. I swim to the other side of the pool as quietly as I can, straining to hear the Elder's words. Does she mean my people in general, or Havar and the others, back in Atmeltan?

I catch a sound from Kygga that might be acceptance, the echo of a murmured reply, then they're both gone.

Unsettled, I slip from the water and pad after them a few paces, but I've no idea which direction they've gone, and the catacombs are unfamiliar. I'm also naked, my sodden hair plastered across my stomach and back, and though the air is warm, my bed calls to me.

I ponder the conversation as I slip back up to my little house, comb my hair, and dry myself beside the fire. Midvyk doesn't seem to trust me. I wonder why someone as powerful as her would consider me a threat, but she mentioned my Eangen bloodline, and our priests and priestesses. The Eangi were formidable, once. Perhaps it's not far-fetched to think I might be too, and that fills me with a daring, nervous hunger.

I peel back the bed coverings and slip beneath. I feel a momentary pang of absence at the emptiness of my bed. Havar and I haven't spent a night together, but that doesn't mean I don't wish he were here, with his warm skin and unfailing support.

The longing, however, is short-lived. I can't imagine him here with my siblings. Nor at the Barrow in the morning, nor the ceremony that will answer the question that has tormented me since my mother's death. When I might, if my father's blood proved true, come into my power.

These things are between my siblings and I. Ogam's children.

I push the thought of Havar aside with a little too much ease, and slip into a deep, exhausted sleep.

In the shifting, eerie green illumination of the Northern Lights, the settlement of the Winterborn takes new form. It's much larger than I thought last night, and high, ice-slicked ridges protect the village from the worst of the wind. Near the colder edges of the settlement, some houses are even built into the cliffs in something close to Algatt style, elevated above the snow and accessed by staircases.

On the ridge above the village, goats wander under the watchful eye of several figures, enveloped with furs and armed with bows. I see a sledge among the houses too, pulled by immensely shaggy horses whose breath billows in the cold and mouths are rimmed with frost. Figures divest the sledge of bags, crates, and bundles while others greet the drivers, embracing them, offering them steaming cups, and pulling them into houses.

"I thought this settlement was a secret?" I ask Arune when we meet outside my house.

"Only to some." Today, my half-brother wears a pale gray kaftan lined with white bear fur. It ruffs up around his ears and brushes his smooth-shaven cheeks, but his head is bare. His usual simple plaits twine back from his temples, and the rest of his hair is windblown. "We need supplies, as anyone else does, and there are some Duamel we trust to fetch them."

I eye the drivers for another moment, then glance around the settlement again. "Did the Duamel build all this too?"

He nods.

"So there are other villages nearby?" I look through a large cleft leading down the mountain, but I see no signs of another settlement. The mountainside and valley below are desolate, layered with snow and natural rock formations. Hot springs stand out darkly against the white of the slope, draining down to the plains in steaming waterfalls, and there are no unnatural shapes that might be houses.

"In a way," Arune replies, distracted as three more Winterborn approach; Kygga, Midvyk, and Siru. They're out of earshot, but not for long.

I ask on impulse, "What did the Elders say about the pedestal in the cave? Below the Old Gods' tomb?"

"Ah." He frowns at me. "They're handling the matter. There's nothing you need to think about—other than the Barrow, and your ceremony."

"I'd prefer to know," I push.

"Thray, one thing you'll learn quickly here is that there are divisions." Arune lowers his voice as the rest of the party closes on us. "They're practical. Do not concern yourself with problems that aren't yours. Your siblings are more than capable."

That tempts me. "Then there *is* a problem?"

Arune gives me a tolerant glare, but we're too close to the others now to continue the conversation.

"Thray," Siru says with a warm smile, and gravity about her large Duamel eyes. "Follow us."

The peaks of the mountains aren't visible from the village, but as we depart up a narrow, serpentine path, one comes into sight. It's high and nearly barren of snow, scoured by the bitter wind and dominated by a barrow of white stone, layered with wind-carved ice. Gray stone pillars interrupt the walls at intervals, carved with watching faces and stylized interpretations of wind, snow, and storm.

There are no springs here, no latent warmth. The thin, frigid air steals my breath and my lungs ache. Slate grinds and ice crunches under my boots as I slow, but my siblings continue a few more paces and spread out. Most of them gaze at the Barrow, giving me a thin degree of privacy. Only Arune watches me askance, pale light casting his face in partial silhouette.

The power of the place pulls at me. It joins with the beat of my heart, quickening the rush of my blood and hollowing me out. The icy wind makes my eyes water, and I sense a presence. That presence feels like Arune's, Kygga's, and Siru's. It feels like my own.

"I thought you said his body wasn't here." I direct my words at Siru, but I speak to them all. "He left nothing to bury."

"We are what he left behind," she replies, watching the Barrow with a quiet reverence, and more than a little sadness. "We are his body."

"This was the last place I saw our father. The last place any of us did," Midvyk says, her soft voice loud in a sudden stillness. Kygga's attention has turned to the wind, and we're shrouded by quiet.

Strands of hair drift into my eyes, and I brush them aside.

Midvyk continues, "He did not tell us he was leaving… If I hadn't looked up the cleft at the right moment, no one would have seen him go at all. He vanished into the wind without explanation. The next we heard of him, he'd begun to break the seals on the tombs of the Old

Gods. We Windwalkers tried to join him, but he was gone before we arrived. So we searched, and traveled, and discovered a world beyond the mountains to the south. We discovered Eangen and Algatt, and heard of our father's death from the lips of those peoples and their fallen gods."

"Eang murdered our father." Kygga picks up the tale. "She killed the child that grew in her own womb. Part of herself."

Because our father nearly destroyed the world, I think in the quiet of my thoughts, but I dare not speak that aloud.

"Eang is dead too," I remind them, concerned by the direction their anger might take—namely, toward my mother's people, who still bear the cruel goddess's name. "Her priestess killed her. Eang used and despised her people as much as she did her son."

"That may be." Midvyk looks up at the twisting lights in the night sky. I sense I've broken some unspoken rule by interrupting them, but Midvyk lets it slide. "We built the Barrow and assumed his rule of the Duamel. Now, we *are* Ogam to the Duamel. He lives on through us, his sons and daughters."

I think of the presence again, the one that feels like Siru and Kygga and Arune. I have the feeling that Midvyk's claims aren't simply poetic—there is true power in Ogam's unified children, and it is vast.

Siru finishes, "You need to understand the weight of that, of this history, if you are to be one of us."

If. The word hangs in the air like a threat, gentle though it is. For the first time, I'm frightened of what it will mean if I am not immortal, if I do not belong here among my father's children. If my fate is to go home, marry a good man, and lead a quiet life—to live, die, and be forgotten by the Waking World.

I look to the Barrow of Winter, ice-covered and indomitable, then to my siblings and the centuries in their eyes.

Silent, I bow, and hope that they cannot see the sudden dread in mine.

Drums ripple through the meeting house as I follow Siru inside. Light and warmth spill around us and a dozen emotions slash through me at once—fear, elation, hope, relief. I battle to keep myself calm, but my hands tremble.

The central table has been removed to reveal a natural pool in the chamber floor, so deep I can't see its bottom. It's not a hot spring—it doesn't steam, nor does it move. Light plays off the smooth surface, intermingling with the reflections of two hundred siblings crowded in at all sides. They cluster and murmur, but as I come into sight, their conversations die off.

Blood pounds in my ears and time begins to skew, not just at the sight of the water and the possibilities associated with it. This is it. This is the moment I find out what I am, what my future will be—temporary, filled with the threat of death and the promise of rest beside my mother, or endless and assured, adrift in a world devoid of those I love.

I scan the faces around me. Siru. Kygga. Arune. Midvyk. That long cold future—that's theirs too. A future without death, yet saturated by it. How can they smile?

"Step into the pool." Siru's voice wheedles through my fugue. "Stand in the shallows until I tell you to step out. You'll go under, but when you resurface, you'll know if you're immortal."

I balk. I stare at her, then Kygga. "Under?"

Siru's gaze is gentle. I haven't shared my fear of drowning, but I've no doubt she picked up on it. "This is the only way."

"How?" I ask, my thoughts turning frantic.

"The water is more than it seems." Siru puts a gentle hand on my back and prods me toward the pool. Kygga stands beside it already and I see Arune off in the crowd, watching with an inscrutable expression. "It will show you your answer."

I force myself to comply, though it takes all my will, all the determination of a lifetime of questions. If this is the only way, I must comply. I must.

I take off my outer clothes with shaking hands. Left in my undertunic, bare-legged and barefoot, I take Kygga's hand and let him help me step over the jagged, rocky edge of the pool and onto a smooth shelf, just beneath the surface on the other side. There's a gravity to his gesture, a sense of responsibility on his part, that lends me courage.

The water is lukewarm around my bare feet. I draw a deep breath into my lungs and count my heartbeats, lengthening them in preparation for the plunge. I do not think of the sea that tried to swallow me. I do not think of my mother, listless on a riverbank. But I do think of my father, alive and present in my blood, and the blood of my siblings around me.

Stepping up behind me, Siru begins to unbind my hair. When it's loose and free about my shoulders, she brushes her knuckles across my upper arm in a soothing gesture, and steps back to stand with Kygga.

"Give yourself to the water, little sister," Siru says softly. The rest of the room is silent, and somewhere at the edge of my consciousness, I register that there are none of the drums Arune promised in this ritual. The water, too, he failed to mention. Where would the blood come in?

What does that matter, here and now? Arune is Arune, flippant and mischievous. Perhaps he lied.

He is pale-faced and quiet, half-shadowed in the lamplight. He looks neither flippant nor mischievous now. He has darkened, his expression neutral except for a tightness around his lips that might be wrath. He glares at Midvyk.

Siru's voice cuts through my observation. "It's time."

Fear flutters through my stomach and the distrust that's been with me from the beginning of this venture writhes. But I can't stop, not now.

Before I can change my mind, I tear my eyes from Arune and step from the ledge. Water envelopes me in a rush of bubbles as I plunge downward, eyes and lips clenched closed, muscles taut as bowstrings. My head is full of the slamming of my heart but I let myself begin to drift, holding my breath close as the bubbles disappear, my tunic floats up around my hips, and my hair billows around my head.

My world becomes one of warm water. Panic batters me and leaves me light-headed, the reality of my underwater suspension all too close and real. But gradually, I begin to drift and reach for the answer Siru promised I'd find here, below the surface.

Power trickles in. It drifts across my skin in a haze of silver-edged gold. I open my eyes and look up, watching it settle on the surface into a barrier—a mirror—between me and the outside world. I glimpse my own eyes, wide, green, and staring back at me. I see my hair, adrift across my face, and the great yawning darkness below my pale feet.

Where is my answer? I stare up at myself, waiting to glimpse some change in my own face, or be caught up in a vision.

Suddenly, the water becomes dreadfully cold. I convulse and instinctively strike out for the surface, but the haze of silver is gone. It's transformed into a cap of ice, thick and clear.

I scream in unbridled, absolute terror. The sound remains trapped inside my skull, threatening to crack my eardrums. Bubbles stream from my lips and pool on the ice above me, further distorting the shadows of my siblings above. But I can still see them, watching, unmoving, their forms blurred by the ice. Just as Siru once watched me through the waves of the sea.

Blackness sparks around my eyes. Betrayal. I swim frantically toward the tall form I think is Kygga, and shove against the ice. He doesn't move. Next to him, Midvyk, whose face I can see with the greatest clarity, watches me with a critical kind of pity.

I swim, searching for any weak spots, but the ice is solid and thick. I'm trapped. They've trapped me with the power our father gave them.

They're trying to kill me.

TWENTY-SIX

The reality of impending death scorches through me. There is no power to this water, no answer here. Drowning is the test.

Either I pass, or I die.

I stop fighting for a dizzy moment, not because I've regained control, but because I'm too overwhelmed to move. I think I see Arune through a smooth section of ice, watching me with emptiness in his round Duamel eyes, but I can't focus on him. I'm a child again, abandoned by my playmates in a winter forest. I'm a young woman, standing next to my mother's sodden body on a riverbank. Then I'm a grown woman, curled into Havar's side on a cool, windy cliff by the sea.

How did I leave him behind in Atmeltan? How could I choose these killers, these monsters, over—

I slam my palm into the ice with a hollow thud. Once. Twice. I've wasted all my breath on screaming and blackness steals across my vision like smoke from an extinguished candle. My lungs begin to seize and my body convulses, bare legs twitching against the backdrop of the pool's bottom.

I am drowning, like my father. Like my mother. The awareness comes in swells and eddies as moments slip by. I can no longer strike out. I hang suspended and my hair drifts in a cloud around my head, sheltering me from the watching eyes as time loses all meaning. There's pain in my body and there's fear in my heart, and then there's... nothing.

I've no awareness of how long I drift, but my next conscious understanding is anger. It rushes toward me like a serpent from the deep, digging its teeth into my flesh and burning through me like blood fever. My thoughts are incoherent, but there is clarity to my fury. Clarity and rage.

I look up at the ice and scream. There's no more air left in me, no bubbles to stream upward, but the feeling is there. And the force.

The ice shatters into particles so fine, they drift around me like snow as I claw to the surface. I seize the side of the pool and fling myself into the air, every limb on fire with a new, blazing strength.

I land on my feet beside the pool. My siblings scatter, jostling into one another, their shouts muffled by trickling water and sodden hair. Wet shanks slick my face as I turn on them, water pouring from my lips. But for all my rage, my body works against me.

My knees buckle. I vomit, convulsing and retching all over the stones. It's the only sound in the chamber, aside from the splash of water and the brush of shifting bodies.

When there's air in my lungs, I look up through bloodshot eyes. I see Siru, watching me without compassion, and rage blinds me again. How could she betray me like this? How could she lure me from home with the promise of answers, speak to me so kindly, then lead me to death in the way that terrified me most?

I feel shame, too, beneath my rage. I trusted the Winterborn when my grandfather warned me not to. I tricked the Eangen into following me to Duamel. I came here of my own volition and climbed into the pool. I'm horrified. I'm ashamed.

I slap the feelings aside, overtaken with a livid, blazing *want*. I want to shatter the Winterborn, like I shattered the ice. I want to tear them to pieces for tricking me into my death, for making me trust them. I want to—

I scream again. The ice I broke is my father, but the scream? It's my grandmother. It's the Eangen bloodline she blessed—my mother's blood, my aunt's, and the warrior Eangi who once dominated their world. The sound fills the cavern to bursting, drowning even the startled shouts of my siblings.

Only when my breath is gone do I realize their startled shouts have turned to laughter—and roars of approval.

Hands grab my arms. I slap them away, emitting a second, feral bellow. "Do not touch me!"

Too late, I realize I'm speaking in the Divine Tongue. But what does it matter now? I'm blooded.

I'm a Winterborn.

Kygga steps back, holding up bloody hands in surrender. Bloody? I blink, realizing that silvered blood streams from his nose, his eyes, and ears. It's smeared across his cheeks and hands where he's tried to swipe it away. He's not angry, though, or even shocked. He looks euphoric, emotions unveiled in a way I've never seen before. His eyes glisten as he looks down at me, and I see relief in them.

"You're one of us," he says. He wipes at the blood under his nose again and glances at it, then laughs and turns on the rest of the room. "She's one of us! Welcome your sister!"

The shouts and cheers redouble. I weather the barrage, my gaze fixed on Kygga's bloody hand and face.

My scream did that. My scream—Eang's scream—made an immortal bleed. Is this my power, then? Not ice, not wind, but something like the fire Eangi once wielded? The power to shatter and break?

Kygga is not the only one bleeding. Siru wipes blood from her upper lip with the back of a hand, eyeing me like a hound might eye a whip. Her caution dismisses my wonderment and restokes my anger.

"Stop looking at me like that," I snap, my voice cutting through the room with unnatural force—or, perhaps, it's entirely natural now. "Isn't this what you wanted?"

Without a word, Siru turns and leaves. I see a few siblings slip after her but more fill the spot they vacated, replacing Siru's caution with grins and cheers and jostling shoulders.

I turn slowly, surveying the lot of them, and my gaze snags on Arune. There's blood on his face, like everyone else. He takes up a few droplets of silver-tinted liquid, licks it off his finger, and starts toward me with a grin, but I glimpse a shadow around his eyes—or, at least, I think I do. It's gone before I can be sure.

"So, little sister," he says, sidling up to me. "You are one of us, and you've true power. What will you do with it? What will you make of your immortal life? Will you protect or destroy?"

I'm still so lost in my shock that it takes a moment for his words to register.

"She'll stay with us," a sister declares, moving to throw her arm around my shoulder, but I shift out of the way.

"Give her space, Saben." Kygga steps up, pushing the crowd back with warding hands. "Give her a moment to breathe."

I can't appreciate the intervention. Looking up at him, I see his face through the ice again. Watching me die. "You murdered me. You lied to me."

Kygga's lips twist in a resigned smile. "It was the only way."

"What if I hadn't survived?" I shoot back. "How many of your own kin have you murdered?"

"You *did* survive." Arune whisks between us and takes my face between his hands. I strike his hands away, so instead, he barrels me into his arms and crushes me to his chest. My second question receives no answer. My vision is full of my wet hair and his bloody ear, but I glimpse the others crowding in, grabbing my hands, thumping me on the back, and trying to tug me into embraces of their own. No one seems to care that I'm barely clothed, sopping wet, and made them bleed with a scream. Nor do they care that I protest and shove them back.

Arune still holds me tightly, his mouth close to my ear. "Wait," he whispers, so soft I barely hear him. "Smile. Accept them for now. Please."

It's his tone, more than his words, that still me. There's worry in it, and a warning so sincere that the coals of anger and betrayal in me wane. Their heat doesn't fade entirely, but I relax in Arune's embrace, and he lets me go. He smiles and spins me around, presenting me to the press like a proud parent while Kygga laughs over us.

But Arune's touch is too firm, and his warning rings in my ears. *Wait.*

I close the door to my chamber, but there's no quiet to be found now. The sounds of celebration fill the settlement as my siblings take full advantage of an excuse to drink and eat and dance and sing. There are drums again—the sisters' drums, carrying memories of other revelries in their rhythms. Bonfires burn on the stone paths between the houses, whose doors stand carelessly open.

I strip off my frozen, sodden tunic and throw it on the floor. Naked in the light of the hearthfire I stare down at myself, seeing my familiar body through new eyes. This skin is still mine, with its muscle and scars and peculiarities. But now I know this flesh will never die. My blood will rush and my heart will beat until the long, lonely end of time. And then… what will become of me? Even if the priesthood takes me back, what is there for me in Eangen?

The room blurs into a haze of tears. The anger and rage that led me to lash out before has fled, and I'm bereft.

There, into that void, flows homesickness. It wraps its fingers around my ribs and squeezes, crushing me with its suddenness and ferocity. Tears stream down my cheeks and I can't move, suspended in the center of my chamber.

I miss my mother, Sixnit, indomitable and faithful, sacrificial and strong, who once stood beside Hessa as the world was remade. I miss Vistic, the man who should have been my brother, but could not be. I miss Hessa, her knowledge and her capability, and the security of her command. I miss Thvynder—a voice and a consolation, the knowledge that I cannot come to harm. I miss Havar with a pain that borders on mourning. No, it *is* mourning, because I know now that I can never be with him. Even if the priesthood takes me back, there is no future in

Eangen for me now. No matter what position I might find for myself, no matter what place I carve, every bond I make will end in grief and a pyre.

Memories cloud before me until, finally, Vistic resurfaces. I imagine my brother beside the White Lake, lost to his duties, his eyes upon the water that once sheltered Thvynder.

The water that drowned my father. The water that could free me, if I've the courage to slip below the surface again.

I wipe tears from my face, taking solace in the movement and the warmth of my own skin.

My imaginings of my immortal life are vast and terrifying, too broad to comprehend—but in that lake, there is an end. It's always been there and it always will.

What will you make of your immortal life? Arune's voice asks me again.

Strength seeps back into me. I have no answer, not yet, but I can see the edges of one. So, for now, I'll follow Arune's mysterious command. I'll smile and I'll wait. And then I'll find out why he asked that of me, and why Siru looked at me with such foreboding.

Going over to my pack at the foot of my bed, I crouch. I dig out my pale blue kaftan—the one I awoke in the day my grandfather saved me from the savn, and thwarted my first attempt to discover my immortality. The one gifted from Aita herself, with its cloth that never wore out, and color that did not fade.

I dress, selecting other gifted articles of clothing from a nearby chest and slipping the kaftan over the top. I belt it and fix my bone-handled knife in place, lengthened into a sickle sword. Its bare edge gleams, dull for the moment, but at a flick of my will, it will be sharp again.

I leave my hair free, wild, and unbound. Then I step out into the snow, and return to the revelry.

There's a feast, more singing, and more drums. Names and faces blur together, each coming with well wishes and welcomes that I barely hear. No one seems to mind my distraction. I can't imagine previous

Winterborn reacting well to being drowned by their own kin, and perhaps they expect my blank expression and smoldering resentment.

Some are gentler than others. They touch my hand and offer me soft welcomes, with hints of solidarity in their gazes. Some laugh and prod me, unbothered by my lack of a response. Some bring me gifts, which pile around the chair where I sit with Arune hovering nearby. He seems to have taken on a guardian role, and I do not protest. I don't intend to let him out of my sight until he's explained himself.

Wait. Accept them for now. Please.

I'm offered food, but do not eat. I'm plied with drinks, but do not touch them. Even when Kygga hands me a cup of what seems to be simple water, I dump it on the floor without a word.

Anger flashes through his eyes. He's cleaned the blood from his face and hands, but I remember how it looked, scarlet and silver on his pale skin. "It's done now, Thray. You have the answer you wanted."

"Where's Siru?" I ask. Like Arune's, her response to the ceremony is an outlier. I need to speak with her.

"How should I know?" Kygga glances across the room, gaze stolen by something I can't see, and starts to stalk away.

"Stop pretending to be ignorant, Kygga," I call after him coolly, and it barely hurts when he reflects the chill back at me. Maybe in a century I can begin to forgive him and the rest of the Winterborn for what they did to me, but I've never lived a century before. Perhaps that won't be long enough.

"I won't fall for that again," I add. "You know a great deal more than you admit."

Kygga shakes his head and strides away.

I look over my shoulder at Arune, who lingers close enough that I can smell the smoke and wind scent of him. "You and I need to speak."

"When?" he asks.

"As soon as possible."

Arune looks over the room, assessing it, then gives the barest nod. "Follow me."

Cooler air wraps about us as we slip out through a back door, but it's a relief after the press of bodies, the watching eyes, and reaching hands. I let Arune lead, winding us through the settlement toward a door set directly into the rock of the mountainside. As we go he picks up handfuls of snow from domed rooves and scrubs the blood around his fingernails, wiping away the reminder of my power.

As he opens the door, I hear a distant flutter of wings. An owl descends through the night, surrounded by fresh snowfall. It's not the owl Vistic set to follow me, but a new one, tiny and gray. It settles in a tree—one of the few in the village—and turns its full-moon eyes on me through a veil of fine white flakes.

I feel a pull, a whisper at the back of my mind. A message.

"Thray," Arune calls.

Afraid he'll see the bird, I pointedly ignore it. But when he ducks through the door first, I glance back at the messenger.

It ruffles its feathers and settles in to wait.

TWENTY-SEVEN

Arune waits for me in a tunnel. It's warm here, and as we travel under the skin of the mountain I see archways leading not to steam and pools, but firelit chambers full of Duamel.

There are Duamel here? How can I not have noticed them before? A whole village of men and women and children go about daily routines in the close heat of the caves. I hear the splash of water, see a woman stacking wood and a man sharpening an axe. I see children playing and another woman weaving, sock-clad feet wedged between the stone weights of her loom.

Startled, I blink hard. The woman vanishes and I see a handsome young man instead, punching holes through a piece of leather with an awl. He holds a length of leather twine between his teeth and as I stare at him, his eyes gloss over me. He will not meet my gaze.

"He already belongs to someone," Arune calls back to me. "Best not to look too long."

Disconcerted, I lengthen my strides to catch up. The woman at the loom—was she a vision or a trick of the mind?

"Belongs?" I repeat. "These are the families of the Winterborn?"

"Yes. The husbands and wives and petty offspring."

I narrow my eyes at his use of 'petty.' "You don't approve?"

"Lovers do not tempt me and I need no family outside my siblings." Arune gestures me toward a staircase, which descends downward. "This way."

My siblings have families—or at least, some of them do. Have they reconciled themselves to losing their spouses and children one day, or do they simply not care? Are these Duamel little more than whims and entertainment for ageless immortals, or is there love and sacrifice here too?

I think of Havar, of curling into him on cold winter nights and sitting with him on the sunlit rocks on summer days. I feel his gaze, heavy with want, and the warmth of his hands.

I imagine him here, avoiding the eyes of my duplicitous siblings in a land of eternal darkness and cold. For a second I feel a flush of selfish desire. Then I see the end of his short life, children raised in a world without dawns, and an inevitable row of cairns on a snow-swept plain.

Havar is Iesa, the sea and the boats and a comfortable Eangen life. This place, with its uncertainty and shadows, is not for him.

I try to think practically, reasonably, but my chest aches so fiercely that I stumble. I stop walking for a breath and brace on the stone walls of the tunnel, anchoring myself in the feel of cool, smooth stone.

Arune doesn't notice my falter. After a single shuddering breath, I begin moving again.

My brother leads me down the stairs, through several tunnels, and finally into another series of caves. Bowled tallow lamps are set in nests of dark iron and shed flickering, bluish light. They blur in my vision, and I blink away a haze of exhausted tears.

"Father made these chambers," Arune explains, ignoring my sniffling. He opens a door, set into a frame of hefty stone slabs, and gestures me through.

I eye him, then the door, and briskly brush at my damp eyes. I don't know how I've found trust for Arune amid so much betrayal, but I suppose there's nothing more he can do to hurt me.

All the same, I ease a lamp from the nearest iron nest before I go through the darkened door. Light spills around my boots and I step onto a floor laden with reed and carpets. I run my eyes over a table in the center of the room and a hearth on the far wall, a rack burdened with clothing, and a series of chests piled with a random assortment of goods, from tools to instruments. There's a bed too, simple but large and thick with blankets.

This is where Arune lives. It's clear from the way he moves about the space, closing the door and crouching to build a fire with familiarity and ease.

"We can speak here." My brother holds his hand out. "Can I have the flame?"

I crouch beside him and he lights a curl of wood off my lamp. He transfers it to the tinder nest he's tucked into the fire and watches it take, flares of orange heat curling up fine wood shavings and turning dried moss to smoke.

"They did this to you too," I observe, watching him. "The 'ceremony.'"

He puffs gently on the tinder. Flames leap up, washing his face with clean firelight, and he sits back into his heels. "Yes."

"Why didn't you warn me?"

Arune shrugs. "I did."

I have a sudden urge to smash the lamp, so I set it aside and force myself to breathe.

"You should have told me what they would do," I clarify. "You lied. You said it was just a ceremony. You and Kygga and Siru all lied."

"If we'd told you, you wouldn't have gone through with it. It was for your own good in the end, but it would have been better for you to find out through more... natural means." He speaks calmly, almost distractedly, but at the last he meets my eyes. "I did encourage you toward those."

"I wanted to live, even if it was a mortal life." The venom I feel doesn't make it into my voice. To my own ears I sound exhausted, hurt and weakness as blatant as the scars on my hands. "But if I'd died tonight..."

"You didn't." Arune sits facing me, forearms resting on crooked knees. "Now you know what you are, and you can decide what to do next."

Yes, I need to think of what to do next. But my mind shies away from such practicalities. I shift to face him too, legs crooked to one side. "Siru thought it was you who instigated the riot in Atmeltan. Was it?"

"As I've explained, it would have been better for you to die there. Or did you enjoy being murdered by blood kin?"

There's no guile in his expression or voice—he truly believes his way was for the best. "But people died in that riot. *My* people nearly died."

"They'll die anyway."

I recoil. "You're callous."

Arune smiles a crooked, melancholy smile. "You're too fixated on me right now, Thray. What of Kygga and Siru? Why did they stop me from ending you before you got here?"

I pause, taken aback at his question, and my silence prompts him to go on.

"When Siru left you in the city, she came to the Elders." Arune leans forward, elbows on his knees. "She expressed her concern that, as the only child of Ogam and an Eangen, you might manifest unpredictable power after your blooding. And, as a priest of the southern god, your loyalties might be… questionable. There was debate whether to let you be blooded at all, at least not until they knew you could be trusted."

I snort, unable to stop myself. "Because murdering me would absolutely earn my trust."

Arune smiles again, this time drier. "They've been immortal too long to understand you. This life… it changes the mind, the priorities. Some of them went through the drowning. Others were blooded by the siblings through other means, equally intentional. Some of them resented it, as you do, and left us. But eventually, after centuries of loneliness, they returned here. They're a fatalistic lot, in that way."

Would I be the same one day? The thought passes through my mind, chilly and ominous.

"Did you resent them?" I asked Arune.

"Yes, though I never left." He scratches at the embroidery on the hem of his kaftan. "I was angry. I was hurt. But I couldn't bear to be alone, not then."

"How long ago was this?"

"Forty years."

I look him over with fresh eyes. Arune is young compared to the rest of the siblings I've met. Very young. Young enough that his mother might still be alive, if…

"Your mother is the one buried in the barrow, near the coast," I say, realizing the truth as I speak it.

"Was, yes." There's a new shadow behind his eyes. "Thray, you must be very, very careful what you do next. How you act. What you say. You can be angry—that's expected. But after what you did tonight… Their fear about your loyalties may gain footing."

"They're afraid of me."

"They should be." He gives a shallow laugh. "We all have Eang's blood, but yours is the first to remember the power of it. You made a room full of Winterborn bleed. None of our magics can directly affect living things. But you clearly can, and what you showed tonight is likely just the beginning."

"How do you know that?"

Arune shrugs. "What you did was instinctual. Once you master that force and direct it? We've no idea what you can do." An idea lights his eyes. "I'll take you out, alone, and we can… test your limits. I'm curious."

I shake my head, not dismissing the idea entirely, but just for the moment. "Later. What will the Winterborn do if they decide they can't trust me?"

Arune starts to say something, then presses his lips into a line and looks away for a long moment. "That remains to be seen. But in the meantime, you must prove your loyalty to them."

"You keep saying 'them,'" I point out.

Arune rubs a hand over one smooth cheek, glancing into the fire. "Well, I hope you won't lump me in with the rest of our ill-behaved family. I'm helping you, after all."

I take a minute to think and he lets me have it. Silence overtakes us, backed by the crackling of the fire.

"What exactly are they afraid I'll do?" I finally ask. "Seek vengeance for my own murder? Surely I wouldn't be the first to do that."

"No." Arune shakes his head. His expression changes, closing and bracing. "The Winter Night is long, little sister. Too long."

My chin drifts to one side. "The land can't support life for much longer."

Arune leans forward again, closing the space between us. I resist the urge to shift back, facing him head-on.

"Yes. They've their eyes on the Algatt Mountains. Eangen. Other lands were explored over the summer—Siru spoke of many of them. But none suit our people so well, or come with such... satisfaction."

"Eang's land," I summarize, shock and horror emptying my face.

He nods. "The land of our father's murderer."

"The land of our grandmother."

Arune *tsks*. "Rage for a father we loved is greater than love for a grandmother who killed him."

"You're not talking about a peaceful migration."

"Your people would not accept the Duamel peacefully."

My fingers twitch with tension, but I clench them and ask, "When will you invade?"

"As soon as the Inheritor can mobilize, but they've been preparing with Attan for two years—since the first year of darkness ended, and they realized a great shift was likely to come. There's talk of invading this spring, when Grandfather's power wanes. Not that they consider him much of a threat—he rarely interferes with humans—but there are only so many Icecarvers and moving an army will be difficult in the deep cold."

This spring. The fair winds that Siru promised would carry the Eangen and me home are the very same ones they plan to invade on. "Are you forcing Attan to do this?"

Arune stares into the fire now, his mind's eye elsewhere. "The Inheritor will gain a rich land and an immortal queen to blood his children with. A new dynasty in a new land."

"What queen?"

"Siru."

I remember Siru's vehement refusal to marry Attan, and the way her fingers curled on the arm of the throne. "She doesn't want that. She wants power, but not through Attan."

Arune shakes his head. "No one wants her to marry him."

Suspicion twines through me. "Will she kill him when the invasion is over?"

My brother shrugs. "That, I can't say. He's useful, and Father ordained that his branch of the bloodline will rule, so it may be best to keep him for a time." He adds, more slowly, "There was talk of giving you to him, assuming your power wasn't anything too dangerous."

"I've already chosen a husband," I snap, because I still can't face the reality that Havar's and my future will never be. "Kygga told me the Duamel don't consider marriage pledges binding for long, but it still matters to us. And *give* me? You can't give me to anyone. I'm my own, and I am going back to Eangen in the spring."

As I say the words, I wonder if they're true—and not just because of my newfound immortality or the looming threat of my punishment from the priesthood. If the Winterborn intend to invade Eangen, I can have no peaceful homecoming.

The weight of responsibility presses on my shoulders. My mind searches for a way to escape it, but I can't. I believe Arune. I saw the Inheritor's warriors and his savn war dogs. I've lived in the endless Winter Night, and I know how dangerous my siblings are.

Just when I think the weight of revelation will crush me, I catch Arune's eyes. He's silent, watching me struggle, but there's concern there, and a warmth that belies our frigid world.

"If you don't prove you're trustworthy, you won't be going back to Eangen. You won't even leave this village," Arune tells me, low and warning—but hinted with promise, a whisper of a way out. "You must prove your loyalty and pledge your power to the Winterborn."

"Pledge my power?" I thrust the thought aside, indignant, and scramble for another avenue. "The Winterborn can't take the south. They must know that. We've the Miri on our side, and the armies of the

Eangan and the Algatt. The Ascended Emperor of the Arpa will answer our call. It's a hopeless cause."

"I'd think Thvynder would be the greatest threat, wouldn't you?" Arune says, so calmly my skin chills. "Why don't you mention the God-Killer?"

"Their protection goes without saying." I wave a hand dismissively. But panic seizes me in a quivering fist. Thvynder would be the greatest threat, if they were in Eangen. But they're not. They're far away, and my people are unaware of their own vulnerability.

But if my siblings don't know of Thvynder's absence, I can still stop this. They might be duplicitous, but they're not stupid. They won't risk the wrath of my God.

"Thvynder destroyed the Gods of the Old World in an instant," I remind Arune. "I don't know how much you've heard of that day but… There is no chance of this invasion succeeding. Please. Believe me."

There's a strange expression on Arune's face, one I can't read. He's silent for a long time, and in the silence I feel my blood begin to rise— not in anger, but dread.

He knows. Somehow, Arune knows that Thvynder is not a threat.

"You should be more careful, little sister," Arune says with a sorrowful smile, "what you say to the wind."

TWENTY-EIGHT

A rune allows me to stay with him that night, and though my trust in him is a precarious thing, I've no intention of returning to my own chambers. My brother comes and goes, fetching my belongings before he leaves again, and I'm finally alone.

My body is exhausted, but my thoughts are frenzied. I sit by the fire with my bone-handled sword at my side, staring at the far wall with unseeing eyes as I wrestle with revelations, threats, and courses of action. They all blur together, but slowly, like a basket of tangled yarn, I begin to order them.

Firstly: my homeland is under threat, and it's my fault. A Windwalker overheard my useless prayer to Thvynder, likely Kygga on the training grounds at the Inheritor's keep. Now the Winterborn know the Algatt and Eangen lands are without their greatest protector.

Secondly: I am immortal. The implications of this are too huge for me to grasp—not the least of which is Havar and his mortality. I agonize over what I will say to him, what I'll do if I don't marry him. Will I live out my days alone? Join the Winterborn and inevitably fall to their corruption?

Third: I cannot sit by while my siblings invade Eangen. I have the answer I sought, but what if the cost is my home?

Eangen is transient, a new voice reminds me. That voice is calmer and cooler. Detached. Everyone there, everyone I love, will die one day. Perhaps Vistic will live long, before the God's soul is reborn into someone else, and Miri like Gadr will remain until their untimely ends. But even if the priesthood forgives my trespasses and allows me to return, everyone will, eventually, leave me. Then I'll be alone, with no one to remember me except my grandfather and Ogam's children.

The fire pops beside me as a log crumples in upon itself. My mind does the same, unable to bear the reality of my situation. I watch a fresh wash of sparks dance up into a cleverly hewn chimney.

Slowly, I pull my thoughts away from that yawning eternity and think of the months between now and the southern spring. I must warn the Eangen, even if it means risking the priesthood's wrath. I must get Havar, Darag, Seele, and Branan out of Atmeltan. But Arune told me that unless I earn my siblings' trust, I won't even leave this mountain.

A solution, it seems, is already there. It was in Siru's eyes as she sat in the Inheritor's throne, Arune's words and Attan's face, back in Atmeltan—his appraisal, his hunger, and his need.

There was talk of giving you to him, assuming your power wasn't anything too... dangerous.

My skin crawls, but I steel myself. My power has proven itself dangerous, but only if I can't be trusted to wield it.

With the right words, the right tone, and the right posture, perhaps my siblings can be convinced to send me to Attan in Siru's place. Once back in Atmeltan, I can secure the safety of Havar, Darag, Branan, and Seele, and figure out how to get back to Eangen in time to raise the alarm.

It's no simple plan. So much hinges on my ability to convince my siblings of my sincerity. But if there's one talent my father left to me, it's deception.

It's long into the sleeping hours, as I lie on my back and stare at the firelight playing across the ceiling, that I remember the little gray owl and its waiting message. How could I have forgotten? If the bird is still there, I can send him to warn the Eangen this very night.

I check my knife at my belt and hasten for the door. I half expect to find it guarded but there are no Winterborn in sight, and the Duamel have long ago gone to sleep. I glimpse a father pacing with a fussing baby, but other than them, I'm alone.

I slip out into the night. It's still snowing, fine and frigid, shushing against my hood as I raise it against the cold—despite the warmth of the ground, the wind funnels up the ravine tonight, and the difference in temperature is stark. I immediately feel the fine hairs in my nose prickle as they freeze.

I rub my nose and look for the owl, but he's nowhere in sight. I peer here and there in the night, but still, there's no sign of him.

I unfurl a finger to draw summoning runes in the smooth, pale snow beside the doorway. But just as I crouch, I hesitate. The worst of my problems began because I didn't consider what the wind might see and hear.

I touch my priestess's Sight. Sure enough, I see a silver haze on the breeze high above me. I'm being watched. Of course I am.

I give no sign that I've seen them, turn the rune into a simple marking for memory, and turn to go back inside. The silver presence slips farther away and I pause with the door open, half of my face bathed in the warmth and light of the caves.

"Grandfather," I whisper into the cold. "I need you. You were right."

There is no reply.

"Ah, so you are coming." Arune materializes next to me as I string my white bow, dropping my hip into the curve of the weapon to bend it. Hair a windblown mess around his pretty face, he watches me fit the string and step free. "I thought you'd stew for a few more days."

I give him a wan smile and reach up to make sure my arrows are well in reach at my shoulder. I prefer carrying them at the small of my back, but the snow is too deep outside the village.

Two days have passed since my blooding, two days that I spent in solitude and contemplation. Since I'd already made up my mind about how to go forward, this was only half for show. My body needed rest after lengthy travel and my unexpected murder, and the quiet of Arune's chambers had provided the safety I needed.

Now half a dozen of my siblings mill about, snowshoes strapped to their backs in preparation for our hunt in the forest below. Sleds wait nearby, and the sky above is lit by wisping blue-green Northern Lights.

"Who says I'm not still stewing? I'll stick an arrow in something before today is done," I say to Arune, "and I don't particularly care if it's an animal."

The threat feels like it comes from someone else, but at the same time, I mean it. I pull up my gloves, one of my many new gifts— soft, fur-lined dark leather—and add, "Don't worry, it likely won't be you."

"That's sweet of you. Best make it Siru," my brother says, indicating our sister as she strides up, clad in black wolf fur with her hair uncovered, braids silver as Winterborn magic in the night. "She heals fastest."

"Let's go," Siru calls to the group, oblivious to our conversation, and we start off through the snow.

Once we leave the shelter of the clefts, the wind blows steady, cold, and bitter. Even when we traverse the steaming waterfalls of hot springs, rimmed with ice, the wind barely loses its bite.

I shoulder my bow and follow in the footsteps of the Winterborn, but as time goes on and we descend into a hidden, forested valley, we spread out. I take the chance to look around for a messenger owl in the darkened trees—either the one Vistic set to watch over me, or the gray from the day before—but neither are here.

Worry tugs at me. I need to find an opportunity to write summoning runes during this hunt. If the owls are nearby, they'll come when it's safe. I can take the gray owl's message, whatever it is, and send word home immediately.

"What exactly are we hunting?" I ask Arune when I stop to put on my snowshoes. Still distracted by thoughts of owls, I fumble with the straps.

Arune, light-footed and hazed by a silver glow when I touch my Sight, watches me lace and tighten the straps around my boots.

"I can't imagine there's much game left in an endless winter," I add.

"The land seems to be less aware of the night. The animals have begun to change their migration patterns slowly, but there's still grass to be grazed on, for those that can find it beneath the snow, and the hot springs always attract game. For now."

I lower my voice. "If the Winter Night ended, would you still invade Eangen?"

Arune glances up at the dancing sky through the trees. "Yes," he says, unequivocally.

"Hush," one of our sisters hisses from up ahead, and the pair of us fall silent.

Time slips by as we stalk through the forest. There's no conversation, no sounds except the occasional rattle of branches and the brush of cloth. Hot springs speckle the valley, producing steaming creeks and waterfalls that cut through the deep snow. Above these waterways mist condenses on ice-laden boughs, dragging them down and snapping them, and the tracks of small animals lattice the powdery ground.

In the heart of the forest, beneath a series of sheltering ridges, the trees grow more thickly. Here the snow has yet to build up and there are signs of animals grazing—scuffed deadfall, torn-up roots, lower boughs, and trunks stripped of bark and needles.

"I'm surprised there's anything edible left this close to the settlement," I murmur to Arune.

"We leave out enough hay to keep them coming back," he whispers in return, pointing to a few clumps of dried grasses, frozen into a large hoofprint. "We bring it in with our supplies, when the Duamel venture to civilization. It's a luxury—we've enough livestock in the catacombs to keep us fed. But there's little else to do in the Winter Night than hunt."

"We'll split up." Siru's voice lifts over the group. "Spread out, send the wind if you run into trouble."

Arune immediately grabs my hand like a child, grinning broadly. "I'm with the youngling," he declares, waving our bound hands for all to see.

I nearly pull away as the rest of the group organizes, but his grip is easy, familial, and I'm suddenly reminded of playing with Vistic in the forests around Albor—him pulling me along as we slide down snowy hills like river otters, as we prepared to jump into quiet summer lakes, or wriggled our bare toes into thick beds of autumn moss. The memories are sharp and clear, clearer than they've been in years—or, perhaps, simply closer to the surface.

I'm beginning to care for Arune, but the feeling is a dangerous one. I have to summon one of the owls and warn Eangen. I have to get home.

I pry my hand free. Arune just winks. "Let's go."

We set off through the trees again, following meandering hoofprints that I suspect belong to some kind of deer. Slowly, the rest of the party fades and I try to let the space between Arune and I broaden, but he frequently stops to wait for me and listen to the wind.

"Why don't you scout ahead?" I suggest, gesturing to his slight footprints. "Surely you're sick of walking by now."

He continues to stride forward. "I am, but there are savn in these woods."

"I'm immortal, what danger are savn now?" I ask, the truth of the words prickling at me. The thought is not an unpleasant one.

"Just because you can't die doesn't mean you can't be harmed," he reminds me. "Unless you've Siru's healing abilities, getting your throat torn out will take a fair bit to mend."

I cringe. "How does that work? What if I lose an arm?"

"Those take *years* to grow back." Arune shakes his head. "But losing your head is the only one that's truly problematic."

I pale and smirk at the same time, amused and unnerved by the image. "What happens then?"

"Hopefully a kind sibling is there to bring the pieces of you home," he replies. "A few stitches to put you back together, a few months of death-sleep, and you'll recover. But if not? If a savn tears your head from your body and leaves bits of you strewn across the forest?"

I find I've stopped walking, waiting for his conclusion with bated breath.

"Ice," he says eventually. "Ice will shroud you and bury the meat and bone that is *you*, like a grave. Years will pass, and you will sleep in your own wintery barrow. But eventually, you'll awake, the ice will crack, and you'll claw back into the world, whole once more."

I shudder and force myself to start walking again. "Has it happened to you?"

"Me? No. It's rare—we are hardier than mortals, after all, and generally heal faster. We don't get sick, and after a few centuries of experience, it's hard to make a mistake great enough to end up in that position." Arune shakes his head. "Midvyk did, once, when she was young. It was her blooding. She was crushed in a landslide, but it was the bear that found her, legs trapped in the press of earth, who tore her to pieces. It was twenty years before the ice returned her, but Father went to her resting place, every chance he could."

I can't see Arune's face, striding behind him as I am, but I hear his voice tighten. My throat, too, constricts at the thought of our father's lost—or, in my case, unknown—care.

"I'm not all that fond of Midvyk, but I hear it was not easy to see," Arune adds, glancing back at me. He paints on a grin. "Or convenient. So be careful, little sister. I've no desire to waste time checking your icy grave every day for the next twenty years."

I manage a wan smile in return. As heavy as the thought of spending decades recovering in ice is, I have a task to complete.

"I need to relieve myself," I say to Arune. "Go on ahead, I'll catch up."

He nods and picks up his pace, vanishing beyond a row of conifers.

I step behind a broad tree and see to my needs, then, checking I'm still alone, I pull off one of my gloves and draw the runes for summoning into the snow. Then I rest the tips of my fingers beside them and will a scrap of my priestly magic into the symbols.

The runes pulse with it—the expected amber-gold of the Vynder priesthood twined with a new, Winterborn silver. Then the magic fades, and the runes revert to little more than subtle furrows.

"Thray!" Arune's voice comes to me on a thread of wind, hushed but urgent. "Hurry! You'll want to see this."

I glance at the runes one last time, then hasten after him. Ducking through the conifers, I squint into an especially dark patch of forest. In the snow just below me I can see the indentations of the hooves Arune and I have been following, but Arune's steps are gone altogether now.

"You left no trail," I chide the wind.

I can hear amusement in his voice as he says, "This way."

A thread of wind tugs at stray strands of my hair, pulling me away from the hoofprints and back into an area with greater light. Grays and blacks are washed in shifting green from the sky and I see a meadow of sorts, heavy with snow, beneath a steep, white-laden slope.

I join Arune, who is crouched in the clearing, and follow his gaze.

As I do, sound shifts—Arune has teased the wind into a muffling cloak around us. I detect a roaring, deadened but present, and I recognize a thrum beneath my feet.

I look more closely at the slope, now picking out glistening sheaths of ice beneath the mantle of snow. I see mist rising from a pool too turbulent to ice over. The mist is so fine it freezes into a haze about the entire clearing, hanging like the river-mists I remember well from my childhood.

At a flick of Arune's hand the mist swirls, glistening like fallen stars.

There, between us and the falls, is a stag. It's shaggier than any deer in Eangen, stockier and heartier, but no less graceful. I draw a sharp breath as it lifts its head and surveys the clearing, its great rack of antlers slicked with ice. Its coat is thick with it too and as it takes a step, I hear the softest tinkling.

A finger pokes my cheek. Startled, I look over to find Arune watching me with anticipation. The roar of the waterfall fades. Arune has muffled us.

"Beautiful, isn't it?" he asks.

I rub at my cheek, more to restore heat than to dispel any pain. "It's incredible."

He purses his lips. "Should we kill it?"

The stag picks its way slowly back over the frozen part of the pond, making for the trees. "Do we need to?"

He shrugs. "We won't die of starvation."

I sink into my squat, forearms on my knees, bow before me, and backside in the snow. "Then let's let him go."

Arune nods and we both fall silent again, watching until the creature vanishes into the shadows of the forest. The mist remains, sparkling the faintest blue and green in celestial light.

"I want to take Siru's place," I confide to Arune. "I can't marry Havar—I care for him too much, and his life is too short. I... I know it's best to move on, now, before that care can grow. But I feel nothing for Attan, and I think marrying him would go a long way to securing my place among the Winterborn."

He looks at me but doesn't say anything. His eyes crease with curiosity, but I feel his suspicion too.

"I can't stop the Winterborn from invading Eangen," I say, hoping my words aren't prophetic. "But I can put myself in a position of power to make a difference, if it's taken. To have Attan's ear, and a say among our siblings."

Arune's eyebrows lift in consideration. "I see. All right."

"That's it?" I stare at him, twisting to kneel in the snow. "That's all you have to say?"

"Well, I thought of it a while ago. But I figured you weren't in the best mood to be told what to do."

I frown at him. The cold is starting to make my joints ache and the skin of my calves feels bruised from the cold, but this conversation is too important.

"It won't be easy," he points out. "You're asking for a position of great power."

"A position no one else wants."

"True." He glances out over the mist and waterfall again. "Ask for Kygga to stay by you, as your keeper. They'll send someone to spy on you regardless, so pick who it is. Kygga's a liar, but he's better than most. Midvyk trusts him, and he feels protective of you. You being the youngest and all, with those freckles and Eangen eyes."

I *tsk*. "I don't appreciate that."

That's a lie, though. I might not like how my siblings see me, young and naive, but my foolish heart thaws at Arune's teasing and the thought of Kygga's care. I remind myself that both still watched me die, but I'm starved for allies.

"You might not appreciate it, but you can use it," Arune points out.

I straighten, shifting my bow to my off hand and offering Arune the other to help him rise. "You're an excellent conspirator."

He takes my hand and stands, eyes crinkling. "I do what I—"

That's when the savn parts from the shadows behind him in a blur of fur, muscle, and flashing teeth.

TWENTY-NINE

I stumble backward as the savn's teeth seize Arune's neck. Winterborn and beast hit the ground with a horrific, snow-muffled thud. The wind snaps back to life around me and sound rushes in—growling behind me, growling before me, and terrible, terrible silence from Arune. He's limp, face-down in the snow. I can't see his wounds, but I see a dark stain of blood beneath the pawing savn.

I cry out, half in terror, half in rage. The stink of the beast fills my senses for one blinding moment, feral and fetid and canine. It's the scent of old blood and dens, danger and—

The savn who took down Arune looks up at me, growling low in its chest. It's barely a pace away. I know I should run, yet the sight of Arune's bloodied head, pinned beneath claws, arrests me.

I draw my bow and put an arrow in the beast's eye before I know I've moved. It rears back, a yelp of pain breaking off as it crumples next to Arune and lies there, twitching.

I curse in relief and start forward, dropping to a knee and reaching for one of Arune's limp hands.

But there hadn't just been one growl, in the night. The dead beast's mate slips into the frozen mist of the clearing. My bow is still in hand. The waterfall drowns the sound of the monster's coming but I see its jaws part, its body shift as it prepares for a marrow-shattering roar.

I roar first. I don't nock an arrow. I don't draw. All my instinct, all my murderous intent, I unleash in my scream.

Snow flies into my face as the lunging savn skids to a stop at my feet. It lies on its side, great head lolling and eyes reflecting the thin light.

It does not get back up. It doesn't even twitch like its mate does. Yet I register a strange, lingering movement—not in the lifeless beast, but around it. More mist has joined that from the waterfall—this one coming from the savn's twisted, collapsing frame. It's glistening red and black. A blood-mist, drifting from the beast's shriveling corpse.

I stare. The waterfall roars—or maybe that's blood in my ears. Slowly, I become aware of mist melting on my cheeks. I wipe at them with the back of a hand and it comes away streaked with pink flecks.

The fog in my head breaks. I curl over and vomit, retching in the snow beside Arune.

This is me. This is my power when unleashed against mortal creatures instead of my immortal siblings. Ogam's ice and Eang's blood-boiling scream have united in me, and the results are brutal.

Slowly, the convulsions fade. I register approaching shouts and pick out Siru's voice, nearly upon us.

I crawl to Arune and turn him over, struggling to make out his pale face in the snow and shadows. There's blood—it looks black in the night, threaded with silver.

My brother stares up at me. His neck has been savaged so brutally I nearly throw up again, but his eyes are still lit with consciousness, if dimly. I shudder in relief—part of me had been terrified that my power had hurt him too.

There's a message in his gaze, if I can interpret it. Cautioning? A question?

Then we're surrounded. Siru crouches across from me, grabs Arune's face, and turns it toward her with no fear of injuring him further, or causing him pain. The bloodied mess that's his neck contracts, torn muscles limp and sinews frayed beneath a coating of silvered blood.

"You'll heal. Stay calm," she instructs. Her eyes snag on me for a moment, then she tears them away. If I didn't know Arune's life was in no jeopardy, I'd have sworn that I saw fear in them. But is it fear for him, or fear of me?

I am still on my knees as my siblings gather in the clearing and see the dead savn. The blood-mist has faded but it speckles their clothes, their cheeks, and fur trims. Siru stares at the shriveled corpse of the second savn as two siblings gently place Arune on the sled.

There are words, questions, but I ignore them until the others leave.

"You did well," Siru says when we're alone, looking from the shriveled corpse to the natural one, with my arrow in its eye. "Arune will be fine, though I'm surprised the beasts got the better of you."

"There was a stag," I tell her. My mouth feels odd, as if it doesn't quite belong to me. "He muffled us so we wouldn't disturb it. We couldn't hear them coming."

Siru nudges one of the savn's paws with her boot and makes a disapproving sound.

I look back down at my hand, streaked with blood, and notice my fingers are shaking. I make the observation from a distance, as though my consciousness has divided—half of me lingering in shock and horror, the other half taking charge.

That second part of me welcomes the shaking. It urges the tears to well and the horror to crease my face. It forces me to lift my head too, showing Siru all of it.

"But he'll be all right?" I ask, my voice thick. "I didn't hurt him too?"

Siru's expression slackens with sudden compassion, but she pieces her mask back together quickly. "You didn't hurt him," she says, coming to crouch before me.

"But I could have." My voice, helpfully, cracks. I hold her eyes, willing her to see each tear. "I hurt you all, already. I didn't... I didn't expect this. Any of this."

Siru looks at me for a long moment, then pulls off her gloves. She picks up a little snow and gently uses it to clean the blood from my cheeks, following its icy passage with brushes of her thumb.

"I can help you," she tells me. "This power of yours—perhaps it's not unlike mine, in its wielding. When I was first blooded, it came sporadically to me too, and in great violence."

Genuine relief flickers through me. "Thank you."

She finishes cleaning the blood from my cheeks and, picking up my bow, rises to her feet. "Come. Give me a week, and you'll have this monster under control."

Monster. I shudder to think of my power that way, but she's not wrong. It's violent and feral and raw in a way I've always insisted I was not.

"I'll find a way to repay you," I promise.

She waves her hand dismissively and starts to walk, following the path the sled left in the snow. "Just never use your power on me again, and we'll call it even."

For the next seven days, I sleep in Arune's chambers with one ear to his labored breaths. If I'd acted more quickly, if I'd been more aware, perhaps my ally wouldn't be lying in a death-sleep. But there's nothing I can do, other than talk to him as I tidy his chambers, and smooth his hair back from his pale face. There's a freedom to his unawareness, and in the space his silence leaves, I find my affection for him strengthening.

But given my pending betrayal of the Winterborn, the feeling is bittersweet. I feel that Arune, more than anyone, might understand what I'm about to do—but even if he awakens, I know I cannot confide my whole plan.

Every night when the Winterborn sleep, I slip out and look for an owl. I must be discreet, pretend that I'm simply stretching my legs or looking at the stars. But the birds never come, and all I can surmise is that the constant watch of Windwalkers over the camp keeps them away. It's the same watch that prevents me from slipping away.

I've no choice other than to press forward with my plan.

I spend every minute of the Winterborn's 'day' with Siru. It's challenging. She's a good teacher, patient and insightful, and in the light of her kindness, I struggle to keep my anger sharp as she guides my power from reckless and untamed, to moderate and leashed.

"Your power is not only tied to your emotion," she decides on the first day, "but your instinct. That's why you injured the savn, but not Arune—your instincts identified the threat and directed your power toward it. Now, think of the ice as a threat, and shatter it."

I look from her to a pillar of ice. We're on the mountainside below the village, and Siru's frozen the water from a hot spring into a column the height of a man. The wind drifts around us and stars speckle the sky overhead, reflecting in the warm, steaming water.

I relax my hands at my sides and stare at the pillar, gathering my thoughts.

Siru doesn't mention how I used my power on all the Winterborn at once, that first time after the ceremony. The incident is heavy on my mind.

"Do you think that the more opponents I face, the less effect my power has?" I venture, still eyeing the pillar.

Siru shrugs. "I suppose we'll find out. Go on."

I push my will toward the pillar, imagining it as some looming threat. Nothing happens. I try runes next, sketching them in the air and breathing on them. I'm not inexperienced with magic, given my place in the Vynder priesthood, and runes are a useful medium. Another is voice, but I'm reluctant to scream again. It feels too vulnerable, too primal.

But the pillar doesn't shatter, no matter how I will, or try to trick my mind into seeing the ice as a charging enemy. I try again and again, until finally, I yell in Eangen, "Break!"

The pillar shatters. Both Siru and I duck, shielding our faces, but the ice turns to dust and falls like snow.

Siru breathes out a steadying breath, then cracks a smile. "You're truly our grandmother's daughter, then. Use your voice."

Day after day, I find a greater grasp on my power. It's enough to control it—and enough to hide its full extent. I'm cautious with each command, each lift of my voice. A single pillar, I shatter with a word.

Two, crumble. But the more we add, the greater my power is spread. It naturally lessens the impact on each pillar—but not to the extent I allow Siru to believe.

Finally, when I face twenty pillars on the barren, mist-wrapped mountainside, they break in a cacophony of cracks, but only a few collapse.

Siru looks over at me, and I spy a dozen Winterborn lingering on the upper slopes, watching me. I feel a stab of fear, wondering if they've come to assess how much of a threat I am, but the feeling eases as a few siblings laugh and toss echoing compliments down to me. A few others stay quiet, their expressions more cautious.

Kygga points to an icy pillar. "You missed one."

I glance at it, the word, "Shatter," on my tongue, but I don't speak it aloud. "You do it then," I prod him.

"You walk on the wind," he challenges back. He glances between Siru and I, and I realize how close together we stand.

"Glad to see you two getting along," our brother adds and waves us by, up the icy slope and past the trickling waterfalls toward the village. "Come. The hunters took a doe today, and I'm starving."

We feast together in the central hall. There's little formality to this meal, with Winterborn coming and going as they please. Some stay late into the evening, like Siru, Kygga, and I. Once my belly is full of venison, root vegetables, and hot flatbread with butter and herbs, I find the opportunity to take the next step in my plan.

Siru rises to fetch more wine, leaving Kygga and I alone for a short time. I'm nervous, and don't bother to hide it.

"Kygga," I begin.

He keeps eating from his bowl, where he's let his meal blend into an impromptu stew, but he meets my eyes.

I'm quiet for a moment, gathering my words. I've planned this conversation for days but all at once, I doubt myself. What if he doesn't believe me? What if all I do is prove I can't be trusted?

"I know Siru is going to marry the Inheritor," I admit. "And I know that's the last thing she wants."

Kygga lowers his bowl and swipes gravy from his beard. "Who told you that?"

"Arune."

"What else did Arune tell you?"

I hesitate. The answer to this question is the greatest risk yet, but if I don't take it, the lie I'm building will crumble too quickly. "That she's doing it because you need the Inheritor's army to conquer Eangen and Algatt."

Kygga's stare is hard and fixed. "How do you feel about that?"

"I'm angry," I admit. "Or, I was. I suppose I still am. But I understand too, I think. I see the night outside, just like the rest of you. I think of the village you and I stopped in, with so little food. The only way forward for these people is to leave Duamel. But I also know my people wouldn't let them stay without... force."

That's not entirely true, but for the sake of my lie, I believe it.

Kygga doesn't speak, still watching me.

"I want to take Siru's place," I confide. "Though 'want' isn't the right word... I need to. If this is the future, I want to be at the heart of it, where I can ensure my mother's people are safe—just like my father's people are."

"You want to be queen?" he clarifies. His gaze slides across the room, checking that no one can hear us, and I feel the air around us tighten in a way I'm familiar with now.

"I do."

"That's a great deal of power for the Elders to give you. You've only been among us for... what, eight days?"

"Yes," I concede. Across the chamber, I see Siru stop to converse with Midvyk and several other Elders. I'm grateful for the distraction. It gives Kygga and I more time. "That's why I want you to come with me. Be my... warden, handler, whatever you would like to call it. Spy on me as you will and make sure I uphold the Winterborn's interests."

Kygga turns to face me fully. "What? You're serious about this, Thray? What about Havar?"

"We can't be together. I can't watch him grow old and die."

I expect Kygga to make some calloused argument, to point out the Duamel lovers and sons and daughters serving in this very chamber, but he doesn't.

"So you'll take a husband you don't love," he summarizes.

"He can die whenever he pleases," I affirm. "Attan's of our bloodline, so maybe our children will be immortal."

"Some of ours are," he acknowledges, and I wonder whether the catacombs house his own family. "But when Attan dies you'll still be in power."

I shrug. "I don't care what happens then. What I want is as little bloodshed as possible for the Eangen *and* the Duamel. This is the only way I can see to get it."

Kygga falls silent again. Looking across the room, I see Siru beginning to extricate herself from her conversation with the other Elders.

"I haven't forgiven you all for what you did," I admit, placing the final nail of my argument and raising the hammer. "But... I don't want to be alone."

Kygga looks at me sideways, pained understanding leaking through his suspicion, then Siru passes through our silencing barrier. Sensing the change, she gives the pair of us a curious look, then settles back down between us.

"What are you talking about?" she asks, setting down the pitcher of wine without refilling our cups.

Kygga and I exchange a look, a question in my eyes, a warning in his. He ducks his chin.

I turn my gaze to Siru and, picking up the pitcher, refill her cup and hand it to her. "I have a proposal."

THIRTY

Torches and lamps line the streets of Atmeltan. Firelight plays off the faces of their bearers; hushed, wide-eyed Duamel gathered to welcome an envoy of Winterborn through the lower gate, where we disembark from the sledges that have brought us south on the frozen river. Horns blow somewhere in the night, answering and building off one another into a melodic cacophony of sound. Drums beat, carried by Diviner priests, and the air stirs with thoughts of reverence, hope, and awe.

Siru strides at the head of our company as we leave the wind-harried docks, bathed in shifting blue and green winter lights, and begins the ascent to the keep. I follow at her shoulder in Aita's gifted kaftan, bow on my back and bare, blunted sickle sword at my hip. I fix my eyes ahead, locking all feeling behind the same mask my sister wears.

Windwalkers materialize around us, stepping from graceful eddies of snow. Kygga falls in at my side, shadows and firelight dancing across his handsome face. He wears a new sword; a broad, single-edged weapon slung at one hip. His kaftan is a dark red, black when it meets the shadows, and his white hair is drawn up into a knot with a series of tight braids.

Seeing him, I feel a momentary pang of anger, then a rush of mourning. I strive to keep it all from my face, but he notices.

"Arune will be well," he assures me, misinterpreting my expression.

I tilt my chin in a half-nod and coax my face back to impassivity.

The Duamel watch us as we stride past, their usual bleakness skewed by the magic of the drums. They smile and murmur, stare with awe and bow.

Sympathy mixes with brooding resentment as I look at them. There are those in this crowd who will march south to invade my home, yet it's the Winterborn who push them forward.

I am a Winterborn. That is what the Duamel need to see as their reverent eyes behold my face in the patterned light of lanterns and the blazing beacons of torches. A Winterborn is what my siblings need to see as we pass through the lower city, through the market where Seele nearly died, and through the long climb to the Inheritor's keep.

Just below the great round fortress, the citizens of Atmeltan fall away and their place is taken by warriors. They bear long spears and short bows, the layered scale armor and shadows within their helmets, which transform their child-like eyes into ambiguous, abyssal hollows.

The doors of the keep open to meet us. The frigid draft rushes around us, stirring our clothes and driving us into the central chamber.

"Thray!" Havar's voice snatches my concentration to the side. He shoves at a wall of warriors, trying to get to me. But when our eyes meet, he slows. He pales and steps back just as Darag, Branan, and Seele appear behind him.

Darag murmurs something to his brother and puts a hand on his arm, while Seele stares at me as if I am a stranger. Branan's expression is more guarded, more calculating.

Havar's crestfallen face draws me back to him. My lips flutter apart, instinct urging me to call to him, to explain, but now isn't the time. He will have to wait.

Siru sweeps into the central chamber ahead of me to a ripple of drums. The Inheritor's court, the Diviner High Priesthood, and other guests line the tiers of the room and the central fire blazes with oppressive heat.

The Inheritor stands before the flames in traditional, broad-belted robes, a savn pup asleep at his heels and his hands clasped over the slight arch of his belly, at ease in his domain.

"Cousins," he declares as we pool on the highest tier of the chamber. "Word of your coming brought me great joy. Tell me, what is the meaning of this? Why are we blessed with so many of Ogam's Get?"

Behind us, the door to the hallway closes with a weighty *thunk*. Siru stands at the forefront of our group, her hair bound into masses of braids and twists: an empress without an empire, a goddess in perception, if not reality. I and our siblings are a small immortal army in the heart of the Duamel court.

The chamber grows quiet, awaiting Siru's reply.

"We come to honor our bargain," Siru says. She turns to me and gestures with one scarred hand. "My sister Thray has consented to be your queen, Inheritor. Make the most of your time together. Spring will be upon the south soon, and in two turns of the moon I expect our armies to be ready to march."

The Inheritor looks to me. I see surprise in his eyes, and momentary displeasure. Then his gaze becomes more assessing. Letting his hands fall to his sides, he comes to the edge of the lowest tier.

Behind him, the savn pup opens its eyes. Head resting on its paws, it stares after him dolefully.

The shallow, broad steps between Attan and I seem too short. My resolve crackles, and I think of Havar out in the hall. What I'm about to do will devastate him. Will he forgive me?

Does it matter anymore?

I take one step down, then another. Kygga does not follow, and the lack of him at my shoulder is like a cold draft. I wish Arune were here, but I would have had a much harder time hiding my plans from him. Perhaps it's best he remained in his bed, sleeping and unaware.

"So, you're the one who's condescended to be my wife," the Inheritor says. No one else in the room dares to speak. "Thray. I am… surprised. I'd expected Siru." He glances at my sister, but instead of regret or displeasure I glimpse suspicion in his gaze. "Tell me, why this sudden change?"

This is it. Now is my moment to speak.

"You intend to take my mother's land," I state, continuing to descend toward him. I pass Siru, our sleeves brushing, and she steps aside. "You'll need a queen who knows the people and their ways."

"A queen with divided loyalties is not what I need," the Inheritor replies, his eyes narrowing. I'm only four steps away now.

I smile, and the curve of it on my lips reminds me of Arune. "My loyalty is not divided. My loyalty is to my blood—the Winterborn, the Eangen, and the children I will take from your body, Attan. I've a hundred lifetimes ahead of me—pledging this one to you means nothing to me. Will I intercede for the Eangen? Yes. Will I rule them? With absolute power."

I reach the last step and remain there, looking down at my supposed husband. His face tilts up, his eyes delving into mine, and I see the moment when his caution turns to hunger. The corners of his own lips contract and, though the suspicion does not entirely leave his eyes, his pleasure is genuine.

"In that case." Attan reaches out to take my hand and draw me down the last step, before turning to the assembly. He raises his voice and looks around the room, taking in every courtier, every priest, and every servant. "Bow, my people, to your coming queen."

Kneeling Duamel transition into speeches and pledges from the priests, then a feast of staggering proportion. Exhausted as I am from my journey—and as eager as I am to leave the Inheritor's presence—I force myself to sit through it all. Behind my impassive expression and occasional smiles, my mind drifts to the plans I will enact, their variables and their pitfalls, and the edges I still need to iron out. When my anxiety rises, I drink fermented milk, and when my plate sits untouched, the servants wordlessly clear it away.

Attan seems unbothered by my lack of appetite or conversation. He eats and drinks well but speaks only with a handful of confidants, hunters who accompanied him on his last savn hunt—which is the main topic of conversation. They hover around our table like aunts at a naming, speaking of the savn in the kennels, bragging about their roles in the beasts' captures, and reminiscing about the solitude and camaraderie of life on the hunt. They even pass around the savn pup who sat beside Attan's throne and laugh when it whines and bites them.

"How does one tame a savn?" I ask, interrupting one hunter mocking his wife's requests for him to spend more time at home.

"I'll show you later," the Inheritor responds without looking at me. There's a warning behind his words that makes my hackles rise, but I keep my ire firmly leashed. He seems to check himself, for his face turns slightly toward me as he adds, "After the ceremony."

A low horn sounds across the room. Per lowers the instrument and steps aside for a flood of servants. The Inheritor's sycophants scatter with hasty farewells, while the servants clear all but our cups. One even takes the savn pup, who growls and yips as it's borne away.

The torches are extinguished and the light shrinks inward to a few oil lamps. With rustling robes and the scuff of calloused feet, priests and priestesses form up around the central hearth. Their shadows stretch over us like the spokes of a wheel, echoing the huge beams of the ceiling above.

As the room falls silent, they begin to chant. At first they beat a single drum and repeat the same, repetitive line in a round—an ode to a midwinter night, which they sing with increasing volume and melody until each voice severs into its own, unique lines. Harmonies and images wash over us, mournful and sweet and awed. They ebb and flow like Northern Lights, hush like frozen streams, and rush like snow on the wind. I feel it all, see it all, and my skin prickles.

The beauty of it takes me aback. Something of that surprise must be visible on my face, because the Inheritor leans in and murmurs, "Do your people not sing?"

I continue watching the priests. "Are the Duamel not my people too?"

He smiles, the subtle smile of someone with a secret they never intend to share. "You seem eager for this union, Thray."

Unsure of how much he's insinuating, I ward off the question with a shrug.

"Your Eangen lover may be displeased," the Inheritor comments, as the priests begin a second song. This one remembers my father, the rhythm of the seasons, and the blessing of his children.

"It's a pity," Attan goes on. "Havar is a fine hunter, one I'd value. Perhaps we can keep him close? If he'd consent. I'm sure that would comfort you, and I'm not the jealous kind."

Shocked, I stare at him and try to glean more information from his face, but my would-be husband's attention is on the priests.

I decide not to mince my words. "Are you suggesting I keep Havar as a lover?"

Attan sips his wine. "I said we."

Unease prickles up my spine. There's no chance Havar would agree to such an arrangement, even if I myself was at ease with it. Still I say, "I'll speak with him tonight."

"Good. Do that, then visit me in my chambers."

I twist to look at him with a raised brow.

He laughs, just low enough not to interrupt the priests' songs. "I've no intention of playing your husband until we're wed, Thray, and I hope you'll give me the same courtesy. After that? We'll make the best of things, I'm sure."

I almost feel a flash of... is that offense? I shouldn't care if this man wants me, but to be laughed aside is something else.

"You said you want to know how the savn are trained. Meet me at my chambers and I'll take you to them," Attan clarifies. "Presuming you aren't too tired? I sleep little."

I'm exhausted but push it aside. I've denied myself a hundred times in the last few days—what is one more? "I'll be there."

The Inheritor looks back to the priests. Goosebumps prickle across my skin, and I can't resist wrapping my arms across my chest as the priests bridge into a final song.

Finally, the feast ends. Guests and priests disperse, the Inheritor leaves without a word and, with a grim knot in my heart, I rise to find Havar.

THIRTY-ONE

I sink onto a fur-laden cushion in the Eangen's chamber as protests ring around me.

"They can't do this to you."

"This is ridiculous!"

"You're Iesa's priestess, you have to come home!"

I raise my eyes to Havar, whose own protests have faded. He stares at me with an agonized kind of disbelief, underlain with unfurling anger.

"Stop," I say with finality. My voice has far more impact than I intend, cracking out like a whip, and the Eangen fall silent. Fear and surprise flicker across their faces—all except Havar's—but my regret is brief. "Listen to me. This is not real."

"It better not be," Havar snaps, no trace of kindness or understanding in his words. "I've waited for you long enough, Thray. I won't do this. I won't be pushed aside and played with so you can curry favor with your siblings."

I swallow a surge of frustration. "Havar, you and I can… we'll speak later. I have to go meet Attan soon, but there's information you all need to know right now. Just listen to me."

Havar's expression still burns, but he doesn't interrupt again.

I lower my voice and, careful to speak only in Eangen, explain: "The Winterborn intend to invade Algatt and Eangen with the Inheritor's armies in the spring—two months. I've put myself in the best position to stop it. *That's* why I agreed to marry Attan."

Shock empties Seele's face, but Branan curses. "We told you!" He turns on the others, gesturing between Havar and himself. "We told you there were more warriors coming into the city, I told you"—he looks at Seele—"not to trust your 'friends,' not to—"

"Branan." Seele's shock has faded into a cool, high-browed glare. "Stop." Branan glowers at her.

Havar tells me in a more level voice, "There are newcomers in the city, billeted out into houses, but they're not refugees. Atmeltan is swelled to bursting. They said it was for a religious festival, but Branan and I suspected differently. They're warriors. I see the way they move, the way they watch us."

His words are hardly shocking, but cold seeps through me all the same. "Then your suspicions were well-founded."

Branan throws up his hands in exasperated satisfaction. "See?"

Darag ignores the younger man, looking to me. "Did you send an owl to warn Eangen?"

"Thvynder won't let this happen," Seele mutters, squaring her shoulders.

I shake my head, addressing Darag's question. "None answered my summons. I think the Winterborn have interfered with them. We must warn home ourselves."

"How?" Branan asks. "They won't let us leave, not now."

"They will let *you.*" I begin to pace, conscious of their eyes following my every movement. But instead of irritating me, as it once did, I feel stronger for it. I have their attention. "I'll insist the Inheritor send you home."

"He'll suspect you've told us about the invasion," Havar counters.

The coldness in his voice is a knife between my ribs. "Yes. So I will have him send you to Imel until the spring thaws. You'll be far too late to warn the Eangen. Seele, you've friends there? Work you can claim you must do?"

The other woman nods. "Dova will do anything for us. You saved his son."

The memory of my near drowning, of clutching the small boy in the frigid sea and pushing him back toward the surface, stirs in the back of my mind. But there's no fear to it anymore, no haze of terror at what might have been, or worry that it might happen again.

I have died. I have drowned. The water holds no terror for me anymore.

"Attan will have us killed as soon as we're out of sight of Atmeltan." Havar's voice clouds with the same dread we all feel. "He'd never risk us warning the Eangen."

"I will convince him," I reply, more coldly than I intend to. "Trust me in this. Then, once you're in Imel, escape and head south. Can you sail yourselves home, if you have a boat?"

Branan and Seele look at Havar and Darag.

"We can," Darag grunts. "So long as the southern river isn't fully iced over."

"We can go overland to the sea if we have to. There are small coastal settlements where we won't be recognized and can buy—or steal—a boat, if Dova can't secure us one," Seele puts in. "We can do it."

Darag grunts in unhappy assent and Branan nods slowly, but Havar isn't convinced.

"We're safer together. All of us." He somehow makes his concern sound accusatory. "What will you do alone?"

"I'll take another path," I say evasively.

"The Windwalkers will follow you," he reminds me. "Whatever path you take. They may follow us too, for that matter. All this is too risky."

"I'm going home," Darag declares, jaw tight. "If I have to walk every step alone, I will get to Sare and my children. How long do you think it will take Attan to chain us up if we stay here? We need to go now, while there's still a chance he'll be arrogant enough to ignore us."

I'm grateful for the big man's support. "He's right. As to the Windwalkers—I doubt they'll spare one for you, especially not once you're in Imel. Kygga will follow me, that's true. But I can lose him."

"How?" Branan asks, concern etched around his eyes.

I force a smile, though this is a part of my plan I've yet to iron out. "Let me worry about that. All we need to concern ourselves with now is making sure the Inheritor doesn't realize you know what he's planning."

"I'm not leaving you behind," Havar bites out.

"I have a plan." I soften my voice, drawing up the warmth that used to be between us. "It's not as if they can kill me."

That silences all of them except Branan. Standing straighter, he observes, "But they can trap you, and hurt you, and make you suffer."

"Now, that's unhelpful," I point out dryly, but my humor doesn't land. Havar looks at me as though he intends to physically stop me from going through with my plan, Seele's expression is overwhelmed and sad, and Darag looks past my shoulder as if the answer to all our problems is beyond the shuttered, curtained window.

I say, "I will be fine. You must trust me."

Havar finally begins to relent, though his resignation is a bitter, chilly thing. "It seems we have no choice."

Darag nods. Branan still doesn't look happy but he doesn't contradict me, and Seele's gaze slides around the room in a way as if she's already mentally packing.

"I'll convince the Inheritor to send you away," I reiterate, moving toward the door. "Be ready to go by morning."

The Inheritor leads me through the palace to a network of catacombs, separate from the bathing chambers.

I'm spent after my conversation with the Eangen, but I note every door, turn, and staircase as I follow him through the damp cool of the subterranean world. Our footsteps echo but beyond the occasional direction, the Inheritor doesn't speak. I sense anticipation from him. He wants to show me the savn—but to what end, I can't be sure.

Beyond a heavy door, yips and howls ripple up a passage toward us. The fine hairs prickle on the back of my neck and I brace. I know what's coming. My scars ache in preparation for it, and my fingers itch for my bone spear. But I'm fascinated too, determined to face the beasts who can no longer tear me from this world.

Light emanates from a series of cisterns, sunk into the earth—or, at least, what were once cisterns. Their rooves arch high above, domed like Duamel homes, and I see shuttered windows laid into them. With a shock, I realize these are the abandoned buildings beyond the training yards.

Now the cisterns and a network of tunnels serve as enclosures for beasts no human has any right to tame. There's a long central passage connecting them, each accessed by vaulted archways, and more tunnels lead off into the darkness. Further enclosures of wood and iron spread out beyond them, and their barred gates reveal pacing inhabitants.

Torches are studded here and there, but the light is hardly a comfort. It simply makes the savn's eyes glisten, and girds their shaggy, hulking forms in shadows.

"How did you do this?" I murmur, more than a little awed and unnerved.

"My affinity," Attan says.

I hesitate, unsure of what he means.

"I do not have Ogam's immortality, as you know," the man says. "My blood is too thin for that. But I am not completely devoid of power. It comes from my human bloodline, one of the many tribes that once roamed this land and became the Duamel. An influence over beasts. It's a subtle thing, not like the version some of your siblings possess. A mere affinity, as I said. Latent. Unobtrusive."

I look at him sharply. Some of my siblings possess a power over animals too?

"But as slight as it is, it has been of great use in this endeavor," Attan says, and waves his arm to encompass the entirety of a central chamber. "It allowed me to begin. And look where I am now."

Savn keepers in practical tunics, trousers, and light armor stand aside as we enter, bowing low. Other than the squat, shuttered windows, there are no openings, and no stairs or ladders to reach them by. These kennels can only be accessed through the tunnels.

But there must be another exit. One into the training yards, perhaps?

"Bring Nir," the Inheritor says to one of the keepers. She bows and vanishes through an archway. As she passes the iron bars on each cage, trapped savn rise to their feet, shifting or coming up to the bars. One growls, but the others simply watch without hostility.

The keeper vanishes around a bend and the Inheritor turns to me. "You've fought savn?"

"Many times."

"They are terrifying creatures," Attan says with reverence. "We'd never seen them before your 'Upheaval.' And when they arrived, they changed. They adapted, both in their appearance and their ways, within a handful of generations."

The keeper reappears, accompanied by a huge female savn. Her head is higher than the keeper's shoulders and her fur is streaked with white about her eyes and ears, down to the tip of her nose. It gives her broad face a distinctly angular appearance.

"Nir is the third generation of savn in my keeping," the Inheritor tells me. "They've adapted, you see. They learn, and they teach their pups subservience better than I ever could."

"You make them sound docile." I eye the beast. "I thought you intended them for war."

The savn's gaze sweeps Attan. She slows. Smiling at my words, the Inheritor steps forward and makes a gesture with his right hand— thumb tucked into his palm, fingers straight and rotating outward.

The savn shifts into something close to a bow. Without hesitation, the Inheritor strides up and, digging his fingers into the fur at the back of her neck, swings astride as easily as if he's mounting a horse. The keeper backs off, fading into the background as the Duamel always seem to do.

I stare at Attan and the beast. I can't help it. I've seen savn riders before but both Attan and the beast are so calm, it's jarring.

The savn unfolds back to her full height, but Attan barely sways and gives no sign of fear.

"We do have saddles, of a sort." The Inheritor speaks mildly, reaching forward to fondle the creature's ears. She bends her head back, leaning into his scratching. "But when I first began taming them, I always rode like this. Southerners are horsefolk, as I understand it?"

I nod, still captured by the image of Attan astride the savn—and the thought that perhaps I, too, could ride one of the beasts. I'm simultaneously terrified and elated. With that kind of power and speed… I might just be able to race the wind itself.

Distractedly, I add, "More so the Soulderni, but yes."

"Horses do not do well in an endless winter night," he tells me. "We have hardy ponies, as I'm sure you've seen. Some of them have survived. But the snow is difficult for any southern creature."

"Not the savn," I finish for him.

"No," he smiles, "not the savn. Soon, I'll have hundreds of riders in the field. By the end of my reign, they'll be revered throughout creation."

I remain silent.

Attan slips from the back of his beast and gestures to the keeper, who rematerializes from an archway and leads the beast away—again with a gesture of the hand, this time fingers outspread and rotated down like a spread fan. The savn falls into step without looking back.

"Will you teach me to ride?" I ask.

Attan's face breaks into a grin. "Not if you're this terrified."

I recoil a little. "I'm not terrified."

"Your body betrays you." He reaches out and takes one of my hands. At his touch, a shaking I hadn't known was there stills. He strokes his thumb over the back of my hand, feeling each bone and tendon, then lets it drop. "Some instincts are not easily overcome. But I'll teach you."

Surreptitiously, I flex my hand at my side and try to shake the memory of his touch. "Thank you."

Attan's attention shifts away from me. "We should both try to sleep now. The betrothal ceremony tomorrow will be long. And tedious. But it serves its purpose."

Something about his demeanor changes as we begin the long walk out of the kennels, back into the darkened tunnels, and up into the keep. He seems quieter, more thoughtful. Perhaps it's just the shadows, but he looks like a different man—a leader with burdens, rather than a young man with too much power.

"I have hope, Thray," he admits at the top of the staircase leading back into the keep. "For a world beyond the Winter Night. For the sun to rise on my people, and for them to no longer sicken and starve for reasons beyond our control. I will conquer the south. I will see my children rule summer lands before I die. But I do not do this out of selfishness. I want you to know that."

Though he's talking about conquering my homeland, his tone and manner resonates with me. I believe him. But even if his motives aren't entirely corrupt, my siblings' are.

"Then you are a better leader than I anticipated," I say, hoping I sound coy instead of rude.

A smile quirks the corner of his lips, and the burdened ruler is gone. His hand rests on the door latch. "Ah, I hardly blame you. Sometimes I surprise myself."

He pushes the door open and we slip into the light and warmth of the keep's corridors. He starts off toward his chambers and I glance the other way, toward mine.

"Attan," I call after him.

He glances back.

"Send the Eangen away," I say, though the words taste sour on my tongue. "It's best if they're not here, given what's coming. I won't put them at risk, and I need them out of sight. Send them to Imel tomorrow. Please."

Attan watches me for a long, quiet moment. "Havar didn't take well to your proposal?"

I shake my head, and allow a fraction of real pain to show on my face. "No."

I catch one last flicker of that other man behind Attan's eyes. Weighty. Reserved. Hidden.

"You've told them of the invasion?" he asks.

"No," I reply earnestly. "I wouldn't put them at risk like that, and I don't want… They would despise me if I told them. I don't want them to know. They can't know. Send them away, please."

He makes a considering sound, face half-hidden in the shadows. "That seems profoundly unwise."

"Ask anything of me, and I'll give it. If you do this."

Attan glances back at me, gaze assessing. There is a long moment of silence, distant threads of voices the only thing to be heard.

"You will owe me four favors, one for each of their lives. Four things that, when I ask them of you, they must be done without question. I may ask them tomorrow. I may ask them in twenty years, or even on my deathbed. But you will grant them to me."

I let out a long, slow breath. Dread raises gooseflesh on my skin and cinches around my lungs, but I nod.

"Good." Attan inclines his head in return. "I'll arrange a sledge for tomorrow. Tell them to be ready by noon."

"Will you give me your word they'll be safe, and unharmed?" I venture. I sound more tentative than I feel, but that's intentional.

"You have my word, on Winter's grave. And I have yours?"

I sift through his solemn tone and the tired lines of his body for any deception. I find none. "On my long life, I swear."

He makes a satisfied sound and starts off down the corridor again, glancing back at me in the half-light of the lamps. "Goodnight, Thray."

"Goodnight, Attan."

THIRTY-TWO

I return to my rooms and sit in the quiet for a long, tense moment before there's a scratch at the curtain to the Eangen quarters.

"Come in."

Havar pushes the heavy fabric aside. He's shirtless under an open kaftan, his hair pulled back in a simple knot.

"What did Attan say?" His voice is somehow empty and rife with accusation all at once.

"He'll send you to Imel and vows you'll be safe. Then it's up to you, and Seele and her friends." The words feel flimsy, and our plans brittle as old bones. My chest is tight, burdened with an ever-increasing weight. "Havar, I don't want this."

He holds my gaze for a moment, then steps into the room and lets the curtain fall closed. He comes over to the bed and sits beside me. And though I could touch him if I reached out my hand, the gulf between us feels vast.

"You will never marry me," he says, and it's not a statement, not a question.

My heart staggers in my chest. I don't want to talk about this now. I need a clear head. I need to stay focused on my next steps.

But he needs to have this conversation. I see it in his face, and in the tension in his shoulders and around his eyes.

I swallow my own desires and speak the words I've never dared to say before, not so plainly. I've hinted at it, danced around it. But now I lay the truth bare.

"I can't watch you grow old and die, Havar. Watch you fade while I stay young. I can't watch our children die, either."

The silence that falls is that of a funeral pyre—thick, deep, and overwhelming.

"I can't ask you to, then." He says the words as if this is a truth he's long prepared himself for. "The road ahead of you is… it will be lonely, I imagine. But my love for you hasn't changed. I'm willing to—"

"Don't." I try to hold my tongue, but my next confession rattles out of its own accord. "Don't love me, Havar. Thvynder didn't send me here. I lied. I don't even know if there's a place for me back in Eangen. I don't know what the priesthood will do. I told you we'd been sent by our God and it was a *lie*."

Without a word, Havar stands. He goes back to the curtain leading to the other chambers and puts a hand on the doorframe, steadying himself before he looks back at me. There is little surprise in his eyes, and what is there is muted, dull.

I catch my breath. Did he already know?

"What will they do to you?" he asks. "If you go home?"

If. That small word cuts me to the bone.

"Atonement will have to be made," I admit. My whole self revolts against this topic and I want to physically draw back, not to speak of it, but I can no longer ignore it. Perhaps if I can convince Havar that my fate doesn't terrify me, I can convince myself too. "But they cannot kill me."

He slowly shakes his head in disbelief. "Can't or won't? I may not be a priest, but I know what the White Lake did to your father."

A chill creeps over me. "They wouldn't," I say, but I hear the hitch in my own voice. Until the revelation that a Windwalker had overheard my useless prayers to Thvynder and learned of the God's absence, perhaps that was true.

But matters are different now. Not only have I lied and dragged four Eangen into my deception, I've handed our enemies the greatest secret the priesthood held. The tinder for invasion had already been laid, but I'd been the spark to ignite it.

"Hessa is my aunt," I protest, reminding myself of this as much as him. "My uncle is the Shepherd of the Dead. Vistic *is* Thvynder, in a way. They wouldn't…"

"So you think favoritism will save you?" Havar huffs a ragged laugh. "Even if they let you live they will exile you, Thray. They will send you away. You knew all this when you left and you…" He rakes a hand over his face, trying to compose himself. "I didn't want to believe it. I don't want to believe it."

I stare at him, thoughts of the White Lake and exile colliding with the implication of his words. "What?"

"Part of me hoped it wasn't true but… You truly risked everything, your place in the priesthood, your home, *our* future, for this? For *them*?"

I'm a confusion of defensiveness and shock. I stare, and I'm horrified when tears prickle at my eyes.

"You knew?" I manage. "All along?"

"Suspected. Feared." His smile is brittle, and a little nostalgic. "I wanted to marry the most influential woman in Iesa. I fell in love with her. And when part of me whispered that she was lying, I didn't mind, because I told myself I'd do anything to be with her and have that future I wanted for us. I trusted you not to put us at risk without… without a plan, a way out."

"H-how?"

"I saw the way you looked at Siru on the beach, that first day. I know you." He stares past me, past the bed and the stone walls. "You don't realize how much you show on your face, Thray. I saw your guilt that night by the altar in Iesa. And I saw your hunger."

"You came anyway?" I manage. "Does Darag…"

"No one else knows. And yes, I came anyway. I wasn't about to lose you, even if your lying infuriated me." His jaw flexes. "I thought you'd be worth it. I thought, by being with you, I could keep you from sinking in this… other world. I thought I'd be an anchor for you, but you wouldn't let me. You abandoned us."

A tidal wave rises in my chest, cresting and about to break. This is it. This is the end. Yet a small voice inside me whispers that this was inevitable. Right, even.

"I'm sorry," I say, though it feels vague and half-false, and I can't find the edges of it. I'm sorry and resigned, relieved and heartbroken all at once.

Havar's hand slips from the doorframe to his side. His smile is tighter now, emotion getting the better of him. "I hope the priesthood is merciful, Thray. Thank you for interceding with Attan. I'll do everything in my power to get us back to Iesa."

Us. Darag, Seele, and Branan. But not me. And for some reason, that's when tears prick at my eyes.

He lets the curtain fall closed behind him. I watch the heavy fabric sway, the curves of its shadows shifting across the floor. For a sparse moment, I let myself feel. I let myself grieve and ache and regret and fear, freely and uncontrollably.

But when the curtain stills, I do too. Breath by breath, I pull composure into my body and set my gaze firmly on the door to the hallway. Then I rise, pull on my hood, and leave the keep.

In the Temple of the Sleepers, I sit on the side of one of the beds in my undertunic as Rana lights the brazier and sets a bronze bowl over the coals. She adds oil and herbs and, after a long stretch of quiet, they begin to steam. Without looking up at me, the other priestess grinds more ingredients in a mortar, then sprinkles them in.

"You are sure you were not followed?" Rana asks quietly.

I nod. I glimpsed silver on the wind on my way here, but heading away from me. There are many Winterborn here in the city for the betrothal, and Kygga does not follow my every movement. Yet.

"Then please, lie down." Rana gestures to one of the beds in its alcove. Sweat prickles across my skin but I pull a light blanket over myself, a thin barrier of protection as nerves skitter up my spine. My eyes burn from the unspent emotion of my conversation with

Havar and dread of my punishment, but as I settle back in the bed, the pain eases.

I've purpose, for now. A task to perform.

Rana pulls the curtain closed and fastens it on both sides of the alcove.

The smoke from the brazier begins to fill the small chamber. My instinct is to breathe shallowly but I resist, deepening my breaths and letting my belly round with each inhale.

The smell, taste, and feel of the smoke fills my senses. It's heavy and oddly humid, making me feel as though I can't get enough air, and I instantly feel dizzy. It reminds me of the basin with the hot springs, where Arune tried to let the wolves blood me.

I shift myself deeper into the bed and close my eyes. I've endured the spiritual transition into the High Halls before, at my ordination.

There's no danger, I assure myself. *No reason to be afraid.*

This is Fate.

I hear the rustle and tap of a loom, offsetting the beat of my laboring heart. I feel my spirit begin to drift in and out of my bones as the widow root lures me into a smothering haze.

For a time, my pulse and the loom are all I hear. Then, one by one, other sounds slip in—my nervous breaths, the rush of the wind, the rustle of reeds.

I feel cold rock and grit beneath my bare feet. I force my eyes open and find myself standing on a stone plain, punctuated by folds in the rock where water collects and plants have managed to root. It's not winter here, instead, the air is cool with summer fog. It shrouds the landscape, thick and heady, but I spy the glow of an eerie, muffled moon to one side.

I frown. Fog is the High Halls' natural defense against those who don't belong within its borders—namely, living, natural humans. But with my bloodline and Thvynder's blessing, it should dispel for me. So why hasn't it? Is the Sleepers' drug to blame, or is Fate doing this?

I begin to walk in the direction I think will take me to the loom. The soles of my feet pass from cold stone to crunchy, flaking lichen, then to cool, damp moss. The latter gathers where the sheets of rock have cracked or thrust up against one another, and it feels like home.

All at once, the sound of the loom surrounds me. I settle my feet into one patch of soft, springy growth and look up into the mist. Moisture prickles across my exposed skin and I resist the urge to wipe it away.

There's no doubt in my mind now. Eirine is Fate. They're one and the same.

"Goddess Fate, I am here and I am listening," I say.

My own voice whispers back to me, the words altered, "I listen."

I shift, unsure what to do. Am I being mimicked, or is Fate telling me to speak?

I venture a question. "What is the Winter Night?"

My own voice responds again, sourceless and surrounding. "They brought it upon themselves, Ogam's Get. The cold and the weeping, and the beasts in the shadows."

The words come with threads of feelings and wisps of memory— no, not memory, foresight. I see a rising sun and a priest in a Sleeper's robes, slipping through a forgotten tomb. I see him stand before the keep in Atmeltan, take up a great, carved hunting horn, and put it to his lips. He blows a long, strident call, so mournful and full I feel it in my chest. And as the last notes fade, the sky begins to lighten.

The same events play in reverse. The sun fades, the horn lowers and is tucked away, back onto a pedestal in a darkened cave, which I know well. Darkness and winter encompass the land once more.

I see the Duamel weep. I see their fear and grief as the seasons refuse to change, the snows do not melt and the savn multiply. I see swords tucked away, spears gathering dust under beds and forges gone dark.

The vision fades. I stand in the moss again, surrounded by fog and hush, and I understand what I've seen with a simple clarity. The horn was what lay on the pedestal in the Tomb of the Old Gods. The Sleepers did take it, and when it's blown, the Winter Night will be broken.

"But who made the Winter Night to begin with?" I ask. "You say they brought—"

"—it upon themselves, Ogam's Get," my own voice replies, disembodied and repeating the exact words it said earlier. "The cold and the weeping, and the beasts in the shadows."

"It was punishment?" I press, though I know I can't linger on this topic much longer. I've no idea how long I have here. "From whom?"

The same answer repeats a third time, and when the last word fades, I venture a new question. "Where is Thvynder?"

No words come to me then, but I perceive a distant thunder. It reminds me of falling asleep with my head on my mother's chest, and feeling the rumble of her voice beneath her ribs as she told me stories.

"Beyond," my voice says from the mist.

"When will they return?"

"When they return."

I clench my fists in a wave of frustration. "We need them."

Your people need you, a new, voiceless voice says. *Protect them.*

I inhale sharply, trepidation clashing with joy. Thvynder. The new voice is Thvynder.

Until that moment, I have not realized how deeply my God's absence has burdened me. Now, I feel a wash of consolation. Strength and assurance comes with it—a lost child returned to their mother's embrace.

But Thvynder's words make me want to retreat, and not just because of my lies and deception. I feel a wave of immense responsibility, so heavy I feel as though I'm being crushed.

My people need me. *My people.*

"How can I help them?" I ask. "I'm only one person."

There is no response, either in my own voice or Thvynder's. I feel my God's presence fade, leaving me alone with Fate. But Thvynder has spoken. I have my answer. My purpose.

I'm a Vynder priestess, and I've a responsibility to the Eangen regardless of my immortality. Whether or not I can bear watching them die, whether or not I'll face terrible repercussions upon my return, I must fight for them. Fight, and hope for mercy.

I swallow a knot of unsorted emotion and level my chin.

"When will Thvynder return?" I ask again.

I taste embers on the wind and glimpse a dead ash tree in a winter evening, as the light of the setting sun slips from its face and fades over the western horizon. Foxfire ignites in the newborn darkness, tracing every line of the ash, every crack in its bark and division of barren branches. The glowing tree fills the eastern sky, and unbroken emptiness lies beyond: the edge of the world, the border of creation.

The vision fades. I hesitate, unnerved, but Fate's visions aren't known for being immediately coherent.

Or perhaps I'm simply asking the wrong questions. There are many things I could ask Fate, but I doubt the deity will appreciate an unending list of inquiries.

One by one my questions fall away until the last and most personal remains. But it sticks to my tongue, and it takes a great effort to force it out into the misty air.

"When will I die?"

The mist eddies. I think that, again, Eirine will not respond, then I taste water on my tongue. I feel it in my lungs and nose—a vision so clear, so real, that I suppress the urge to panic. I'm drowning again. I know the feeling well and the memories, the instincts it summons—

I draw clean, moist air into my lungs, reassuring myself, but the vision doesn't end. I'm still underwater. I see my hands before my face, blurred by water thick and white. There are scars on them, and the little finger on one hand is missing.

I float in the White Lake. My final escape.

My fated end.

The vision begins to fade. I hear a voice I distantly recognize as Rana's, hushed and urgent, followed by another, deeper female tone. With shock, I realize it's Per's, the chief priestess of the Diviners.

"... as the army leaves..." Per murmurs. "They're speaking of spring."

"I can keep it hidden," Rana replies firmly. "I'll be ready. We all will."

There's a moment of quiet and a rustle of robes. When Per speaks again, there's fondness in her voice, and the firm warmth of imparted courage. "The sun will rise," she murmurs.

"The sun will rise," Rana murmurs back with a smile in her voice.

Drug-induced haze wraps around me again. Disembodied and unanchored, I drift, unable to focus until I feel cold, bitter air rush into my lungs. I hear Rana's and Per's voices again, but their words are blurred.

My curtain flutters in a cool draft as Per slips out the main door, and I glimpse Rana in the center of the chamber, a bundle in her hands. With a flutter of surprise, I recognize it as the same one the Sleeper priest took from the chamber below the tombs of the Old Gods. A gilded rim slips out from the edges of its wrap.

Rana notices the rim too. With reverence she uncovers the item halfway and holds a horn toward a lamp. Light traces across inlays of silver and a delicate array of engravings, but they're too distant for me to make out the details.

The temple door closes, the draft subsides, and my curtain falls back into place. Ensconced once more in privacy I sit up and pull on my clothes, making no effort to hide the sound of my waking. By the time I push the curtain aside myself, Rana sits by the fire, and there's no sign of the bundled horn.

It seems that the Sleepers have their part to play in the coming days, as I have mine. So I do not mention the horn, or the conversation I overheard.

"Did you see what you hoped to?" Rana asks.

"More." I step out into the room with one hand on the wall, prepared for lingering dizziness, but there is none. "Thank you."

She nods and watches as I pull on my hood and mittens. She hides her secrets well, but I sense tension about her, and when I move to leave, her relief is palpable.

"The sun will rise," I say, just before I slip out the door.

Rana's face pales in sudden fear, then fades into tentative understanding. "The sun will rise," she promises.

THIRTY-THREE

At dawn, I stand by as the Eangen throw their packs onto a sledge on the ice-locked river. Duamel move around us, loading goods, saying goodbyes, and casting my people and I furtive glances.

Seele embraces me. Darag wraps a gruff arm around my shoulders and hugs me. He must know what transpired between Havar and I the night before—I see it in his eyes when he looks between his brother and me—but he doesn't seem to hold it against me. At least not now, at the moment of our parting.

Havar himself says nothing as he climbs into the sledge. I try not to let my eyes linger on him—or to feel the ache lancing across my chest.

Branan is the most understanding. Before he climbs onto the sledge he takes my forearm in a firm grip and meets my gaze.

"Be safe," he charges me, then adds in a lower voice, "for what it's worth, I know this is the best way forward."

My control almost cracks then. I squeeze his arm in return.

"Whatever happens, you'll always have a friend in me," he promises.

Then he lets go. He climbs up as the Duamel drivers check the harnesses on the horses, brightly painted tack jingling in the crisp, cold air.

Despite my resolve, I look to Havar to find him looking at me. A long, pained moment passes, and though a dozen placating promises leap onto my tongue, some comfort to leave him with, he reacts first.

He smiles. It's thick with regret and sadness, but it's also gentle. And I know that it's as close to forgiveness as I can hope for.

The drivers call out, the locals scatter, and the horses begin to move with a stamp of hooves and a clink of tack.

I retreat to the shoreline and watch until the sledge is swallowed up by the snow.

The first two days pass in nerve-fraying tension. I can't execute my plan until Havar and the others arrive in Imel and have time to contact Seele's friends, but I'm left guessing over timing, and increasingly agitated.

I sit with Attan each evening while his court feasts. He and the hunters laugh and recount events I've no knowledge of. I see little of Per or other Diviners, and when I do glimpse the Duamel High Priestess, she's detached. If Rana has mentioned me to her, she gives no sign of it, so I follow her lead and do not interact. I can't risk exposing her allegiances.

Kygga is his usual quiet, uncouth self, but he notices my tension.

"You'll get over Havar," he tells me on the second day as we walk to the main chambers for another of Attan's feasts. "Train with me tonight, after dinner. It will do you good."

And so I do. For three days after that I train with Kygga, drawing on his centuries of expertise and storing each tip, each tactic and refinement away for the battle to come. The battle against him.

Finally, on the fifth day, I can bear the waiting no longer. I pace my bedchamber until the keep falls quiet for the night and gather my possessions before the door to the neighboring now-empty quarters. If I hold my breath, I can still imagine that I hear Darag snoring, Seele stoking the fire, and Havar calling my name.

But they're gone.

Within the hour, I intend to be too.

A savn growls, low in her chest. I freeze, crouched inside one of the den's long, short windows, just beyond the training ground. My braids flutter in the draft of the open shutters, but the breeze does little to mask the stink of the beasts—damp, blood, earth, and shit.

The den spreads out below me, with its passages and enclosures. The tops of the walls form a network of footpaths from my vantage point, and it's those I intend to take to my destination.

Carefully, I pull the shutters closed behind me. The cold, clean draft cuts off and I lower myself down toward the top of the nearest wall. My shoulders and arms strain, supporting not just my own weight but the weight of my pack, weapons, and heavy winter garb. Then my boots land lightly on the top of the nearest wall. The skirt of my kaftan rustles and something in my pack clacks, the only sounds in the sudden silence of the pit.

In the enclosure beside me, the pregnant female savn eyes me from a darkened corner, glinting eyes narrowed and belly still swollen with pups. I'd considered involving her in my plan tonight, but one look tells me she's in no condition for flight.

I scan the other enclosures. One has a huge male, his bristling fur black and gray and his paws twice the size of my skull. He looks calm, pacing in the dim light, but I disregard him too.

I travel along the tops of the walls until I find Nir, the beast Attan introduced me to not long ago. Stocky and muscular, she paws over and looks up at me, head cocked to one side.

My courage flags for the space of one, thin breath, then I speak.

"Nir," I say, trying to sound as calm and commanding as Attan had. I may not have the power that allowed him to begin taming these beasts years ago, but neither do the savn keepers.

I drop down on the outside of her cage and look at her through the bars, holding my breath against the fear and the stink.

The savn retreats a step, eyeing me. I resist the instinct to do the same and instead hold out my hand, praying she doesn't smell the blood thundering through my skull. If she doesn't obey me as she did the Inheritor and the keeper, if her instincts take over...

I snap my fingers and make the gesture Attan did. Nir backs off another step, then stops, watching my hands for another prompt.

Relief makes me shaky.

"All right, monster," I murmur. I slowly lift the latch on the barred doors and open it wide. "Are you ready to run?"

Nir grumbles, low in her chest, and I swear she sounds pleased. She holds still as I slip into her enclosure, dig my fingers into the thick hair across her shoulder blades and, with one leap, land on her back.

For an instant I wonder if I should have taken the time to find a saddle. But the space behind her massive shoulders is oddly cradling, and her fur is as thick as a blanket. It brushes my legs as she shuffles, the pair of us adjusting to one another, and I tighten my thighs. The feel of her muscles flexing and the smell of her, so close, is a truly terrifying thing.

But it's also exhilarating.

Leaning down, I murmur in the Divine Tongue, "We need to leave the city as quickly as we can, but quietly too."

She huffs, but lower than before—almost as if she understands the need for stealth.

I pause. Perhaps she truly does. The Divine Tongue, after all, is universally understood, and the savn are descended from creatures that escaped the High Halls. Who knows what blood is in their veins?

"Do you understand me?"

She turns her massive head to look at me and bares her teeth in an impatient growl.

"Right, I'll take that as a yes." I shift my legs, pinning them as I might on a horse, and bury both hands into the scruff of her neck. "Then go. Outside."

Nir slips through the tunnels with ease. We pass no guards, no keepers at this time of night, and when a rising tunnel ends in a heavy, iron-studded gate, I open it without hinderance.

Nir and I emerge into the practice yards behind the keep. Between my entering the den and leaving again, it's begun to snow—thickly enough that I suspect my grandfather has a hand in it.

"Are you here?" I murmur to the drifting flakes. "Can I rely on your help tonight?"

The flakes swirl against my cheeks in affirmation, and my tension eases. This can work. This *will* work.

The snow muffles Nir's footfalls as we stalk through the veil of white, making for the back gate I noted while watching the Duamel train.

The guards on the walls topple at a hiss of my Winterborn magic. I'm careful not to kill them—no blood-mist blooms in the night. But they won't rise soon, either.

One topples all the way off the wall and lands at our side with a clank of armor and puff of snow, then all is quiet.

Nir waits, poised, as I slip down and unbolt the gate. I open it with a soft creak, grateful that the servants have recently cleared the snow, and beckon to Nir. She prowls through, nose to the ground, and stops on the other side to look out over the cliff's edge.

As I start to close the gate my gaze snags on the toppled warrior. His helmet is askew, over one eye, and his tall shield fallen to one side.

In a burst of inspiration, I take the shield and sling it over my back, adjusting my bow and quiver so they're still accessible. The shield isn't light, but if any guards farther down the wall decide to loose arrows at my back, I'll be protected.

I close the gate behind us.

Nir doesn't flinch as I mount up again, bow and shield clinking. Her gaze is still out over the cliff. What is she looking at? The view is obscured, but the weight of it is there—a sense of great emptiness, of vastness and...

A flicker of silver on the wind. Kygga?

I drive my heels into Nir's sides. "Run!"

The animal leaps—not down the switchbacking trail that laces away from the gate, but straight off the cliff. I swallow a scream. Snowflakes lash my face and my body lifts from Nir's back, thighs slipping, feet scrabbling. We're falling, and all I can do is dig my fingers into her fur and hold on.

She lands with a sliding thud and a burst of snow on the steep mountainside. My bow, shield, and pack clatter, dragging at my shoulders. The breath is knocked out of me, but Nir is unbothered.

She runs. She leaps down the mountainside with the surety of a goat, simultaneously thrilling and terrifying. I don't have the air in my lungs to shout. I can barely open my eyes. Tears drag across my frozen skin and bury in my hair.

"Thray!" Kygga's shout is all around me, twined with the roar of wind in my ears. "Thray, stop!"

I couldn't if I wanted to. Nir's descent is controlled madness—all I know is cold, starving lungs and the erratic slam of my heart.

Then Nir lands on even ground with a coiling of muscles and a victorious, bone-chilling roar. I cling low, face buried in her ruff.

"South!" I shout, though it comes out as a panting growl, and tug Nir right.

A gust of air grabs at me, and I swear it's Kygga's hands. But Nir moves so fast, his grip is formless, ineffectual—and even when the wind turns to torrents, buffeting me and howling in my ears, she does not stop running.

She doesn't stop when the snow ceases and the night clears into a bone-cracking cold and pale, colorless Northern Lights. She doesn't stop when Kygga materializes ahead of us, body braced and sword extended. His hair is wild and he bellows a wordless challenge—a beast in his own right. But then one of my white arrows sprouts from his shoulder, he tears it out, and vanishes. Nir thunders over the space where he stood, and I don't miss the shimmer of silvered blood in the snow.

Over frozen rivers and lakes, the savn runs. I feel the muffled, hollow thud of her footsteps on the ice in my bones. Over flat, snow-swept plains she flies with what I can only imagine as a lifetime of captivity burning through her veins. And in no time at all, the mountains to the south-east of Atmeltan close in upon us. I'd laugh at how wonderfully my plan is working, if Kygga wasn't still on the wind—a flash of silver dust.

I try to turn Nir farther west, intending to round the mountains and head south along the coast, but will we even get that far? The beast must tire eventually, and then Kygga will be upon us.

"We have to lose him!" I shout to the beast, though in her frenzy, I'm not sure how much her taming still holds sway.

"Thray, don't do this." Kygga's voice pleads, and I hear the pain in it. "You won't escape. Midvyk has caged your owls, and the journey to Eangen over land will take weeks. Stop, now."

So that's where the owls went. I'd suspected as much but confirmation is harsh, a stab of isolation and betrayal.

"You won't stop me," I snap.

"That beast is tiring." My brother's voice is right beside my ear now, soft and warning, and at the same time I feel the change in Nir—less power in her leaps, the growing rasp of her pants, the sweat-slick fur under my fingertips. "Will you truly fight me, Thray?"

I curse at him in response, and with the curse comes power. His presence shudders but does not fade, a silver streak on our heels as the high walls of a mountain valley soar around us.

The snow grows deeper. Nir diverts out of the valley and up onto a narrow ridge that might have once been a road, when the world still knew springs and summers. She barrels through small trees that shudder and dislodge their heavy mantles of white. I brush my face clear on one shoulder and blink just in time to see Kygga materialize in the path ahead of us.

I start to reach for my bow, but Nir's movements are growing ever more labored. I almost slip and barely keep my seat.

"Stop!" Kygga shouts.

Nir slides to a halt before my brother. Her body shudders with great, raking breaths and her head sags, her energy spent.

I slip from her back and land in snow up to my thighs. I curse, gripping her fur for balance, then pivot to face Kygga.

He watches me struggle, a shadow of pity in his eyes. "Thray, this is useless. I'll follow you wherever you go. If we fight, I will win."

My power surges in my throat, ready and eager to prove him wrong. But I bite my tongue. Despite his betrayal, despite his condescension and his lies, there's still a tie between us. That tie isn't just his footprints, breaking up the snow on our long journey to the Barrow of Winter. It's not how he cared for me after the wolves attacked. It's that when I look at his face now, hair wild and dusted with snow, I see our father.

"Then help me," I say, though even as the words leave my mouth, I know it's futile. "This isn't right, Kygga. You're not heartless. You're not a fool, either. Thousands of Duamel will die invading Eangen, and peace will not come swiftly. You and the Winterborn—yes, you'll survive. But what of *them*?"

I pause, letting my question and its reality sink in before I continue: "Let me go. Let me warn the Eangen, at least. Better yet—come with me."

Kygga's eyes have a glitter to them—at first, I think it's fury, then I see his clenched hands tremble at his sides. One reaches across his waist, and he draws his sword.

At my side, Nir lets out a low growl. I soften my grip on her fur and shuffle forward to peer into her huge face.

"Go on," I tell her. "I don't want him to kill you. Please, go."

She stares back at me for an instant, then heads back the way we came. Soon, she's little more than a shadow, marked by jostled trees and cascades of snow. Then she's gone.

I shrug off my pack, along with my shield and bow and quiver. I move carefully, watching for any hint that Kygga will take advantage of my distraction, but he does not.

"Grandfather," I murmur under my breath. "Grandfather, are you still close? I'll need you, soon."

A tendril of wind brushes my cheek, full of the taste of frost, and my stomach stirs in fear.

I draw my knife, flick it out into a sword, and face Kygga. "Break."

Kygga flinches back, braced for the power of my attack, but it doesn't come.

There is a crack from high, high up the slope above us. It reverberates through the valley more times than I can count, sending birds to sudden flight from the forest below.

Kygga stares at me, all color leached from his face. Then, in a flash of wind and silver dust he's before me, grabbing my sword arm by the wrist.

"What have you done?"

THIRTY-FOUR

A rumbling begins, shuddering through the snow beneath us and the air around us.

Kygga looks up the mountain and begins to back away.

At first I see nothing, then a disturbance on the upper slopes catches my eye. It moves like water in the moonlight, gathering and tumbling and spreading. The shivering of the ground doubles, the trees around us shed snow like shaking dogs, and I know there's no escape. I'm not Kygga. I'm not the wind. No matter what direction I run, no matter how fast I sprint, there is no outrunning this fate.

Unless Grandfather comes for me.

"I'll find you," Kygga shouts, dragging my wide eyes back to him. There's no threat in his words now, just a promise, and it almost consoles me. He's pale in the moonlight, glancing from me to the oncoming tide. "I *will* find you."

I smile sadly.

The expression gives him pause, but only for a moment. He presses three fingers to his forehead in a Duamel salute and vanishes. And despite all that's transpired between us, his absence opens a well of fear in me.

"I cannot die," I whisper to myself, watching the avalanche spread across the entirety of the mountain wall. The cold air shudders in my lungs and I'm on the brink of pissing myself, but I repeat the words like a prayer. "I cannot die. Grandfather is close and I will not die."

The roar and tremor of the avalanche fills my senses. I bite my lips to stifle a scream, but as the last line of trees between me and the snow vanishes in a mudslide of churning, groaning white, I can't silence myself any longer.

I scream a challenge as the wave swallows me whole.

I awaken to the crackle of a fire. My eyelids are leaden and my senses drift. Slowly, unhurriedly, I sift through my memories. They're piecemeal and vague, more feelings than facts. It takes time before I find one that stirs me into full wakefulness: the avalanche roaring toward me, and Kygga'a hand on my wrist.

I will find you.

Opening my eyes, all I see is a blur of firelight and walls of ice. An ice cave. I try to reach for my knife, but my entire body screams in pain.

I must have screamed aloud too, because someone crouches over me. I try for my knife again and gain a little movement, but when my fingers scrabble at my belt, the blade is gone.

I pant and blink in a mad flutter of lashes, trying to clear my vision.

"Hush." A big hand presses down into the center of my chest, holding me gently to the ground. No, not ground—layers of cedar boughs. They tickle at my bare hands and neck, and their scent surrounds me. "You will worsen your injuries."

I know this voice. The fight leaves me in one pained breath. "Grandfather," I wheeze. "You came."

The hand lifts and this time when I blink again, his face becomes a little clearer. Snow-white skin. Pale beard and hair, unbraided but smooth. His iceberg eyes search my face, ensuring my submission isn't a trick, then he sits back onto his heels.

"I feared you were Kygga," I manage.

"He still searches for you in the valley." Winter rests his hands on his thighs. He wears trousers and tunic in various shades of gray, with a heavy cloak and sashed waist. "You may go on your way unchallenged, once you heal."

My relief is thin. "I don't have time to heal. I must warn the

Eangen." My mind is moving faster now, and multiple realizations hitting me at once. "Can you go to Eangen for me? Can you send the wind to Hessa or—"

"Thray." Winter subdues my rambling questions with a calm, level look. "There is more happening in this world, and I am not everywhere at once, even if there is snow on the ground. You have your role to play, with Fate's guiding hand. I have mine."

"What is your role?" I sit up, slowly and painfully. Every muscle feels torn and my head aches, but I manage it.

"The Winter Night." He looks directly into my eyes, and I could swear he's never truly looked at me before. "Too long I've left my grandchildren to sully the north and abuse its people. I will help ensure Fate's worshipers lift the shadows."

Half-formed suspicions worm through my belly. "Didn't you create the night to begin with? To punish the Winterborn?"

"No. The Winterborn created it themselves to control the Duamel. Their power over the people waned after Ogam died, so they needed a new tool, a new reason for the Duamel to need them—and convince them to leave their homeland, helping them exact vengeance on the Algatt and Eangen."

Cool betrayal slips over my skin. "How is that possible? They're powerful but... to do something like that?"

"The Tomb of the Old Gods." Winter glances at the fire as a log collapses with a crackle, rush, and plume of sparks. "You've seen the Duamel's drums, the ones made by your sisters? It is the same magic— magic gathered and placed into an object. They took the lingering magic of the Old Gods, left in the tombs, twisted it, and bound it to an object of their creation."

"A horn." The pieces come together as I speak. I distantly recall Arune listing other instruments the sisters had made, and that there was a horn among them. Did Arune know what that horn had been for? Did Kygga?

"The Sleepers took it from the tombs," I tell my grandfather. "It's in

Atmeltan, with the Sleeper priestess Rana. The Diviner High Priestess, Per, is working with them."

Winter inclines his head in understanding. "Which is why I must go to Atmeltan, to protect and aid them against your siblings."

"If you lift the Winter Night now, perhaps the war can be avoided entirely."

Winter shakes his head. "It will take time to unlock the horn's power. Your siblings are not fools, and it is not without its safeguards. But more than that, the Sleepers need the opportunity that the Winterborn's departure will bring. They are not strong enough to face the Winterborn, the Inheritor, and the Diviners at once. When the armies are beyond Duamel borders, we will lift the night and seize control."

"So this is a play for power." I look at my grandfather more critically. "You rarely bother with humans, Grandfather. Why do this? Why back the Sleepers?"

"Because the Winterborn are my blood," he replies, and the sound of his voice resonates in the ice all around us. "Their wrongs are mine. Ogam's wrongs are mine; he claimed the Duamel, then abandoned them to the machinations of his power-drunk children. So, I will atone."

The weight of his vow settles on me, startling and unexpected. "So you'll let the Eangen be slaughtered, just to give the Duamel an opportunity to rise up?"

Winter looks at me levelly. "The Eangen are your task."

I bristle. "That's selfish, Grandfather. You're powerful enough to face the Winterborn in Duamel. Lift the night now and help—"

"I am not," my grandfather states. "If the battle is fought in Atmeltan, the Sleepers will be annihilated and I will be bound."

I stare at him, aghast. "That's not possible."

His chin drifts to one side quizzically. "Did you not see the tombs of the Old Gods? The White Lake where Thvynder was held? There is great power and cunning in this world, and even the most formidable of beings can be brought low."

Perhaps he has a point. "Then… You said this is my task. Why? I can warn the Eangen, I can fight, but I'm not enough. And after what I've done, *I'm* the one they'll bind, Grandfather."

The thought makes me shiver. All at once, the cave around me feels like my own barrow of ice.

"What they do to you is a question for tomorrow. You are a Winterborn, Thray, and you've power none of them possess." He still watches me as he speaks, and I can't look away. I can barely breathe. "For years I protected you from that power. I stopped your blooding and diverted the Winterborn's gaze, to protect you. But you went north. You forced your blooding and revealed yourself to them. Now events are in motion that cannot be stopped. But this is Fate; all is Fate."

His frequent referrals to Fate are beginning to chafe. My head spins, and not just from my injuries. I *tsk* in disbelief. "If this is all Fate's doing, why can't she stop the Winterborn?"

"Fate weaves time, but has no physical self. She can only guide people and events, nudge them into a better telling. She cannot rewrite what must be or physically intercede," Winter explains, unhurried as falling snow. "The Winterborn's invasion of the south will be. Your blooding had to be. But the timing and events that bring these things to pass… that is what we fought to change, to give the Sleepers a chance to lift the Winter Night and reclaim Duamel."

I'm still struggling to pull the pieces together, but one reality is clear. "I can't fight the Winterborn alone. They can't die. They can barely be slowed. If you hadn't come to me when you did, I may never have escaped Kygga."

"You won't be alone. You'll have the Vynder, Gadr, perhaps even Aita," my grandfather says, factual instead of soothing. He unfolds and straightens to his feet in a fluid motion. "And they are not the only ones who cannot die. An avalanche took you yesterday, and in one night you healed as much as a mortal would in two weeks—if they ever awoke."

Rather than comfort me, the thought stirs up a host of confusion and pain. I thought I'd walled it off when I learned of my siblings' plot and decided to warn the Eangen, but now it creeps over and around my barriers, wedging into the cracks like the roots of a mountain pine.

Winter watches the agony crease my face. His doesn't soften, but he holds my gaze as firmly as before. "With the power you've been given, you can take the world and make it what you wish. You can protect your people long after this generation's bones are ashes, and you *will*."

His words align with Fate's charge, and I believe them. A tentative courage creeps through me, but its edges harden into something harsher.

"I don't want this," I say truthfully. "I'm a terrible priestess. They will cast me out, or drown me in the White Lake like Eang did to my father."

"Yet your task remains." Winter glances at the mouth of the cave, and I sense his desire to leave. "Atone. Fight for them, and fight well. And if in the end they still turn against you? Leave. The world is far bigger than Eangen, Thray. Understand your role in it, and you'll find the will to keep going."

Winter's voice hardens, but in that, I hear something new—emotion. I wonder, through my tears, if Winter did care, once, for mortal lives. And if now he truly cares for me. "Your purpose is different than mortals. Beyond theirs. Once you accept that, purpose will bring you peace."

I want to protest, to mourn and complain, but the words won't come. "I don't want to be alone," I say finally, and as raw as the words are, they sound flat. Unfeeling. "I don't want to leave them. I don't want to be cast out. I don't want them to die."

"You will never be alone." He looks down at me and gives a small, almost imperceptible shrug. "I've told you before that you will have me. And, sordid as they are, your siblings—perhaps some of them can be redeemed. Face the future with us, or wither away. I cannot choose for you."

His final words are harsh. I'm almost grateful when he moves toward the mouth of the cave and, with one more backward glance, slips away into the shadows beyond.

I don't know if he will come back. I don't know that I want him to. But as the last of his footfalls fades from the cave, I feel something inside me crack.

I cry. I choke and sob until my throat is hoarse and my eyes burn. I kick at the fire and burn myself, scattering coals across the uneven, icy floor. I strain sore muscles and make my head spin in agony. But the pain feels like pleasure, because pain reminds me of mortality and, just for a moment, I can pretend that it's mine.

Winter does not return. By the time I fall into an exhausted fugue the remnants of the fire are little more than orange-edged coals, flickering away the last of their heat into a world of unforgiving ice.

And then, exhausted, I sleep.

THIRTY-FIVE

I awaken bitterly cold. I unfurl stiff limbs and stagger to my feet. It doesn't look as if Grandfather returned. The scattered coals of my fire are long cooled and snow scuds across the floor from the cave mouth. It clings to my clothing too, and a pile of gear set neatly beside the cave entrance.

I've been unconscious, in the cold, for a long time. A mortal would have died by now, slipping away in their sleep. But I'm alive.

Once again, my immortality shows its value.

Value. The thought takes me off guard, reminding me of my grandfather's admonitions before he left. But I'm only just crawling back to consciousness—I don't let myself think too deeply yet.

Next to the cave entrance lies my pack, a new heavy cloak, my bow, my knife, and my commandeered Duamel tall shield. Combined with the sleeping roll, all the gear I'd assumed was lost in the avalanche is here and accounted for.

Winter has provided for me, again. He's saved me, again, as I trusted he would. But that feels bitter in light of all I've learned—the reality that he could warn the Eangen himself with little to no effort. Yet he's left me to wade through the snow with the future of my mother's people on my shoulders.

Was he always heartless, I wonder, or did his immortality make him so? Will I become the same, in time?

I've no desire to become like him. Or the Winterborn. I must be something different.

I mutter a curse and stagger to a corner of the cave to relieve myself, then make my way to my pack. As I search for food I glance out the cave entrance, down a short tunnel, and outside.

Light. Daylight. It pours through a high, narrow cleft, glistening off piled snow and smooth walls of ice.

"How?" I croak, startling myself with the sound of my voice.

I leave the pack, nearly trip on my bow, and catch myself on the icy wall beside the opening. I squint, blinded after months of firelight and moonlight. But slowly my eyes adjust and the land before me takes shape.

Mountains rise, snowcaps shrouded in cloud. The wind is sharp, but it clears my mind with one, swift gust.

I step just outside the cave mouth, boots squeaking in frigid snow, and turn around. I stand at the foot of a glacier in the embrace of a broad mountain. The glacier's side rises above me, blue heart mottled with white cracks and black twists. Below it, down the slope, a barren section of coastline churns under a shrouded winter sun.

All I can do is stare. It's been so long since I saw a landscape by daylight, the details stagger me. The snow-laden forests. The glint of frozen waterfalls. Ridges of rock erupting from a blanket of white. The rim of the ice-laden shore of the sea, with its peninsulas and inlets.

The last feature prickles at the back of my mind. I recognize one inlet in particular—the arch of its arm and its arrangement of three, small islands. We sailed through here with the Duamel. We camped on that shore and encountered the Algatt.

I'm in Algatt territory. My grandfather hasn't left me to trudge through the winter for weeks on end. He's carried me all the way to Gadr's land.

Gadr, who met me in the forest around that inlet and warned me that there was a door to the High Halls nearby.

Hope bursts through me, and a spark of shame at my earlier resentment toward Winter. Even if he didn't act out of love, he has helped me.

Between myself and the coast, there's a village. Smoke trails into the sky and I can make out the subtle irregularities of snow-covered roofs. They'll know where the door to the High Halls is and I can slip through. In hours, or even minutes, I'll be in Albor.

I need only get off this mountain and walk to the village. It's three days' travel, at most. But sore and weak as I am it may take longer, and I've no idea how much time has passed since the avalanche. The Eangen and Algatt will need time to prepare for the coming conflict. Palisades are not constructed in a day, particularly with the ground frozen solid.

I need to move as quickly as I can. I look back at my pack and the tall Duamel shield, then turn my gaze to the slope below—a smooth, relatively unobstructed descent carved by a recent landslide. Fallen chunks of glacier rise up here and there, but between them are natural indentations from spring runoff; broad, clear paths.

A grin steals onto my face. I laugh aloud, awed at my own insanity— but what do I have to lose? I already endured an avalanche and at least one night in the murderous cold without a fire. I'm immortal, Winterborn.

For the first time, that truly feels like a boon.

Still, when I stand at the top of the slope with my pack strapped to my back and the shield in hand, I almost change my mind. Fear makes my heart pound like a drum and the brisk mountain cold scalds my cheeks.

Yet I set the shield face-down in the snow and sit on it, gripping its straps and wedging my heels to either side. I adjust my pack and drag a few bracing breaths into my lungs. Then I shuffle my makeshift sled forward.

One nudge. Two. Three. The shield begins to slide and I stifle another half-terrified, half-reckless laugh.

I lift my heels, just enough to gain speed, and slip between two toppled chunks of glacier. I keep my heels down and lean, controlling my speed and trajectory as best I can until a jagged outcropping forces me to jerk my feet in. The incline snatches me up, I let out a bracing shout, and I burst onto the open mountainside.

For a moment, as I careen down the mountain toward the meadow and forests of coastal Algatt, I wonder if this is how Arune and Kygga feel as they ride the wind. Despite a childhood sliding across ice and tumbling down hills, I've never moved so fast. There's no breath in my lungs. The air darts away before I can draw it in and snow half blinds me. The edges of my clothing snap and billow and my hood flies back. The wind tears at my hair and burns my cheeks, but I do not care. I'm lost in the thrill and exhilaration, and the terrifying knowledge that there is nothing this mountain can do to kill me.

The tree line, however, is rushing up fast. Just in time I stick out one hand to claw at the snow and guide my path into the belly of a buried river.

The forest swallows me, but still I'm flying. The snow cushions my sled from what I'm sure must be small waterfalls and rapids in the summer, and by Fate alone, it seems there's nothing more dangerous in my way.

When the incline lessens I lean forward, digging both hands into the snow and trying to slow myself. It seems to be working, until the trees up ahead vanish and I'm faced with an open expanse of sky.

I've just time to understand the danger before the shield is airborne. I look down and there, beneath the cascade of dislodged snow, I see a frozen waterfall. Some six paces below it meets the surface of a lake in a muffled roar, then vanishes beneath a mantle of ice.

I hit the ice with a crack and clatter. I tumble and skid until I come up against something hard. Winded, I lie still for a moment.

I wipe snow from my eyes. My shield lies a dozen paces away but my pack is still on my back, along with my bow. I'm against a bank of ice, huge chunks pushed up by the waterfall, stacked like pieces of plate armor and refrozen. But the ice before me, recently formed and clear as crystal, is latticed with thin, white cracks.

I go still. Are the cracks old, or new? Are they actively branching toward me, or is the crackle I hear just the sound of the waterfall?

The ice beneath me shifts, ever so slightly, and I see a new crack skitter up to my feet. I move instantly, clambering over the scales of ice and skidding down the other side. More cracks resound across the lake as I break into a run, charging for the shoreline. I'm a dozen paces away before my foot breaks through—only to land on a second layer of ice, just below. Still, I fall hard and curse, jerking my leg free as frigid water swells from the hole in the ice. Splayed on all fours, I crawl the rest of the way to the shore.

Algatt hunters wait for me under the trees, red-cheeked and bundled against the cold. One steps forward, his snow-crusted beard spilling from a hood of thick fur and an arrow laid to the string of his bow.

I gulp, feeling starved of air. I don't think I've taken a proper breath since I stood at the glacier and I'm starting to feel woozy for it.

"Peace," I pant. "Eangen. Priestess of Thvynder."

The man looks at me for another moment, and I realize that I know him. He was with Gadr in the forest, the night the Duamel camped on Algatt shores. But he doesn't appear to recognize me.

I wonder if I've made a mistake. There are those in the world who don't respect the priesthood or the bonds of peace between the Eangen and the Algatt. There are corrupt men and women in all places, and if I—

I reach for my knife.

A grin splits the man's face. "No need for that, you mad woman! A shield? A *shield*? What do I think when I see this *thing* flying down the mountain? Oh, a priestess? No, a mad woman!"

His coastal Algatt accent is among the thickest I've ever heard, but there's no threat in it. He breaks off into a gale of laughter and his companions follow, crowding in to clap me on the shoulders and help me to my feet. They marvel at my unbroken bow and barrage me with questions that I haven't the breath to answer.

"Ignore Torfin. There's no need for your weapons," a woman tells me, seeing my hand still lingering around my knife. "Why are you alone out here? Who are you?"

I stare from her to the boisterous man for a moment, then collect myself. "My name is Thray, niece to the High Priests of Thvynder. And I must speak to Gadr."

The hall in the Algatt village is full of warmth. I sit by the fire as my limbs prickle and feeling slowly returns to my fingers. Torfin, the laughing man from the lake, is here along with two dozen other adults and nearly as many children. This village isn't large and everyone is present, watching and waiting and pressing me with food and drink. But despite their vigilance, their good cheer startles me after months with the subdued Duamel. These are a people who know the sun will rise each morning, and spring will come again.

The village priestess hovers, refilling my cup of hot mead from a pot whenever its halfway empty.

"He still hears our prayers," she tells me, offering me a steaming ladle for the fourth time. "He'll come, though it may take a little time."

"How much time is there?" The huntress from at the lake's edge sits nearby, her dark blonde hair flattened by her hood and temples smudged with blue paint. Her windburned cheeks remain red and she's hardly touched the bowl of thick stew at her side.

I haven't said a word about what I need to tell Gadr, but the Algatt aren't stupid. They remember the Duamel on their shores last autumn, and they know whatever news I carry is important enough to merit an Eangen priestess personally traveling in winter.

I glance down at my feet, newly clad in borrowed socks of thick wool, and sniff. The Algatt deserve to know what's coming, but just as when I brought news of the Duamel ships to Iesa, I don't want to cause a panic. Gadr is their leader. Not me. I'm… something else. Something apart.

Fate and my grandfather's words about my purpose drift back to me, hedged with fresh meaning, but at that moment the door of the hall opens and Gadr strides in. His head is bare and his expansive beard spills over the chest of his thick, belted coat.

He takes one look at me and the crowded villagers, and snorts. "You're all looking very serious. Back so soon, Daughter of Ogam? Did you bring me my gift?"

My return smile is humorless, a little sad, and my gaze grim. I rise, setting aside my cup and offering the Miri a half-bow. "I have, Gadr, though it's a bitter one. I've brought you war."

THIRTY-SIX

The standing stones are sheathed with ice, on the side of the cavern that faces the sea. Ancient, square runes that are neither Eangen nor Algatt crawl up each looming monolith, and though I can't read them, the power of the place weighs on me.

"This was the sacred place of Addack and his people," Gadr says as he picks his way ahead of me into the sea cave, his voice echoing above the drum of waves at low tide. The space is huge, four times my height and stretching far along the coastline toward the inlet to the north.

I follow him with my pack on my back and my bone-handled knife transformed into a staff, which I use to keep my balance on the treacherous cave floor. There was no time for sleep before we departed—my clothes had barely dried by the time Gadr and I left the warmth of the hall. But my exhaustion is an increasingly distant thing, tamped down by purpose.

"It was before Eang slew him," I observe, stopping just within the circle of stones. The monuments are alone in the cave, as the cave is alone on this stretch of shore. Before our descent down a treacherous path, I could see all the way to the mountain where Winter left me, and the glacier where I began this final leg of my journey. Even now, at the memory, I feel a belated wash of fear—and satisfaction—at my mad descent.

"As Eang was prone to do," Gadr affirms. "Are you ready?"

He's come to stand at the center of the stones and, following his gaze, I touch at my priestess's Sight. A slim golden crack appears in the air at the very center of the ring, warm and glistening, fine as a crack in a pot. But this crack is in the fabric between the worlds, the High Halls and the Waking World. Already, the door swells with light, stretching and broadening to accommodate Gadr.

The Miri eyes me, one side of his face washed with gold. "You've been bodily in the High Halls before, with Hessa and Imnir?"

"Yes. I can navigate it."

Gadr grunts. "Good. Eat nothing, drink nothing. No matter how great your need is."

I give him a wan smile. This was a lesson every child in the known world knew. "I know better than that."

Something passes around his eyes. It might have been bitter humor, or a thread of unexpected pity. Then he takes another half-step closer to the rift and its brightness doubles, scattering the gloom of the day and casting shadows stretching in every direction, from both us and the standing stones.

The light wavers as Gadr steps through and vanishes. The rift immediately begins to fade but, before it does, I dart inside.

The world stretches and skews. Suddenly, I stand in the orange and gold of an autumn sunset. The standing stones still reach high above me but we're no longer in the cave and the season has shifted. Instead of snow, fallen leaves rustle around the bases of the monoliths. Forest crowds in and though I can hear the sea, it's no longer in sight. The sky, too, is obscured by arching branches and leaves of umber, yellow, plum, and scarlet.

"You can find your way to Albor?" Gadr stands nearby, watching me with a nearly paternal scrutiny.

"Yes. You go to Imnir," I say, naming my uncle and High Priest of the Algatt. "Let me warn the Eangen."

Gadr sucks his teeth for a moment, still considering me, then nods. "I'll see you soon. Send an owl."

He leaves without a backward glance.

I remain in the circle a moment longer, breathing in the kinder air and closing my eyes against the afternoon sun. It drifts through the whispering leaves and warms my cheeks. It comes with a hundred memories of home and, gathering them close, I reach out an empty hand.

In the air, I sketch three Eangen runes. The first is for request, the second for travel, and the third for home—not Iesa, but the Morning Hall where I grew up, in Albor.

Without opening my eyes, I begin to walk. The air shifts around me and the rich scent of warm deadfall and stone is replaced by a brisk summer wind and blinding light.

I open my eyes. I'm still in the High Halls, but now I stand knee-deep in a meadow of poppies, before a wooden shrine. The shrine is all angles, simple and stark, with gray, weathered rooftiles and a forgotten offering bowl inside. Before me thick forest cloaks the mountain's feet, while at my back the peak of Mount Thyr interrupts the High Halls' divided sky. No longer shrouded by autumn forest, the heavens here are marked out by four distinct quarters: the deep violet Realm of Death in the west, a sunrise east, a blue-skied south, and a lingering darkness in the north, vague with the shifting veil of white Northern Lights—sourced from the White Lake itself.

Between myself and the shrine is another rift. This one will take me to the Waking World just a few hours outside of Albor. I'll be home. I'll deliver my message and face the repercussions of my deceit. Perhaps it will be exile, perhaps death—which I will be forced to flee. Perhaps another kind of atonement, but that seems too merciful to hope for.

"Vistic," I pray to the sweet air of the High Halls. "Can you hear me?"

Immediately I feel a tug at the corner of my mind, and a voice drifts toward me, carried on the magic of the High Halls. "Thray, where are you?"

"Come to Albor," I reply. "We've much to discuss."

I sketch another rune in the air. The golden rift before me flashes wide, and I step back into the winter brightness of the Waking World.

Snow mushrooms the roofs of Albor as I leave the tree line and cross shrouded fields, following deep ruts from sledges.

Situated on a rise and surrounded by a high ring wall, Albor is easily one of the largest and most defensible towns in the south. Its gates stand open to the bright day and inside I glimpse villagers moving to and fro on daily errands. Hauling and chopping wood, fetching water, passing around infants, and clearing snow.

Children playing outside the wall are the first to notice me. Shouts go up and several dart back through the gates while the rest stand, snow-caked and flushed, watching me approach.

Soon after, a baying dog streaks out of the gate. A cluster of figures comes after it, and I'm close enough now to make out Hessa's face. She wears a hastily donned cloak and her braided hair is uncovered. I've caught her off guard, but she's not alarmed. The children must have recognized me.

The dog's barking turns from warning to joyful, and I can't help but smile as huge paws land on my shoulder. I stagger and grab her head, trying to scratch her ears and stop her from licking my face all at once. "Nui, down!"

Oblivious to my pleas, the hound lands a wet tongue on my eye and pulls off my hat with a sly bite. She drops back to all fours and trots away with the hat between her teeth, and for all her decades of life, she still looks like a puppy when she shakes it like a captured rabbit.

I leave her to it. The villagers are paces away now, and Hessa watches me with guarded, questioning eyes.

I self-consciously smooth my sweaty hair and give a slight bow. "Aunt." There's more relief in my voice than I intended to show and my eyes feel wet, but perhaps that's just from the cold, or Nui's kiss. "Can we speak privately?"

Hessa glances at the people around her. I recognize my uncle Nisien, a tall, dark-skinned Soulderni, and Hessa's children, the twins Berin and Yske. They're nearly twelve now, and Berin is already taller than his mother, with her black hair and casting of freckles. Yske takes more after their Algatt father, with blonde hair and pale eyes. Despite the passage of time, her cheeks are just as round as the day I left Albor, and as our eyes meet she smiles shyly in welcome.

"We should really speak privately." I look back to my aunt. "Please."

Hessa nods. I expect her to open her arms for an embrace but she just steps aside and gestures me up into the village. Stuffing my hurt under an icy mask, I start walking. Nui, my hat hanging from her teeth, precedes us through the houses at a stately trot.

The Morning Hall, seat of the Vynder priesthood and memorial to the Hall of Smoke, rises above me. Its pitch is steep to shed the snow and wings have been added to both sides with equally severe degrees. The ends of all beams are carved with the heads of animals, from bears to crows, and smoke drifts out its huge central chimney. Heavy oak doors are inlaid with runes, declaring the purpose of the hall, its occupants—the Vynder priesthood.

Once we're inside, Hessa sheds her cloak and beckons me into one of the wings, where her own living quarters occupy two rooms. They're small and warm, their windows heavily shuttered and covered with embroidered drapes. Bundles, sacks, and crates stuff the ceiling beams above and the wooden walls are hung with clumsy weavings—Yske's doing—shelves of jars and implements, and painted runes. A shield hangs central, marked with the head of a lynx in fine knotwork. The floors are layered with reed mats, old furs, and coarse knotted rugs. The whole of it, from the children's beds along one wall to the small table by the hearth, is achingly familiar, scented with sage and woodsmoke and leather.

Only Nisien follows us into the room, though the twins and Nui try. He prods them back out the door with a soft, firm command and snatches my hat from Nui before he closes the door in their disappointed faces.

"What's happened?" Nisien asks as I shrug off my pack. He sets my hat on the table.

I lower my burden with a clatter of bow and pull my hood over my head. Despite my composure my hands tremble, the two halves of me warring inside—my new, determined self with a message and a plan, and my old self full of childhood memories and fear of what Hessa will do when she learns the whole truth.

Nisien notices my shaking and takes the hood, hooking it onto a peg beside the fireplace. "Sit by the fire, Thray. You must be exhausted."

Fatherless as I'd been, Nisien stayed close when I was a child. But when I became a woman, the distance between us had grown. Now, the new lines around his eyes and the gray in his short, clean beard look foreign to me, but the kindness in his gaze is familiar.

I give a half-hearted smile. "I am. My journey has been long. Though not as long as I expected."

Hessa sits on a stool and watches me settle on a bench across from her. She's barely spoken since we met at the gate and I try not to let her silence unnerve me, but the quaking in my hands remains. I exist in two states at once—cool and determined, nervous and instinctual.

"Where are the Eangen who went north with you?" she asks.

"They are coming south by boat," I reply. "I came through the High Halls. They're several weeks behind me at least."

The High Priestess nods. "Then tell me why you've come."

"The people of the north, the Duamel, intend to invade Algatt and Eangen in the spring. They're led by two hundred of Ogam's immortal offspring." I'm relieved that it's my new self who speaks, clear and concise. "It is an invasion long planned. But now they have learned of Thvynder's absence and intend to take advantage of it."

"How did they find out?" Hessa asks. The contours of her face are more severe than I remember in the firelight.

"One of them overheard my prayers... My attempts at prayers." I hold her gaze, willing steel into my spine. "It was my fault. They move on the wind, and I didn't know to look for them until it was too late."

I hear Nisien shift on his feet. He pulls up another stool and sits, lengthening his long legs out toward the fire.

Hessa takes a moment to digest this. "How large is their army?"

"Ten thousand warriors, two hundred Winterborn. They intended to march south overland come spring, but that may change now that I've escaped. They have the power to break the ice and control the wind. The winter seas will not hinder them as much as we might hope. They have mounted warriors too. They ride savn—they're fast, and vicious." As I talk my confidence renews, and I lean forward. The warmth and light of the fire washes over my right side, while the left remains shadowed. "And the Winterborn are more dangerous than I can describe. Ogam is dead, but together, they're just as powerful as he ever was."

My words are met with a span of silence before Hessa speaks. But rather than questions of the upcoming invasion, her focus remains solely on my face. "What happened to you? How did you escape?"

I hesitate. "My story is… not simple."

"I want to hear it."

"As do I," Nisien adds.

I take a moment to gather my words. "I went to the Winterborn willingly. They promised their Elders could tell me if I was immortal. But I was tricked. They… They drowned me. I lived. And so I got my answer."

I try to go on, but my tongue won't move. I feel Hessa's and Nisien's eyes like physical forces, and I meet neither of them.

"Then I learned of the invasion," I continue. "I intended to send an owl, but the Winterborn captured both the bird you sent to follow me and a second messenger. I fled as soon as I could."

I see anger slip into Nisien's eyes—toward my siblings, not me—but he doesn't speak.

"The second message was from Vistic. We feared for you. How long ago did you leave?" Hessa asks. Her expression is more opaque than Nisien's, and it makes my chest ache.

"Two weeks, I think." When they look taken aback, I add, "I don't know. I left the Duamel capital not long after midwinter—a fortnight, at most. There are no days in Duamel, only endless dark. An avalanche took me right after my departure. My grandfather found me and brought me to Algatt. I healed for a few days, I think, then I found Gadr and came to you."

"Midwinter was three weeks ago," Hessa tells me, lost in thought. "I've no idea how Winter moved you so far so quickly, but we can only pray the Winterborn do not have access to it."

"They can't reach the High Halls, if that was how he did it," I assure her. "There are no doors in Duamel that I saw. But many of them can travel with the wind as Ogam did. They could already be close, spying." I think of Kygga, and his vow. "Though the last they saw of me I'd been buried by the avalanche, so perhaps that will have distracted them for a time. We have some… sense of where one another are, and they will eventually realize I've escaped, and where I've gone."

Hessa abruptly reaches across the fire and grasps my hand. "Thray, there's more we need to discuss and I want to know everything you've been through, but I have to say something."

I hold still. Her hand, smaller than mine, mottled with scars and rough with callouses, clasps my fingers tightly. Is this it? The moment when I'll learn my punishment?

"I am glad you are home," my aunt says.

My eyes burn. I blink hard and look at the fire, trying to hide my face from her and Nisien.

"As am I," the man echoes. "You should never have gone north alone."

"I wasn't alone," I correct, squinting at the fire. "I took four Eangen with me."

"They weren't even priests," Nisien points out, hardening further.

Hessa breaks in. "That's a matter for another day." Unspoken, I hear the truth that I lied to my Eangen companions about our divine mandate, and her warning rings again.

There will be a price to pay.

"Yes," I agree, focusing on Hessa's hand upon mine. "The Algatt will begin preparing for war within the next few days, and Vistic is on his way."

"Then we wait for his arrival," Hessa says, releasing my hand and sitting back. "But for now, rest."

THIRTY-SEVEN

Vistic arrives in the night. When I awake in the musty warmth of my mother's old home, he kneels on the hearth, breathing life into the coals. I've no sense of time—the windows are shuttered and heavily curtained—but as I watch, flames lick across birch kindling. Each smoke-darkened beam and dusty shelf takes on new clarity and contours, and though they're familiar, there's no way I can pretend life is as it once was. This house has no soul anymore, no heart—only memories, empty chairs, and an abandoned loom.

Vistic looks over at me. His herringbone cloak is hung by the door, beside my own kaftan and hood, but his boots are still on his feet—there are no reed mats on the floor, not with the house empty most of the year. They still glisten with melting snow, as do the tracks he's thoughtlessly left on the pounded earth.

For a moment I'm struck by the carelessness of that act, so human and childish, then I look into his golden eyes and remember what he is.

"War is coming," I say. I turn to lie on my back, avoiding his uncanny gaze. "Have you spoken with Hessa?"

"No. I came right to you."

I draw a long breath and close my eyes, pushing the last threads of sleep aside. "Then I've much to tell you."

I recount everything to him, from spying the ships in the fog to reuniting with Gadr in Algatt. I tell him of Attan's savn warriors, Arune's dubious aid, and Kygga's vow to find me. I describe the Barrow of Winter, Siru breaking the river ice, and the eerie endlessness of the eternal night the Winterborn have made. I tell him of the tombs, and the mysterious passage within, and Rana's secrets.

By the end of my tale, we both sit next to the fire on an old blanket. He's removed his boots, and they gently steam next to his folded legs and knitted socks. I'm growing hungry and thirsty, not to mention I need to relieve myself, but the quiet after my tale is something I don't want to break.

Vistic saves me the trouble. "Then we prepare for war. There is no other way."

"Will you call on the Arpa?"

He moves his boots away from the fire. "Yes. The Soulderni should make it north in time, at least. Do you know when and where the Winterborn will make landfall? I assume they'll come by ship."

I brush a thumb over the nails of my opposite hand, torn to the pink by travel and trial. "Kygga must have given up his search by now. He and the Windwalkers may already be on the way to Eangen, spying and searching for me."

"I haven't sensed them yet," he says, a reassurance rather than a contradiction. "But I'll instruct all Vynder to keep watch. We will be ready."

"They're immortal," I point out. "How can we hope to stop them? They can be injured, but they'll only recover and come back. Even if we tear them to pieces, we're only postponing the inevitable. And capturing and drowning them in the White Lake is... complicated."

The last sentence feels dangerous on my lips, and I watch my brother's face carefully.

"They can be bound, if it comes to that." My mother's son makes a considering noise, staring at the blanket between his folded legs and mine. "But Omaskat and I will find a more permanent solution."

His vow raises gooseflesh on my arms. I believe him.

"There's also the matter of your actions and punishment." Vistic looks up, holding my gaze. Outside the winter wind picks up, rushing against the shutters and over the chimney top. "I'd ask you to remain until after the battle is won. Fight with us."

"Of course I'll—What do you mean, remain?" Dread empties my face and I hold myself carefully still, determined not to betray my growing fear.

"You will be exiled, after the Winterborn are pushed back." Vistic still holds my gaze. There's the barest softness around his eyes, but it's so thin I decide it must be wishful thinking. A brother who cared for me could not be speaking these words.

Exile. I should feel relief, but the word sinks into me like a stone into mud. The emptiness of the house swells again, every shadowed corner taunting me with a life long gone.

"You expected something less?" he asks.

"More. Less. I don't know," I admit, knotting my fingers in my lap. "I feared the White Lake. I hoped for… a labor of atonement? Public disgrace? Losing my post in Iesa—that I assumed."

At the mention of Iesa, worry for Havar, Darag, Seele, and Branan flickers through my mind, but I'm too overwhelmed with my own fate to think on them long.

Vistic falls quiet, and I realize how foolish I'd been to hope for more leniency. Panicked questions flutter through my mind, more solid now, more tangible. Where will I go? How will I live alone for years, perhaps even decades?

I tackle the last query. "How long of an exile?"

"A generation."

My breath rattles in my lungs. In Eangen, a generation is largely accepted as twenty years. Nearly as long as I've been alive.

It takes me a long moment to realize I'm staring, and I haven't said anything in reply. I'm immortal, I remind myself. Twenty years should be little more than a blink for me.

But it's not. It seems like an eternity.

I conjure a memory of Hessa's face, Nisien's too. If I go into two decades of exile, will I see them again? Before the rise of Thvynder and the peace, constant war meant anyone living past sixty was uncommon. Now it's possible, but in Hessa and Nisien, I cannot see possibility, only pessimism and impending loss.

Vistic fills the silence. "You claimed a divine mandate for a private quest, deceived your people, and put them at risk. They may even be dead, we do not know yet. You manipulated the ones you were set to protect, and you did it knowingly, in the name of your God. You betrayed the greatest secret this priesthood holds. If these were the days of Eang, you would be put to death without question."

"Is that supposed to make me feel better?" Two decades of exile, loneliness, and struggle surge before my eyes. I press my hands into my thighs, trying to hide their shaking. "I made a mistake. A selfish, short-sighted mistake. That's all."

"But you do not regret it," Vistic states. "Not truly."

My panic blackens into frustration. "No," I snap. "I needed to visit the Winterborn. I deserved an answer, and Thvynder wasn't here to help me."

"I was," he reminds me in a low voice.

"You? You wouldn't have listened. And sending an owl would have taken days that I didn't have. I'd have had to wait another year. I'd have married Havar and... We'd have no knowledge of the invasion. Now my 'mistake' might just save us."

Vistic looks straight across the hearth at me, arresting me in place. "Thray," he says, and my stomach coils in dread of what he might say. "I am sorry for your pain, and I am sorry your trust in me is so thin. I'm not the brother you need, I know. But I have my role in this world, as do you. We must fulfill those roles and face the consequences of our actions."

He sounded like Winter.

"I know," I say, my head a cacophony of anguish and relief and frustration. He lets me have the silence for a time and I wonder if he regrets his decision to banish me. But when he speaks, it's on another topic.

"I will fight beside the Eangen and the Algatt," he decides. "Perhaps the Watchman too."

As angry as I am at my brother, fear for him ignites. "You're not immortal, Vistic. It's too risky."

"A risk that Hessa and every other human will take," he says, and I've the sense that he's speaking to himself rather than me. "Besides, my soul will simply be reborn."

"The shard of the God will be reborn in another body. It won't be you, not truly." I press my palms into my eyes, unable to bear his nonchalance.

"That is as it should be. I'm sorry, Thray, for the way things are. I need to go see Hessa now but... I am glad you're home."

I hear a shift of clothing and look up to see my brother on his feet, gathering his boots to leave. I'm overwhelmed past the point of exhaustion, but that fatigue smooths the edge of my unrest and blunts my dread.

I do not have the will to respond.

The next day, Albor is buried under one of the heaviest snowfalls in living memory. Villagers labor to keep doors, walkways, and even chimney caps from being smothered, while a veil of impenetrable white seals the settlement off from the world. There's no wind, leaving the endless flakes to pile precariously on branches and fenceposts, and the top of Albor's ring wall.

Only one traveler comes in during that time, a woman from Urgi astride a massive Soulderni horse. She comes for the birth of a grandchild, who arrives shrieking into the world five days later, while the snow still falls. The muffling weight of the storm softens even the child's first, baffled cries.

I sit by while Hessa conducts the dedication in the Morning Hall. The majority of the village is there and, combined with the roaring fire, the close heat makes sweat trickle down my spine.

I watch Hessa dip her fingers into the birthblood, saved in a bowl, and draw runes on the naked infant's chest. I listen as she murmurs prayers and accepts the child's name from his parents. His mother begins to sing, and soon every voice in the hall is raised in unison.

I feel tears in my eyes, though I do not shed them. The power of this moment is a familiar one. There's comfort in it, in the expectation and fulfillment and repetition. But soon we'll face the Winterborn, my time of exile will come, and everyone I see in the hall now will know of my wrongdoing. The distrust they've harbored my whole life will be proved true, and I'll be alone.

There will truly be no return to Iesa, no marrying Havar, no sitting at Ossen's right hand and performing ceremonies just like this for the coastal people. I will never hold my own child at the head of a hall and begin a mother's song.

But for the first time since I learned of my punishment, these thoughts do not hurt quite so badly. I know my next steps. I have a purpose, and in that, I find strength—just as my grandfather said I would.

First, I face my siblings. First, I fight to keep the people in this hall alive, to preserve them and the way of life that brought me into being— and, I hope, to redeem myself a little in their eyes.

Then I will face my exile.

The days begin to pass with increasing swiftness as the Eangen prepare for war. I cherish each sunrise over the next two months, rising early and pouring all my efforts into helping the Eangen ready themselves. I train and fight, pray and perform my duties with more diligence than I ever have. I'm building a memory of myself. These months, and my actions in the battle to come, will be my legacy.

Eangen's armies move to the coast, swelling villages like Iesa to bursting. Before the snow melts and the rivers break up, a Soulderni legion crosses the wall to the south and heads for the Algatt-Eangen border. Such efforts are not easy in the winter, but by the time spring draws close, we are prepared.

When the first snowblossoms appear on the mountainside above Albor and the last leaves fall from the oaks, Gadr comes to the Morning Hall.

"Your former lover and his companions brought word to the Algatt, on their journey home," the Miri says, standing with Hessa, Nisien, and I beside the hearth in the Morning Hall.

Relief makes my stomach weak. They're home, though I doubt I'll ever see them again.

"Before they escaped, the Sleepers informed them of the Winterborn's plans," Gadr continues. "They'll come ashore at the inlet near the standing stones, where you camped with Siru. I've owls marking their progress south, and they'll be there within a week. My Algatt are already gathering, and the Soulderni are in place."

Five sunrises later, in a circle of stones by the sea, I stand by as Hessa's war chief Sillo holds the rift open with one upraised hand. Eangen Vynder priests and priestesses stream through and regroup in the echoing cave, lowering packs and casting their gazes through the broad mouth toward the sea. The coast is still rimmed with ice, buckled and stacked by the never-ceasing tide and waves, and the wind howls through the cavern.

I hold my bone spear loosely at my side and peer north over the ice-laden coast. No Duamel drums drift across the dark waves, but I feel them like a storm over the horizon. The ships are coming. Soon, my siblings will be here.

I lead the newcomers out of the cave and up the path to the world above. False spring has come and gone and the oversaturated earth is crusted with ice. The air is sharp and harsh in my lungs and only the bravest grasses reach quivering shoots into the harsh morning. Blown snow clings to every crevice and the footprints of humans, horses, dogs, and deer are imprisoned in the mud.

Here and there, the markings condense into broad pathways of churned earth. One such path leads to the camp where three thousand Algatt warriors wait, along with a thousand Soulderni horsefolk. Their tents and campfires spread down the tree line to the north-east and their Vynder trudge out to meet us, wind whipping pale hair and beards against a backdrop of colorless earth, drifting smoke, and sleeping mountains.

With Eang's axes strapped across her back and her lynx-painted shield slung over one shoulder, Hessa strides past me to meet her husband, Imnir, Shepherd of the Dead and High Priest of the Algatt. Their relationship has never been a simple one, and I've yet to hear the word 'love' pass between them, but there's warmth in the way Imnir pulls her into an embrace, and relief in the way she reaches up to scratch his gray-blond beard.

Vistic appears behind Imnir, his tawny Eangen skin and smooth black curls marking him out among his Algatt and mixed-blood companions. He keeps his head raised, despite the cold wind, and his golden eyes find me.

I go to him. I haven't seen him since his visit to Albor, but this meeting feels easier than the last. More even-footed and less taut with the pain of the past.

"Thray." Vistic doesn't reach for me but stops a pace away, one hand on the sword at his hip. The fingers of his other hand hang loose, brushing the thickly embroidered hem of his tunic, visible through the divide in his short, herringbone cloak. Our mother, I remember with a spark of painful memory, made both.

The sword, however, is unfamiliar. It's a handspan longer than any Eangen or Algatt sword I've seen, with a double edge and a short crossguard, blade hidden in a boiled leather sheath capped with bronze. The hilt's grip is tightly wrapped leather and its pommel a simple triangular stone, the same color as the rest of the crossguard; a milky, opalescent white.

Vistic catches me staring at the weapon. He doesn't seem perturbed by my lack of greeting but watches my face like a teacher might a student, waiting for the moment of revelation. Though there's barely a year between our births, this is an expression I'm used to.

Suspicion creeps through me, and with it both unease and hope.

"It reminds me of the Lake," I say searchingly.

"It was cooled in its waters," he replies. He still hasn't moved forward, but his pastoral expression eases somewhat. He looks more like a warrior and less like a priest then—loose-muscled, keen-eyed, and calm, as his mortal Eangi father might once have been.

My suspicion solidifies. "A weapon against immortals."

"The Winterborn think Thvynder's absence means there is no one left to stop them. They are wrong."

"You can kill us with that?"

Something else passes through his eyes at my use of "us." "If I must."

It's my turn to study his face, searching the minute expressions there. The longer I look into his eyes, registering the weight, responsibility, and assurance in them, the more I understand him. He's looking at me and the rest of the world as though he's not part of it, as an outsider, burdened with purpose and responsibility.

My distant sense of the Winterborn's approach rises, sounding to the beat of my heart.

I smile. It's neither joyful nor smug, but there's genuine warmth to it, and it draws a startled half-smile out of him in response. I step closer and reach out a hand. Hesitant, he returns the gesture and we clasp forearms. His long, slim fingers somehow feel warm, despite the cold and thick fabric of my sleeve.

"I'll do what I can to dissuade the Winterborn," I promise him, squeezing his lean, muscular forearm in return. "But if it comes to it, kill one of the Elders. I'll point them out to you. Their deaths will have the greatest impact."

And the greatest justice, I think, recalling the way Midvyk delivered me to my blooding. Still, I reflect that the impending death of an immortal sibling should grieve me; yet I feel only a cool, distant vengeance.

Blood, I know now, does not equal kinship. Blood does not dictate loyalties. And as I look at my mother's son, I wonder where he fits in that new understanding. My grip softens on his arm.

Horns sound and Vistic and I both look up. Eangen and Algatt war horns cut through the frigid air, turning to discordant moans before ending in ascending cracks, one by one. No sooner does one end than another begins, forming an endless circle of sound that fills my senses to bursting.

Only when the last droning note fades do I hear the Duamel drums in truth. Vistic and I look to the sea as, on the horizon, a snowstorm takes shape like shreds of carded wool and smears of muffled, twilit cloud.

Vistic releases my arm. I hold a fraction longer, unable to pry my own fingers away, then will myself to let go. We turn, standing shoulder to shoulder in the face of the coming storm.

THIRTY-EIGHT

The coming of the Winterborn is heralded by snow and ice and drums. The sea freezes along the shoreline with a sound like thunder and bursting sap, sheathing the waves around the inlet from north to south. The ice stretches a hundred paces out to sea, creating a broad, slick expanse of no-man's land so clear and so quick that I spy bubbles trapped within the ice.

I settle my feet on the solid rock of the windswept peninsula that guards the inlet. To the south, just out of sight in the sea cave where the standing stones lie, Gadr and a dozen of the Algatt's best Vynder guard the door to the High Halls. I'm not sure if the Winterborn realize the rift is here, but if anyone is capable of protecting the High Halls, it's Gadr.

The inlet is where the army will make its stand, on the beach before the windblown pines. Eangen and Algatt line the eastern shore, round shields ready, black-painted eyes narrowed against the wind. Spears point up into the sky and axes flash, swung in agitation or grated against shield rims. Out of sight, Soulderni riders range up and down the coast, guarding our forces from flanking attacks, and ready to plunge into the melee when the summoning horn sounds.

Billows of snow roll inland, buffeting us, tossing hair and beards and lashing clothes. Beside me, Vistic narrows his eyes against the flurries and rests a hand on the hilt of his sword. A pace away, Hessa unshoulders her shield and stands with Uspa, whose hounds prowl through the two dozen Vynder at our backs.

Duamel drums hammer, snow collects on my frigid cheeks, and silver glitters in the wind in swift, lithe streams.

"Windwalkers," I murmur to Vistic and Hessa.

The High Priestess nods. "I see them."

The Windwalkers draw closer to the shore, skimming across the ice and twining with gusts of snow. Despite their speed there's a languidness to them, a lack of caution that reveals how little they know about the Vynder and our Sight.

They think themselves invisible. They're wrong.

Between one breath and the next, the silver streams close in and transform. Windwalkers lunge from the snow with weapons already in motion—swords thrusting, axes arcing, spears darting. But the Vynder are there to meet them, equally in motion, equally prepared.

A few Windwalkers falter in shock, then they all scatter back to the winds. Some reappear at random, pacing the sea ice like wolves in the snow, waiting for an opportune moment and murmuring between one another.

Three streams of silver descend upon us again. Hessa hisses. The sound is feral and low, sending shivers across my scalp that have nothing to do with the cold.

The three Windwalkers instantly snap back into flesh and blood. They stumble to the ground, stunned and disoriented. I recognize them all, though I recall only the name of one. Saben, one of the sisters who enthusiastically welcomed me after my blooding. Her eyes flick to me now, shock and confusion momentarily burying any animosity.

She's blocked from sight as Vynder charge. I remain where I am, watching the other Windwalkers for any sign of assault. Kygga will be here, I know, as will Midvyk, and I suspect they'll come directly for me.

After a scuffle, the Vynder retreat. There on the snowy, rocky shore, Vistic holds Saben by the hair and lays his sword across her throat. Held by his arms and Hessa's magic-smothering power, there's nothing Saben can do. Nowhere for her to go.

The other two Windwalkers Hessa brought down are hauled back and thrust to their knees.

Vistic shouts to the wind, "I am the Vestige of Thvynder, Soul of the God-Killer, and this land is under our protection. I will end the long life of any Winterborn who stands against me."

Laughter ripples on the wind. It turns and swirls, driving snow into our eyes at the same time as, out on the ice, the rhythm of the Duamel drums ceases. It's replaced by a creak of wood as ships slip into sight of the shore, prows cradled by carefully wrought channels in the ice. Warriors begin to disembark and form up, their armor and flashing steel interspersed with tall, white-haired Winterborn in heavy kaftans. Icecarvers and Stormbringers. I can't tell which is which with the distance, but Siru will be among them.

Back on shore, Eangen and Algatt horns resound, echoing across the ice and the cliffs around the inlet.

"End us? You cannot *end* us. You cannot even slow us." Midvyk materializes a dozen paces away on sea ice, visible through a swirling tunnel of snow. The ends of her skirts flutter around her high boots, where carved savn claws rattle as she strides forward, well into bowshot. "Bleed us, break us, and we will come again."

For the briefest of moments, Vistic glances to me. There's a quiet in that gaze, and the remnants of a question. He's seeking absolution, perhaps, for what he's about to do, and in the face of Saben's end, I find I can't manage to give it—at least, not aloud. I barely know her, but she looks like me, and she carries my father's blood in her veins.

So I let my silence be my answer.

Vistic's gaze returns to Midvyk.

"Then know I take no pleasure in this," he says. His voice changes as he speaks, deepening and broadening from the voice of a man into the voice of a god.

Then he begins to draw the sword across Saben's throat. Blood spills, a trickle at first, and then a torrent. It runs over her collar and down the front of her kaftan to pool around her knees.

She sways in Vistic's grip, and he gently eases her to the ice.

Absolute silence wraps around us. The Duamel army still approaches and the wind still howls down the coast, but I do not hear them. I feel nothing, either—nothing save the threads of Saben's immortal life, fraying and unwinding at Vistic's feet. For a moment I see them in the air too, delicate strands that run from her to me, to Midvyk, and every other Winterborn in sight. Connecting us.

"Move back," Hessa's voice commands.

The Vynder retreat. Blinking hard, I follow them. Vistic moves last, with his long, blood-slicked sword dripping onto the ice. We take the other two captive Winterborn with us and, for now, they're too stunned to resist.

Saben is left alone, framed by blood and scudding snow.

Midvyk vanishes and rematerializes over Saben. She doesn't crouch, doesn't cry out, but she stares in hollow horror as our sister's life drains away. More Windwalkers materialize around her, gathering like pale crows.

Blowing snow snares in Saben's silver-tainted blood. It melts at first, then slowly begins to shroud the blood in white.

The Winterborn in our captivity begin to strain, cursing and shouting and pleading. I cannot look at them, but Vistic goes to them, sword still edged with crimson blood. The threat of his presence brings them to a strained, disbelieving hush.

My blood begins to hammer behind my eyes. I see disbelief and fear blossom in the Winterborn, and despite knowing this was coming, I feel the echo of their horror. I feel pain too, pain in my very blood.

In the truest sense, I can feel Saben dying, because a part of me is dying too. Did they feel this same pain during my blooding? Would they feel it now if I was the one lying on the ice, open eyes staring toward the snow-hazed sky?

I feel a presence at my side and turn to look down at Hessa. Her touch is light, one gentle hand on my back, then it's gone. But it gives me the strength to level my chin.

Blood does not equal kinship.

Midvyk steps over Saben's body. Footprints of crystalizing blood follow her as she takes three steps toward us.

Behind her, more Windwalkers materialize and spread out. There are two dozen of them visible now, but Kygga isn't among them. Neither is Arune—but where as Kygga, I suspect, is watching me from somewhere in the blowing snow, Arune may still be in his bed at the Barrow. I can't decide whether that's a consolation.

Beyond the Windwalkers, the Duamel army settles into lines of shields and glistening spears. I can't see the savn riders yet, but I finally spy Siru in the front lines, her myriad braids lashing like a banner.

More Winterborn will die today, and I'll feel each death. But I know Siru better than any of them, other than Kygga and Arune. That increases the pain of her betrayal and manipulation—but it also leaves me in dread of seeing her fall to Vistic's sword.

"Leave now and there will be no more death." Hessa speaks now to Midvyk. "I was there the day your father died, Daughter of Winter. I watched Eang drown him, and I slew her with my own hands. I've no desire to see you throw away your own lives for vengeance, or your father's twisted legacy."

Midvyk's smile is a fractured thing. And though she's too far away for me to see the tears in her eyes, I know they're there. When she speaks again, she doesn't direct her words to Hessa, or Vistic, or myself. She speaks to her brothers and sisters, arrayed at her sides, and hidden upon the wind.

"Kill them."

A wall of blinding snow and wind crashes over us. I hear Eangen war horns blast, then the sound is torn away. I stagger, unable to draw breath, eyes instinctively pinned shut. Even the sound of my own gasp is smothered.

I pry my eyes back open just in time to see a spear spin toward my head. The pain of Saben's death still aches in my veins like a blood fever. But I do not hold back.

I snap out my own spear, smashing Kygga's aside and launching myself into his guard. His eyes widen in surprise, then my spear is a sword.

I slash at his stomach. He sidesteps, spins his spear into one hand, and grabs my arm with the other. He jerks me forward and turns, tossing me out onto the ice like a child's doll.

I come to a sliding, skittering halt. Kygga advances, shouting at me, but his words mean nothing. Halfway to my feet I stagger in another blast of wind and slide backward half a pace, then he's upon me.

I dodge an attack and hack out my own. I block, duck aside, and thrust. The snow is so close and the wind so intense, I can't breathe. But when a nearby shout snatches Kygga's concentration I dart in, narrowly avoid his driving elbow, and slash my blade across the back of his legs. The cut isn't deep, but it does its task.

Kygga's knees hit the ice with jarring force. There's betrayal in his eyes but rather than hurt me, it makes my indignation boil.

"Do you think I want this?" I demand, braced in a low, wary guard. Everywhere Windwalkers and Vynder clash, and down the ice I see the first savn riders materialize from the storm. The body of the army is nearly upon us, and drums continue to pound.

My temper unfurls. "I don't. But I should. I could see you from under the ice, Kygga. Watching me die. You lied to me!"

"You are a child," he roars back, rising to his feet in a haze of silvered power. The edges of him blur briefly but he retains his form, blood trickling down the backs of his calves. He ignores it—his body does not rely on muscle and bone, though his face is gaunt with pain. "A selfish, short-sighted child. And like a child, I will protect you from yourself. In a hundred years, you'll thank me. You'll come back to us."

"You're blind!" I close on my half-brother again, sword transitioned back to a spear. He retreats, blocking blow after blow. The accusation is a gamble, but at least it might distract him. "The Elders made the Winter Night, Kygga! Midvyk. Siru!"

Kygga falters, just the barest amount—enough for me to knock the head of his spear aside and give myself an opening to strike. But

314

I don't. I step back instead, emphasizing my words with the action. "They *made* the Duamel suffer. So they could keep them under heel. So they could use them."

Kygga stands momentarily, spear loose in his grasp, then his expression clouds with renewed anger.

He doesn't speak. He doesn't accuse me of lying or show any sign of believing me, but thrusts his spear straight for my thigh. The wildness of the blow is the only sign that I've unsettled him.

I sidestep with ease, strike his spearhead with the butt of my weapon, and pin its head to the ice. Then I twist and drive the head of my own spear toward his immortal chest.

Just before the tip pierces the heavy, dark green of his kaftan, he vanishes.

He materializes behind me in a haze of snow.

"Believe me, Kygga!" I spin and barely block his attack, too close, too fast. He wields his spear with two hands on the shaft, both ends coming at me in a flurry of movement. I lose grip on the ice and skid backward, barely keeping my footing under his barrage. "I'm not lying!"

"We all lie," Kygga growls. The shaft of his spear strikes my fingers and I cry out, nearly dropping my weapon. The next strike hits my head in a glancing blow. Black sparks across my vision and I stumble.

I clumsily raise my spear to block the next blow, but it doesn't come. I look up to see a hatchet sprouting from Kygga's side. He roars in pain as Uspa thunders past, one blood-spattered hound ahead of her, one at her heel. The priestess glances at me, pulls another hatchet from her belt, and vanishes back into the snow.

My instincts take over. Before Kygga can recover, my sword is a staff and I smash it into the side of his head, as he just did to me. He drops to the ice and blinks stunned, disoriented eyes.

I hesitate, staff raised for a second strike. "I'm telling the truth. The Elders made the Winter Night, and if you don't know that, they've manipulated you as much as the Duamel."

"Thray," he wheezes.

I bring the staff down on his temple and he goes still. The sight of him lying there is a knife in my stomach but it's also a mercy. If he's out of the action, at least Vistic can't hurt him.

A roar of rage makes me spin—nearly a second too late. Midvyk and another Windwalker throw themselves upon me with darting swords and impossible swiftness, flowing seamlessly from flesh to wind.

A blade plunges for my chest at the same time as a swirl of silver passes through the corner of my vision. I start to turn, barely remember to block the thrust to my chest, and duck just as the tip of another spear drives at my eye.

I scream. The second Windwalker buckles with a plume of blood-mist and a ragged gasp. His knees hit the ice, hands scrambling, sword lost. His face, gaping up at me, is deathly pale and blood-mist drifts around him—but even as I watch, color begins to return and the mist fades. He's recovering.

Midvyk only staggers, blood streaming from her nose, eyes, and ears. I open my mouth to shout again, raking frigid air into my lungs, and she vanishes.

A dagger of ice punches toward me from the side. I throw up an arm at the last instant, taking the blade to the forearm instead of the throat, and unleash my waiting shout.

Another Winterborn collapses in a haze of frozen blood, her open eyes staring up at me in pain and shock from the blood-spattered snow. Not a Windwalker—an Icecarver, judging by the unnatural blade in my flesh. The rest of the army must be upon us, but the storm hides them from sight.

The Icecarver's eyes flutter closed and she slips into unconsciousness.

Pain assails me. I stare at the dagger, stunned and momentarily unable to decide what to do. But the blade slips free of its own accord, the ice shattering as its bearer's consciousness fades.

Midvyk materializes between me and the felled Icecarver, grabs my spear with one hand, and jerks me forward—right onto the blade of her outthrust sword.

THIRTY-NINE

Just as the blade bites into my belly, a shield smashes into Midvyk's sword arm. It's followed by the flash of a rune-laden axe and the leering grimace of a knotwork lynx—Hessa, shield pivoting, axe a blur. The Windwalker disintegrates to silver haze.

Hessa lets out a hiss that reminds me of dead gods and empty tombs. Midvyk snaps back into flesh and bone, her expression creased with rage. She strains, obviously trying to vanish again, but Hessa's power pins her in her flesh.

"I warned you," I pant. I clutch my wounded arm but the pain is fading—my blood thrums hot and I barely feel the cold. "I told you we are not helpless."

Midvyk snarls like a caged wolf. In the same moment, more war horns sound, interspersed by shouts from war chiefs among the Eangen and Algatt lines. Shields. Archers. Prepare. I realize the wind has lessened, and the snow. But why?

My question is answered as a horde of savn riders tears out of the waning storm in a flood of ravening jaws, rippling howls, and shouting riders.

They surround us in an instant. Midvyk breaks from Hessa's hold and vanishes before either of us can move.

A savn leaps at my head. I cut it down. I kill its rider with thoughtless efficiency, any conflict I might have felt barred by visceral instinct. Hessa remains with me and we fight side by side as the ice and snow beneath us turns red with blood, then brown. I feel it dripping down the hand of my injured arm. I taste it on my lips and smell the thick, canine carrion reek of the beasts.

With every moment, I search for an opening. I should find Vistic and, with him, try to regain some control over the Winterborn. But there's no break in the blood and chaos, no moment to breathe or search for my mother's son.

I scream my frustration, and four savn and their riders drop. Unlike Midvyk, these riders are only human and blood-mist swirls thick on the wind, melting on my sweat-streaked face. The men, women, and beasts do not rise again.

I brush aside passing nausea. The snow is thickening again, dimming the world around me and smothering the sounds of the battle. Hessa stares at me with a grieved kind of shock over the desiccated bodies of the savn and riders. There's memory in her expression too. Memories of the Eangi she once was, and her bone-shattering scream.

"It's my power," I tell her, my voice dull in my own ears. "Eang's and Ogam's combined."

Hessa's throat is visibly tight, but she holds her chin level. "Then use it."

The wind abruptly changes direction. I follow it, expecting to see Windwalkers materializing for an attack.

Half a dozen of them spread out in formation across the ice. Between them, cracks form, cracks that widen until open water is revealed.

The first sea serpent slithers out in silence. I feel the thud of its weight as it settles, though the dripping of water and the rattle of scales are stolen by the wind. The size of the creature threatens to overwhelm me, its body as thick and round as the great trees that line Eangen's southern coast. Its serpentine face is framed by an arc of horns, each as long as I am tall and curved backward like a taut bow.

A nearby Winterborn grabs at one of these horns and leaps up. She lands with expert lightness, setting her feet as if the horns are merely a ladder. Her body now shielded by the creature's deadly fan, she lets out a howl.

That howl is taken up by her companions. More serpents rise. More Winterborn leap into their deadly crowns, and they and the beasts slice away into the snow.

I remember long ago, Siru telling me that she rode the serpent from whose teeth she'd made her bracelets. I remember when Attan spoke of his influence over beasts, and that it was far more subtle than that of my siblings.

But this… this I never imagined.

At my side, Hessa curses and hefts her axe. One of the serpents is coming directly toward us, its scaled body making the ice creak and crackle. No Winterborn rides this one's crown, but it seems to need little direction.

Despite the size of the creature, despite the shock of its arrival and the imminence of its threat, I find a knot of calm in my chest. I inhabit it, reach out a hand, and touch Hessa's shoulder.

The older woman looks at me over her shield, then slowly steps back.

I step forward to take her place. And when the serpent is mere paces away, the ice moaning and shuddering beneath my feet, I say, "Break."

The serpent jolts, shrieks, and writhes. Blood-mist blooms in the air but the creature's momentum carries it on. Hessa and I step aside as the serpent slides past, scales scraping a huge furrow in the snow.

As I stare after it, blood-mist drifting past me, I see a Winterborn appear beyond the serpentine corpse, staring just as I am at the desiccated beast.

Siru meets my eyes. She holds them for a moment over the distance, and her lips ripple back in a snarl. Then she takes off into the storm, making for shore and the dark mouth of a cave in the cliffs. The sea cave, where the standing stones and the door to the High Halls lies.

"She can't know," I say to Hessa, who, still half-stunned by the serpents, searches for her next target. "She can't know about the rift."

"She's not going to the rift." My aunt points, and as Siru hits the elevation up to the cave mouth, I see a figure I swear is…

Havar. Havar is running ahead of Siru, sprinting up into the sea cave. Havar, with half of a broken spear in his hands.

I go very still. I'd known there was a possibility he'd be here today, but I hadn't bothered—or had the courage—to seek him out.

"I have to—" I look at Hessa, who shows no signs of moving.

A chorus of terrified screams shudders through the storm, followed by Algatt and Eangen horns. The serpents have reached our forces.

"Go," Hessa says, sights the nearest serpent in the direction of the screams—a ripple of opalescent scales in the storm—and takes off at a run. In moments, the snow conceals her.

I nearly follow, torn at the image of her facing the beast alone. But Hessa has survived a dozen battles. Havar needs me more.

I pound toward the cliffs. The closer I come, the more details I make out—high rock, clinging scrub, swaths of snow. Havar, lunging into the cave. Siru is barely three paces behind him and lingers in its mouth with her back to me, and her eyes, no doubt, on Havar and the standing stones. She stalks forward out of sight.

I thunder after them and scramble up to the sea cave. I rake my eyes through the dimness. I see the standing stones and a smattering of bodies, but there's no sign of Gadr and the Vynder who were supposed to guard the rift.

The only two living creatures here are Siru and Havar. She has him backed into one of the standing stones, the tip of her spear at his throat. Above Havar's knot of black hair, runes stretch toward the ceiling, inscrutable and ancient. I'm sure this isn't the first time blood has spilled on their hallowed ground.

Looking up at me, Siru lifts the spear slightly. The flat of its head taps Havar's bearded chin and he lifts it, chest heaving and eyes flicking from me to my sister.

"Thray." Siru's voice echoes. She's spattered with blood, her mass of twisted and braided hair wild about her shoulders. Like the rest of the Winterborn she wears no armor aside from her thick kaftan, and her gaze is chilly.

From the end of her spear, Havar watches.

"Siru," I reply, and despite my fear for Havar, my voice is as hard as her gaze. "Leave him."

"Then stop the Vestige," she snaps. Havar lets out a hiss, anger and frustration making his chest shudder. "Stop him and I will not kill your lover."

"He's not my lover."

"Then you shouldn't care if I drive this spear out the back of his skull."

I flinch and Siru smiles a flat, bleak smile. But even that wavers. "They killed one of us, Thray. They killed our sister. Your sister. You felt her die, I know you did."

"The Vestige is my mother's son. He's my brother too," I tell her, mirroring her smile. "Everywhere I turn, I'm bound by blood, but where is my family?"

Havar makes a sound. It's so thin and bitter that it takes me a breath to realize he's laughing, and my afflicted heart breaks.

"We're right here," Midvyk's voice answers.

More figures step up into the cave and materialize in drifts of snow. There's at least a dozen Winterborn now, weapons ready and eyes hard.

I've no choice but to step farther into the cave, distancing myself from my stalking siblings. I stop in the shadow of one of the standing stones, spear low.

Watching my progress, Midvyk joins Siru. She casts a glance at Havar, and though she's never seen him before, she must realize who he is.

"You'll join us one way or another, whether this century or the next," Siru tells me. She softens her voice, but there's something else in it now—a hint of prophecy, of a truth I understand but can't face yet. "When they're gone, we'll remain, and your loneliness will drive you mad."

"Leave the Eangen in peace. Leave Havar. *That* is the only way to save yourselves."

"What do you care for them?" Midvyk demands, throwing a hand toward the cave's long, low mouth and the churning lines of combatants on the ice, savn and serpents and humans just visible in the maelstrom.

"They live, they die, they rut and breed and are forgotten. You're immortal, Thray. You're so much more than them. I know you see it. I know you crave recognition."

"I *am* them," I hiss back. "They're my people."

"Then we'll bleed them from you like poison from a wound," Siru states, all emotion gone from her voice. The tip of her spear now rests against the throbbing vein in Havar's neck. "For your own good, little sister. You came to us and we will not abandon you, no matter how hard you fight or how badly you betray us."

Midvyk's eyes narrow. Siru's vow, I sense, does not hold true for her.

I can see no way forward. I look from Havar's pinned form and the Winterborn barring my escape. Half of them are silhouetted against the light and the snow, their faces obscured. Others I recognize. Some once accepted me with open arms and broad smiles. Others treated me with caution. But now they all stand against me.

That's when Vistic steps from the rift in the center of the standing stones. Golden light blazes for all who have the power to see it, throwing the Winterborn's faces into bright relief and casting the shadows of the standing stones across the snow-swept floor.

Gadr and half a dozen Vynder come with him, dragging two more Winterborn. Winterborn who, to all appearances, found their way through the rift into the High Halls. Now they're barely breathing, hanging on the edge of death, and as they re-enter the Waking World, my awareness of their pain swells. Again I glimpse threads in the air, binding them to me and every other Winterborn.

I take a step toward them as Siru's expression slackens. Even Midvyk shows momentary surprise, then anguish as our siblings' blood smears the cavern floor.

"Make your choice now," Midvyk says to me, gathering herself together. "Or I will kill the Vestige, take that sword, and put it through your chest."

Through her pain, Siru shoots Midvyk a startled look. "Mid, no. She's young, she's—"

I don't hear the rest as Gadr draws up to my shoulder. I can't look at him and my head is a mess of tension, but his voice is warm in my ear. "You don't need to be here, woman. Go into the Halls. I'll finish this."

I shake my head. As conflicted as I am, the thought of walking away holds no allure.

If this is anyone's battle to fight, it's mine.

I take hold of the fragments of my resolve and look to Vistic, who surveys the Winterborn with a gravity so cold it rivals Midvyk's.

I transition my spear into its curved sword form, and nod to Gadr and Vistic. I don't dare look at Havar, but my feet turn toward him, and my muscles tighten.

The space between my nod and the Winterborn's attack is less than a breath, but that's all I need to scream. The Winterborn shudder, some crumpling, some staggering, others weathering the barrage. Blood-mist drifts on the air.

I direct the brunt of my power into Siru. Her hands waver on the spear and she convulses, her head snapping back and her spine twisting in sudden pain. Havar moves. He seizes the shaft of the spear and thrusts it away from himself, kicking at Siru's legs as he does.

My scream turns to echoes. Silver twines through the air like whips, Windwalkers materialize, and I throw myself toward Havar.

Havar's kick lands, and he knocks Siru's legs out from under her. The floor beneath Havar's feet promptly slicks with ice and he loses his footing, transitioning his fall into a lunge at the last instant. The pair of them slam into the icy floor and skid, entangling in a blur of punches and clawing hands.

My attack weakened Siru, but she's not helpless. A dagger of ice materializes in her hand and before I reach them, she stabs it into Havar's side.

I go blind with rage. Suddenly I'm on top of her, slapping her clawing hands from my face. She doesn't notice my sword in her chest until I jerk it free and roll away into a crouch. She stills, panting and staring down at herself.

Around us, the cavern is chaos. I see Havar weakly roll to the side, trying and failing to get to his feet, while Gadr smashes a hurtling spear of ice from the air and sinks his axe into the thigh of one of my brothers. All around him battles rage, and Vistic's sword flashes.

I turn back on Siru, ready to bring down the hilt of my weapon on her head. A hand sinks into my hair.

Kygga jerks me backward. He grabs my left wrist and twists my arm behind my back, releasing my hair and grabbing for my sword arm as he does.

Pain blinds me, and not just from tearing muscles. In the heat of the battle and the numbing cold, I'd forgotten about the wound to my forearm. My bone sword hits the ground at the same time as my legs are kicked out from under me. I go down.

I scream—or try to. He manages to clamp a hand over my mouth, wrestling me onto my stomach as more Winterborn close in.

"I believe you," he growls in my ear. There's pain behind his voice, but it's awash in a sea of anger. "I believe you about the Winter Night, but it changes nothing. Submit, Thray. I'll do what I can to save you. Siru may forgive you, but Midvyk will not."

I go still, not in submission but exhaustion. I can't reply. I can barely breathe through his hand. My lungs shudder in my chest and my nostrils flare.

But I can still see Havar. He meets my gaze through a barrier of converging Winterborn boots. He clasps his bleeding side with one hand, chest shuddering and fingers covered with blood. He looks as though he wants to call to me, but he can't.

I'm glad for it. The only way he'll survive this is if the Winterborn forget he's here.

"Thray!"

Beyond Havar, Vistic moves. I see him close the space between us and hear my name again, distant through the cold stone grinding into my ear and the weight of Kygga's arm. But I still can't move. I have no voice to scream with, not even to redirect the sword in Vistic's hand—because that, in the moment, is all I can think to do. I remember footprints in the snow, and the man who left his bowl of porridge for hungry, tired children. I remember the pain of Saben's death in my own body, and the thought of its cause being Kygga—I can't bear.

I'll find you.

I'll do what I can to save you.

Kygga follows my gaze. He sees Vistic charging toward us and his grip on me loosens as he spins, snatching up my fallen sword. I break free and scramble to my feet, grabbing at Kygga's tunic to pull him behind me.

"Stop!" I shout, stumbling over my own words. "Not him! Vistic! Kygga—stop!"

Kygga's fist connects with the back of my head and I hear a crack, see a wash of black. But I don't let go. I twist and drive a knee into his groin, shove him backward, and seize his wrist, trying to reclaim my sword.

In the melee, I glimpse Vistic still fighting his way toward me. Then Kygga's free hand clamps around my throat and he pins me against a standing stone.

"Don't try it," Siru warns, deadly calm. She unfolds next to Kygga, her wounds already healed while mine bleed freely and my vision begins to blur.

Vistic's sword tears through Siru's shoulder. She darts away but the sword keeps moving through the space where she was, twisting over Vistic's head and slashing down at the next accessible target.

Midvyk staggers, blood blooming across her chest.

Vistic presses his advantage. One step. Another flash of the blade.

Midvyk falls to the cavern floor. Silvered blood spills, wide eyes dimming with each, gushing pulse.

Deep in my chest, I feel another thread untether. Midvyk's long life is coming to an end.

Vistic levels his sword at Siru's throat. Looking down the long blade, still covered in our siblings' blood, she stills.

Kygga eases his grip on my neck, but doesn't let me go. In his hand, my sword has reverted to its passive form—a small, bone-handled knife—and he stares at Siru, dark eyes momentarily full of helplessness and premonition.

"Eangen and Algatt are not yours for the taking," Vistic says, panting, stray hair caked onto his sweaty forehead. "Leave with your lives and do not come back."

Siru tenses as if to throw herself at him, careless of the sword. Kygga abruptly turns from me and grabs her around the waist, hauling her away from both Vistic and I. In his haste, he drops my knife with a clatter.

"Stop," Kygga pants, watching Vistic's blade and looming form. "Midvyk is dead, Siru. Saben's dead. Stand down. Order a reprieve!"

"Impossible!" Siru sputters in rage, but that anger quickly collapses into tears. "She can't die! We can't die!"

"I felt it, just like you did." Kygga holds her close and for the first time, when his wrathful eyes find me, I'm not the focus of their rage. I see a warning for me, though, one laced with grief and disappointment—one that will carry long into eternity.

My own well of my resentment is empty, and I sense the sorrow flicker across my lips. I brush the back of my hand over my mouth. The other hangs bloodied and useless at my side.

The fight leaves Siru last. She drops her weapon and the other Winterborn follow, one by one.

FORTY

Soon after, Duamel horns lilt. Eangen and Algatt respond, and as the snow clears to show a brutalized battlefield, the Winterborn retreat.

Kygga leads Siru away in a flood of Duamel and my other siblings. They bear Midvyk's body back to the boats—along with the bodies of Saben, several other dead, and numerous wounded. Around them, the corpses of sea serpents and savn bleed, and Eangen, Algatt, and Soulderni warriors gawk at the kills. Near to the shore, I see one gore-splattered Vynder prying teeth from a serpent's yawning maw, wheedling a knife into pale, bloodless gums while his exhausted comrades recover nearby. They're all equally covered with filth and injuries, but I recognize them through the blood. All Vynder. All men and women I'd once worshiped alongside, and was now cast out from.

Duamel warriors regroup farther afield, and, from my vantage in the mouth of the sea cave, I see Attan ride forward astride a huge savn. Hessa and Vistic meet him, and parley begins.

I should go to them, I know. But instead I hasten back to Havar's side and take his hand in mine. His breathing is shallow but he's alive, blood oozing from the wound to his side.

"I'm sorry," I say, pushing the bloody hair back from his face. "I'm so sorry."

He looks up at me, barely turning his face, and pulls a weak smile onto his lips. "I never liked Siru."

I smile back, infusing my expression with happiness I can't feel. "I'll see you're looked after. Just rest. I'll be back."

I leave him in the care of Gadr and his Vynder. I climb down from the cave and cross the ice where Hessa, Vistic, and Attan confer. I'm slow, weakened by blood loss, but I need to finish my part in all this.

"Ah, my elusive bride," Attan says as he looks me over, taking in my blood-splattered hair, face, and clothes. He's unbloodied, the fur of his grand muskox-hide cloak rustling in the breeze. Beneath him, his savn mount shuffles and sniffs the wind.

Attan continues, "I don't expect you're here to beg forgiveness."

I shake my head and beside me, Hessa steps back to let me lead. But I feel her eyes on me, weighing.

"No," I concede. I glance around, ensuring there are no Windwalkers listening on the air. But with Hessa so close, none dare. "But I am here to tell you that the Winter Night is over. When you return north, the sun will have risen over Duamel again. Spring will come, and your land will heal—there is no need for more blood to be spilled. Follow the Sleepers and their goddess, Attan, and trust Per—she is their ally."

Attan is speechless. He stares at me for a few breaths, lips parted in shock, then he gives a short laugh. "I'd say I don't believe you but... I find that I do. How is this possible?"

I look toward the boats, where I can just pick out a few of my siblings moving about. The body of a serpent lies between us, its crown of long horns an arc against the sky. "The Winterborn created the Winter Night to manipulate you and your people, Attan. They're not deserving of your worship. None of us are."

For a moment Attan's expression remains astonished, then darkness creeps in.

"With the help of my grandfather, Winter, and Eirine, their magic has been broken." I draw a steadying breath as pain washes over me anew, and wet my lips. "Duamel is free, though I assume your fight there is not entirely over. Trust Fate. She will protect you, if you serve her."

The conflicts in Attan's face still rage, but he makes a visible effort to contain himself. The leader I glimpsed in the catacombs reappears, and he sits straighter in the saddle.

"Thank you for this news… I will act upon it, if your word proves true, and the time is right," he says levelly. "Though for now, speak of this to no one else. Consider that the first and most mild of my requests. Remember, you still owe me three more."

I nod, supressing a twist of foreboding at what he might one day ask of me. "Of course."

Attan turns to Hessa and Vistic, then to the carnage on the ice behind us. "I do not suppose peace will be easy to forge after this, but if what Thray says is true and I have my way, the Duamel will never again venture south for war."

It's Vistic's turn to speak. "Good. Though if your people serve Eirine, you will find kin in the south."

Attan smiles tightly. "Perhaps. I must go. We'll gather our dead and wounded and depart. High Priestess. Vestige. Thray."

With that, he turns his savn and rides away. I'm left standing with Vistic and Hessa on the ice, and as Attan's presence fades, I feel the reality of the next step welling up between us.

"I'll be gone by tomorrow morning," I say, turning to look at them both. The last of my strength flees, but I do not feel grief or fear. There's no hope in me that my banishment will be revoked. I'm exhausted, and with that, resigned to my fate.

I find Darag and Branan with a knot of warriors from Iesa. I bring Havar to them, but do not stay. We speak little. Darag squeezes my hand and Branan gives me a stiff hug. They don't know of my exile yet, but there's a finality to that embrace.

I crouch beside Havar where he's propped against their stacked packs.

"I hope one day I can earn your forgiveness." I speak low enough that Branan and Darag cannot overhear. "For deceiving you and putting you at risk. I do regret what happened, Havar."

"Ah, so it only took a knife in my side." Havar gives a thin laugh. He reaches out to take my hand, and his fingers are cold. "My forgiveness can't be earned. But you have it, regardless. And I hope you find happiness, Thray, wherever you go next. Just promise me one thing."

"Name it."

"Don't be alone." He squeezes my hand more tightly, stopping me from pulling away—because he knows I will. "Don't be afraid to love, or lose. No, don't look at me like that. I know I can't understand your position. But a life without loss is a life without joy. And besides, there are those in this world who love *you*. Their pain is as valid as your own, and their love, in my humble opinion, is what will make eternity bearable."

My hand is stiff in his, but I manage to nod. I'll take his charge with me, even if I can't quite grasp it yet.

"All right," I concede. "Good... Goodbye, Havar."

His hand slips from mine. "Goodbye, Thray."

As night draws close, I leave him. I have my wounds tended, staring into the distance as a healer cleans, stitches, and binds me. I drink my fill from a pot of hot honey wine that tastes of pine and home, and with its warmth in my veins I set off to find Hessa.

She speaks quietly to Imnir in the Vynder's section of the camp. I watch her from the shadows and find that though Havar's words still ring in my ears, I can't bear to say goodbye.

Instead I watch my aunt converse with her husband, cracking a small smile here and there. Her eyes never rest for long, watching the movements of her wounded Vynder, turning an ear to their conversations. Ever the leader, ever the caregiver.

I glance over the other Vynder too, saying silent goodbyes as my gaze alights on each of their faces. I see Uspa, and think of how her children will be grown the next time I see them. Hessa's children will too, for that matter. They'll be the next generation, standing tall, with their own challenges, loves, and perils. Their own places in the world.

As to Vistic, he's nowhere to be seen.

"You may regret not saying goodbye." I turn to see Nisien behind a nearby tent, hood pushed back from his short hair. "But no one will blame you for it."

I smile a melancholy smile. "Well, I'd never leave without saying goodbye to you."

He pulls me into his arms and I let myself anchor there for a long minute. We're of a height but I bow my head, resting it on his shoulder as I did as a child, when he'd held me and told me stories of the Upheaval and hunting monsters, and crossing the vast plains of the Soulderni Ridings on the back of a swift horse.

I hold him until emotion clogs my throat, then I pull away. "Give Hessa my love," I say, though the final word is among the hardest I've ever spoken.

He nods, eyes glistening with tears, and I slip away into the night.

Campfires burn. Voices call and shadows move between the tents. There's joy and grief all across the camp, around each fire and in every silhouette. But with every pace I pull myself farther and farther away, and by the time I reach the bitter cold on the outskirts of the camp, there's only determination in my steps.

I make my way to the coast, to the cave and the standing stones. An owl, guarding the rift, glances at me from her perch atop one of the stones.

I slip into the High Halls in a surge of golden light. It's the deep of night on the other side, but the moon is bright on a mantle of fresh snow.

I immediately start for the cluster of trees where I stowed my pack before the battle, but come up short as Vistic unfolds from the shadows of a standing stone.

"Where will you go?" he asks. His breath barely mists in the air and the cold is a gentle thing, clean and crisp.

I check my pack, ensuring my bow and quiver are accessible, then pull the straps over my shoulders. I tug my Duamel hood free, but don't raise it yet.

"North," I say. "Or perhaps east. I haven't decided yet. But I will leave Eangen, I promise."

He glances at the ground between us and it occurs to me that he doesn't know what to say. His humanity seeps to the surface in this moment, and he allows me to see it.

"I would change the verdict, if I could," he admits. "But I cannot make an exception. Even for my family."

The crack that Havar's charge left in my control opens a little wider. I can't help myself. I close the space between Vistic and myself and embrace him, as Nisien embraced me. I hold him tightly, letting the years of callousness and resentment trickle away.

He wraps his arms around me in return. There's awkwardness to his hold, as if he's forgotten how to do it—all bone and muscle digging into my back, and beard in my face. But it's honest and sincere.

"I think I understand now, why you stay separate," I tell him as I step back and let my hands return to the straps of my pack. "Why you hold yourself back from the world."

He smiles, short and a little sad. "Sometimes it's difficult. Sometimes it's far too easy."

"I hope…" I trail off, then hold his gaze and speak again. "I hope we can both find a middle ground."

He holds his eyes closed for a moment too long—regathering his impassive exterior. "Perhaps we can," he agrees, golden eyes opening once more.

I check my bone-handled knife at my belt and glance at the northern horizon. Enough emotion. I need to leave, before my courage fails.

"I'll see you again some day, brother," I promise.

Vistic nods, his shoulders straight and back, and his eyes gentle on my face. "Goodbye, sister."

I turn my feet north and begin to walk.

EPILOGUE

D awn over the Hinterlands is pink and gold, violet and orange. I watch it from where I sit, cross-legged in the mouth of the Tomb of the Old Gods. The stone is cold but the sun is warm and when the wind blows, it tastes of thawing earth and new growth. All around, the snow is beginning to retreat, and meltwater trickles down the sides of the mountain in ever-broadening streams.

The last of the winter wind coalesces into the form of a man with windblown hair and singular braids, twining back from his temples. An owl wings over us in his wake, brown and black with a pale moon face and a black fringe.

"You found me," I observe, smiling up at him. "And you've brought my owl back?"

"Yes, yes, I did. I've become quite attached to him. Though the other one wasn't fond of me, he's gone off south." Arune sits beside me, crossing his legs and sinking down in one fluid motion. He mirrors me, palms on his knees, and the owl lands on his shoulder. It churrs, rustling its feathers, and begins to preen.

"You're lucky it was me who found you," my half-brother continues, frowning at the wing buffeting his cheek. "You took a risk coming here."

"I wanted to see the sunrise," I explain, shrugging his caution aside. "And I wanted to make sure you're safe."

"Well, I am. No thanks to you."

I ignore the jibe—he delivers it without ire. "I'm glad you're all right."

"As am I." He sighs and looks east, down the line of the mountains toward the rising sun. There's a forced lightness to his tone as he continues, and I see sorrow coil through him. "I thought my timing terrible, missing the battle and all. But it was nice to rise with the sun."

"I'm glad you weren't there," I admit, following his gaze. "Arune... About Midvyk and the others..."

"She's the one that lured me to my blooding," Arune replies, gaze still on the rising sun. He lifts his chin, angling his face to catch more of its warmth, and his chest rises and falls with a deep breath. "The pain is not as great as you'd expect. I can't blame you for what their vengeance forced you to do, Thray. I did, for a time. But I can't. Many of the others are with me. Most didn't know the Elders made the Winter Night. I only suspected. In any case, Midvyk and the Elders went too far."

Relief makes my knees weak, and I'm glad we're sitting down. "Kygga?"

"His loyalty is to Siru, but it will take a long, long time for him to forgive her."

"Will he forgive me?"

Arune shrugs. "I expect so. Eternity is long, and all we have is each other."

I nod, once, and we continue to watch the sunrise. The snow between us and the blinding orb glistens with gold, each wind-carved pattern highlighted with the promise of spring.

"The Sleepers actually succeeded," I murmur.

"Yes," Arune affirms. The owl stops preening and settles in, watching the landscape with wide-eyed attentiveness. "The horn was blown over Atmeltan on the same day the Winterborn attacked the south. The first new dawn was summoned, and the night banished. Duamel will rejoin the rest of the world in the light of day. And the rule of the Four Pillars, apparently."

"Then Attan did convert," I observe, unsurprised.

"Of course he did." Arune gives a soft laugh. "You haven't met the new priests yet, have you?"

I shake my head. "I've been avoiding civilization."

"Probably for the best, it's usually the least civilized place. Fate has gifted her priests with a kind of foreknowledge as I understand it, and a marginal control over the movement of time. They may not be immortal, but it's rather hard to slay someone who foresees your every move. So the Sleepers have established power over Duamel and I expect them to retain it. We won't intervene, in any case. We'll find other ways to occupy our time."

I look at him curiously. "We, as in the Winterborn, or you and I?"

He cocks his head to one side in thought. "I meant all of us, though I do like the thought of you and I as a 'we.' Our siblings are scattering to the winds, looking for new places to call home. Though some remain at the Barrow. I've decided I'll join the former. You know what? You and I should travel together, see more of the world."

A flicker of hope stirs inside me, but I gesture to my feet. "I'll slow you down."

He waves a dismissive hand. "It'll be good for me, especially after my convalescence. Where would we go?"

"I once had a vision of a great tree in the east." I indicate the rising sun. "We could find it."

The owl shifts its long talons on Arune's shoulder but is otherwise unperturbed. "Perhaps. Farther north there's a great sea that stretches to the edge of the world. The Unmade. Then there are all the territories of the Arpa Empire to the south, and in the west there are islands and lands that Siru mentioned, all places where two immortals could make their names known."

A smile creeps into the corner of my mouth. "So many choices."

"Indeed. How long is your exile?"

My smile retreats a little. "Twenty years."

"Pfft, so little? Spend them with me. We'll explore, learn about the world beyond Eangen and Algatt and Duamel and Arpa. Gods know, the Eangen will soon enough, and you'll be prepared to help them."

I do not take long to decide. I remember Havar's charge not to be alone, to risk love despite the pain, and hold it close. It's what has carried me north, in a way, and given me hope that Arune would find me here. I can't wholly commit myself yet, but I'm willing, for now, to begin to try.

A few, temerarious heartbeats pass before I truly grin, slow and a little crooked. If I'd ever met my father, perhaps I'd see him in that expression.

I look to the west, south, and east. I feel a presence on the wind then, a brush at the back of my mind. Grandfather. Spring is coming to Duamel, and his power is waning. But I sense him all the same—just a touch, an acknowledgement. An affirmation.

"How about that tree in the east?" I ask.

Arune shrugs. "Sounds interesting enough."

I rise to my feet. Drawing my bone-handled knife, I lengthen it into a staff and stretch a hand toward my half-brother, who smiles and grasps my wrist. As he pulls himself to standing, the owl takes off and, without waiting for a command, begins to soar toward the rising sun.

"Come on, then," I say. "We'd better start walking."

GLOSSARY OF NAMES

A

Addack—A coastal tribe of the Eangen peoples and the name of their former Miri god.

Aegr (*Ahy-ger*)—An immortal bear demi-god, healed by the woodmaiden Liv, and thereafter protector of young women.

Aita (*Ahy-tah*)—A Miri, former goddess. The Great Healer who resides in the High Halls of the Dead.

Albor—The seat of the Eangen High Priesthood.

Algatt—The mountain peoples residing between Eangen and the Hinterlands.

Arpa—The empire to the south of Eangen.

Arune (*Ah-rune*)—A Windwalker, son of Ogam. Thray's half-brother.

Atmeltan (*Ah-mel-tan*)—Capital city of the Duamel.

Attan (*Ah-tan*)—The Inheritor of the Duamel, being their chief ruler and inheritor of the right to rule, as ordained by Ogam himself.

B–D

Berin—Son of Hessa and Imnir, twin to Yske and named after Hessa's late father.

Branan—A huntsman of the Addack village of Iesa.

Darag—Brother of Havar.

Diviners, the—The primary religion of the Duamel, which worships the sons and daughters of Ogam.

Dova—A Duamel merchant with a young son. A friend of Seele.

Duamel (*Dh-wah-mel*)—The people once called the Erene, dwellers of the far north and worshipers of Ogam.

E

Eangen (Een-gehn)—The peoples called after the fallen goddess Eang, who live between the Algatt Mountains and the Arpa Empire. Comprised of multiple smaller tribes, including the Addack, the Iskiri, the Meadan, and the Dur.

Eirine (*Eye-rin-ee*)—A god of destiny and time, worshiped by the Duamel cult of the Sleepers.

Elin (*Eh-lin*)—Duamel, son of the headwoman of Imel.

Erene (*Air-een*)—An old Miri name for the people that became the Duamel.

F–H

Fate—One of the Four Pillars, creator of the High Halls. Now bound within time itself, she governs and guides the destinies of all.

Four Pillars, the—The four original deities of the Hall of Smoke world: Thvynder, Imilidese, Fate, and Eiohe.

Gadr (*Gad*, or *Gad-er*)—A Miri, former god who rules the Algatt as king.

Girda (*Geer-dah*)—Wife of Ossen.

Havar (*Dar-ahg*)—Thray's betrothed, of the Eangen tribe Addack, of Iesa.

Hessa—Warrior and High Priestess of Thvynder among the Eangen, wife of Imnir, aunt to Thray, mother of Berin and Yske.

High Halls, the—The Realm of the Dead.

I–M

Icecarvers—Winterborn who can manipulate water and ice.

Iesa (*Eye-ee-sah*)—A small Addack-Eangen coastal town.

Imel (*Ihm-el*)—A city of the Duamel.

Imnir (*Ihm-neer*)—High Priest of the Algatt and Shepherd of the Dead, husband to Hessa and father to Berin, Yske, and Uspa.

Inheritor, the—Chief ruler of the Duamel, a descendant of Ogam who inherits the right to rule, as ordained by Ogam himself.

Kygga (*K-eye-geh*)—A Windwalker, son of Ogam. Thray's half-brother.

Midvyk (*Mid-vih-kh*)—A Windwalker, daughter of Ogam and Elder of the Winterborn. Thray's half-sister.

N–R

Nir (*Neer*)—A savn war beast.

Nisien—A horseman of the Soulderni plains, former Arpa legionary, protector of the north, and uncle to Thray.

Ogam (*Oh-gam*)—Son of the Miri Goddess of War, Eang, and her consort, the Elemental Winter. Killed by Eang during the Upheaval for his crime of releasing the Gods of the Old World from their tombs.

Omaskat (*Om-ah-skat*)—The Watchman of Thvynder.

Ossen (*Oh-sen*)—Headman of Iesa.

Per—A High Priestess of the Diviners.

Rana—A priestess of the Duamel Sleeper god Eirine.

S–U

Saben—A Winterborn Windwalker.

Savn—Monsters originating from the High Halls that merge wolves and bears.

Seele (*Seal-ee*)—Merchant, an Addack woman from a village south of Iesa.

Siru (*See-rue*)—Daughter of Ogam and a devotee of Aita. Thray's half-sister.

Sixnit—Mother of Thray and Vistic, an Eangen woman of Albor. Died sixteen years after the Upheaval.

Sleepers, the—A cult of the Duamel that worships the goddess Eirine.

Stormbringers—Those among the Winterborn who can manipulate the weather.

Thray (*Th-ray*)—Daughter of Sixnit and Ogam, niece to Hessa, Imnir, Nisien, half-sister of Vistic and the Winterborn.

Thvynder (*Th-vin-der*)—One of the Four Pillars of the World, an ancient and original deity of creation and order, represented to the Eangen, Algatt, and Arpa peoples by the Watchman Omaskat and the Vestige Vistic.

Upheaval, the—The series of events that brought about the end of Miri worship in Algatt, Eangen, and Arpa, and led to the reawakening of Thvynder.

V–Z

Vist—First husband of Sixnit, mother of Vistic. An Eangi in service to Eang prior to his death during the Upheaval.

Vistic—Son of Sixnit and her first husband Vist, Vestige of Thvynder, and bearer of a piece of the God's immortal soul, though he himself is mortal.

Widow root—An ingredient in yifr.

Windwalkers—Those of Ogam's children who possess his ability to move with and control the winter wind.

Winter (person)—An Elemental spirit, counterpart to Summer, capable of taking human form. Father to Ogam, lover of Eang, and grandfather to Thray and the Winterborn.

Winterborn, the—Ogam's children among the Duamel.

Winter Night, the—The perpetual night that reigns over central Duamel.

Yifr—A drink that the Eangen and Algatt High Priesthood use to travel spiritually to the High Halls of the Dead.

Yske (*Yih-sk-ah*)—Daughter of Hessa and Imnir, twin to Berin, and named after Hessa's cousin, who perished during the Upheaval.

ACKNOWLEDGMENTS

It takes so many dedicated and creative individuals to bring a book to life, and I'm so grateful for each one of them. Firstly, an endless thank you to my agent Naomi Davis for believing in my work and always having my back. Thank you to my genius editors George Sandison and Elora Hartway – my books would be a shadow of themselves without your insight and creativity, and knowing you're on my team is such a consolation.

Thank you so much to Katharine Carroll and Lydia Gittins for getting my books out into the world, and to Julia Lloyd, for creating Barrow's absolutely incredible cover – it's the cover of my dreams for this book, and seeing on my shelf every day brings me so much joy. Thank you.

To my writer friends, my beta readers and brainstormers, my cheerleaders, I could not do this without you. To my agent-siblings of the SFF Powerhouse, Kritika H. Rao, Gabriela Romero Lacruz, Essa Hansen, Chelsea Mueller, Rachel Fikes, Melissa Caruso, Sue Lynn Tan, Prashanth Srivatsa, Sunyi Dean, and Nadia Afifi, your encouragement and advice, listening ears and solidarity keeps me writing every single day. My critique partners Cheryl Bowman and Stephanie Rinaldi, and my incredible mother (who still reads every one of my books multiple times) – thank you so much for your unending patience, wisdom, and gentle critiques. To my debut buddies Genevieve Gornichec and Mallory Kuhn, thank you for keeping me sane and for standing with me in the chaos that is publishing.

My family, you got my here. I love you and appreciate you every day.

Finally, thank you so much to you, my readers. You make every word, every battle, every bleary writing session worth it, and you never cease to amaze and inspire me. Thank you.

ABOUT THE AUTHOR

H. M. Long is a Canadian fantasy writer, author of *Hall of Smoke* and *Temple of No God*, who loves history, hiking, and exploring the world. She lives in Ontario, but can often be spotted snooping about European museums or wandering the Alps with her German husband.

DARK WATER DAUGHTER
H.M. Long

Mary Firth is a Stormsinger: a woman whose voice can still hurricanes and shatter armadas. Faced with servitude to a deathless pirate lord, Mary offers her skills to his arch-rival in exchange for protection - and, more importantly, his help in sending the pirate to a watery grave.

But Mary's dreams are dark and full of ghistings, spectral creatures who inhabit the ancient forests of her homeland and the figureheads of ships. Her new ally has his own vendetta, complete with revenge and a lost fleet, locked in the eternal ice of the far north, and disgraced pirate hunter Samuel Rosser is close on their trail. Samuel will stop at nothing to restore his good name and claim the only thing that stands between himself and madness: a talisman stolen by Mary herself.

Finally, driven into the eternal ice at the limits of their world, Mary and Samuel must choose their loyalties and battle forces older and more powerful than the pirates who would make them slaves.

Come sail the winter sea, for action-packed, high-stakes adventures, rich characterisation and epic plots full of intrigue and betrayal.

JULY 2023

TITANBOOKS.COM

HALL OF SMOKE
H.M. Long

Hessa is an Eangi: a warrior priestess of the Goddess of War, with the power to turn an enemy's bones to dust with a scream. Banished for disobeying her goddess's command to murder a traveller, she prays for forgiveness alone on a mountainside.

While she is gone, raiders raze her village and obliterate the Eangi priesthood. Grieving and alone, Hessa – the last Eangi – must find the traveller and atone for her weakness and secure her place with her loved ones in the High Halls. As clans from the north and legionaries from the south tear through her homeland, slaughtering everyone in their path Hessa strives to win back her goddess' favour.

Beset by zealot soldiers, deceitful gods, and newly-awakened demons at every turn, Hessa burns her path towards redemption and revenge. But her journey reveals a harrowing truth: the gods are dying and the High Halls of the afterlife are fading. Soon Hessa's trust in her goddess weakens with every unheeded prayer.

Thrust into a battle between the gods of the Old World and the New, Hessa realizes there is far more on the line than securing a life beyond her own death. Bigger, older powers slumber beneath the surface of her world. And they're about to wake up.

For more fantastic fiction, author events,
exclusive excerpts, competitions, limited editions and more

VISIT OUR WEBSITE
titanbooks.com

LIKE US ON FACEBOOK
facebook.com/titanbooks

FOLLOW US ON TWITTER AND INSTAGRAM
@TitanBooks

EMAIL US
readerfeedback@titanemail.com